THE HERON DYNASTY

With indomitable spirit and unflinching courage, the first Herons strove to create a bold heritage out of the primitive Oklahoma wilderness. From the homestead rushes of the Indian Territory through the turbulent years of World War II, the vast Heron petroleum empire burgeoned into international prominence.

Now, in *The Survivors*, the third generation of the clan confronts the conflicting challenges of post-War prosperity and Cold War hostilities. And as the age of jet travel opens up new international frontiers—from the oilfields of Oklahoma and the Middle East to the motion picture studios in Hollywood and the battlefields of Korea—the Heron inheritors will once again test the legacy that their forebears so nobly forged.

Whitney Stine, a native of Garber, Oklahoma, who now lives in Upland, California, has had many best-selling books, including *Mother Goddam*, the story of the screen career of Bette Davis; *The Hurrell Style*, for which he wrote the text accompanying glamour photographer George Hurrell's famous portraits; and *Stardust*, the three-generation saga of a famous acting family.

Other books by Whitney Stine:

THE OKLAHOMANS
THE OKLAHOMANS: THE SECOND GENERATION
THE OKLAHOMANS: THE THIRD GENERATION

THE OKLAHOMANS:

The Survivors

Whitney
Stine

PINNACLE BOOKS NEW YORK

This is a work of fiction. All of the main characters and events portrayed in this book are fictional. In some instances, however, the names of real people, without whom no history could be told, have been used to authenticate the storyline.

THE OKLAHOMANS: THE SURVIVORS

An original Pinnacle Books edition, published for the first time anywhere.

First printing, October 1983

ISBN: 0-523-41926-0
CANADIAN ISBN: 0-523-43036-1

Cover illustration by Norm Eastman

Printed in the United States of America

PINNACLE BOOKS, INC.
1430 Broadway
New York, N.Y. 10018
10   9   8   7   6   5   4   3   2   1

For India—
who understands the
anguish of creativity . . .

THE
SURVIVORS

1

Ebb and Flow

The nightmare must have begun the moment that Letty had dropped off to sleep.

She was first conscious of the wind blowing her long blonde hair into her eyes; then she felt a fine dust hitting her face with gale force. She brushed her hair back from her forehead and looked down at her hands. Why was she wearing red gloves? Then it occurred to her in a flash of remembrance that her body and clothing were stained with the rich red soil of Indian Territory.

In the confusion of suddenly being plunged back into the past, it took a moment to realize that she was sitting upright in a buckboard, and that the two horses pulling the vehicle were stained pink with the same dust that was settling over the hundreds of conveyances that were taking part in the Cherokee Strip Land Rush. How well she knew the date: September 16, 1893!

At this point in the dream, Letty realized, with a rush of emotion, that she was involved in a scenario out of times gone by, half forgotten over the last fifty-eight years.

In wonder, she brushed the red soil from her hands, which were now gleaming white—not the spotted, veined hands that she saw every day. Questioningly she brought her fingers up to her face, and smiled with relief. Her jaw was firm, the skin fit tightly over her high cheekbones, and long blonde, fine-as-cornsilk hair cascaded around her shoulders. Miraculously, in this dream world, she was an eighty-year-old woman, with a twenty-two-year-old body!

Letty was at first fearful of looking at the form beside her, afraid to look upon the handsome, young, virile Luke with whom she had fallen in love. Then, with the full knowledge of the past, she remembered that he was riding a horse up ahead and that she was sitting beside his brother Edward and his wife, Priscilla.

She caught a glimpse of Edward's strong profile against the moving scenery of time, and quickly shielded her face with the poke bonnet, lest he look in her direction and see the old woman that she was inside. But his eyes were staring straight ahead as he skillfully guided the team of horses through the conglomeration of vehicles and horse-flesh—all obscured by the swirling clouds of red dust. In a time of grave danger, he was performing magnificently.

Then, emotionally absorbed by the intense excitement of the Land Grab once more, she experienced the thrill of taking part in a historic endeavor as hundreds of horsedrawn vehicles rushed pell-mell toward the ulimate goal: a hundred and sixty acres of free land, wrested from the Cherokee Nation to be presented free and clear to the white man.

As the choking red dust rose a hundred feet in the air, Letty felt the poke bonnet loosen from her head. She was standing up, and Edward was gradually pulling the reins to the right, away from the horde of rushing settlers that surrounded the buckboard.

They were climbing a small hill now, following Luke's trail. Once more she smelled the pungent, white, frothy sweat of the galloping horses. As the buckboard reached the top of the incline, the flames of the prairie fires leapt up against the horizon: fires set that very morning by the U.S. Cavalry so that the grid of markers setting off each one-hundred-and-sixty-acre tract could be more easily found by the claimers.

Then, as in all dreams, there was sudden transition, a short passage of time. She was first conscious of the dry, pithy odor of dry prairie grass as she sat on a slight mound, holding a still form. Whose head was she cradling in her arms?

From the terrible distance of her eighty years of life, she

was filled with sudden horror. She dared not look down into that tortured face again. *Oh, please, God*, she beseeched, *don't let me go back, return me to the present*. Tired and weary, she desperately wanted to rest. Yet relentlessly the scene continued: she could not quell the baffling slide of history.

But then the very atmosphere changed and she felt a sudden chill. Time stood still; even the motion of the wind in the trees ceased. She had the distinct impression of being caught in some nameless time warp that could not be changed until she permitted the scene to continue. She— Letty Heron Story Trenton—was the catalyst. She closed her eyes tightly and thought, *Very well, then, I shall see it to the end!*

She took a deep breath in preparation, opened her eyes, and looked down into the face of her dying husband. Luke had been shot by a *Sooner*, a camper who had erected a tent on the claim a day previous to The Run. Apparently Luke and he had engaged in a shoot-out over the property, because the man lay dead a few feet away.

Luke's strength was ebbing; his dark eyes were staring out of a bloodless, white face, and she thought, *Oh, my God, he's looking at a frail, old, wrinkled woman with white hair, instead of his beautiful young Letty*. She had now aged in the dream. But no, although his eyes were open, she knew that he was blind. His face wore such a blank look that she was afraid he did not know who held him.

But when his jaw brushed her hand, she knew that his sense of smell had returned and he recognized her perfume. She started to cry; the burning tears of an old woman splashed down on the face of her young husband as his lips formed the words *I love you*.

It was then that Letty began to scream.

"Mama! Mama!" the deep voice cried. "Wake up!"

While her shoulders were being gently shaken, it took a few moments after she opened her eyes to realize that she was back in her upstairs bedroom at the Heron clapboard in Angel, Oklahoma.

She was feeling calmer now, as the nightmare receded into a comfortable position in the far distance. Letty looked up into the worried face of her stalwart fifty-seven-year-old son, Luke Junior. His soft brown eyes carried the frightened look of a mongrel puppy. He was trembling, and it occurred to her that this was the first time in years that she could remember him showing an emotional reaction.

"Are you all right, Mama?" Luke asked, and his voice was almost tender.

Regaining composure, she brushed a strand of white hair back from her temple. "Yes, thank you . . . Luke." She stumbled over his name because a short while ago she had been holding in her arms, his dying father, whom he had never known. Luke Senior had been unaware of her condition; she had planned to tell him about her pregnancy after he had staked the Heron claim.

"Was it a very bad dream, Mama?"

She looked into his dull eyes and restrained herself from giving a sharp answer. "It was very real, that's all," she said simply, recalling the blood on her husband's shirt, ". . . and in color."

"Do you want to talk about it?" he asked, and his voice was very gentle.

She gave him an odd look. Was this the same tone that he used when he made love to his wife, Jeanette? Why should she want to confide anything in him? "Not really," she replied, and her voice was strong. How could she explain what it was like to go back sixty years and occupy a twenty-two-year-old body when one was eighty inside? She gave him as kindly a look as was possible at the moment. "I'm all right, son"—she could still not call him Luke—"please go back to bed."

"Are you sure that you don't need anything?"

She shook her head and managed a smile. "Good night."

"Good night, Mama," he replied, and, closing the door gently, went into the hall, where the rest of the family, still dressed in nightclothes, were waiting. "She's fine," he whispered. "It was only a bad dream."

While they went back to their rooms, he motioned for Jeanette to follow him downstairs. She removed two curlers from her forehead, yawned, and padded down to the kitchen, glancing slyly into the back hall, but Hattie, the maid, was nowhere to be seen. "That woman could sleep if a tornado blew away the roof, and stripped off her sheets!" she muttered, filling the old-fashioned coffeepot with water, and trying to remember where her mother-in-law kept canned goods. With all those oil millions, one would think that Letty could afford an electric perker. Jeanette gave a disgruntled sigh. It was a wonder that she was not still using a wood-burning stove!

"Where in the hell does your mother keep the coffee?" she demanded as Luke came into the kitchen.

"I'd think you'd be more concerned with her condition than trying to make coffee at this time of night!"

"Well, what would you suggest?" Jeanette answered tartly. "This side of the Heron family being temperance, I doubt if there is even medicinal wine in the house." She paused. "How is she *really*?"

He raised his eyebrows. "Okay, I think. I suppose the nightmare had something to do with Bosley's funeral this afternoon. You know, Jeanette, she looked so tiny in that big bed, so frail, like a little sparrow." Then he mused as he turned away, "She's sleeping alone for the first time in years. . . ."

She gave him a long look. "I dare say she'll get used to it," she replied dryly. "I have."

"And just what do you mean by that?"

"Please keep your voice down. Everyone has been awakened once tonight, no sense rousing them out again. At least Bos wasn't on the road all the time."

"Don't be bitchy, Jeanette," Luke replied quickly. "Do you think I enjoy visiting all the field offices and attending the openings of all those new Heron service stations?" He went to the door. "You'll find the coffee in the icebox."

She laughed. "The 'icebox'?"

"All right! The *refrigerator*!"

Letty turned on her side and immediately started to dream again. Strangely, she was in the same bedroom, but the furnishings and wallpaper were different. What year had she ordered that bird pattern from France?

She was wearing a print cotton house dress, and

remembered purchasing the material at Baker's Mercantile store in Angel; she had sewed her own clothes in those days.

The smell of the climbing roses wafted through the open window, so it must be summer, but *what* summer? With her lovely, unlined hand on the sill, she looked down into the front yard and saw the gleaming white roadster in the driveway.

Then, with an awful certainty, she knew the date: October 29, 1929. Before turning from the window, she knew what she would see, so she closed her eyes tightly and took a deep breath in order to be prepared for the scene.

She opened her eyes. "Good morning, George dear," she said evenly, thinking that she had made proper provision for how he would look. She knew that he would not appear as the same man with whom she had fallen in love in 1902. He had been tall then, broad-shouldered and incredibly handsome, with high mixed-blood Cherokee cheekbones and sparkling, porcelain-blue eyes; a big man, who weighed two hundred pounds.

Now, the blue eyes and the cheekbones were all that was left of that beautiful face. Cancer had ravished his body to the point where Luke could pick him up in his arms and take him to the window to watch the bees working over the roses.

Looking again at that almost unrecognizable face, which she had placed in the uncharted areas of her memory bank—so that she would remember what he had looked like before that last, long illness—she was suddenly aware again that she was dreaming. Would she still be young when he looked at her?

She was filled with apprehension, but when he opened his eyes and twisted his mouth into a semblance of a smile, such love was reflected from his face that she was ashamed of herself for being apprehensive. Then his smile faded and she felt an incredible, all-consuming loneliness; there was such an empty space inside that she could not bear to look at the form on the bed. A sob escaped her throat, and then she began to cry and could not stop. . . .

* * *

A half hour later, Letty was sitting on the sofa in the living room and sipping coffee that scalded her throat. Although she was outwardly composed, she was still shaking inside. It had been embarrassing to awaken the household after the first dream, but to rouse everyone again, after the second, was unforgivable.

To take her mind off the dreams, she examined Luke's and Jeanette's faces: seated on the loveseat opposite the couch, holding nine-year-old Murdock, they did not look as if they were still in love. All of her three husbands, Bosley included, had somehow managed to keep the inward fires stoked, and, looking back, she still loved them, perhaps in slightly different ways, but the warm feelings of passion were still there.

On the west side of the room, sitting by himself as usual, Luke Three looked undeniably handsome in his new Marine uniform. The strange one in the family, he was a throwback—like his uncle Mitchell, who occasionally disappeared on long "vacations."

Luke Three had just returned from three years in England, where, it was rumored, he had worked in a Heron British service station under another name. Now he had joined the armed services and was on his way to Korea. What was it about the Heron boys that almost always made them misfits?

Patricia Anne Hanson, curled up in Bosley's rocker, was a different type of person entirely, Letty reflected. Of course, as she was the only offspring of Clement, Letty's son by George Story, Cherokee Indian blood gave her a foreign look. She was smart, all right, having graduated in the top ten of her class at Phillips University in Enid. But that was before she married Lars Hanson, who had taken over the practice of Doctor Sam, Born-Before-Sunrise, their late, great Cherokee friend.

Letty placed the empty cup on the coffee table and smiled wanly. "I'm so sorry to be such a bother. I don't know what got into me—dreaming things that happened so many years ago, things that I'd almost forgotten about death. . . ."

"Why, Mama," Luke exclaimed, getting up quickly,

"you didn't say anything . . . about people passing away, and all—"

"Didn't I? Well." She pointed her finger at him, cutting him short. "It's of no matter, son"—she still could not call him Luke. "If you'll all excuse me, I'll go back to bed."

Luke Three arose. "Grandma, I can move a cot into your room. . . ."

"That's a kind suggestion, but I wouldn't hear of it. I'll be all right." She paused and looked around the room. "You see, the problem was, I shouldn't have gone back to sleep right away after the first dream. That was the mistake. Now, enough time has gone by that I'm certain I won't be bothered again." She controlled herself carefully, so that she wouldn't sway as she got up from the sofa. "Good night, everyone—for the second time!"

"I'll go with you," Jeanette put in quickly.

Letty turned at the stairs. "No. This is something that I must do for myself."

No one understood what she meant, until her slight form had disappeared up the stairs, and then Luke, Jeanette, Patricia Anne, and Luke Three looked at each other in surprise. It was the first time they realized that Letty Heron Story Trenton was a very old woman.

The telephone rang in the Bridal Suite at the Stevens Hotel in Angel, and Clement Story answered sleepily. "What?"

Luke paused a moment before addressing his half-brother further. It rankled that Clem and Sarah always stayed at the hotel instead of the house. "Are you coming over for breakfast?"

Clement glanced at his watch. It was seven o'clock in the morning. He seldom arose before noon, being accustomed to fronting his orchestra until two and then having supper before going to bed at four. "No." He kept his voice even, wanting to tell Luke to go soak his head. "There is no sense in sending Hattie into a tizzy. For some reason, she always feels she has to make biscuits and country gravy especially for me, and that's a lot of trouble. Sarah and I will be stopping by on our way back to Kansas City after lunch."

While no one appreciated more than Luke the fact that Clem was one of the most famous bandleaders in the United States—and even parts of Europe—there were times when Clem's show business ways intruded on their friendship. Of course, granted, now that Hattie had moved into the bedroom on the lower floor, there was only one small bedroom left unoccupied; it was still ridiculous that Clem and Sarah had to sleep in what was called a Hollywood "king-sized bed"—and the Stevens Hotel had installed one especially for them.

"I think you'd better come over before then, Clem. We were up half the night with Mama."

Clement shook himself fully awake. "What's wrong?"

"Bad dreams. She had two of them and her cries awakened the whole household—well, at least everyone except Hattie. It was awful, and then, of course, she tried to pass it off."

"I suppose Bosley's death is just getting to her," Clement replied slowly. "Maybe we shouldn't leave her alone, Luke."

"Well, she has Hattie."

"Yes, but she's hardly what you'd call a companion. She's getting old herself."

"You better come over. We've got to toss around some ideas."

My God, Clement thought, *you aren't conducting a Heron board of directors meeting, Luke.* Aloud, he said, "All right. No sense going back to bed now. We'll be over shortly." He hung up the phone and looked lovingly at his wife, Sarah, who he knew was awake, although she had her eyes closed. "Honey . . ." he said insinuatingly, and touched her cheek. She was looking very Indian this morning, he thought, but how could she look so beautiful at forty-seven, when he, at the same age, knew that he looked ten years older?

Recognizing his tone at once, she opened one eye and held the sheet open in invitation. They always made love in the morning, because Clem was always too exhausted to think about romance after a gig. But, she reflected, he was still very much the romantic she had fallen in love with so many years ago.

She was a fortunate woman, because so many of her contemporaries indicated that the act of love had become commonplace and was utilized purely as a physical release. Phoebe Landers, a close friend in Kansas City, had confided that her husband and she had not kissed each other in years, aside from a "good morning peck" on the cheek before he went to work in the morning, and they made love twice a month!

"Come on in," she said cheerfully, "the water's fine."

He threw back the sheet and opened her nightgown, then bent down and kissed the gold ankle bracelet, with the tiny diamond heart, that he had given her during World War II. He brought his lips up to her outer thighs, hips, breasts, and finally reached the back of her neck, which he had recently discovered was one of her erogenous zones. "I didn't think we had any secrets." He had laughed. "You never told me that was one of your excitable areas!"

She had given him a long, amused look. "Only because I didn't know it myself!" He had kissed her lovingly on her nape and she had shivered deliciously, just as she was doing now.

He began to run his tongue along her cheek until he reached her mouth. He kissed her very deeply, they shuddered in each other's arms, and their passion built.

"Let's pretend this is our wedding night," she said softly. "After all, we're in the Bridal Suite."

"Yes." He laughed. "Only because it happens to be the *only* suite in the Stevens Hotel!" Then he turned her adroitly on her side and, after a while, as they kissed, he was ready and moved within her slowly and lovingly, painstakingly bringing about the quivering response that he loved. Half of his enjoyment was bringing her to a peak of excitement, and then making the feeling last by swaying and undulating his body in concert with hers.

Oh, how wonderful it was to have an experienced lover! she thought as her vibrating body sent tiny shocks up and down her spinal column. *Oh, how she loved him! When she felt the sweet throbs and the wet gush within, the moment*

*was very precious. With menopause behind her, and no
worries about contraceptives, she was a willing receptacle
for his seed, which seemed indeed to spread and lubricate
her very being.* Still joined, they lay for a long time
together, until he finally arose.

"Come on, my sweet, it's time to go see Mama."

Mitchell Heron and Charlotte Dice lay loosely in each
other's arms in the ornate gilded bed in the great white
bedchamber in the Federal Restoration mansion next to the
Heron claim.

"This is all so new to me," he whispered in her ear, "this
feeling of doing something that I shouldn't."

Charlotte stirred in his arms. "Even with someone
you've known for more than fifty years? After all, we grew
up together."

"That's what I mean, it's so incongruous." Mitchell
knitted his brows together, which deepened his eyes and
gave him a squint. "Isn't it funny that you and I end up
married?"

"I wouldn't exactly call it funny, Mitch," she replied
defensively.

"Oh, I don't mean *funny* funny!"

"Humorous?"

"No."

"Peculiar?"

"I mean *strange*."

She laughed. "I'll go along with that, yet us getting
together in middle age has its compensations. For one thing,
we know what we're doing, getting married at this age."

He gave her a quick kiss on the ear. "Thank you for
implying I'm a good lover." He kissed her again. "You're
fabulous"—he grinned—"for an heiress."

"Thank you, sir!" she countered playfully. "But you
aren't one of the ten neediest cases, either, according to your
last financial statement."

He looked at her incredulously. "You mean you checked
me out?"

"Of course."

"What do you mean, *of course*?"

"Well, Mother—who everyone thought was a dumb bunny—told me years and years ago (after the monthly oil checks got to be seven figures) to always find out what any man that I planned to marry was worth."

"And did you have all of them checked out?" he asked darkly, not at all amused.

"No."

"Why not?"

"Because," she said quietly, pulling at the blue ribbon on her sleeve, "if you want to know the truth, you're the first man who actually wanted to marry me."

He threw her a quick look and got out of bed. "I can scarcely believe that, Charlotte. After all, you're an attractive woman, and—"

"And rich?" She went on with a touch of sarcasm, "Thanks!" She paused. "Why are we having this conversation?"

He paused in front of the Louis XIV chiffonier. "I think it all started when you had me checked out at the bank. Are you a friend of the chairman of the board? I thought some things were confidential."

"Mitch, you're making a mountain out of a molehill," she replied crossly, getting out of bed and arranging the chiffon nightgown around her rather plump body. "I shouldn't even have mentioned it. My lawyer was naturally curious, and since he's in Washington and doesn't know how successful your furniture stores are—and you having the name of Heron—he was naturally curious. It's as simple as that."

She combed out her medium-long brown hair with quick strokes. "And as for cash money, you know damned well that when Mama and Papa died, they stipulated in their will that I wasn't to receive the bulk of the estate unless I moved back here to Angel and occupied this overdone monstrosity for ten years."

She peered into the mirror and applied red to her generous mouth with two slashes of the stick in a defiant, final gesture. Then she began to pace in the opposite direction, in front of the gilt pier glass that had come all the way from Paris, France. "So, Mr. Mitchell Heron, for the next eight years you're going to be supporting me, whether you like it or not—that is, if I decide to marry you!"

They stopped pacing and faced each other, and it simultaneously occurred to them how ridiculous they both appeared, striding up and down, crossing each other's paths every moment, and they burst into laughter and fell into each other's arms.

He looked down into her face. "Let's go back to bed, my poor little rich girl!"

"Not unless you have an encore up your sleeve."

He grinned broadly. "What I have in mind is *not* up my sleeve—or, at least, wasn't the last time I looked!"

As they lay down on the satin quilt that her mother, Fontine, had made in therapy for her arthritic fingers, Charlotte thought of all those young, golden boys whom she had bedded over the years—the ones that she had paid and the ones that she had not—and realized once more that she was a fortunate woman indeed to be engaged to Mitchell Heron.

Those golden boys had only cared for their own pleasure—those explosions of seed that every young man coveted above all else—and they hadn't really cared a damn for her, a brutal, but truthful fact that she had faced a long time ago.

Those golden boys wanted the run of her luxurious Washington apartment, expensive clothing, gold and diamond accessories, the convenience of her car and the use of her body—in that order.

But when it came down to the final tally—and she loved hard, smooth bodies—she was grateful now for a not-so-young body that had a brilliant, mature brain attached to it, a body that lifted her along to ultimate fulfillment. She kissed Mitchell warmly on his lips. *To hell with the golden boys!* she thought as she climbed over him and expertly began the machinations of love.

Mitchell lay quite still, imprisoned by a plump leg on each side of his thighs, and relished the moment: this was a new experience for him, which he was fully prepared to enjoy. But because he was so relaxed and Charlotte was so tense and concentrating on the pleasures of the moment, he had to allow his mind to wander or he would spend too soon.

He wondered idly where Charlotte had acquired her expertise in making love. Obviously, she had far more experience than he, and she was accomplished in arts that he had only read vaguely about in Henry Miller's *Tropic of Cancer*, which had been published when he had lived in France. He hadn't cared very much for erotic writing in those days, but now he was sorry that he had not paid more attention to some of those explicitly sexual passages. Not that he felt himself a novice by any means; he had certainly enjoyed a few affairs over the years, but he was not quite the Lothario that he would have liked to be. . . .

Once, quite early in their relationship, Charlotte had been on the brink of confiding in him, but he had placed his finger over her mouth and indicated that, at this stage of the game, what was past should remain past. If she had confessed sexual derring do's, he would have felt bound to reveal something about himself that no one in Angel or Enid knew anything about. He had one tightly kept secret in his life.

He smiled to himself, because very likely she would have burst into hysterical laughter had she known that his long vacations were not spent in Tahiti or Guatemala, but on secret missions for the government of the United States of America.

It was certainly incongruous, he admitted. Who would have thought that Mitchell Heron of the Heron Furniture Stores, with headquarters in Enid, Oklahoma, had been parachuted into France during World War II, on a mission that, it turned out later, had to do with the development of the atomic bomb? Or that he had most recently returned from impersonating a Viennese psychiatrist in a caper that took place in Germany? On second thought, she probably would not laugh at all, but think him laboring under some gigantic delusion.

Frankly, lying in the garish upstairs bedroom of a Federal Restoration mansion in Angel, Oklahoma, with an experienced lover laboring sweetly over his supine form, he found it hard to believe that he had successfully assumed the identity of either Monsieur Michel Bayard or Herr Doktor Professor Schneider. Then even his musings failed to suppress his passion, and he rose up to meet her expert gyrations and their bodies were fulfilled simultaneously—which was, in itself, a rarity.

Luke Three lay between the cool sheets in the small back bedroom of the Heron clapboard that he had occupied during high school, when he had lived with Grandma Letty and Grandpa Bosley. He had discovered the joys of sex by himself, in this very bed. At odd moments—like now—he was most pleased with his body. In fact, his personal equipment had been one of his proudest possessions and greatest joys since the age of fifteen, when his Cherokee friend, Doctor Sam, Born-Before-Sunrise, finished the hormone injections that had made him a big man—in every sense of the word. Until that time his underdeveloped penis had resembled that of Murdock, his nine-year-old brother.

As Luke Three ran his hands up and down his body, inciting that pleasurable response that he loved so very much, he was thankful that he could give himself the same—well, perhaps not quite the same—enjoyment as a member of the female sex. Until he met the right girl, he had no intention of getting married.

He had learned how to charmingly refuse older ladies who wished to go to bed with him, when he did not want to go to bed with them; charmingly seduce young girls whom he wanted to go to bed with, and who didn't want to go to bed with him; and charmingly walk deftly between the two points when he was not sure about either. . . . But he had also discovered that what he had in his pants did not necessarily give him *entrée* to any bed that he wanted to enter.

But for now he would do his tour of duty in Korea, the same as he had in World War II, when he had run away to join the Marines at the age of seventeen. There would be plenty of time after he got back to decide whether or not he wanted to rejoin the Heron Oil Company or go into another type of work.

Wouldn't it be great, for instance, to work in a male

whorehouse? Oh, he could satisfy any woman alive, he knew that, and then he would be able to try out all of those fantastic positions and techniques that he had seen illustrated in those pornographic books he leafed through in that bordello in Antwerp when he had visited the Heron field offices in Europe with vice president Robert Desmond.

Then, with his hand busy under the sheet, he continued the fantasy to its natural conclusion, and finally lay trembling, moist, and exhausted. He would have to take a shower the first thing in the morning—but now he remembered the shower was located in the new suite that Bosley had had installed for the visit of their Saudi Arabian friend, Muhammad Abn, in 1945. Well, Luke Three consoled himself, he would have to be content with a tub bath, even though there was something obscene about the feel of cold porcelain on his bottom.

Patricia Anne Story Hanson, looked at her pale face in the old-fashioned mirror above the washbasin in the upstairs bathroom of the Heron clapboard. She disliked using makeup in the daytime, but she looked like the Witch of Endor, having been awakened twice during the night. But the violet circles under her eyes were not caused wholly from weeping over the death of her stepgrandfather, Bosley Trenton, either. She had tossed and turned during the early part of the night, worrying about her husband, Lars, who was undergoing a series of tests at Walter Reed Hospital. But she was actually too upset to think about that ordeal.

There was no need to impress the immediate family, but she wanted to look as good as possible for her father, whom she had not seen in some time. She did not want him to feel that her marriage was a mistake and was falling apart because of her husband's health. She loved his music, and he was a glamorous public figure; it was a thrill to see him perform in the movies. And although she did not have a television set, Lars and she had been invited over to the chief-of-staff's bachelor pad to watch Clem's appearance on Ed Sullivan's *Toast of the Town* variety show.

She dexterously applied the pancake makeup, taking care to wet the sponge well, so that her skin would not look caked. Her thoughts went back to Lars, with whom she had dated for several years while he was studying the effects of the hallucinogenic mushrooms, the background work of which Doctor Sam, Born-Before-Sunrise, had pioneered.

Sam's research had dealt mainly with the use of the drug on terminally ill patients, and he had successfully aided George Story in a gentle passing, minus that terrible agony after morphine was no longer effective. He had used the drug himself when he lay dying.

But it was also Sam's theory, and Lars had agreed with the summation, that minute measurements of the mushroom compound might be useful medication for schizophrenic patients. Apparently the drug separated areas of the brain. As it disassociated the brain waves, causing a malfunction, the terminally ill were able to endure extreme pain, so that suffering became only one more preoccupation of the body—like breathing, urinating, or defecating.

But Lars made the mistake of experimenting with the drug himself, and at first there were no side effects. Then, much later, at odd times, even without taking the drug, he was thrown into a flashback of his former experiences. Apparently that was the danger: the substance stayed within the body. Once he had jokingly referred to the drug as J and H, and when she had asked what the initials stood for, he had said, "It's like Dr. Jekyll and Mr. Hyde. There's no physical change, of course, but mentally there is a similarity."

She adroitly used an eyebrow pencil while the pancake makeup dried, but when she looked carefully into the mirror again, for all of her painstaking work she looked like a slick mannequin in a cheap department store window. The Witch of Endor was preferable to that Glossy Look. "To hell with it!" she exclaimed bitterly, and, soaping her face, blindly reached for a huck towel. Again she looked into the mirror, blanched, and decided to go downstairs for breakfast sans makeup.

As if everything else was not enough, she began to feel the twinge of menstrual cramps. The fact that she was also terribly worried about both her grandmother and her husband did not improve the situation. Whenever she was emotionally upset, the cramps always became worse.

Before leaving the bathroom, Patricia Anne Story Hanson pushed the brown pancake-makeup-stained towel into the bottom drawer of the lavatory stand, and she composed her face carefully before going down the stairs. If there was one thing that she hated more than funerals, it was showing oneself at seven o'clock in the morning.

Letty glanced at the illuminated dial of the clock on the bedside stand. It was time to face the world. She was tired, very tired, because she had not permitted herself to go back to sleep after that last dream. Having frightened the family out of their wits twice in one night, she had no intention of achieving a third!

She had never before reacted to an occasional nightmare in a theatrical manner. Now, was it because she needed attention? Was it because she was—for the first time— alone? Then, suddenly, she wanted to feel strong arms around her; she desired to be held, to feel the beat of a man's heart next to her breast.

Automatically, her hand went to the other side of the bed. Then she remembered that there was no one there. She began to sob into the pillow, because no one would be there—*ever!*

2

Gathering Clouds

The thunderstorm broke at eleven forty-five a.m. on August 15, 1951.

"And now, I pronounce you man and wife," the Justice of the Peace intoned nasally, glancing over his Ben Franklin spectacles at Mitchell Heron. "Now," he said firmly, rather than kindly, "you can kiss the bride."

As Mitchell brushed Charlotte's lips with his own, a lightning bolt flashed through the gray sky and illuminated the room. "You can't say we don't generate electricity!" He laughed, brushing a bit of imaginary lint from the lapel of his new dark wool suit.

Charlotte gave him a long, amused look and adjusted the corsage of white camellias on the shoulder of her powder-blue dress. "I hope you have an umbrella in the car," she said with a worried expression, looking out of the window at the rain that splashed down relentlessly on the red-brick paving of Blackwell, Oklahoma.

"Why must you always be so practical?" he countered lightly. "How can I manage a bumbershoot while I'm carrying you out to the car?"

She shook her head and laughed, noticing that the J.P.'s mousy wife, who had acted as witness to the ceremony, was signing the marriage license. "In the first place, my good man, you'll surely get a hernia if you attempt to lift me. Remember, I've gained twenty pounds since I stopped smoking!"

She paused meaningfully. "Now, will you be serious for a

moment? Should we stay at the Blackwell Hotel tonight? That country road back to Enid, through Medford and Pond Creek, can be miserable. It's no fun being stuck in the mud."

"With you, my sweet, it would be glorious!" He grinned like a little boy who had been caught examining his first nude female statue. "Let's take our chances."

"You're not being yourself, Mitch. If I didn't know better, I'd swear you'd had something alcoholic to drink."

He raised his thick eyebrows. "I don't need that kind of stimulation. It's not every day that I get hitched." He paused. "I always wondered what the state of marriage would be like to an old confirmed bachelor like myself. You know, I *do* feel kind of drunky. How about you?"

"Sober as a judge," she answered with a straight face, refusing to look at the J.P. "But I do feel a bit giddy." She gazed out the window at the downpour. "I guess this rain business runs in the family. Mama and Papa were married during a deluge in San Antonio, and you can't say that they didn't have a happy marriage. Maybe the rain will bring us luck."

"Amen," said the mousy wife of the Justice of the Peace in such a bored, skeptical tone that Mitchell wondered if she thought marriage in general was a mistake. She had obviously witnessed hundreds of marriages, and perhaps had gained second sight as to those that would endure and those that would not. Or more likely, from her sour expression, she was only experiencing an attack of indigestion; she looked a bit green around the gills.

He thrust a twenty-dollar bill into her hand, and at that moment, as if on cue, the rain suddenly ceased. The J.P. glanced over his spectacles again and testily advised, "Don't mean to get rid of you folks, but you'd better skedaddle while there's a let-up."

"Good idea," Mitchell replied, and pumped his hand, then kissed his startled wife on the cheek. "If you ever need any new furniture, come to my store in Enid, and I'll give you a discount."

The J.P. and his mousy wife exchanged glances. "Oh," he exclaimed, "so you're one of *those* Herons!"

"Yep," Mitchell replied smoothly, "the black sheep of the family."

The J.P. smiled broadly, displaying a gold eyetooth. "Isn't that a coincidence? It was family gossip for years that Great-Aunt Leona, who founded the Barrett Conservatory of Music in Angel, may her soul forever be preserved, had some Heron Oil Company stock once upon a time."

He took a pinch of snuff and sneezed enthusiastically before handing the small tin box to his wife. "But none of us ever knew what happened to it. For some reason the family didn't have much truck with her. I have a photograph of her somewhere, a white-haired old lady sitting in a big wingback chair in front of a fireplace in her big house in New York City." He adjusted his spectacles. "You being born in Angel, did you know Leona Barrett Elder?"

"No," Mitchell replied quietly. "Now, if you'll excuse us, we'll take off between showers." He held out his hand. "Remember what I said about the furniture."

Charlotte was still giggling as they got into the 1952 Chrysler. "Why didn't you fill him in on his fabulous great-aunt, Mitch?"

"Why should I disillusion him?" He waved his hand and went on airily, "I didn't think it was the best of taste to tell him that before Leona Barrett married Holden Elder in New York City—about 1909—and became a respectable patroness of the arts, she ran The Widows, the most famous whorehouse in Indian Territory!"

The rain continued sporadically all the way back to Enid, but there was so little traffic that Mitchell was able to drive down the middle of the graveled road, thereby avoiding sharp-rutted shoulders.

At North Broadway, he turned at the courthouse. "Excuse me, dear, but I have to stop by the store and check the mail. I'm expecting a big order from an oil man in Tulsa, big enough to pay for our honeymoon in Monte Carlo. I won't be a moment."

He parked the car at the curb, squeezed her hand, and went quickly into the storeroom, where Ida Parrish, the bookkeeper, accosted him at the door. "There's a man who's been waiting to see you all morning long," she said, looking toward the ceiling. "He won't go away."

"I didn't have any appointments set up," he replied with a frown, but did not add, "because I was getting married," for the simple reason that he had not told his employees about his nuptials. Next week he would simply introduce Charlotte as his wife. In the meantime, he would make short shrift of the visitor, who could only be one of the more persistent salesmen.

Mitchell riffled through the stack of mail and smiled as he extracted the fat envelope from the Tulsa millionaire, casually glancing through the glass partition. Sitting in the anteroom, smoking a large Havana, was a little man with magnificent mustachios, who looked exactly like a French civil servant.

At the top of the list of all the people in the world Mitchell did not expect to see on his wedding day was Pierre Darlan. He took a deep breath, selected a gracious smile out of his repertoire of pleasant facial expressions, opened the door, and held out his hand. "What a surprise, Monsieur Darlan!" he cried, with far more enthusiasm than he felt.

The little man threw him a hard glance. He knew him very well. "Why are you not glad to see old Pierre?"

Mitchell raised his eyebrows. "It's just that you always pop up at the most unexpected times."

The man nodded, somehow managing to look like an ancient sage. "Yes, that is true, yet I must wholly blame it upon my—ahem—*our* profession."

Mitchell shook his head. "If you have a job in mind, Monsieur, you can forget about it."

"What is this new attitude?" The tone was amused and pensive at the same time.

"The attitude of a newly married man."

"*Pardon?*"

Mitchell gave Pierre a genuine smile. "I thought that might shake you up! Our vows were said not more than two hours ago in the small provincial community of Blackwell."

"Are there, indeed, black wells in that locality?" Pierre was playing for time.

"Presumably."

Pierre examined Mitchell's dark blue suit. "Is this the appropriate dress for the wedding march?"

"But there was no 'march,' Pierre." Mitchell was enjoying himself hugely. It was not often that he could surprise the Frenchman. "We stood up before a Justice of the Peace."

"Mendelssohn?"

"The only music was 'arranged' by the storm."

Pierre was not amused. He got up slowly, eyes very dark, his complexion more ruddy than it had been before Mitchell's announcement. "I shall be going, then." He bowed formally. "Nice to have seen you again, and good luck on the road of matrimony."

"You mean you came all the way to Oklahoma for this?" Mitchell asked incredulously.

"No, I had something else entirely in mind, but that has now been thrown out of the window."

"What do you mean?"

"I mean, my friend," Pierre said coldly, "you know very well that we cannot use married men, alcoholics, homosexuals, drug addicts, child molesters . . ."

Mitchell's eyes were steely. "You have certainly placed me in a rarefied group."

Pierre held up a warning finger. "Not that we have not, from time to time, utilized all of these types. But the man for the current job must, unfortunately, be single." He bowed. *"Adieu."*

"You will meet my wife?"

Pierre shook his head and picked up his raincoat.

"I don't know how you are going to avoid it," Mitchell replied with a grin. "She's coming through the door right now."

Charlotte hurried into the office. "Mitch, what on earth is keeping you?" When she saw that he was not alone, she colored." "I'm . . . terribly sorry, but I didn't mean to interrupt." Flustered, she started to back out of the room.

"It's quite all right, dear," Mitchell said casually. "An

old friend just dropped by to chat. Charlotte, I'd like you to meet Pierre Darlan, a dealer who specializes, I believe, in the Queen Anne period."

Pierre did not smile, but bowed very stiffly and raised his hat. "*Madame*," he murmured and rushed out of the room.

"Oh, Mitch, I'm so sorry! It got so hot in the car . . ."

"You need not apologize. Pierre never makes appointments." He smiled at a private joke.

"He was very curt. You couldn't say that I've made a conquest there. I disapprove of wives who barge into their husbands' offices unannounced. I promise never to do it again."

"It was my fault, Charlotte, I shouldn't have left you out there so long.

"Did the letter come?"

He nodded. "Yes, with a big, fat check." He paused. "You know, not very often, but once in a very great while, the name of Heron comes in handy. This multimillionaire trusts me implicitly. Oh, he knows my work, and all of that, but I'd never have gotten a deposit this large if his office wasn't next to the Heron Building in Tulsa." He ushered her out of the door. "We'll have a nice honeymoon in Monte Carlo?"

She gave him a long, amused, wry look as he opened the Chrysler door for her. "Not especially. The casino is an architectural monstrosity, the wine is overpriced, and all the beach boys and girls have gonorrhea."

He laughed, and climbed in beside her and turned on the ignition. "Charlotte, do you know one of the great things I like about you? You're great fun!"

As the Chrysler pulled away from the curb, Charlotte repeated the word "fun" to herself. Not one of all those golden boys in Washington had ever said that she was *fun*. They had variously called her "insatiable," "bitchy," "kind," "game," or even "a good lay"—but never "fun." "Why, thank you, Mitch," she said seriously, "that's quite a compliment."

She had created her own niche in Washington society: the inevitable "extra woman"—so handy to hostesses who needed a fourth for canasta; someone to make the table come out to an even twelve, or to sub, at the last moment, for a suddenly indisposed guest at a stage play at the National Theatre.

She had loved that life. Who would have dreamed that Charlotte Dice, the social butterfly, who took so many young men under her commodious wings, would ever be content to be the wife of the owner of a group of furniture stores with headquarters in Enid, Oklahoma? A man who was not particularly young, not especially good-looking or exceptionally well endowed? But content she was and she turned gratefully to her new husband. "Mitch, I want you to know that I love you very much."

He glanced at her in surprise. "What brought that on?"

She smiled at him. "When I get to know you better, I'll tell you."

"If you don't know me by now, you never will!" he joked, but thought: *You have your secrets, and I have mine, my dear. Part of my past will be forever hidden: Michel Bayard and Herr Professor Schneider.* He wondered what sort of job Pierre Darlan had had in mind for him. For one shattering moment, Mitchell regretted that his new status as a married man would forever rob him of working as an undercover operative again. . . .

Then, conscious of Charlotte's presence, he felt a surge of guilt. No, he would not trade present life for a few weeks of danger that always included portraying someone other than himself. That was play-acting. It suddenly occurred to him that all secret agents were really frozen forever in adolescence: a fantasy world in which they always played the "loner"—a role that, no matter under what name, or what disguise, or what nationality, was a massive journey for the ego. A journey that he could nicely live without.

"Merde!" Pierre Darlan exclaimed to his superior, H.R. Leary, as he strode angrily into the office on the second floor of the huge building in Langley, Virginia.

Having just returned from a vacation in Bermuda, Leary brushed the top of his white crew cut with a brown, suntanned hand. "I take it that all did not go well in Enid?"

"He is no longer single," Pierre replied simply.

H.R. Leary, a man whose words were as sparse as his facial expressions, shrugged. "So, we lose yet another man to the hallowed halls of matrimony!" He picked up a pencil and began to doodle idly on a piece of paper, a habit that told Pierre Darlan that his boss was deep in thought—and even deeper in trouble.

The Frenchman went quickly to the corner of the room, where he typed a command on a small keyboard which was attached to the massive computer in the next room. At once, two names appeared on the small screen. Impressed, he looked up quizzically. "Phillips and Hernden are free for the job."

'Dolts, both of them!" Leary expostulated. "Heron is perfect in every way. He speaks both French and German without accent; his Spanish isn't bad; he's a quick study; and, more importantly, he conveniently disappears into the woodwork of his furniture business after each mission." He paused thoughtfully. "Incidentally, what type female finally started his hormones working?"

Pierre smoothed his mustaches and looked like nothing so much as small walrus. "Plump, fortyish, uninteresting . . ." He clapped his hands together suddenly. "Of course!" He turned away, brow furrowed. "I am an idiot!" he exclaimed.

Leary stopped doodling and smiled indolently. "Are you asking for confirmation or repudiation."

"Her maiden name was Dice," Pierre went on hurriedly. "It must be that she is the Senator Dice's daughter."

He went quickly to the computer, typed a name, and a moment later was peering at a screen filled with information. "Very interesting. Plump she is, fortyish she is, uninteresting she is not!" He read from the screen: "'Top security clearance, Justice Department . . . employed June 1938 to July 1949 . . . I.Q. 145 . . . speaks some French, fluent in Spanish . . . traveled abroad on grand tour 1934; London, 1936; France, 1948; Rome, 1949; Paris, 1950; active in Junior League, Bachelorettes, Red Cross, USO . . . smokes . . . social drinker—' Aha!" Pierre clapped his hands together again. "'Married Mitchell Heron, top security clearance, Blackwell, Oklahoma, August 15, 1951.' *Merde!* The computer knows what we do not!''

Leary shook his head sadly. "It's really very funny—ironic, actually—that our organization spends such great amounts of money keeping up-to-date information on such nonentities as this . . . woman, when they won't give us sufficient cash to conscript worthwhile individuals for our common cause. It's disgusting!''

"Absolutely. Yet there is one very interesting thing about Charlotte Dice Heron. Here is a screen full of reports on her various affairs of the heart over the years." He raised his eyebrows. "She apparently went to bed with an entire generation of young men from eighteen to twenty-two!''

"Wonder how she got her clearance?" Leary asked absently, then answered his own question. "Her father was a senator. . . .''

Pierre smiled, showing an array of tobacco-stained teeth. "I do not suppose security felt that her job of recruiting secretaries was endangered by her promiscuity.''

"Nevertheless, why did Mitchell marry her?''

Pierre shrugged elaborately. "Perhaps it is unwise to speculate on such things. It is sufficient that he must be retired from the game.''

Leary nodded. "A pity. I thought he might like a trip through from Paris to San Sebastian, including a tour of the magnificent châteaux of your native land.''

Clement Story stood on the stage of the venerable War Memorial Opera House in San Francisco. The show was a benefit for the Children's Hospital, and he was last on a bill that had already presented seven other performers. Benefits, he reflected, were a pain in the ass. Since only expenses were paid and there was no salary, the stars were usually quite casual about performing, and rehearsals were usually for amateurs only.

He had already performed three numbers, "Tea for Two," "Moonlight Becomes You," and "Red Sails in the Sunset." He glanced out over the huge auditorium, and while the applause lasted, took four curtain calls. His midnight-blue tuxedo was damp, and perspiration was running down the nape of his neck and trickling down his spine.

He was feeling slightly dizzy. A fierce headache, tentacles emanating from his temples, clashed in the middle of his forehead. He was aware that his pain was caused by the multicolored lights which shone mercilessly down from the teasers and tormentors hung above and at the sides of the maroon cyclorama that encircled the stage.

The most disconcerting lights, however, were two powerful blinding carbon-powered kliegs, which blazed down relentlessly from the booth above the peanut gallery. Covered with Shubert Pink gels, the spots gave a rosy glow to his dark, mixed-blood Cherokee complexion.

It was always the same, night after night: after two hours of those lights, he thought he would go mad, yet he must not in any way show his extreme discomfort. He dabbed repeatedly at his forehead with a white handkerchief, which served two purposes: first, his gesture prevented the sweat from streaming into his eyes, and second, his action cued pianist Tracy Newcomb to start the introduction to "The Cowboy Waltz," with which he always ended his gig.

Tracy faked the *clomp, clomp, clomp* of horses' hooves with his left hand and signaled the orchestra with his right. Clement knelt on the apron of the stage and retrieved his guitar, and the crowd went wild.

He smiled widely, waiting for the audience to quiet, giving the appearance of being able to discern every face in the auditorium, when actually he could discern only a vague gray mist beyond the footlights. Then, looking up to Nosebleed Haven, the second balcony, he began to sing in a flat Midwestern voice that sounded like dried leaves rustling in an autumn forest:

> *College frats in sheepskin chaps,*
>   *Shootin' irons stuck down,*
> *In holsters, brown 'n'*
> *Fuzzy from the dew.*

He was on home ground as applause went through the auditorium like a thunderclap. As always, he smiled shyly, as if surprised at the sound, and then, wide-eyed, addressed the first balcony:

> *Teenage cats in Stetson hats,*
> *Gum in their jaw,*
> *Instead of a chaw*
> *Of leafy dried and green.*

After more applause, he addressed the main floor with his eyes and did the third verse. It was then that he knew that he could not make that last high note that ended the song. He would retard. He stepped back and, nodding from side to side, bleated out the chorus:

Teenage cats in Stetson hats,
College frats in sheepskin chaps,
Three-piece suits in roun-tip boots,
Middle-aged curs in silver spurs,
Foreign dudes are havin' feuds,
All sippin' their malts, discussin' faults,
And doin'—the cowboy, yes, doin' THE COWBOY WALTZ

He retarded, but the orchestra behind him roared on, leaving him wavering somewhere on the bottom side of the note. He bowed, cursing to himself.

During the quick blackout, he was conscious of a scurrying sound backstage, as the seven other stars on the program joined him for the finale, the chorus of "There's No Business like Show Business"—which none of the stars had practiced together. Clement had instructed the orchestra to come in strongly to make up for the lack of rehearsal; this time the bastards paid attention to what was happening, and the music was so loud that he could not even hear his own voice.

As they all bowed low, he felt the curious wind that always preceded a standing ovation, which they all damned well deserved, having performed free. It was a rite of passage.

The stage lights faded to black, and before Clement ran into the wings he hissed at Tracy Newcomb: "Goddammit, when I retard, you *retard!*" When the auditorium lights came up to full a moment later, the stage curtain had closed: the concert was over.

Before the audience could arise and filter backstage, Clement was in the limousine on his way back to the Fairmont Hotel on Nob Hill. Let the others wear their mouths out smiling to fans and crimp their fingers around stubby pencils, signing autographs.

The first thing that he had learned in show business was the absolute necessity of conserving personal energy. The most talented genius in the world, whether he sang for his supper or wrote equations on a blackboard, could not perform on nonexistent physical force. When the drive, the spark, the enthusiasm, was missing, there was always the danger of reaching for the bottle or the syringe or the pill— to replenish that which had been frittered away and was lost.

Too often he had seen fellow performers, stoned to their gills, giving what they thought was the performance of their lives. But what the audience saw was a highly animated puppet with an unreliable, often harsh voice, and an intense stage presence that detracted from the performance.

He was fond of remarking to friends that the only thing that he was hooked on was sex—which always got a laugh. It was only lately that he did not think his witticism very funny—especially on those occasions when it was easier to turn over on his pillow and pretend that he was even too sleepy to say good night.

Sarah handed him a whiskey and soda from the bar in the back seat. "How did it go tonight?"

He took a long pull from the glass. "A little ragged, even for a benefit. The only thing I kept thinking about was how many famous people had stood on that stage. The most renowned stars of opera, ballet, Broadway, and the movies —internationally known orchestras and the most prestigious symphony conductors."

"But surely you didn't feel intimidated?" she cried, and when he did not answer, went on forcefully, "But you're a star!"

He smiled wryly. "What's a star, Sarah? I don't class myself in a league with Enrico Caruso, Alexandra Danilova, Arturo Toscanini, Leopold Stokowski, Helen Hayes, or Paul Whiteman. And those performers who appeared at the benefit tonight certainly aren't in that league." He looked at her quizzically over the rim of the glass. "I'm just a halfbreed Cherokee Indian from Angel, Oklahoma—remember, Squaw?"

She smiled and suddenly looked very beautiful. It had been a long time since he had called her "Squaw." "I don't agree that you're any less a star than the others, Hotshot!" she said, addressing him by her favorite nickname.

"Well, the crux of the matter is, let's just say that I didn't give my best performance, that's all, and the orchestra, back there picking their noses, didn't follow me when I had to retard at the end of 'The Cowboy Waltz.'"

"What do you mean 'had' to retard?"

He poured himself another scotch. "What do you think the word 'had' means?" he spat out angrily. "The voice, the wind—or, as Helen Traubel always said, 'the instrument'—GAVE OUT! Does that answer your goddamn question?"

She ignored this unusual outburst and tried to be sympathetic. "Everyone has an off night now and then, dear."

"Don't patronize me, Sarah!" He sat the empty glass on the tray secured to the seat. "I'm dead tired, from the inside out. The only real three days off I've had during the last nine months was Bosley's funeral. You can't count transportation time between gigs.

"Somehow, I worked in that movie for Metro-Goldwyn-Mayer and I did Ed Sullivan's *Toast of the Town* television show twice." He began to cough. "I'm beat and, furthermore, I think I'm coming down with a cold. If I get laryngitis—"

"Honey, you should have changed into a dry suit after a concert."

"You know very well," he groused, "I couldn't spend any time backstage or I'd be cornered for autographs. That's for kids new to the game. I'm pooped as it is, without being stuck for another hour or so, signing my name and being pleasant to people I don't know. I can't put myself through that routine anymore. Do you realize that I've been performing steadily since 1918? Thirty-four years!''

The limousine came to rest under the ornate portico of the Fairmont Hotel, which also protected a group of youngsters holding a huge sign that read:

CLEMENT STORY S.F. FAN CLUB

"Jesus Christ!" Clement swore under his breath. "What in the hell are those juvenile delinquents doing here?"

Sarah, who took care of his fan mail, leaned over urgently, at once the professional. "See that fat girl in front, with all the pimples? She's Mary Jane Fulmer, president of the club. She writes those passionate letters, and the last one included an autographed picture of herself." Sarah smiled tightly. "Which was a switch."

"Have I written to her?"

Sarah nodded. "Yes. The Number Three letter."

He nodded. The Number Three letter was civil, but worded in such a way as to discourage future correspondence.

Clement closed his eyes tightly, and a startling transformation took place. He squared his shoulders, lifted his head, opened his eyes wide, and, placing a friendly grin on his face, stepped out of the limousine onto the curb to applause, cheers, and whistles.

"I'm real pleased at the reception," he said warmly. "It does my heart good to see you all here."

He searched the front line and picked out the fat, pimply girl. What was the monster's name? Ah, yes. . . . He grinned, and said very casually, "Hello, Mary Jane," noting that, from the look of ecstasy on her face, she was precariously close to orgasm.

He did a quick head count. There were twenty teenagers. "Let's all go inside," he said cordially, moving toward the hotel entrance so that he would not be surrounded, "and I'll treat you all to hot fudge sundaes at Blums." He turned to Sarah. "And I'd like you all to meet . . . my helpmate."

Sarah, who did not feel like a helpmate at all, managed a

fleeting smile as he took her arm and they led the group into the red-and-white ice-cream parlor.

An hour later, after the door to the suite was locked and bolted, Sarah turned angrily to Clement. "Really," she said furiously, "it's getting worse! You are behaving like—oh, I don't know what, so patronizing and folksy. If you had said 'you all' one more time I would have retched—and that 'helpmate' bit really topped off the evening! Where in the hell did you get that? *Cosmopolitan* magazine?"

He smiled thinly. "But you *are* my helpmate, and also my wife, lover, mistress, and expert cook—"

"This is no time to be funny," she retorted, but, looking into his eyes, she saw how utterly exhausted he was and her heart softened. "You're so tired, you probably don't remember what you said. It's all right. I've forgiven you for a lot more."

He took her in his arms and held her tightly. "I love you," he said softly, "and when we get into bed, I'll prove it."

They undressed and changed into nightclothes and then climbed between the lavender-smelling sheets. When she turned on her side, facing him, she saw that his eyes were closed and he was breathing evenly.

"Oh, my dear, my very dear," she whispered fervently, "what is happening to you?" His personality was changing; very gradually, he was becoming a man she scarcely knew. It was as if all of his old values had turned inward. "Oh, Clem," she murmured, "come back to me. . . ."

Sarah opened the San Francisco newspaper to the entertainment section. There were photographs of the eight stars who had appeared at the benefit at the War Memorial Opera House, starting with the Oak Rhythm Boys at the top and ending with Clement on the bottom. She frowned. The most important performer on the bill—his picture should have headed the grouping. The review began:

BENEFIT MIRED IN THE PAST
By Jared Rosenblum

A capacity audience attended last night's Children's Hospital benefit at the War Memorial Opera House. It is hoped that the funds raised from the star-studded social event will compensate for the lackluster musical stylings provided by the eight famed performers in an ambiguous evening. . . .

Sarah raised her eyebrows and hurriedly skipped down to the end of the review, which dealt with Clement:

. . . Clement Story and his Cherokee Swing Band closed the evening, and let it be said for this popular entertainer that he pleased his fans, who turned out in great numbers. Musically, however, he seemed ill at ease, as if the confines of the huge auditorium were less a home than his windswept Oklahoma prairie. It may well be that he was discomfited, coming on so late, after younger, more enthusiastic performers had been given their chances. . . .

Sarah shifted uncomfortably in the easy chair and took another sip of coffee, then nervously continued reading:

He began the set with "Lady Luck," the familiar theme song of his popular radio show, which he sang in a strident, offhand manner. "Tea for Two," "Moonlight Becomes You," and "Red Sails in the Sunset" seemed ill-advised standards from what must be a prodigious repertoire.

He had not had a critical review like this for a very long time, and her palms were watery.

His voice became thin and noticeably frayed, too fragile and increasingly edgy, though finely backed, as usual, by the strong, vibrant, and inventive arrangements (credited on the program to the gifted William Nestor). The orchestra is still very fine, even having lost many of its original Cherokee members.

Sarah was shocked but had an uncomfortable feeling that the worst was yet to come.

Clement Story almost redeemed himself with his sign-off song, the plaintive and amusing "Cowboy Waltz," but even here, accompanying himself on the guitar, he seemed weary and distracted, with a lets-get-this-over-and-go-home attitude, and when the orchestra came in on what was obviously supposed to be a touching evening . . . it was not . . . touching.

She would discard this newspaper before Clement arose, and since she handled the mail, she would also destroy the cutting when it arrived from the clipping service.

Mr. Story, who is celebrating thirty-four years in show business, should take a hint from Walter Huston, who did not really have a voice, either, and yet who can forget the loving attention given to the words of "September Song" from *Knickerbocker Holiday*? It is hoped that the maestro takes heed and performs his lyrics with the same scrupulous concentration to detail.

"Squaw." It was Clement's voice from the bedroom. "Order some ham and eggs from room service, will you please?" He was in a good mood if he had called her "Squaw." She had already crumpled the newspaper when she made the decision to show him the notice.

She had never hidden a review from him before; they had always been honest with each other, and there was always the real danger that someone, sooner or later, might mention the article. She ordered breakfast, then called, "Hey, Hotshot." She made her voice sound light. "You're not very hot this morning!"

His laugh echoed from the bedroom. "Give me time, I just got up!" He came into the living room, toweling his head. "We've got to catch a plane or I'd—" He paused, seeing the strange look on her face. "What's wrong, honey?"

"Oh, sometimes I think the critics in San Francisco are perpetually constipated, that's all."

"I take it that the notice is not one of the more glowing of my career?" His tone was bantering, yet she could feel his anxiety.

"Rosenblum didn't like the evening, period! Not that he singled you out particularly—"

"That bad, huh?" He threw the wet towel on the parquet floor of the entryway and picked up the paper. After reading the first paragraph, he sat down beside her on the sofa, his brow furrowed.

Sarah nervously lighted a cigarette and then answered the knock on the door. The elderly waiter, who had been with the Fairmont for many years and who had waited on them on other occasions, wheeled in the table with its silver, damask, fine porcelain, crested flatware, and crystal goblets.

"I hope I'm not out of line, Mr. Story," he said, arranging two side chairs around the table and removing the plate warmers, "but Jared Rosenblum is getting senile. He's been on that paper for forty years. He should be retired. He's lost touch." He paused. "I thought you were just *fine!*"

Clement finished the last paragraph of the review, took the check, and added a five-dollar tip before he signed the bottom with a flourish. "Thank you," he said kindly, "but I'm feelng somewhat senile myself this morning."

The waiter bowed himself out of the room as if he had just served royalty, and Clement got up slowly and seated Sarah before sitting down himself. He took a forkful of hash-en-cream potatoes, masticated thoughtfully for a moment, and then pushed the plate away. He took a sip of coffee. "Maybe old Rosenblum is right, Sarah," he said thoughtfully. "I didn't feel right about last night, and not having much of a voice to begin with, I know I sounded strained."

He got up and went to the window and looked at the Golden Gate bridge in the distance. It was so clear that he could see Alcatraz Island, and beyond, a bevy of sailboats in the middle of the bay. "I'm going to tell Max not to book me on any program where I have to sing more than one song." He paused. "I do remember Walter Huston singing

'September Song.' He was wonderful; just this old man on the stage singing about what it was like to grow old, and looking back over his lifetime."

He rubbed his jaw thoughtfully. "I must have seen *Knickerbocker Holiday* after it had been on Broadway for many months, yet Walter sounded like he was singing the lyrics for the first time. I was very moved. I remember there were tears in my eyes." He drew in his breath, and his voice was cryptic. "I doubt that anyone had tears in their eyes last night when I finished 'The Cowboy Waltz.'"

"But it's an entirely different sort of song!" Sarah protested, coming up behind him and placing her arms around his shoulders and laying her head forward on his back.

"In content, yes, honey, but 'September Song' was Walter's signature tune, just as 'The Cowboy Waltz' has become mine."

He paused, and turned in her arms. "You see, Sarah," he went on quietly, "by rights, everyone in the audience *should* be moved, even though it is a novelty with no shmaltz. It's *my* song, like "When the Moon Comes over the Mountain,' is Kate Smith's, or 'When My Baby Smiles at Me' is Ted Lewis's. Those songs are so identified with the performers that it's touching and moving to hear them sing those old numbers. Christ, if I can't do justice to Billy Nestor's words, I better quit show business!"

She kissed him on the mouth quickly, and then stood back. "I hate to rush you, dear," she said soothingly, "but the plane won't wait."

He blinked his eyes. "Where is the next gig? I've forgotten."

She patted his cheek. "Home," she said softly. "We're going home."

3

The Promise

It was February 14, 1952, and Enid was bathed in the cold light of an unfriendly sun.

Mitchell Heron slid into his usual booth in the dining room of the Hotel Youngblood, and was poised to order the special of the day, liver and onions—which Charlotte refused to prepare for him at home—when he looked up into the smiling face of Pierre Darlan, who was seated in the next booth, having a cup of coffee. Mitchell showed no surprise, but nodded coolly as if the Frenchman were a distant acquaintance.

Pierre summoned the waitress. "Transfer my check to the next booth, please." He got up slowly, and it seemed to Mitchell that he had aged since they had seen each other last, six months before; he appeared more frail.

"Won't you join me?" Mitchell asked cordially, raising his eyebrows slightly.

"Merci!" Pierre smiled widely and, with some difficulty, slid into the booth. "The voice is kind, the eyes are not. Why are you not happy to see the Frenchman? What are you eating, my friend?"

"The special."

Pierre glanced at the menu. "To quote a very young friend of mine, 'I think offal is awful.' No, I shall have the Swiss steak, which I am certain bears little relationship to either that famed European country or to the noble sirloin."

Mitchell gave the order to Gracie, the blonde waitress, well past her prime, who always waited upon him. He knew

38

Pierre well enough to ascertain that he was in a good-to-excellent mood, and when he was in a good-to-excellent mood he wanted something very badly. He dispensed with preliminaries. "What do you want of me?" he asked in French, taking a long sip of coffee, refusing to look at his visitor. "You are, of course, aware that not only am I still married, but divorce is not even contemplated?"

Pierre pulled at his mustaches and shrugged. "Have you and Charlotte been together long enough that you both *appear* married?"

"What kind of a question is that, Pierre? My God, don't married people always look *married*?"

"Not necessarily."

"This conversation is, at best, idiotic. Don't tell me that you traveled all the way from hell and gone to question me about my marital status?"

"You know me better than that, my friend." Pierre removed a leather tobacco pouch from his inside coat pocket and began to dexterously pack a pipe.

"I thought you gave up smoking."

Pierre grinned. "I did, but I've taken it up again." He paused. "It gives me something to do when someone is sent out into the cold and doesn't return on time. I must have smoked a barrel of very bad tobacco when we had difficulty bringing you back from France that time." He went on with his ritual, placed the finished brown fag in his mouth, and brought out his tiny European lighter, which he flipped repeatedly until he finally raised a flame. "Why do not you play the game with me?"

"What game?"

They were interrupted by Gracie, who swallowed a wisecrack when she saw the men were engaged in a serious conversation, placed the steaming plates on the table, and disappeared before they could order more coffee.

Pierre paid elaborate attention to the Swiss steak, which Mitchell conceded looked far more appetizing than the liver and onions. "You have not taken your honeymoon?"

When Pierre asked a question in that manner, Mitchell reflected, it meant that he knew the answer. "No, we've had a rush of business at the store that just lasted until a week ago, and we haven't been able to get away. A money-man in Tulsa is building a hotel, and the Heron Furniture Company is one of the suppliers."

"Well, Monte Carlo can be hectic in the spring, at best," Pierre put in casually.

"Goddammit!" Mitchell threw down his napkin. "If you know everything, why are we continuing this charade?"

"A highly overrated game, charades."

Mitchell was angry. "Will you please tell me what you came to tell me and then get the hell out?"

"Do not be cross with the old man," Pierre said gently, "who must do things his own way."

"Well, *his* way is getting worse!" Mitchell replied testily. "And why are we speaking in the third person?"

Pierre took a bite of the Swiss steak, nodded his approval, and wiped his mustaches with the napkin, before replying. "I have in my pocket a trip for a worthy honeymoon couple, through the magnificent château country of France, ending in the picturesque city of San Sebastian, Spain." He took another bite of the Swiss steak and chewed thoughtfully. "We surmised that you and your wonderful bride might like a peaceful, expense-paid honeymoon."

Suddenly Mitchell lost his appetite for liver and onions. "Why are you including my wife?" he demanded in a strong, low voice, strong enough to be forceful, and yet low enough that other people in nearby could not hear.

"Because a honeymoon is not a honeymoon unless there is a woman along."

"Now, suddenly, Pierre, you make jokes!" Mitchell shook his head. "You've always said that married men have no place in the business."

Pierre nodded thoughtfully. "Yes, I have often put forth that theory." He frowned. "Yet, once in a very great while, a job requires a man and a woman to be together for . . . some time, and logistics work against a couple who are not . . .married."

"What do you mean?"

Pierre gestured vaguely. "It was a statement, nothing more. Must I bring out my easel and paint a picture? I do not like to be indelicate, but sharing accommodations with a strange woman to whom one is not actually attracted might be considered one of those logistics."

Mitchell laughed. "It would depend entirely upon the woman!" Then he turned serious. "Saying I would agree to such a trip, there is a catch, of course."

"*Naturally*. A very small one, my friend, but a catch nonetheless."

Mitchell placed his fork and knife neatly on the edge of the plate. "Well?" His voice was flat, yet he was filled with excitement. He had not realized until this moment how he had missed that feeling of being in jeopardy—in danger, and the possibility of being captured, exposed, detained, that always existed around the next corner.

Then all anticipated joy went out of him. Whatever the odds, he could not place Charlotte in peril. He shook his head. "Thank you for thinking about me, Pierre," he said politely, reverting to French, "but we can't possibly go."

"*Non?* And, why not, pray tell?"

"One word. I thought you might have guessed."

"And what is that word?"

"Charlotte."

Pierre leaned forward. "I admit that our department has shown, shall we say, somewhat less regard for details than usual, perhaps, but I assure you H.L. Leary is not an idiot. Charlotte Heron, *née* Dice, possesses a number one security clearance with the State Department. Agreed that we are not on too friendly terms with them at the moment, but . . ."

Mitchell stared at the man across the table. "You can't mean that Charlotte is to be in on the mission?" He was incredulous.

"*Certainly*. She is a very important part of the scheme. You are newlyweds, remember?" Pierre paused. "Perhaps a bit long in the tooth to shower each other with overt affection in public, but newlyweds just the same—a most difficult state of mind to fake."

"But she knows nothing of my—activities," Mitchell protested. Starting to slide out of the booth, he was held by Pierre's strong grip; the little man might look old and frail, but his fingers were viselike.

"Sit down, my friend." Pierre's voice was gentle and persuasive. "I have been with this job for so long now that I sometimes am accused of performing certain tasks very badly. It has been said that I have lost my diplomacy."

Mitchell smiled coldly. "You have not lost your touch, only I don't fall for the old routines anymore. Charlotte knows nothing of my 'secret life.'"

And, reflected Pierre Darlan, thinking about all of the young men in her past, *you also know nothing of hers!* Aloud he said, "She has been, shall we say, investigated. Our sources, who must be nameless, believe that she will wholeheartedly cooperate."

"Why must sources always be anonymous? If they're privy—and I use this term advisedly—to a lot of information, why in the hell can't they come out and say so?"

Pierre looked at him blandly. "The point is moot."

And so am I! You don't understand what I've been saying, Pierre." He was adamant. "I *never* want Charlotte to know about me having worked with your . . . organization!" He set his jaw. "We have started a new life together, our pasts have been wiped out—that was our agreement. It never occurred to me that you would ever want me for another assignment after I married. No, Pierre, I am no longer available."

"This is all quite touching, this baring of the soul." Pierre smiled mirthlessly. "But there are other points to consider. It is not mandatory that we must confide in her. In fact, looking at the project from another angle, it is probably best that we keep your duties confidential. You're darling wife will provide the window dressing, and perform her duty without ever knowing—"

"No, no, Pierre." Mitchell shook his head. "It's all too complicated. Get someone else for the job and let me alone."

The Frenchman's lips curled behind his mustaches, contemptuously. "One little foray behind enemy lines during the Hot War, and one tiny excursion into occupied territory during the Cold War, does not a *past* make!"

Pierre folded his hands under his chin and looked like nothing so much as a confidant of Lucifer about to deliver an epitaph. "This mission is *important!*" His voice became steely. "Do you think I would come all the way to Oklahoma if this job was not crucial?"

Mitchell regarded him with amusement. "Our country isn't at war, so you can't say that our national security is involved," he retorted. "That business of trying to stir up any patriotic feelings that I may have won't work this time."

A sad, weary expression flashed over Pierre's face. He was very pale, and his voice trembled when he spoke. "Oh, my friend, my dear friend, you know so very little. If I should reveal to you that this little thing that we are asking you to do involves *more* than national security, what would you say?"

Mitchell regarded his companion wryly. "I would shout, '*Merde!*' I'm on to your tricks, Pierre. You think that if you can reach me emotionally, I'll say yes, and the next thing I know I'll be in Georgetown, going through extensive preparations: day and night briefings, having my hair dyed orange, going blind looking at scratchy old films, and Lord knows what else." He shook his head. "No, thank you. Get yourself a new boy."

"There are many ways to hang the cat!" Pierre took a long breath and looked as if he had lost all energy and was going on nerves alone. "This time there is no interrogation, no briefing, no hairdressing. All you do is go to Paris, join a château country motorbus tour that will eventually go on to San Sebastian, enjoy yourself, and one moment of one day receive an article. That is all." He paused significantly. "And the most gracious Charlotte need never know."

Mitchell squinted at him. He did not wish Pierre to know that he was weakening. "And how do I convince my dearly beloved to take a motorbus trip to Spain, when I had promised her a honeymoon on the Riviera?"

Pierre gave him a quizzical look. "*Mon ami,* Have I not seen your powers of persuasion before? I do not for one moment doubt your abilities. Remember how you convinced the hospital personnel in Berlin that you were Herr Doktor Professor Schneider? Surely the task before you is more simpler."

"Simple!" Mitchell was pleased at last to have an opportunity to correct his mentor. "You don't know my wife," he replied laconically, and from habit reached for the check. He had already paid Gracie when he gave a short laugh. "I thought that lunch was going to be on you?"

Pierre smiled widely. "There are two reasons why I did not pick up the check. First, I do not approve of paying for unconsumed food"—he indicated the liver and onions with a nod of his head—"and secondly, the organization is very short of money just now, and my expenses have been sharply curtailed."

Mitchell's eyes twinkled. "You cheap son-of-a-bitch," he said affectionately.

It was then that Pierre Darlan knew that he had won. "Come up to my suite," he said, "so that we can talk in privacy."

Upstairs, Pierre turned from the large false mantel, where he had unwisely shaken the ashes from his pipe, and continued the conversation, "You will drive to Oklahoma City on the 25th of July. A long time from now, no? But we must plan far ahead this time. Please arrange for the Chrysler to be parked in the Skirvin Tower Hotel parking lot."

He removed an envelope from his vest. "Here are the tickets for your connecting flights to New York and to London, and then Paris, where you will join the motorbus tour."

"What about passports? I have mine, but Charlotte . . ."

Pierre did not look at him. "Hers was renewed on May twenty-eight, nineteen forty-eight, when last she went to France."

Mitchell's eyes narrowed. "For some reason, I always underestimate you people."

"But we can leave nothing to chance," Pierre put in gently.

Mitchell smiled grimly. "Of course not, but you think nothing of disrupting people's lives and creating havoc—"

"—where none existed before?" Pierre finished for him.

"Ah, *mon ami*, a complaint that I have heard many times."
He paused. "I must not detain you."

"You mean this is all?"

Pierre nodded. "The interview is at an end."

"But, what are we to do? Isn't there any interrogation?
Where will the briefing take place? In Georgetown?"

"Oh, no, we haven't used that place since you were sent
to Germany," Pierre explained patiently. "As I explained
before, there is no interrogation. You and Charlotte are
playing yourselves." He held up his hands, palms upward,
and made a furtive little gesture. "After all, it is your
honeymoon."

"But the job," Mitchell cried, "the *job*!"

"Ah," Pierre replied with a light laugh, "it will take care
of itself."

"And just what is that supposed to mean?" Mitchell
retorted angrily.

Pierre's light manner disappeared. "Your contact will be
on the bus."

"But what is the *password*?"

"You've been out of the business for too long, my friend.
Passwords in a simple operation of this type are no longer
used."

Mitchell was growing more and more distraught. "But
how will I know the contact is genuine?"

"Oh," Pierre Darlan replied almost as an afterthought,
"the person will be carrying a small silver makeup mirror
engraved with the initial L."

"You're positively the most exasperating man that I've
ever encountered!" Mitchell raged. "What do I do when I
see this lady waving around the mirror? What am I to do
after the contact is made?"

"Oh," Pierre replied suavely, "you take the makeup
mirror, *naturally*."

Mitchell closed his eyes tightly and then, like a little boy,
counted to ten, opened his eyes, and glared at Pierre. "Why
go through all of this intrigue?" he shouted. "And what am
I to do with this very feminine mirror?" His eyes narrowed.
"Isn't it highly improbable that a man would carry such an
article around in his suitcase? How can I explain the

damned thing to Charlotte? You forget that I'm not going on my honeymoon alone!"

"I forget nothing. Use your head, my friend. Is not your dear aunt's name Letty, and does not Letty begin with the letter L? Would she not appreciate such an excellent antique?"

"My God, Pierre!" Mitchell exclaimed, exasperated. "Do you take joy in provoking your operatives? I could have a heart attack."

"Your heart, if not your logic, is in perfect condition, or so says your doctor," the Frenchman replied languidly. "But so that you will not be upset further, you will bring this priceless artifact to the Hotel San Lukas in San Sebastian and give it to Flamingo, who, one might say, resides there."

"Oh, my God, Pierre! What or who is this Flamingo? A bird . . . a plane . . . Superman?"

Pierre's eyes twinkled mischievously. "I do not read the comic pages, but I promise you that identification will not be difficult." He paused. "After that, you may pursue the honeymoon of your liking."

"What if I get in a pickle barrel and can't climb out? After all, Pierre, I have someone else to worry about besides myself!"

Reluctantly, the Frenchman pulled a scrap of paper out of his breast pocket. "Here is a telephone number in France that you may use, but only under the direst emergency. Please memorize the number and return it to me. By the way, my code name is now Gibson."

Mitchell laughed and gave him the paper. "If the organization hasn't given up code names, then all can't be lost! But Gibson doesn't sound very Gallic."

"That is exactly why it was chosen. Leary's code is Jacob."

"Pierre, I swear that all you people do is make up funny names that no one ever uses." Mitchell's voice grew heated. "Why not, in the name of the good, sweet Jesus, tell me who the contact is on the bus and dispense with all of this intrigue? Why can't the person just give me the silver makeup mirror in the first place and save a lot of time and worry?"

Pierre shrugged his shoulders elaborately. "Because, *mon ami*, we have not yet conscripted the person in question!"

Clement took a sip of coffee and grinned at his protégé, twenty-four-year-old William Nestor. "My agent, Max, has made out a check in your name for the sum of forty thousand dollars, the first payment on your royalties on 'The Cowboy Waltz.'" He held out his hand. "Congratulations."

William shook hands enthusiastically. His face, in animation, looked very Indian. "I have you to thank, Mr. Story."

Clement shook his head. "When are you going to start calling me Clem?"

William's face twisted. "Maybe in five years or so, maybe never. I have the greatest respect for you, sir."

"And I for you. Frankly, I'm the first to admit that your song is responsible for this new surge of popularity. Remember, I've been around from the year *one*. Thanks to you, kids now come to the concerts. Before the song became number one on *The Hit Parade*, my audience was definitely over thirty." He grinned. "Do you know that I have fan clubs of teenagers all over the country?"

William nodded. "You know, you have a way of changing the conversation around. Please let me finish what I was going to say. I was able to write 'The Cowboy Waltz' because you discovered me in Willawa and sent me to the Barrett Conservatory in Angel—giving me the opportunity . . ." He was very moved, and his fine, dark face, with its high cheekbones and sensitive mouth, was very grave.

"Oh hell, Billy," Clement said with a quick grin, "I'd have done the same for any kid who had your talent. Besides, I didn't discover you, it was Louisa Tarbell."

"Did I hear my name bruited about?" The voice came through the peephole in the door.

"*Entrez*," Clement shouted in an approximation of a French accent, and laughed. Louisa Tarbell was one of the most unusual women that he had ever met, but there was something about her serious mien that brought out the devil in him. She did not possess a sense of humor.

Hearing only her voice, William was transported back to the schoolroom and the mental picture of a tall, thin, plain form in a shapeless dress, with mousy brown hair finger-waved close to her head, standing at the head of the class.

The form in the doorway was still tall and thin; otherwise there was only a fleeting resemblance to that nondescript schoolteacher in Willawa whom he remembered with such fondness. Louisa's figure—much improved by a tight foundation that lifted her rather small bust to a height complimentary to her equally small waist—was swathed in pleated red silk, and her auburn hair was swept away from her face in a beehive style that brought out her deeply set blue eyes. Flawless pancake makeup and lipstick the exact same color as her spiky fingernails completed the New York designer look.

She swept into the dressing room and could not hide her enthusiasm. "I've just been on the telephone with a Mr. Ray Cornwallis of Universal International Studios in Holly-wood—"

"How is old Corny?" Clement asked dryly.

Her eyebrows rose in surprise. "You *know* him?"

"Yep. When he was musical director at the studio in the late thirties, he gave me a lot of good pointers about how to appear before the cameras in a natural way. Then, as chance would have it, he was my commanding officer during World War II, so we go back a way." He paused. "I suppose now that he's turned producer, he wants William on a picture?"

Louisa's mouth was still open. "As a matter of fact"— she turned to William, somewhat upset that Clement had taken the bloom off her announcement—"he wants you to write the title song for a comedy called *Maidie Loves Norman.*

Clement yawned. "Which has to be the bomb title of the year."

Louisa ignored his remark. "What do you say, William?"

He was embarrassed. "Well, thank you!"

She laughed. "I mean can you write a song called 'Maidie Loves Norman'?"

He grinned. "I'll have to get my thinking cap on for sure!"

"Whatever his offer is," Clement said, repeating one of his agent Max Rabinovich's aphorisms, "ask for twenty-five percent more."

Louisa stared at him. "I asked for *forty* percent more!"

"But did you get it?"

She smiled benignly. "After a while." She took a deep breath. "I had to remind him that 'The Cowboy Waltz' made that terrible English film *Jubilee* a success. Of course," she backtracked quickly, "let it be said this instant, Clem, that your marvelous rendition of the song also contributed to the box office of the picture!"

"*Thanks*," Clement interjected dryly. "I'm so glad you mentioned that. It does my heart good!"

"You know that I didn't mean to take away anything from your reputation, Clem."

He laughed. "I'm not offended. How much did you get for William?"

"Twenty-five thousand, including ten percent of the price of sheet music."

He whistled. "Not bad, Louisa. I don't think Max could have done better."

"I take that as a compliment."

"It was meant to be." He turned to William. "Take my advice, my boy, and get a copy of the screenplay of *Georgie Loves Porgy,* or whatever the hell the title is, before writing a note."

Louisa went to the mirror and brushed her hair back from her forehead. "It's in the mail."

"Good!" Clement said. "Corny is a great old guy, but he has a sentimental streak a mile long and a yard wide. Read the screenplay, and write the song *before* you meet him."

"Why?" William asked pensively.

"Because he'll tell you exactly what sort of song *he* wants, which may not be exactly the sort of song that the *producer* wants. Use your own intuitive powers. It's a love song, so you're not entirely out in left field. Your personal expression of emotions will be of the current generation and won't hark back to the era that Corny loves best—the shmaltz of the forties."

William gave him a strange look. "But Mr. Story," he said quietly, "you—"

Clement held up his hand and nodded. "I know," he defended himself, "I've made a fabulous living out of the forties swing era, which I'll continue to do as long as I possibly can, but remember, sport, I never had a hit recording that did anywhere as well on the charts as 'The Cowboy Waltz,' which was not only a change of pace for me but was a damn good novelty as well. That told me something. Right now I'm the 'grand old man of swing,' but I may fall out of fashion tomorrow. So take Corny's suggestions with a grain of salt, or you'll be writing that song twenty different ways."

Clement folded his hands under his chin. "What I'm getting at, William, is write ballads as long as you can, because there's something brewing out there in music. I don't know just what it is, but swing can't go on forever; jazz didn't. There's a brand-new style just around the corner. I can *feel* it!"

"I've never heard you talk so seriously before," William said with a sad half-smile.

"You look at life a little differently when you've been through it all a couple of times. William, I'm tired out of my mind, and people keep . . ." He shrugged. "Oh hell, why am I telling you all of this? You've got Louisa."

She looked at Clement out of the corners of her eyes and said kindly, "Why don't you take a nap before going on tonight?"

He grinned. "I think I will." After they left, he took a long pull of scotch from a silver flask. Liquor always relaxed him. He turned over on his side on the couch, but before dropping off to sleep he thought how lucky William was to have someone like Louisa to look after his business affairs. He wished that he had acquired a Louisa in those early days, after World War I, before he founded his first orchestra made up of mixed-blood Cherokees.

In that intriguing void between waking and sleeping, the face of that charming lady Leona Elder, who had befriended him in New York, came up before his face. She had been the *grande dame* of all Fifth Avenue *grande dames,* and the

Sunday afternoon salons at her mansion were rightfully famous.

Elsie Janis, a famous star of that World War I period, whom he had accompanied on the piano behind the front lines, had taken him to meet Mrs. Elder, who had asked him to perform. He had sung "The Old Chisholm Trail," which for some reason struck a sympathetic chord, not only with the guests but with Lester Mainwaring, who had subsequently given him a contract to play his hotel circuit. That was the beginning of a thirty-four-year career, but how long could he keep up the pace without falling on his face? Sleep came before he could further ponder that important question.

Letty stirred the large pot of baked beans in the oven, and decided that after using the same recipe for fifty years she would not need to taste the mixture to know that it was up to Heron standards.

With age, she had lately begun to realize, food and elimination took on more important aspects. Indeed, to what could older people look forward with greater certainty, at the beginning of the day, than a cozy sojourn in the smallest room in the house, or at the end of the day, than a good supper graciously served? She smiled, because cosmopolitans always called the evening meal "dinner," and she had complied for many years. But she had lapsed back into country ways after moving back to Angel from Washington.

The big house on Connecticut Avenue could now be utilized by any family member on business in the nation's capital, which would not only save expensive hotel bills but be tax-deductible as well. One had to think of such things as income tax these days. Bosley always said . . .

Her eyes filled with tears. It still seemed that he should be sitting in his old chair by the fireplace, or be reading the sports pages of the *Enid Morning News* over the breakfast table. There were times when it seemed impossible that she would never again see his slight form ambling by God's Acres on his way back from town.

Letty was so engrossed in thinking about Bosley that she

did not hear the telephone ring, and was roused by Hattie, who was saying in her slightly nasal voice, "Someone real important is on the line."

Letty smiled and reflected that connections were exceptionally weak on calls from Hollywood or Washington, because everyone up and down the party line—including Nellie, the half-deaf operator—was listening. The possibility of dialing service had intrigued the community for years.

Picking up the telephone, she said distinctly, "This is Letty Trenton speaking."

The voice on the other end of the line was very faint and faded away completely from time to time, replaced by static. The voice was female, she was almost certain. "Just a moment," Letty shouted into the mouthpiece. "Nellie, will you tell everyone to get off the line? I can't even hear who's calling."

"WHAT?" Nellie screamed back.

It was at times like this that Letty wished she was back in Washington, where only the CIA tapped telephone wires. She repeated her question and was greeted by a long series of clicks: neighbors were reluctantly relinquishing the line. "I'm so sorry for the delay," Letty apologized.

The soft, distinctive voice replied, "Goodness, it used to be the same in Gettysburg before dial service was connected!" It was then that Letty knew that it was Mamie Eisenhower on the wire.

"It's so nice to hear from you again," Letty said enthusiastically, trying to remember when they had last spoken. She was certain that it must have been several years ago in an officers' club where Clement Story and his Cherokee Swing Orchestra was making a personal appearance.

"I want to congratulate you, Mamie. I feel certain that you'll end up as First Lady."

"Thank you, Letty, but the General is not at all convinced this is the right move at his age. The responsibility will be so great."

"It's my belief," Letty said with conviction, "that this country needs a military mind to combat the Russians right now."

"This year will be interesting, to say the least. Goodness!"

As Letty thought back, it was Clement more than Bosley or she who had kept in touch since Ike's command during World War II. The Eisenhowers were great music fans, being particularly addicted to the waltz. Letty genuinely liked Mamie, and with Ike having lived in Abilene, they shared a similar Midwestern background.

"I'm calling from the farm," Mamie Eisenhower was saying, and Letty could see the famous dark bangs, which Mamie had worn for years, strung across her forehead, "and the General is in Washington, as usual, so I'm taking today off and calling some of my old girlfriends."

Letty was flattered, because she had not known Mamie well. Were the Eisenhowers Democrats or Republicans? Letty could not remember, but at any rate, Mamie had to be very aware that the Herons and the Storys and the Trentons had turned Democratic with Roosevelt's fourth term. Still, she was delighted that Mamie did not apparently consider political lines.

"I'm looking at my calendar now," Mamie continued. "I heard through the grapevine that you might be coming to Washington for a couple of months. Could you come to Gettysburg as our overnight guest on Saturday, the weekend of May 29th? The General will be here, and Clement, who'll be playing a benefit in Hanover, is coming over for the afternoon. And besides, I want to chat." When Letty paused, Mamie went on, "Letty, do you have your appointment book open?"

"It's in my head. In Angel, one day is much like the next." She considered the invitation a moment, and then said graciously, "Thank you, I should like to come to see you and the General very much. I'll call my son, Luke, in Tulsa and reserve the company plane." She giggled like a young girl. "You know, I've never used the *Blue Heron* personally before."

"Goodness!" Mamie replied succinctly. "Then it's high time you did!"

"Thank you most heartily for the invitation, Mamie."

"You're quite welcome, and I look forward to seeing you

again on May 29th.'" She paused. "Oh, I almost forgot, we'll send a car for you at nine-thirty, which means we'll have a light lunch here at one. Good-bye."

The telephone went dead, then Nellie screamed into her headset, "Well, so it's *Mamie* and *Letty* now!"

Letty, who seldom lost her temper, raised her voice so that Nellie was certain to hear. "Tend to your own business, Nellie Drack!"

Regaining her composure, and yet not at all ashamed of her outburst, Letty held the receiver in her hand for a long time. Normally she was never suspicious of what Bosley had always called "interior motives," yet what was so important that Mamie Eisenhower would invite her to Gettysburg? Was it wholly because of Clem, or was there something else in back of the invitation?

She would soon know: "The proof," as her old friend, Fontine Dice, would have said, "is in the pudding."

4

The Western Experience

The long black limousine left the pink stucco Beverly Hills Hotel at seven in the morning and arrived a half hour later at Universal Studios in Studio City.

Louisa Tarbell looked in dismay at the line of old Spanish-style buildings on Lankershim Boulevard that comprised the front entrance to the studio. "It looks so flimsy," she complained.

William laughed nervously. "Maybe, but think of the history of this place, Lou," he replied. "It's awesome." He was impressed by the fact that one of the bellhops at the hotel had told him that the Cahuenga Indian Tribe had once held powwows on the Universal property: he was on hallowed ground.

The limousine stopped at the gate that led into the parking lot. Philippe, the driver, gave William's name to the keeper, who looked at his clipboard and replied that Mr. Cornwallis was on the recording stage.

Philippe parked the car and pointed to the red light above the door of the sound stage. "When that goes off, we can go inside," he explained.

Louisa looked out of the window at the groupings of huge buildings contrasted with small bungalows scattered here and there. A few workmen were about, and boys on bicycles rode leisurely by, but there were no glamorous females in furs and jewels or intriguing males in fezzes or tuxedos.

"This is all so ordinary, and I'm disappointed," she said

unhappily. "Somehow, I expected a lot of excitement and color."

Philippe smiled. "Making pictures is just an ordinary business, Miss Tarbell," he explained. "All the glamour is up there on the screen. Here on the lot, it's just hard work." The red light above the door was turned off. "We can go in now," he said.

The interior of the sound stage was so cavernous that in the dim light William could not discern the ceiling or the walls of the building. The sixty-five-member orchestra, composed of both men and women, was dressed in extremely casual clothing and seated on wooden folding chairs placed in front of a large, tattered screen.

A young man in white slacks and a blue pullover greeted them with a harried smile, glancing ever so slyly at William's three-piece gray suit and Louisa's pale green princess dress. "Hi," he said. "I'm John. Sit down, please." He indicated two canvas director chairs. "We're just about to have another go at it. Please don't step on the spaghetti—the cables. Mr. Cornwallis will be with you shortly." He waved and disappeared in the gloom.

Louisa pointed to the canvas backs of the chairs, one of which was inscribed with the name JAMES STEWART, the other with SHELLEY WINTERS.

William laughed. "You take Jim, Lou, and I'll take Shell!" He pronounced the names as if the stars were intimate friends, and immediately felt at home, with the orchestra members so close that he could reach out and touch the celeste player.

There was a sudden tapping, which came from a podium at the left of the screen. John, the young man they had just met, stood with raised baton. While the musicians arranged instruments comfortably and checked orchestrations on music stands, orders and signals, none of which either William or Louisa understood, were passed back and forth between several men who obviously had a great deal to do with the proceedings.

John hit the podium once, raised his baton, and a scratchy black-and-white work print of a love scene of a couple on a south-sea island beach was flashed on the screen. The downbeat was given, and at once the stage was filled with the sound of glorious strings.

William was enthralled. The couple, dressed in swim-suits, were at first at arm's length, but as they came closer together, their eyes never leaving each other's faces, the music swelled, dramatically enhancing the feelings of love kindled between them.

The lead violinist, his eyes fixed on the screen, stood up, and as the couple's lips were seemingly drawn magnetically together, his instrument sored theatrically. William tensed, almost in pain, because the orchestra came in a second too late and the effect was spoiled.

But young John continued to direct with the baton in his right hand and his left hand waving in a *pianissimo* warning signal. The scene on the screen faded out, with the lovers still entwined, a shout was heard, and signals were passed back and forth again.

John tapped the podium again. "That was an 'almost,' " he said patiently, and turned toward the violinist. "You were right in there, Peter." He coughed delicately and addressed the other members of the orchestra. "Remember, ladies and gentlemen, the *moment* their lips meet, we must all come in. The take before last, we anticipated, this time we lagged. Watch me, and go to it on the count of four."

"Isn't this all fascinating, Billy?" Louisa said, drawing in her breath with the excitement of being on a Hollywood sound stage and watching music placed on film.

He did not reply, because it was if he were a member of the orchestra, whose sole purpose as musicians was exactly matching what was transpiring on the screen.

The beginning routine was repeated, and this time, as the couple moved toward each other and the violinist began, William counted under his breath: *One, two, three* . . . FOUR!

John gave the signal, and at the exact moment when the lips met on the screen, the music towered to new heights, building, underscoring the passion displayed on the screen. William was deeply moved; this was music as it should be! As the screen faded to black, he stumbled to his feet, shouting, "Bravo! Bravo!"

A tense, embarrassed silence pervaded the giant sound stage as the sixty-five orchestra members turned to glare at him; then there were the usual shouts and signals from the recording engineers in the glass booth, before John tapped the podium impatiently. "Ladies and gentlemen, we shall try again," he said with a sigh. "A perfect take was spoiled by the enthusiasm of one of our guests this morning." He looked at the red-faced William. "Will you please confine your esteem of our work to silent appreciation?"

William blushed until his face burned so badly that he thought his eyeballs would pop from his skull. He realized then that his shouts of "Bravo! Bravo!" had been recorded along with the musical crescendo. He hunched down into his seat, and the session continued.

This time a perfect take was achieved, and another piece of film—an establishing shot of Rio de Janeiro—was threaded into the projector and flashed on the screen. The orchestra switched to a South American beat, the camera tilted up to a shot of Sugar Loaf mountain; then as a closeup of the statue of Christ of the Andes was shown, the music soared with a mystical, haunting hymn played contrapuntally to the Spanish tempo, and William was suddenly emotionally touched.

In his twenty-four years of life he had seen very few motion pictures, and only two until he was eighteen—*Life With Father* and *The Inspector General*—because his mother and father belonged to a church which taught that the devil himself sponsored such entertainments, and forbade members to attend such frivolities.

It was only after Louisa Tarbell had contacted Clement Story, who had given him a scholarship to the Barrett Conservatory of Music, that he was permitted to leave the nest in Willawa and pursue a musical career.

Louisa was entranced at the boy's fascination with the recording session, and tears stung the back of her eyes. Pride welled up in her breast. She was a woman most blessed. How many other teachers, with students touched with genius, were able to start them on the road to fame— and, she might as well admit it, fortune as well?

But even now that the royalties from "The Cowboy

Waltz" were becoming substantial, she could not relax her vigil. Unscrupulous people would want to subvert her William, and that she would never allow. If nothing else, she could hold him in her grasp with her sexuality, and she smiled to herself, because she was an excellent businesswoman as well. "Having a good time?" she whispered.

His eyes were full of wonder. "I'm having the best . . . time of my life," he whispered back. "This is what I want to do—write this kind of music." He turned quickly back to the screen, summoned by the shot of a Peruvian farmer plowing a field against a clouded sky. The music took on a realistic, stark mood and expertly followed the horse up the furrow.

This was what interested him most—freedom to express pure emotion through different leitmotifs, imparting something precious and expansive to the visages on the screen; giving substance to moving shadows. He was convinced that composing for film would be the height of creativity, making "craven images," as his mother would have called them, *live!*

It was time for luncheon before the title music was recorded, but the morning had passed so quickly that William was still in a daze at what he had observed. And Louisa, knowing how moved he was, remained silent, vicariously enjoying his elation. She realized that seeing the musicians plying this strange trade, welding music to celluloid, had been an almost spiritual experience for him.

"Sorry to keep you waiting," a voice boomed out, "but I was looking at some 'dailies' and some problems cropped up."

William turned to see a big, balding man striding toward him, hand outstretched. "I'm Ray Cornwallis."

William introduced himself and shook his hand, then said, "I'd like you to meet my business manager, Louisa Tarbell."

Ray Cornwallis bowed. "Enchanted!" he exclaimed.

But, William thought, he didn't look at all enchanted and took an instant dislike to the man. *This is ridiculous,* he told himself. *You don't even know him! Make an effort.* "I was enjoying myself thoroughly," he said as cordially as he could. "After watching the conductor at work, I think I'd like to compose film music."

Ray Cornwallis patted him on the shoulder and replied in a patronizing tone of voice, "You *are*, my boy, *you are*. By the way, how is my ol' buddy Clem?"

"He sent his best," William replied, although Clement's last words had been "Give him a goose for me!"

"Known him for years. A great guy," Ray Cornwallis said warmly, and his genuine affection for Clement shown through his overly smooth exterior. "I hear he's on the bottle, and that's sad."

"I saw him just the other day," William replied with a frown, "and I didn't notice anything wrong."

Ray Cornwallis waved his hand. "Maybe I heard it wrong. Show business can be vicious." He paused. "But I'm here to welcome you to my home." He indicated the sound stage and the acreage beyond.

William began to warm up to his personality, although Louisa remained distant. "Come on, we'll have luncheon in the commissary. I suppose you'd like to see some stars?"

William acknowledged that he would, but when they came into the large, crowded room, filled with tables, he could only recognize Tony Curtis, who was talking animatedly to someone he did not know.

"This is where I always sit," Ray Cornwallis said, indicating a table near the door. As a pretty young girl got up from a nearby table, he called, "Hi, Piper, I've someone I want you to meet." When she turned and smiled sweetly, he went on in a hearty tone of voice, "William Nestor, I'd like you to meet Miss Piper Laurie."

William stumbled to his feet and awkwardly held out his hand. "Pleased to make your acquaintance," he said, although he did not recognize her face.

"Mr. Nestor wrote 'The Cowboy Waltz.'" Ray Cornwallis said, and then, seemingly as an afterthought, "And this is Louisa Tarbell, William's business manager."

Piper Laurie greeted them graciously. "I'm a fan of yours. Now, if you'll please excuse me, I must get back to the set. Come around later, if you like."

The moment she left, Louisa Tarbell leaned forward. "Is it true that she eats gardenias?"

Ray Cornwallis laughed. "I see you've been reading the fan books, Miss Tarbell." He paused, an amused expression on his face. "I'm sure that gag was dreamed up by our publicity department. Now, what would *you* like to eat?"

After mushroom omelets had been consumed, Ray Cornwallis took them out the rear door and introduced them to a willowy young man named Byron. "I thought you'd enjoy a tour of the back lot, William," he said effusively, ignoring Louisa. "After you've seen everything, Byron will bring you to my office, where you can pick up a copy of the script of *Maidie Loves Norman*."

"Thank you, sir."

"Call me Corny," he replied. "By the way, Piper Laurie is going to play Maidie, and Tony Curtis is going to play Norman. Philippe will take you back to the hotel and pick you up at nine in the morning. I'll see you at ten in my office. Okay?" He waved a plump hand and, turning away abruptly, walked quickly to the recording stage.

After a steak dinner in the Polo Lounge, where Louisa pointed out Barbara Stanwyck, Rory Calhoun, and Sonny Tufts to William, they came into the suite and he grimaced as he looked at the script on the bed.

"I'm going to take a long, hot bath," he said, then paused and kissed her on the nape of her neck, a particularly delicate spot. "Why don't you read the script and tell me the story? I was looking at it earlier, and I swear I can't tell head nor hair about it. It's written in some funny kind of lingo."

She laughed and tweaked his ear. "I suppose, as your business manager, I should become accustomed to reading these things." She settled down on the settee in the corner of the suite and opened the first page of the script.

At once, Louisa was introduced to a strange new language: fade in; fade out; cut to; wipe to; and dissolve to; and such abbreviations as: F.G. (foreground), V.O. (voice over), B.G. (background), P.O.V. (point of view), and O.S. (off scene.)

She learned the script offered involved directions for the

placement of the camera, and that characters were frequently photographed in Long Shot, Medium Shot, Closeup, Over the Shoulder, or in various combinations of all four. She also discovered that the camera could be mounted on a track; placed on a crane; tilted up, or tilted down; moved in slowly, or drawn back quickly; panned to the left, or panned to the right, or an intermediate point between the two. . . .

After becoming accustomed to the nomenclature, she found that the first scene introduced two ordinary people with "ideas of grandeur." She read the entire script, then mixed a whiskey for herself and opened a Coca-Cola for William.

"Come in and sit in the easy chair, Billy," she called, "and I'll tell you about the story." When there was no answer, she went into the bathroom. With his iron bar floating half out of the water, he was lying with his head laid on the back of the tub, sound asleep. She caressed his shoulder, and he opened one eye. "Lie still," she said, "and enjoy yourself while I tell you the story."

"Is it good?"

She sighed. "You be the judge." She paused and nervously wet her lips. She was not very good, she knew, at speaking extemporaneously about a fresh subject. In the schoolroom she could weave an enchanting spell around Beowulf or King Arthur, but to relate a rather silly story in dramatic terms was something else again. "Here goes," she said. "Now pay attention: On their days off from work, an ice-cream vendor (Curtis) and a lingerie saleswoman (Laurie) meet in an elevator, when her heel becomes entangled in the cuff of his pants. . . ."

William frowned. "Yes, go on."

"She removes her shoe, and by the time a cobbler is located and disengages the heel from the cuff, they are in love." She paused. "Curtis and Laurie—not Laurie and the cobbler."

He grinned and splashed water on his chest. "So far it sounds like it would be a better story if she did fall in love with the cobbler. What's he like?"

"Grizzled, sixty, German or Lithuanian type." She gave him a long look. "No, be serious! Anyway, he—Curtis, not the cobbler—introduces himself as a stockbroker, and she tells him that she's a dress designer. The remainder of the story deals with various plot devices wherein the couple tries to hide their true professions from each other.

"The denouement occurs when Curtis, with his ice-cream box on his back, comes into the store where Laurie works, to purchase hose for his mother's birthday gift, and of course they discover who each other really are. . . . Eventually, love triumphs over all, and in the ending scene the happy couple are seen eating ice-cream bars on the steps of his brownstone tenement, and apparently live happily ever after."

"Would you go to see a movie like that?" he asked suddenly.

"No. Would you?"

"No." He got out of the tub slowly, and she helped wipe his back and then his iron bar. "Hey, cut that out." He laughed. "What are you trying to do, distract me?"

"As a matter of fact, yes," she replied seriously.

"It's really pretty awful, isn't it? The script, I mean."

She sighed. "Now, how can something be both *pretty* and *awful* at the same time?"

"You have a point," he replied with a laugh, "but it's really terrible. I wish Mr. Story hadn't told us to find out what the plot was about. It would be easier to write a song about a couple of imaginary lovers, rather than an ice-cream peddler and a clerk."

"Would it help if you forgot about the story and just wrote a love song for Tony Curtis and Piper Laurie?"

"I'll try."

While Louisa took a bath, William decided to forgo putting on his pajamas and, still quite nude, climbed upon the king-sized bed. He looked up at the ceiling. Almost always there was a tune lurking about in his head, which he would hum for several days and then forget. If the melody became truly insistent, he purged it from his brain by transcribing the notes to paper.

But now there was nothing from which to draw; his mind was blank. He smiled ironically. Was this battle with frustration the same as a barren woman experienced when conception was denied her?

Louisa came into the bedroom wearing a peach-colored chiffon negligee. To retain its distinctive shape, she had wrapped toilet tissue around the beehive hairstyle, over which the young man downstairs had labored for an hour.

She glanced with approval at her image in the full-length pier mirror. Compared to that tweedy mouse who had once conducted seventh-grade classes in Willawa, Oklahoma, she felt very languorous and sophisticated indeed. Looking about the luxurious pink and green suite filled with freshly cut flowers, she was very much aware that William's future progress remained in her hands.

However, for the moment, there was a more immediate need. Her look of love was returned fully as she joined him on the bed and kissed his jaw. "Excuse me for not shaving tonight," he apologized, "but since I have to look good at the studio tomorrow, I thought I'd wait until morning."

"I think a black beard is sexy," she replied, "but be careful; I don't want to look like a red, scratched-faced harridan, either." And, seeing that his iron bar was poised in readiness, she whispered, "Turn toward me, but just lie still."

Louisa switched off the bedside light and held him lightly in her arms, moving up until his iron bar was secured, then she began to sway very, very slowly.

He sighed gently in the darkness, savoring the feelings that spread over his groin. The marvelous release of body and mental tensions was the best therapy in the world. This constant renewal of the very forces of nature—and he thought of all the extravagant claims of old-fashioned patent medicines—*did* add an electric shock to the process of creativity, while toning the body and sharpening the wits.

What could all those other young men in the world, who had no lovers who catered to their erotic whims, creatively draw upon? How could they tap into that universal center where all great ideas were born, if they had to live their lives in complete sexual frustration? Was this why there were so many mediocre talents?

Then William could no longer delay the responses of his

body, and sighed in delight and whimpered in contentment as his energy was outpoured into Louisa's eager receptacle; then he slept.

Gradually her heartbeats subsided into a normal pattern. Moist and warm, still in his intimate embrace, she luxuriated in a moment of supreme fulfillment. Then her skin contracted as if her body had been thrust into a snowbank: *What if she lost him?*

Since he had graduated from the Barrett Conservatory of Music, she had been with him almost constantly, protecting him from the occasional attentions of young girls eager to become acquainted with a celebrity. But now, in the course of daily work at the studio, he would most naturally meet some of the most beautiful and desirable women in the world.

There was only one way to insure her hold over him, and that was to see that he was kept physically drained. A young man, no matter how sexually active, could only respond to the attractions of a desirable young girl by conjuring up sexual images—impossible if he was kept satiated. She smiled in the dark. She would satisfy him as he had never been satisfied before.

The historic town of Gettysburg was blessed with huge trees that formed a canopy over many of the streets. Letty was enchanted. From time to time she asked questions of the driver, a young man in his twenties, who gave one-syllable answers until it was plain that he either did not want to converse or was awed by the responsibility of delivering her safely to the Eisenhowers.

She smoothed her blue printed silk foulard with shaky fingers, praying that she was not overdressed for the occasion. At home, she usually wore plain cottons when people came to call, but Mamie had probably brought back a Paris wardrobe. The lush, rolling countryside reminded Letty of Oklahoma's green country beyond Tulsa. This verdant landscape was a far cry from the prairies of the Midwest, and she could see why the General, who had lived so long in Abilene, Kansas, was especially drawn to the area.

The driver turned down a country lane, and on the left could be seen an old three-story square house on a slight incline, and as the car came up the drive, Mamie Eisenhower came out of the front door and waved. She was dressed in a pink flowered dress that was expensive enough to be flattering, and yet informal enough for the country.

She held her arms wide, and when the driver opened the door for Letty, she held out her hand and kissed her on the cheek. "It's so good to see you again," she said in that soft voice that was so engaging. "Goodness, it's been a long time, hasn't it?"

"Too long, Mamie," Letty agreed with a smile.

"My, you look as pretty as a picture!" Mamie Eisenhower exclaimed. "I didn't know what to wear today. This country living is so new to me. We've just returned from Paris, you know, and it's so dressy over there. Do come inside. A cold luncheon is on the table. I hope you like salmon?

"Your room is at the top of the stairs. Only one bathroom in the house as yet!" She laughed and winked. "It's rather primitive! But we'll change all of that when we remodel."

Letty smiled crookedly. "Mamie, I think it was about nineteen twenty-two or three before we installed plumbing in the house at the farm in Angel. Until then, we had a . . . privy."

Mamie Eisenhower lowered her voice. "If Ike doesn't win we'll settle here right away and start to work on the house. Otherwise . . ." She rolled her blue eyes, then, hearing a step, held her forefinger up to her lips. "Ike?" she called.

"Miss Mamie?" The remembered voice came from the kitchen, and a moment later he came into the room with a wide smile on his face and beads of perspiration on his shiny bald head. "Hello, Letty," he said, extending his hand. "Please excuse how I look. I was out counting the cattle, and time got away from me."

"It's good to see you again, General."

He laughed. "I'm *Mr.* now, but everyone forgets. I've been in uniform almost all of my life, and if I had my druthers, I'd put on a pair of overalls right now!"

"Why don't you wash up for lunch, dear?" Mamie Eisenhower said. "I'll have the driver bring up your case, Letty."

After the salmon, potato salad, a mixed salad with a green dressing and prune whip had been consumed with great relish, for they were all hungry, the trio relaxed in the high-ceilinged living room. "That was such a good dressing; what is it?"

Mamie Eisenhower looked fondly at her husband. "It's Ike's favorite, and it's called Green Goddess." Her blue eyes sparkled, and she ran fingers over the bangs on her forehead. "The secret ingredient is . . . anchovies!" She laughed gaily. "The color comes from two drops of green coloring." It occurred to Letty that she was extremely good company.

"I've always thought that if I'd not gone into the military," the General put in, "I'd have maybe opened a restaurant. I can't cook anything elaborate, but I can put a small meal together. I find that cooking is therapeutic."

Mamie giggled. "When we first got married, I couldn't cook, and Ike helped out even then. I'm afraid I'm not much better now. But nutrition is very important, especially to the elderly."

As if taking a cue, the General excused himself. "I'm writing a speech," he explained, "that's giving me fits. What time is Clem due, Mamie?"

"He can't get here until after five. He must be at the benefit at seven-thirty."

"Good, then we can have dinner together."

"No," Mamie Eisenhower replied, "he said he never eats directly before performing. He'll only be here for an hour. We'll eat at seven."

The general waved and after he left the room, Mamie Eisenhower leaned forward. "We'd love to go to the benefit tonight," she confided, "but with this political situation, the news media would be after the General, and it's not fair to the performers."

Her voice grew more confidential. "Then too, he doesn't want to make a statement so soon. There was such a furor when he resigned as the Commander of the NATO forces and was persuaded to have his name entered in New Hampshire. He's certain that Bob Taft is going to get the nomination." She paused. "I'm not so sure."

"I've been thinking a great deal about the political situation in this country, Mamie. As you know, I'm a friend of Bess and Harry Truman. The President appointed my late husband, Bosley, to an important post to work with President Hoover, mainly, I think, because we had known him for some time, and it was the first time in so many years that he'd held an official position."

"That was nice of Harry to do that." Mamie smiled impishly. "But Herbert was the best man for the job!" She paused and grew serious. "Which brings up another question, Letty. If Ike should be elected President, I'll have to be active. Oh, in moving around all these years, I truly looked forward to retirement. We've lived in thirty houses, you know! I want to be *Mrs*. Ike for a change."

She smiled suddenly and looked very pretty. "If I . . . do become more active, there are only two or three things that I would like to become involved with; one would be a program to help the elderly."

Letty was becoming interested. "They've"—she laughed —"*we've* become neglected. Oh, I don't mean me personally. I've had a full, rich life, but in general, sons and daughters are refusing to take care of their folks, the way the older generation took care of theirs."

Mamie nodded. "And, Letty, I'm afraid it's going to get worse when money begins to get tighter and tighter in the future." She took Letty's hand. "That's why I wonder if I can count on you, if the occasion arises where I can be in a position to help the oldsters?"

"I don't know what I could do, Mamie." Letty suddenly felt helpless and infirm.

"First of all, you'd be an *example* of an active and alert woman who is still very much involved in projects that she believes in." She paused. "In a way, you would be a spokeswoman for all of those millions who are over sixty-five."

"Let me think about this when I get back to the farm."

Mamie's eyes twinkled. "Do that, and, as I say, we have time—at least until November!"

Letty had only just washed her face, after taking a short nap, when she heard a car in the driveway. She looked out of the upper bedroom window and saw Tracy Newcomb crawl out from behind the wheel of an Oldsmobile and open the door for Clement.

By the time that she had combed her hair, added a little lip rouge, and come down the steep stairs, animated conversation was emanating from the living room.

When Letty came into the room, Clement kissed her on the cheek and called her his "best girl." He was wearing very strong aftershave, she thought, and then, when he moved away, she recognized the very faint odor of alcohol under the scent. Surely, she said to herself, the fresh Pennsylvania country air was playing tricks on her sense of smell!

She shook hands with Tracy, and he gave her a strange, guarded look, and then she understood why he had been driving. She sat down on a high-backed chair and clasped her hands in her lap, hoping that Clement was far enough away from his host and hostess that they would not discern that he had been drinking. She was silent as the General spoke about amusing army experiences, and Clement kept his conversation to a minimum.

When the hour was almost up, and it was quite dark outside, Clement told a political story about President Truman's piano-playing being sometimes more proficient than his foreign policy. The General laughed and held up his hand. "No Washington talk today, that's the rule of the house here in Gettysburg."

He rubbed his chin. "There's something that I've meant to say to you for a long time, and it seems we never get to spend more than a couple of minutes together every three years or so, so here it is. I've been very grateful to you for the time that you've spent entertaining the troops. It seemed that when I went into the field after you'd been there, there was an entirely different attitude among the men."

Tears welled up in Clement's eyes. "Why, thank you,

sir." Letty, however, wondered if the emotion was caused by the General's compliment or by the drink.

The General glanced at his watch. "I know you have to go soon, but before you do, would you sing a song for me?"

Clem smiled widely. "I suppose you'd like to hear 'The Cowboy Waltz.'"

The General frowned. "I don't believe I know that one," he said.

His wife laughed. "It was just the number one song in the USA for months, Ike."

He rubbed his bald pate. "Don't chide me, dear! You'll have to excuse me, Clem. I miss a lot of the 'pop culture,' as the kids say. I've always traveled too much to suit either me or Miss Mamie." He grinned. "I was thinking of 'The Old Chisholm Trail.' A couple of verses would just be fine. You know, of course, the trail started down in Santone and ended in Abilene?"

Without asking, Tracy brought the guitar from the car. Clement flexed his hands a moment, as Letty had seen him do a thousand times since he was thirteen, cleared his throat, and sang:

> Come along, boys, and listen to my tale.
> I'll tell you of my troubles on the old Chisholm Trail.
> Coma ti yi youpy, youpa ya,
> Youpa ya,
> Coma ti yi youpy, youpy, ya. . . .

Letty had not heard him sing the old tune for many years, and the old cowpunchers' song brought back memories of those years before Oklahoma became a state when men ate, slept, and worked in the great out-of-doors. She thought: *My life has spanned so much actual history. I was barely twenty-two in 1893, when we made The Run, and this song wasn't new.* . . .

When Clement finished, the Eisenhowers applauded, and Tracy said, "Aren't you going to clap for Clem, Mother Trenton?"

She laughed. "I've never thought it proper for relatives to lead a claque!"

Good-byes were said, and they went outside to wave as

the car disappeared in the darkness of the countryside. Letty was glad that Clement had left before some sort of incident had given him away. Watching him perform, and seeing his control, she knew that he had been in the habit of drinking for some time. She knew that today was no accident.

Her heart was heavy. Sam, Born-Before-Sunrise, had told her that a child born during a storm would have musical talent, and Clement came into the world during the worst thunderclaps that had hit northwestern Oklahoma in many years. Was there also some fatal weakness embedded somewhere in that genius?

5

The Neophyte

*The tickets for the French châteaux to San Sebastian tour,
booked through a travel agency in Oklahoma City, arrived
special delivery at Heron Furniture headquarters in Enid
on May 27, 1952.*

Mitchell swore under his breath. Having been involved in
expediting several large orders that required two trips to the
manufacturing facility in Guthrie, he had put off telling
Charlotte about the change in honeymoon plans.

In fact, he had mentally blocked out the Episode Pierre
entirely, but the presence of the fat itinerary on his desk
could not be ignored, and he found himself glancing at the
manila envelope periodically all day.

The moment that he opened the back door to the house in
North Enid, the odor of fish filled his nostrils, and he smiled
to himself. He appreciated the fact that Charlotte was what
his Aunt Letty called an "aromatic cook." He swore that if
she boiled water, the very vapor would have an appetizing
smell. His former housekeeper, Mrs. Briggs, could cook a
twelve-course dinner, and the kitchen would still smell like
Lysol!

After being single for fifty years, a simple action like
coming home at night took on a very special glow; he truly
looked forward to opening that door to a potpourri of
delightful smells.

And although he did not rush into Charlotte's arms, and
she never wore a Mother Hubbard apron, he nevertheless
felt the pull of the same sort of old-fashioned domestic life

that he was certain that Herons had enjoyed in Angel in the days just after the Cherokee Strip Land Rush.

Charolotte, dressed in a navy-blue dressmaker suit that made her look slimmer than she actually was, and holding a spatula in her hand, kissed him briefly before returning to the stove.

She laughed. "Mitch, isn't this just like my mother—frying catfish in a dress that cost a hundred and fifty dollars?" She wiped her hands on a towel. "Actually, I haven't had time to change." She sighed. "I sometimes wonder if I was cut out to chair meetings of the Ladies Aid? Then I have to remember that I'm not Charlotte Dice, I'm Mrs. Mitchell Heron"—she cast an amused glance in his direction—"and expected to become a Mr. and Mrs. America of the community—or a reasonable facsimile thereof!"

"Don't underestimate your abilities," he replied lightly. "You could run every social organization in Enid with one hand tied behind your back, and still have time to be my wife, mistress, cook, dishwasher—ad infinitum."

She frowned. "Not when I can't spend full time here in Enid. By the way, next week we must do penance in Angel. I hate for you to have to get up forty minutes early to be at the store by nine."

"It's not that big of a problem," he replied gently. "I rather enjoy the week each month that we spend in your house over there."

"I still don't know why mother and dad did this to me, Mitch." Charlotte faced him. "And yet I suppose we have them to thank for us getting together after all of these years. It would never have happened in Washington." She thought about all of those golden boys, and she suddenly looked at him with such love in her eyes that he was embarrassed; then she turned back to the sizzling fish encased in their cornmeal batter, nicely browning in the hot lard.

Taking Charlotte in his arms, he always thought, *This is the way that life should be . . . this caring . . . this feeling of being needed . . . of contributing to the welfare of another person . . .*

Instead of the completely selfish attitude that he had

displayed all during his bachelorhood, this business of being responsible for someone else was somewhat frightening; he had never even owned a pet animal because he had never wanted to be tied down, and then when he became an operative for Pierre Darlan, he had to be away a great deal. . . .

Now he was married, and the organization still demanded his cooperation, yet he could not turn them down, because—and they knew this—he needed that extra sense of danger; it was like a strange kind of drug that one had to take every few years or wither away.

"I thought it was the end of the world," she was saying, her voice a bare whisper, "when the lawyer read the will stipulating that I had to live in Angel for ten years before the money in the estate reverted to me."

"The money doesn't mean a good damn to me, you know that," he replied quietly, "but it was good to get the ruling from the lawyer that as long as you kept a closet full of clothes in the Dice house, and we spend seven days out of thirty-one over there, you weren't violating the terms of the will."

"Yes, thank the good sweet Lord for favors granted. Anyway, I'm looking forward to the trip—to get away from *both* Angel and Enid."

Mitchell realized that it was time to make a move, and he came up behind her and placed his hands on her shoulders. "I was wondering if you were hell bent on going to Monte Carlo?"

She turned off the gas burner and swung around in his arms. "Why, no, not especially. Why?"

He hugged her close. "Have you ever been through the château country of France—maybe ending up in San Sebastian, Spain? It's a beautiful old town and just over the French border on the Bay of Biscay."

"No, actually I've always wanted to go through all those old castles, but when I was younger I naturally craved the excitement of Paris." She paused thoughtfully, thinking about the young men that she always brought along, who would have been bored into infinity if they had been asked to climb one staircase or admire one chandelier. "I've 'done' the Mediterranean. Oh, Mitch, this sort of trip is a marvelous idea!"

A wave of relief swept over him as he broke away gently and looked down into her eyes. "You're not disappointed?"

"Au contraire!" she exclaimed. "I'm happy as a clam. I didn't say anything before, since I thought you had your heart set on the Riviera, but I've never been moved to ecstasy by either Nice or Antibes. So it will be interesting to go somewhere with you that I've never been before." She paused. "Didn't you spend a lot of time in France between the wars?"

He was on dangerous ground. "Well, yes." He made his voice uninteresting. "I peddled glass figurines from door to door. A very boring life. Frankly, I was broke all the time, and I don't like to think about those years."

Neither do I, she thought. Her memories of journeys up and down the beaches were not exactly memorable. On her last trip to Europe, she had brought along a young man from Washington who had abandoned her in Nice without even a note on the pillowcase. She had seen him a few nights later in the casino wearing the Brooks Brothers tuxedo that she had purchased for him, and showing off her birthday present—platinum cuff links. But what hurt most of all was the fact that he was squirming around, and fawning over, a drunken old lady, whose skinny arms were strung from wrists to elbows with diamond bracelets. "Besides," she added aloud, "I don't gamble. Do you?"

He thought, *Not with money—only my life when I'm on a job,* but he shook his head and replied, "I'm much too Scotch to throw my hard-earned loot around. Besides, the casino in Monte Carlo is an architectural monstrosity, the French wine is not only overrated but overpriced." And he did not add that Pierre had told him that all of the beach sluts and beach bums were rumored to be infected with gonorrhea. Not that either Charlotte or he would be playing around, but he supposed that this complete lack of body care was a sign of the times.

She placed a lid on the frying pan to allow the fish juices to accumulate. "To get into the mood for the trip, shall we have a glass of wine before dinner? Clement brought some

Chablis from California that's supposed to be first rate. It's in the refrigerator.

"I assume we'll rent a car in Paris and then drive south through the countryside at a leisurely pace."

He took a deep breath and summoned a light tone. "I thought it would be great fun to do something different. Why not be Mr. and Mrs. America and take a small motor tour?"

"But Mitch"—she laughed uneasily—"you must know the area like the back of your hand! We wouldn't know the sort of people that we'd be traveling with—and is it really worth splitting the cost of the limousine with two other couples?"

He tried not to show his discomfort. "Actually, dear, I thought a motorbus would be more fun."

"Did I hear rightly? Did you say a *motorbus*?"

He opened the bottle of wine with a pop and took a moment to taste the contents while he thought of a reply. "Well," he said casually, with what he hoped was a winning smile, "why not? It will be a new experience." He handed her a wineglass. "I think it might be fun to be thrown in with a variety of people that, under ordinary circumstances, we'd never meet."

She took a sip of wine and pursed her mouth in approval. "It's an interesting concept," she agreed. "That sort of trip just might be what the doctor ordered." She paused meaningfully. "You know, Mother and Dad were in many ways ordinary, salt-of-the-earth people, but when the oil checks began to arrive in generous numbers, they always traveled in style. I was brought up that way, and I've never, ever, gone anywhere without the VIP treatment. I was always the Senator's Daughter, capital S, capital D." She frowned. "Looking back, I think that might have been a mistake. And, at my age, why not rough it for a change?"

"We'll hardly be roughing it, my dear," he said reproachfully. "After all, we'll be traveling first class. The only thing is, you'll have to limit your amount of luggage. Besides"—he grinned—"I didn't know you were a snob!"

"I'm *not* a snob at all," she replied humorously, "but I can tell you one thing, Mitch, if Eleanor Roosevelt had invited me to Hyde Park, I wouldn't have shown up in a *taxi*!"

"Like Aunt Letty and Uncle Bos? That was funny, wasn't it? But Bos told me that during World War II he put out an order that all of the Herons were to abide by gas-rationing rules—no extra privileges, no special priority stickers for their cars, or anything like that. They didn't want to show up at Hyde Park in a gas-gobbling limousine that had been driven all the way from Washington. So Aunt Letty and he took the train to Poughkeepsie and then a taxi on to Val-Kill Cottage. I guess the Roosevelts were properly impressed."

Charlotte placed plates of food—catfish, over-browned potatoes, glazed carrots, and hush puppies—on the dining-room table, and Mitchell filled their glasses. "Let's have a toast."

"To our trip?"

"No." He laughed. "To this splendid repast that's fit for a king." He paused, glass in hand. "But I can't help speculating on just how many times an elegant wine has been served with such a humble dish as *catfish* in the dry old state of Oklahoma!"

"Amen," said Charlotte, raising her glass.

In Langley, Virginia, Pierre was also raising a glass, to the computer, which had coughed up a name that had been wrongly filed under DECEASED. He turned triumphantly to H.L. Leary. "The perfect operative for this Heron job." He repeated the name on the screen.

"Yes, this person was made to order." Leary smiled, for the situation was quite ironic. "Make proper contact immediately. It's a relief to put this all together." He paused and ran his hand over his white crew cut. "It's such a simple little task on paper, and when Mitchell comes back, it will seem like a dream—just like all these miserable jobs do—and we'll forget all the details involved and all the sleepless nights."

"And when he comes back," Pierre announced, "I'm handing in my resignation."

Leary gave a derisive laugh. "Yeah? I've heard you say that at least a million times over the last twenty years.

You'll never throw in the sponge, old boy, because mixed in with all those white and red corpuscles in your bloodstream is the necessary element of danger that gives you the adrenaline that keeps you alive. You *can't* quit—any more than I can—or you'd, quite frankly, die!"

Pierre waved a fragile hand. "No, *mon ami,* this is my last case. I shall retire to my small farm in Normandie and scrape the soil in my garden, well aware that my neighbors will be calling me 'that peculiar old white-haired man with the black-dyed mustaches.' "

"Horseshit!" Leary exclaimed.

"Why don't you use the French expression—*merde*—it is much more elegant?"

"Perhaps"—Leary nodded—"but not nearly so expressive!"

Luke Three lay back in the dugout and lighted a cigarette, while his buddy, Rich Halprin, a nineteen-year-old with severe acne scars, pounded his chest. "Dammit, Heron"— he coughed dramatically—"blow the smoke away from me. You don't know what torture it is to be around a chain smoker when you've given it up."

"I've got to smoke to take my mind off this crappy war. Because I'm a fairly good driver, and my name is Heron, which everyone associates with G-A-S, I was assigned to chauffeur a dotty old shell-shocked major around! Me, a M-A-R-I-N-E!"

"Tough titty," Halprin said with a yawn. "You must be nuts yourself to have enlisted, for Christ's sake, with your money. If I was in your shoes, I'd have me a big fat commission. I'd have had my Dad—"

"Can it, Hal!" Luke Three cried. "I may bitch, but I *want* to be here. I mean not *here*, but in the war. And I've already got one war under my belt. You're so green, you still think there's an Easter Bunny! When are those supplies we've been waiting for going to show up? I'm so damned bored. I don't know how you can slop around in this mud without something to do, Hal."

"I do get tired of playing with myself," Halprin joked.

"Of course if I had something big to hang on to like you do, I might do it so much I'd go bananas."

"A happy thought!" Luke Three said with a grin.

"You bitch so much, but why'd an old vet like you sign up in the first place? I had to, or I'd have been sent to reform school, but with your name and your money—"

"The Heron name has never done me much good, Hal, and the so-called money, either. As far as being sent over here, that's something else again. What in the fuck is a Marine doing in a foxhole? The Second World War was different. We had a purpose, fighting Japs and the Germans. I spent a lot of time not far south from here, among the islands in the East China Sea."

"Any native broads?" Halprin's pitted face got redder.

Luke Three squinted at him. He had never been drawn to females outside his own race, but he replied, "Oh, a few."

"I haven't found Oriental gals are built sideways!"

Luke Three saw that Halprin was serious; at nineteen, had he ever been that naive? At sixteen, he had been sexually active with Darlene Trune. "It doesn't make all that difference."

There was a long pause as Halprin fought to sort out a variety of mental images and did not succeed.

Luke Three, managed with great difficulty to keep a straight face when all hell broke loose. Four grenades exploded nearby, the air was blackened with dust and debris, and the acrid smell of torque was everywhere.

He was frozen in time, and it seemed that the smoke did not clear away for hours, although it was only a moment or two. When he looked up, he could not believe his eyes. The grenade had caught Halprin so completely unaware that he had not even had time to utter a sound. He was looking at Luke Three with complete wonderment, still seemingly waiting for the answer to his question, only his body had been shot away from the chest down.

The old beige-colored two-room clapboard bungalow which bore William's freshly lettered name on the door was located next to the Property Department, within sight of a maze of false-fronted buildings that made up a portion of the giant back lot.

On his first day at the studio, Louisa had brought fried chicken luncheons from the hotel, which they ate on the steps of a huge courthouse-type edifice that was in the process of being converted to an ancient Roman palace for a picture that took place during the time of the Caesars.

An avid movie fan, she had gone to every "change of the picture" at the Criterion theater in nearby Lambert, because Willawa's only theater, the Pearl, had closed after Roosevelt's Bank Holiday in 1933, never having been wired for sound.

She was overcome with feelings of nostalgia as she looked across the street, recognizing the visages of former sets in well-remembered films from the thirties and forties. There was the facade of a mansion used in *Back Street,* with Charles Boyer and Margaret Sullavan, the Western street where Mae West fought off the advances of W.C. Fields in *My Little Chickadee,* and, in the distance, the huge hundred-foot painted "sky drop" used as a background for all those Arabian Nights fantasies with Maria Montez and Turhan Bey.

"What are you thinking about?" William asked, throwing a bare chicken leg into a pile of nearby rubbish.

"Nothing, really." She was pensive. "Billy, just think of all those thousands of pictures that have been shot here at the studio since 1915. Think about all those characters who have lived out their celluloid lives right where we're sitting."

She pointed to the mountain that rose up behind the back lot. "That's where they photographed *The Birth of a Nation.*" She drew in her breath quickly, and her face was flushed with remembrance. "It surely makes one wonder about the real world."

"Yeah," he answered cryptically, "especially how to deal with a bomb like *Maidie Loves Norman!*"

"Still worried?"

"'More than you know, more than you'll ever know.'" He sang the words to the old song. "Oh, God, Lou, what are we doing here?"

"We—or, more correctly, you—are earning forty-five thousand dollars cash for writing one song." She got up slowly and brushed the back of her skirt with her hand, then threw him an amused look. "Right now, the piano in your office is just waiting for the caress of those talented digits of yours."

In the mornings William sat alternately at his desk and at the piano, drinking coffee and thinking. Occasionally he ran his fingers up and down the keyboard, but his mind was blank. He was pleased that, during this dry spell, Corny did not bother him and finally left for a two-week vacation in Palm Springs. At last Louisa could not bear to see William in such mental turmoil, and began a series of walks over the Universal property, until she was familiar with every nook and cranny.

In the afternoons he would pass into one of the projection rooms on the lot and watch rough cuts of pictures in the last stages of production, and during the second week he called for a secretary from the steno pool and dictated letters to almost everyone he had ever known.

One afternoon he waited until two executives filed into Projection Room Number Two and the lights were extinguished, and then took a seat in the back row. Since he arrived after the main tiles, he did not know the name of the picture that he was viewing, but, from the locales and the cast, it was obvious that it had been shot in England.

The plot concerned the bittersweet affair between an older woman, Lisa, and a younger man, Colin, who finally dies of black lung disease in a rainstorm. The unknown actors were most touching, and there was the most appealing cat that William had ever encountered, which had the ending shot all to itself. They were all photographed against the realistic background of a Liverpool slum. There was a raw edge to the film that violently contrasted with the lush film score performed by the London Symphony Orchestra. The music was pretentious, William realized, for an unpretentious film.

After the ending credits flashed on the screen, William prepared to rise, as usual, before lights came up, but he did not rise quickly enough, and, afraid of being discovered on forbidden territory, slouched down in his seat.

"What a stinker!" a fat man in the front row exclaimed. "No wonder they couldn't get a distributor in England. And that title, *Is This Enough*? Can't you just see a reviewer picking up on that one?" His voice was filled with contempt. "You know damned well, Nicol, that the critics will say that *Is This Enough*? isn't enough at all!"

"Hold on, Harry," the second fat man replied. "I liked it. Some things should be cut out, like that dead cat on the garbage dump, and that scene where Colin picks Lisa up from the couch and takes her to bed. But, considering the fact that it was made over there with frozen funds and included in that package of other stinkers, don't you agree it's releaseable over here?"

"Yeah, Nicol, as the lower half of a double bill. But something bugs me, I don't know quite what. The texture of the film is so real, with no makeup, and Colin's pimples and ordinary street clothes and that dirty tenement setting. . . ."

"True, that's one reason why I like it, Harry. A film of this sort, the older woman/younger man thing, could never be done over here. An American company would make them the same age, change the setting to Park Avenue, put Brooks Brothers suits on Colin, cover his pimples with pancake makeup, give Lisa an Edith Head wardrobe—you know what I mean." He puffed thoughtfully on his cigar. "As far as I'm concerned, the film is a small jewel."

"Small jewels aren't going over this year," Harry replied nasally. "What the public wants is color and splash. I think the film works against itself—"

William could no longer restrain himself. He got up and stood with his hands clamped on the seat in front. "What's wrong with the picture is the score," he said with conviction. "It's the music that's going to alienate audiences. Instead of a sixty-five-piece symphony orchestra, what's needed is a little melody played on an oboe now and then. For instance, at the Employee Club party, when Colin falls in love with Lisa, he hits the wrong button on the jukebox, and what comes out but a classical piece!"

He was warming to his subject. "Who ever heard of any kind of employees' club anywhere that stocked Vivaldi? True, Colin expects to play a romantic ballad, and what comes out should be a loud, jazzy piece of some sort. You get the same effect—but it's just as upsetting to Colin because it spoils the sexy mood he's trying to create." He turned away and was halfway up the aisle when Nicol called, "Hold on, young man, who are you?"

"I'm William Nestor, sir," he replied, ashamed now of his outburst, "and I've got to get back."

"Are you on the lot for a special reason?" Harry asked.

"I'm not sure." He turned to leave.

"Just a moment," Nicol said quietly. "I like your thinking about the picture. You hit the nail on the head. Are you a new writer on the lot?"

William shook his head. "No, sir, I'm a songwriter working on *Maidie Loves Norman*."

Nicol laughed. "Well, as of luncheon, the property's been shelved. Tony Curtis refuses to do it, and Piper Laurie's been assigned to another picture. Who brought you to the studio?"

"Ray Cornwallis."

"Oh, that old fart?" Nicol paused. "Excuse me, Corny's okay, only he's been around since the coming of sound." He paused. "Aren't you the guy who wrote 'The Cowboy Waltz'?"

William was beginning to warm up to the man. "The same."

"Well, I'm Nicol Herbert, and this is Harry Leinsinger."

The men came up the aisle and shook William's hand. "Don't you also do arrangements for Clement Story?" Nicol asked, snubbing the cigar out in an oversized tray.

"Yes, I've done many of his orchestrations also."

The men exchanged glances before Nicol went on, "I don't suppose you've ever written a film score, have you?"

William shook his head. "No, but then I'd never written a Western song before I composed 'The Cowboy Waltz,' either." He was being uppity, he knew, but he certainly had nothing to lose. He didn't even know these men.

"You mentioned something about a theme song for the jukebox scene," Harry said. "Any ideas?"

"No, but I think the title of the picture, *Is This Enough?*, would be a natural."

Nicol Herbert nodded thoughtfully. "I'll call the Legal Department. I'd like to put you on the picture. You can pick up a print of the picture, with a separate soundtrack of the dialogue minus the music, in the Shipping Department tomorrow morning. Okay?"

William flushed. "I guess I should check with Mr. Cornwallis first, sir."

The man straightened his back. "That's not necessary. I'll fix it up. I'm in charge of acquiring foreign productions. You'll be working for Harry and me." He nodded. "Good afternoon, Mr. Nestor."

William left in a slightly dazed condition, and Nicol laughed. "He'd do a good job, I feel it in my guts."

"And what if he falls on his ass?"

"Let's face it, his work can't be any worse than what we've got. Wise up. If we work it right, he'll end up doing the entire score—plus the title tune—for what Corny is paying him for one song for *Maidie Loves Norman!*"

6

The Warning

The moonlight was intense, creating a glow beyond the low Korean mountain passes near the town of Cunchon, and the fighting concentrated all along the 38th Parallel.

The company commander assigned Sergeant Luke Heron III as driver for Lieutenant James Foxwood Elliott IV, who was to carry a packet of coded confidential papers to a Major Hardwell at headquarters, an assignment that neither coveted.

They had started out in an old jeep at seven a.m., stopped for chow with a MASH unit, and then run into a series of bomb craters on the road, which had made travel extremely difficult.

At sunset, they were weary, tired, dusty, thirsty, and miles from the nearest village. They should have reached Munsan, where the news pouch was to be delivered, at four p.m. The last canteen of water had been drunk at two p.m.

The lieutenant was a red-headed, twenty-year-old, buck-toothed, ninety-day wonder with a soft, comic, hush-puppy drawl that, even angry, sounded like an actor's voice in a Tennessee Williams play about the Deep South.

Lieutenant Elliott also used language that Luke Three felt was unbecoming not only to an officer, but to the country gentleman that he professed to be. He might behave himself in the company of fellow officers, but he relaxed so completely with his men that they were inclined to take advantage of him in any crucial situation that arose: they did not want a buddy, but a boss. He was tendered very little respect.

"She-it," he was saying as they drove over the rough road that snaked along a dry riverbed, "Ah don't think Ah've evah been as dry in the mouth. You been ovah this road befoah, Sarge?"

"Yes, sir," Luke Three replied with alacrity, "I make this run about twice a month."

"Is there a watah stop?"

"No, sir, not until we get to Witch's Village, where I suggest we spend the night. The road from there into Munsan is even more deteriorated than this one, and very difficult to drive over even in daylight."

"She-it. Did Ah heah you say Witchas Village?"

"Yes, sir. That's as close as the UN forces can come to pronouncing the Korean name. The place has been captured and recaptured by both sides so many times since Northern Korea invaded South Korea on June 25, 1950, that," Luke Three continued airily, "I've heard the natives have two sets of flags and just wave whichever one is appropriate at the moment!"

The lieutenant pounded his knee. "That's a good one, Sarge, but it sounds like an old Witchas tale to me!"

Luke Three thought that he better laugh, commenting to himself that if this was the sort of humor that his superior possessed, it was unfortunate that he did not stay a civilian. Obviously, the fighting was getting to him.

Luke Three smiled to himself. His so-called superior was an ass in more ways than one, and he himself felt old enough to be his father. The lieutenant had a great deal to learn about men in combat, men under pressure, men who might lose their lives at any moment. Luke Three, at twenty-six, knew what fighting and wars were all about, having served in World War II, but that was water under the bridge.

What a naive kid he had been five years ago, before Robert Desmond, the sharp, cultured, somewhat effete Heron executive, had taken him on a trip to Europe to visit field offices. What he had learned under Bob's expert guidance would fill a Heron service station manual, but what he had learned on his own would fill *two* Heron service station manuals. . . .

Even with his war experiences behind him, Luke Three now realized that he had been a country bumpkin. Bob had been his mentor, had sent him to a crash course in social dancing in New York City; taught him to stride authoritatively into a London hotel without looking like a farmer; given him the confidence to order a seven-course meal, including the right wines, without stuttering; coached him in the proper protocol at such affairs as American Embassy luncheons, and how to treat persons like manicurists, barbers, and clerks.

The only thing in which he had no need for schooling was in the art of seduction, a talent which had not been utilized since he had been in Korea. He was far too fastidious to patronize the local Joy Houses. He liked his women clean.

"Ah I'm so thirsty, Ah swear, Ah could drink a gallon of sea watah!" Lieutenant Elliott tried to wet his dry lips with his tongue and did not succeed. "Wah is hell," he groused. "Ah wish MacArthah was still in command, instead of Ridgeway. Truman hadn't atta done what he did, removin' that perfectly capable gen'ral." He shook his head. "'Old soljahs nevah die.'"

"Yes," Luke Three put in, quoting the popular song. "'they just fade away.'"

There was now the sound of artillery fire as Luke Three reached the end of the dirt road. "Excuse me, sir," he said, turning on the jeep's lights. "Better hold on tightly, I've got to detour through the gully and pick up the road about a quarter of a mile down country. A bomb took out this section a couple of months ago."

He expertly maneuvered the jeep through the wash, and when he heard the sound of a plane coming in from the north, he turned off the lights, killed the motor, and parked under the camouflaging branches of an old cypress. Even then, the moonlight was so bright, he was fearful that the pilot could see the black outline of the jeep under the tree.

Luke Three knew the plane was a Soviet MR, and when the plane swooped low behind them, and he turned and looked up, there was a young Chinese pilot at the controls.

Six hundred feet ahead, he dropped a bomb and then sped upward and over a mountaintop before the small explosion rocked the area.

Luke Three sighed with relief, knowing the pilot had dropped his last egg on his way home. If he had been on a regular mission, he would have peppered the road.

"That fuckah!" the lieutenant muttered. "Now we'll never get to the village."

Luke Three counted to ten under his breath as the dust settled thickly over area. "We'll be a little late, it's true, sir"—he kept his voice steady, trying not to sound sarcastic—"but at least we're alive."

"Ah'm so thirsty!" the lieutenant grumbled. "Let's get this show on road."

Luke Three swallowed hard and put the jeep in reverse. "Yes, sir," he replied politely, trying to sound encouraging. "It won't be long now before we reach civilization."

"You call a couple of crappy bamboo and thatch houses civilization? She-it!"

A half hour later, the jeep pulled into Witch's Village, which consisted of a few wooden houses covered over by flattened US Army corned-beef tins, bright calico curtains at stretched-paper windows, thatched roofs, and a muddy street which ran down the middle. Only two dwellings were lighted, one on the inside, which was obviously a residence, and one on the outside, which was just as obviously a Joy House.

Luke Three kept his eyes straight ahead and kept all humor out of his voice. "Which house would you like to try, sir?"

"Sure'n hell Ah'd get everything in that whorehouse except a gallon of watah! And my jouls aren't in too good shape either, after being joshed about all day like a couple of dice. Try the other place."

"Yes, sir," Luke Three said. He parked the jeep and knocked smartly on the door of the hut, which was opened by a boy of about twelve with an orange cast to his skin, whose almond eyes lighted up when he saw the uniform. He was dressed in a blue jacket and black trousers. "Okay,

General? What can do? Who you be? You lost, maybe?" He pointed to himself. "Me Do'm! Okay?"

Luke Three smiled and looked the boy in the eye. "Me no general, first-class Gyrene in second-class jeep. Me Luke. No lost." He indicated his throat and made swallowing noises. "Very dry."

Do'm put his hands in his ragged trousers, shuffled his bare feet in the doorway, smiled, and pointed across the street. "Whiskey? Beer? Wine? Soft talk? Okay?"

Luke Three shook his head violently. "Boiled water."

The boy frowned, then pointed to the Joy House again. "Shower bath? Okay?"

Patiently, Luke Three again made swallowing noises, and the boy grinned so widely that his almond eyes disappeared in his face. "Coca-Cola? Four bits? Okay?"

Luke Three laughed and called back over his shoulder, "Lieutenant Elliott, would you settle for a Coke?"

"At this point Ah'd settle for a bottle of Calso watah!" he retorted, jumping out of the jeep.

Do'm opened the door and bowed them into the one-room dwelling, which was lighted by a rusty old kerosene lantern set on a wooden table. The room was furnished with two stools, a wall shelf, three straw mats, a statue of Buddah, and a pile of Soviet army blankets. The only picture on the wall was a large lithograph of Jesus kneeling in the Garden of Gesthemane, upon which some UN jokester had scrawled:

To Do'm
With Love,
J.C.

The boy produced four Cokes from a cache under a floorboard and solemnly held out both palms, into which Luke Three counted two dollars in change.

Lieutenant Elliott rubbed the dust from the bottles and looked about expectantly, as if looking for ice and an opener.

The boy smiled. "Church key? Two bits? Okay?"

"Hot damn!" cried the lieutenant. "This little fuckah is gonna break us!" He laughed. "His type is what we need at the conference table at the cease-fire talks in Panmunjom. He'd negotiate an armistice in nothin' flat!"

He crossed the boy's palms once more with silver, then opened and upturned a bottle in one swift movement. His Adams apple, thought Luke Three, went up and down like the bellows which Grandpa Bosley used to encourage the flames in Grandma Letty's fireplace.

When the lieutenant plunked the bottle down on the table, it was empty. Luke Three, amazed at the performance, waited for the inevitable belch—which never came, even when the Lieutenant gulped the second Coke in the same manner.

"Shall we make arrangements to spend the night here, sir?"

"You can, but Ah'll be takin' off across the street. Come and get me as soon as it's daylight."

"Yes, sir," Luke Three replied evenly, and when the lieutenant reached the door, took out his wallet. "Oh, sir, would you like a prophylactic?"

The lieutenant laughed. "Nevah use 'em. It's like going to bed with your shoes on!"

"How about a 'pro kit'?"

Lieutenant Elliot paused. "Much too messy." He ran his hand through his rusty mop of hair. "But thanks anyway, Sarge."

Luke Three shrugged his shoulders. Every soldier had been told that many girls in Korean Joy Houses had VD of a particularly virulent strain, resistant to VD drugs, which would cause the muscles of the body to swell.

In fact, an Intelligence unit had supposedly suggested that the infected whores had been imported into South Korea from the north to cut down as many UN troops as possible. He had heard the report was entitled, *The Communist Trick*, which told more, he thought, about Intelligence than about the Chinese Commies.

But he had done what any conscientious enlisted man who had been assigned as a temporary aide should do, and if his superior got the clap, that was his problem.

Do'm mentioned that for six bits Luke Three could sleep on the floor ("Okay?") and then cooked a handful of red rice and made bark tea over a tiny charcoal stove. Luke Three refused chopsticks and ate with a spoon. When the meal was over, he indicated that he would sleep in front of the door in the event that "bandits come. Okay?"

Although Luke Three thought that bandits in the area were a highly unlikely prospect, it was possible that an enemy straggler might cause trouble, and besides, he realized that it was impossible to dissuade a South Korean from anything traditional. It was perfectly logical to the boy that, since money had been accepted for the night's lodging, protection should be provided free of charge. It mattered not at all that the lodger was twenty-six and the lodgee was twelve.

It was sometime before dawn when Luke Three awakened, muscles aching with a painful erection, and realized that he was not alone on the mat on the floor; there was a warm body beside him! The room was flooded with light from the full moon, and he could see Do'm, who was snoring lightly, half sitting up by the front door.

Cautiously, Luke Three glanced at the form beside him. The girl was very young, with high cheekbones, a small but well-formed nose, and a sweetly pursed mouth. Her skin was the color of a very pale Oklahoma peach—more creamy than orange—but her most startling feature, long, almost straight black eyelashes, gave her face an exotic look, far more than the slanted fold of skin over her closed eyes.

In the extreme need of the moment, and since they were already touching, he placed his arm around her slight shoulders. She awakened immediately and pulled away, clutching the army blanket. She stumbled to her feet, eyes wide, mouth trembling, and searched the room with a glance; she saw Do'm, and her shoulders sagged with relief. She uttered a quick command in Korean, which awakened him instantly.

The boy was on his feet in a moment, took in the situation at a glance, and, seeing that Luke Three was fully dressed except for his boots, he exchanged a rapid-fire conversation with the woman, who lowered the blanket. She was dressed in a loose jacket with trousers tied at her ankles.

"Say hello?" Do'm said tightly with a small bow, and it was obvious that he was trying to assume an air of authority with the introductions. "Luke? First-class Gyrene in second-class jeep? Okay?" He pronounced the words very carefully. "T'am? Sister Number One? Okay?"

Luke Three bowed slightly, somehow not feeling at all foolish. "First-class Gyrene in second-class jeep, happy know T'am."

She bowed in return, and her eyes sparkled mischievously as she replied in a musical voice, "English not good, but better than Do'm. I come through enemy lines in middle of night. Very tired, very sleepy, very happy to be home town."

She adjusted the army blanket around her body and looked down at the bare feet. "I see body on mat, think it small child." She fought for the right word. "Ah, brother?" She paused, a blush settling over face and neck. "I not like wild flowers on other side of street."

He nodded and looked at his watch. It was five-thirty, and the sun would be up soon. "I must go," he said.

"You go now," she said. "I fix dress quick. You come back?"

He put on his boots and went outside and smoked a cigarette. The street was quiet, although birds in the grove outside of the village were making strange noises as if they had just awakened and were clearing their throats for a morning song.

He was enchanted by T'am; there was a sweet, touching quality about her that was extremely appealing. She was unlike any woman that he had ever met. What a fool he had been not to stay close to her on the mat, simply enjoying the warmth of her body! Why had he spoiled the experience by touching her?

"Come? Okay?" Do'm called, and when Luke Three came back into the room, he was greeted with the fragrance of bark tea, and a bowl of steaming *congee*—rice gruel—was sitting on the table.

T'am had caught her straight black hair with a comb on top of her head, and even then she was only shoulder height. Luke Three colored; T'am was dressed in a pink brocade Chinese split skirt, such as was brought back from Hong Kong by American soldiers for their Korean girlfriends. He felt a pang of jealousy.

"Sit, please," she said, "I sorry for small food. This is all we have." He began to eat the gruel with a spoon. She stood opposite him, watching him eat. Under other circumstances, Luke Three would have been embarrassed, but there was something so straightforward about her that he was impressed.

In a strange way, he felt flattered by her attention. She had only met him, and to her he could only be another Gyrene, yet she gave the impression that at the moment the only concern was that he was well fed for his journey.

He finished the last sip of bark tea just as the sun was rising. Do'm blew out the kerosene lantern, and T'am bowed slightly. "It is a pleasure having met you," she said graciously.

He smiled. "Do you go through enemy lines often?"

She shook her head. "No. I come home to stay now. I am—was—cooking for black market couple, now closed up for good by fourth-class dogface who take over business." Her voice was without rancor. "Number One Brother and Number Two sister work in Hong Kong, with Mother."

"I come by this village every ten days or so," Luke Three said, heart pounding so rapidly in his chest that he thought his good conduct medals would surely shake. "Is it possible that I can stop and see you?"

She colored, and it was then that he knew that she liked him; he was not just another Gyrene. "Yes. Do'm and I weave mats all the time."

Luke Three smiled widely. "Yes, ma'am," he said, excitement welling up in his breast. "I will see you soon."

They accompanied him outdoors, and he was embarrassed to go to the Joy House across the street without an explanation. "I must bring my superior from that place," he said, turning red.

She nodded. "So long, Luke," she said, turning back to the door, and when Do'm turned to accompany him to the Joy House, she called him back sharply.

Luke Three tried the red door, which was locked. He

knocked twice, and a window opened. "Yesss?" a voice called, then a disheveled head appeared. "Too early? Too late? Come back after early chow?"

"I'm here to pick up Lieutenant Elliott."

The window slammed shut, and a moment later the door opened. "Come?" The woman looked like a fat Oriental kewpie doll who had been left out in the rain. Instead of taking off her makeup the night before, she had smeared cold cream all over her face, which gave her a painted, garish look, as if a red neon light were constantly reflected over her features.

She pointed to a naked form on the floor mat. "He out cold," she said matter-of-factly. She took a billfold, small change, a knife, and a crumpled letter from a drawer. "Check? Honest place?" she said, her glance penetrating and sharp.

Luke Three made a great show of meticulously examining the contents of the wallet. He had no idea of the amount of money the lieutenant carried, but there was a twenty-dollar bill and two ones. He looked up and nodded, and the woman grinned and said, "Paid? Everything copacetic?"

Never having been placed in a like position, Luke Three turned away, as she went about the business of retrieving shorts, undershirt, and socks without a backward glance. "You help? We fix him in fine first-class shape, pronto?"

She had obviously been through this maneuver many times before. He turned away; Elliott's breath was like a sewer in a distillery. He held the pale, thin body while the woman expertly slipped on the socks. It was then that he realized with a shock that all of the lieutenant's body hair had been removed!

Was this some sort of sexual ritual? His mind conjured up pictures of sharp razors, giggling women, and willing participation by the subject. Had the ceremony been conducted while he was sober? No man in the service would permit himself to be shaven, even if the idea might have seemed exciting at the time, because he had to shower with other men; ridicule by fellow officers was anathema.

Self-consciously, trying to suppress his amusement, Luke Three supported the lieutenant's middle, and the woman glided the shorts up his legs, paused at the thighs while she gently placed the lieutenant's genitals inside, and gave a sigh of appreciation as she snapped the elastic around his waist. "Korean men not so well hung," she said matter-of-factly, ignoring Luke Three's red face.

They finally finished dressing the lumpy form, and Luke Three threw the dead weight over his shoulder like a sack of grain, hoping that T'am was not watching the humiliating procedure from across the street. He lowered the body into the jeep, perhaps not as gently as the lieutenant might have wished had he been conscious. Luke Three hated his role of nursemaid.

The woman stood back in the doorway, as if she was afraid of the sun. "No tip?" she muttered.

Luke Three did not know what services had been provided the night before, or at what cost, but he figured that it was worth two dollars to have the lieutenant dressed. In fact it would be worth the money to see the lieutenant's reaction when he discovered that all of his body hair had been shaved off in what was no doubt an orgy.

The woman smiled and cried, "Come back? Hunky-dory?"

He waved, tied a rope around the lieutenant's waist, which he secured to the back of the seat, jumped into the jeep, started the motor, and drove through the deserted town full speed. He did not look back, afraid that he would see T'am's face in the window.

Ten minutes later, as they climbed a hill that would be considered a mountain in Oklahoma, a patch of dense fog rolled in from the west. Luke Three slowed down cautiously and was relieved to see that the road was clear up ahead.

A half hour later, dark clouds rolled in from the coastal area, and a few giant raindrops splattered down, awakening Lieutenant James Foxwood Elliott IV. "Ma mouth tastes like horseshit smells," he grumbled, "and ma crotch burns like the rear end of a red-assed monkey looks!"

Luke Three swallowed hard, wanting to retort: *Then you must be in tip-top shape!* But instead, he remarked innocently, "Gee, sir, then this bit of rain should be refreshing."

The lieutenant glared at him. "Ah'm still kinda woozy." He clamped his hand to his face and reached for his wallet and riffled through the contents. "Thank God! Ah thought Ah'd been robbed. It's all there."

"You do owe me two dollars, sir."

"What for?" His eyes were suspicious.

"The . . . lady . . . helped you get dressed."

"Oh, thanks. Ah was wondering how Ah got put together."

"Did you enjoy yourself, sir?"

The lieutenant spat out of the side of the jeep. "Ah guess so. Ah got drunk and ah got laid, so what else is there?" He shook his head, and then groaned. "Ah'm gonna be sick."

"I'll stop whenever you say, sir," Luke Three replied, slowing down so the bumps in the road would not be so severe, and glad that the rain had stopped.

Artillery was heard in distance, and the lieutenant clutched his head. "Can't we rest somewhere?"

"We've only just started, sir."

"Then for Christ's sake—and mine too—take it easy, Sarge."

As Luke Three turned a steep bend in the road, a convoy of trucks sped toward them, headed by a jeep with colors flying. "It's General Hopper. I'll have to stop, sir. Can you handle this all right?"

"She-it, wouldn't ya just know?" The lieutenant was yellow around the gills, but he ran a comb through his rusty forelock, straightened his shoulders, and managed to sit up with some semblance of respectability.

The jeep stopped, and the convoy, snaking around the background curves, halted suddenly, creating enormous clouds of dust, half clay earth, half animal droppings.

Very slowly and deliberately, the lieutenant climbed out of the jeep, picked up the packet, walked carefully to the general, and saluted smartly, every inch the perfect officer. "Lieutenant James Foxwood Elliott IV reporting, sir." Each word was uttered like a pearl. "Ah'm on my way to headquarters, sir, with an FE 12-8-9-7." He indicated the packet, which was resting under his arm.

"You were due yesterday afternoon, Lieutenant," the

general replied curtly. He had a gray face, a gray mustache, gray hair, and a uniform gradually turning gray from clay dust in the air.

"The road has been bombed out in spots," the lieutenant answered, "makin' travel exceedingly difficult. We drove until after sundown and spent the night in a village."

The general's eyes glittered. "At Witch's?"

The lieutenant managed not to blanch at the name. "Yes, sir, a native boy took pity and offered us a mat for us to sleep on, sir."

"Well, headquarters was moved this morning; the fire bombs decimated almost everything. Give me the packet, Lieutenant, and since the sergeant knows the road, your jeep can head the convoy."

"Yes, sir!" The lieutenant saluted gravely, then climbed in beside Luke Three and muttered, "You heard the old son-of-a-bitch. Make tracks!"

"But where are we going, sir?"

"How the she-it do Ah know?" the lieutenant snapped, "just keep your eyes on the fuckin' road!"

After many delays, while Luke Three led the convoy around the bomb craters that pitted the road and the lieutenant cussed profusely and vomited copiously over the side of the jeep—and not always in the order—the trucks passed through the forlorn Witch's Village.

Luke Three looked in vain, but neither T'am nor Do'm appeared; but the troops cheered relentlessly as the fat madam and three girls appeared in front of the pink door, waving what appeared to be intimate articles of apparel. Lieutenant Elliott hunched down in the front seat, but not before the madam screamed, "Jimmy, Jimmy, Jimmy?"

"Damnedest thing I ever saw, Sarge," he told Luke Three that night after they were back in Cunchon, "that whore out there in the middle of the road, shouting my name!"

"Oh, I wouldn't worry too much, sir," Luke Three replied dryly. "Ever think about how many men there were named Jimmy in that convoy of two hundred and fifty men?"

"She-it!" exclaimed the lieutenant, which was exactly

Luke Three's sentiment when he was permanently assigned as driver to Lieutenant James Foxwood Elliott IV.

Patricia Anne had held her husband's hand all afternoon. Lars had briefly responded that morning, long enough to be fed oatmeal, for which she was thankful; intravenous feeding was becoming painful because he had taken so many needles during his stay in the hospital.

He was tied in bed at his own request, because he was fearful of injuring others. Being a doctor himself, he was not particularly afraid for his own safety, although he remarked casually that he'd read about two accidental suicides, when a couple on an experience jumped out of the window, thinking they could fly. "That was stupid!" he exclaimed angrily to Patricia Anne. "In the first place, the golden rule is that only one person has an experience at one time; the other always acts as companion, as you know."

Being Scandinavian, Lars had a delicate skin that did not take the sun well, and in summer always suffered a series of mild burns. The result was a rather healthy-looking ruddy complexion, and his blonde hair was always streaked by the sun.

But now, having been indoors for so long, his face was completely white and his hair silver-blonde. His head on the white pillow looked almost corpse-like. The first time that Patricia Anne had seen him in the hospital, she had cried out, thinking that he was dead. He had awakened at her outburst, and she had burst into tears.

It had been one of his good days. "I know I look like a *boogie-man*!" He laughed, using an Oklahoma expression.

But that had been several months ago, when his spirits had been much improved because it had appeared he was gaining ground at last. But since Bosley's funeral he had suffered several bad experiences. She had been present during one, when he had shouted nothing but gibberish for five minutes and thrashed about so violently on the bed that he had broken his restraints twice and ended up with ugly bruises on his arms.

She had truly been fearful for his sanity when, with horror in his eyes, he had told her breathlessly that he had been in an anthill and was trying to imitate the sounds of the workers.

Now his eyelids fluttered open, and he smiled when he saw her sitting beside the bed. "I thought I was holding Miss Enema's hand," he joked. "But you're much prettier."

She laughed. "Thank you, sir."

He noticed that her beige dress complimented her olive complexion. "You look very Indian today," he said.

She smiled, showing her very white teeth. "I've heard Mother tell Daddy that lots of times. When I was growing up in Kansas City and Angel, no one ever mentioned my Cherokee blood, although a couple of the boys I used to date sometimes said that I looked 'exotic.'" She laughed. "Daddy said that in the First World War the doughboys called him 'Breedy.'" She paused. "How do you feel?"

"Scrungy. Untie my hands, please," he said. "I want to take a shower."

She looked at him doubtfully. "Shall I call an orderly to help you?"

He shook his head. "No, I'm fine. I haven't had an experience for five days now. If this continues, I may ask to go home. We can get a male nurse." He took her hand. "Oh, Pat, wouldn't it be the greatest thing in the world if I'm finally finished with these horrible hallucinations?"

He paused as she untied his hands. "Surely, dear God in Heaven, this chemical can't be imprisoned in my body *forever!* Oh, if only Doctor Sam was here, he might come up with a solution."

"But he left you all of his files, dear, and I helped you go over every page. You've carried on his research so many steps since then."

"Yes," he replied bitterly, his eyes staring straight ahead. "But I had to experiment further and take more and more of the mixture, not realizing the drug could not be passed out of the body like other wastes. Dr. Sam only used minute qualities of the mushroom compound to benefit those who were terminally ill of cancer and other diseases, when painkillers no longer worked. The drug helped them endure the agony of dying by separating sensations, so that pain became no more important than eating or sleeping."

He shook his head. "I'm sorry to be chewing my cabbage again, when we've been over these same points a million times." He summoned a pleasant expression and tried to be cheerful. "Come on, will you scrub my back for me?"

"Why of course, darling," she said, and then saw his face take on that distant look that always preceded an experience. As his head began to tremble, she fastened his restraints again, then held his hand tightly.

He was traveling down a long pink corridor faintly reminiscent of a long rubber tube. Rather than a sensation of floating, he found that he was sliding along on the soles of his bare feet.

The slippery surface felt pleasant at first, as he picked up speed. He was conscious of a variety of tickling sensations running up and down his legs, and there was an erotic re-evaluation of who and where he was. He was fully aware that he was Dr. Lars Hanson and that he was enjoying a delightful trip; a sensuous journey through a tactile land where only touch and feeling existed.

He was now conscious of a warm wind caressing his body, and, looking down, discovered that his hospital coat had melted away. He was naked. The hairs on his chest moved in the warm breeze, and below, his penis swayed lustfully back and forth in anticipation of some unknown carnal delight.

As Lars became even more physically aroused, the wind increased in volume. He was being propelled forward at greater and greater speeds—until he grew fearful of being able to maintain an upright position because the downward slant of the tube had increased alarmingly. He held out his hands to act as a sort of rudder, so that he would not be tossed end-over-end.

The wind was now at gale force, grotesquely rippling the muscles of his body this way and that, cruelly whipping his penis one moment against his thighs and the next against his stomach.

There was a penetrating, cloying perfume in the pink tube

that was at once both exhilarating and vile. He was repulsed to find himself more sexually aroused than before.

The tube was tapering slightly now, and up ahead he could discern only a pinpoint of light. And as traveling speed increased even more, and he was gliding at such an exhilarating rate of speed, he knew with certainty it would be only a matter of moments before he was thrown forward on hands and knees, even more constricted by the narrowing tube.

The dreaded moment came the next instant, and he could feel the skin on his stomach and thighs burn upon impact. The fiery sensations then turned into soft, undulating waves of pleasure. He was lying on his stomach, with his hands stretched out in front, swan-diving deliciously and joyfully into the narrowest confines of the pink tube—which magically stretched elastically to accommodate him. To his intense pleasure, he discovered the tube was undulating rings of pink flesh. He came.

Lars awakened slowly, drowsily, and moist, sighing with contentment, his eyes dreamy. "Oh, what a wonderful trip!"

Patricia Anne, who knew that look of fulfillment so well, sighed with relief. "It's time that you had a good experience," she said, "after all the nightmares."

"Oh," he said gently, "if you could only have shared that supreme moment of fulfillment, different than I've ever known."

She smiled. "Do you realize that you used the word 'trip' a moment ago instead of experience?"

"Did I?" He paused and considered the idea. "Well, that's what it was—a *trip*. That really describes the feeling much better than 'experience.'"

"Well, I'm glad that you had a good trip this time," she said with a smile. "Only, I'm jealous."

He smiled sleepily. "Don't be, I love you too much." He closed his eyes, and when he was breathing steadily, she removed the notepad from her purse and made the notations, which she had continued to do since that very first trip several years ago. Tomorrow she would question him more fully, so that the data would be kept up-to-date.

Patricia Anne made one final note in the book: *At four-thirty this afternoon, upon awakening from a pleasant sexual hallucinatory projection, Doctor Lars Hanson said (quote): "Oh, what a wonderful trip!"*

She went to barred window and looked out idly over the hospital grounds. Oh, if he would improve to the point where she could take him home. If only an antidote for the poisonous mushrooms could be found!

7

Inward Battles

The wispy room clerk at the small, elegant Tricolor Hotel off the Champs Elysées near the George V hostelry raised his eyebrows and announced with considerable pride that the rooms booked by the Paris-to-San-Sebastian tour would not be ready for occupancy until three in the afternoon.

He reminded Charlotte of one of those slightly effeminate, if undernourished, lingerie salesmen whose territory included most of Manhattan's Fifth Avenue. But when he heard the name Heron in connection with Oklahoma, his icy facade broke; he became coy and twittered, "You must be a member of the family of the great maestro?"

Mitchell was aghast. Outside of his home state, no one ever connected him with Clement. What if possible tour members nearby had heard the exchange? He had no desire to spend the entire trip explaining his connection to either the Cherokee Swing Band or the oil barony of the Herons. "A distant relative," he answered vaguely and, hoping to distract the young man, asked if there were feminine apparel shops in the area?

But the man was not to be put off so easily. "I believe I have all of the maestro's swing recordings. 'Red Sails in the Sunset,' is almost worn out, and I have a scrapbook with hundreds of newspaper and magazine clippings, but not much about the Herons, except Luke and Luke Three. Are you, perchance, his uncle?"

It was disconcerting to Mitchell to hear family names bandied about so easily by a stranger. When Charlotte giggled and turned away, the clerk knew that he had made a *gaffe* and became even more flustered as he sailed into profuse apologies. Mitchell rather enjoyed his embarrassment. "I am Clement Story's cousin," he said with finality, then leaned forward confidentially. "I am here *incognito*. I'm on my honeymoon."

"Oh," the young man replied, rolling his dove eyes. "I should have known!" But it was obvious by his manner that there was nothing in either Mitchell's or Charlotte's attitude that gave a clue to their newlywed status. He changed the subject none too adroitly. "I would give *anything* for the signature of Clement Story!" The threat was implied: *I'll keep quiet about your identity, if you will procure his autograph.*

Mitchell forced a smile. "If you will give me your name and address, when I return to the States I'll see that you get a signed photograph."

The young man turned pink. *"Merci, merci!"* he exclaimed and went into such a long appreciative tirade that Mitchell, who was fluent in French, could scarcely keep up with him. "By the way," he finished, producing a key, "there will always be an available accommodation for Clement Story's *cousin!*"

Mitchell bowed, and winked at Charlotte. Upstairs in the large suite, he shook his head. "That's the first time that's ever happened to me," he proclaimed, "and in Paris of all places!"

"Well," Charlotte replied seriously, removing her navy-blue coat, "you must remember, dear, that Europeans look at fame quite differently than we Americans do. Over here, if you've made one great accomplishment, you're revered for life. I think that's rather nice. Elders are not cast off, and if you've been around as long as Clement, I suppose you become a sort of legend."

He hung up his coat in the spacious closet. "Certainly we have fewer and fewer heros in the States. Actually, it may not be so bad, being the relative of a celebrity. After all, we have Clement to thank for this room!"

He surveyed the furniture. "That Louis Quatorze IV sofa is not a bad piece at all." He paused. "Speaking of furniture, Charlotte, if you'd like to browse around the shops, I've an errand to do. There's a dealer near the Tuileries who might be interested in placing an order now and then." He paused and went on casually, "You can come along, if you like."

"Thank you, dear, but I think I'll just rest." She yawned. "There's something about Paris that makes me drowsy."

"Maybe it's the chestnut trees. Have a good nap." He smiled with relief, because he could not take her to visit Alice B. Toklas.

The cream-colored taxi that Mitchell hailed was new, and the august young driver held his head up proudly, much as if he had slid out of the womb with his nose in the air.

"Cinq rue Christine," Mitchell announced, climbing into the back seat. He had lighted a cigarette before he saw the *dé fense de fumer* sign. He threw the fag out the window and sighed. In the old days, Parisian cabbies would not have dared to forbid customers the pleasure of tobacco. But the war had changed the attitude of the French people much more than that of Americans at home, who had not been forced to play host to the *boches*.

There was now also a new breed of cabby; the one in question was typically young, and quite good-looking except for the dreadful condition of his teeth—probably due, Mitchell reflected, to poor nutrition during the Occupation. The driver pulled out carefully into the traffic pattern, honking his horn vigorously, as if in imitation of all the other taxis. At least, thought Mitchell, the noise pattern in Paris had not changed.

"The literary lady, Gertrude Stein, you seek is laid to rest in the Père Lachaise Cemetery. I can take you there if you like. The gravestone is very simple. A great many former servicemen go there to pay her homage."

"Yes, I know," Mitchell replied sadly, "but I have read that her companion still lives in the apartment. Is this not so?"

"*Oui*. She is there, but it was the great lion all of them came to see, and not the little mouse. You must have lived a long time in France; your accent is very good."

"*Merci*. Yes. But I was here last six years ago."

"Nineteen forty-six was a bad year," the driver replied stoically, "because Paris had not been too long liberated." He turned into the rue des Grands. "We have more or less recovered from the Occupation, as you can see, but francs are still scarce." He turned into the rue Dauphine. "It has been said wrongly by foreign journalists that only two professions are still successful in Paris—the demimondaines and the drivers of taxis." He stopped before a bookbinding store in the rue Christine. "That is wrong, of course. We all must scratch for francs, even the great fashion houses. This is your destination, monsieur."

When Mitchell saw that the cabby had not asked for an exorbitant fare, he asked, "Would you kindly wait?"

"*Oui*. I shall park, and when you are ready to go, ferret me out of the bookbinders. I have a love for beautiful leathers."

"You are a student?"

The man colored. "*Non*. I have no money for the university, but the appreciation of books is still there."

"There are many ex-soldiers driving cabs at home, some with a few years of college. But the economy seems in worse shape here."

The cabby nodded. "All the tourists see only the best places. They do not know that many still do not have enough to eat." He turned and extended his hand democratically. "My name is Etienne."

Mitchell shook hands solemnly, then got out of the car and climbed the narrow stairs over the bookbindery. The musty odor that wafted through the hall—half dust, half tuberose—brought back a flood of memories. When there was no answer to his first knock, he applied his knuckles to the door again.

"*Oui*?" came a faint voice. The door opened a sliver, and he was staring into one dark eye. "*Oui*?"

"I am Mitchell Heron," he said softly in English.

"You are a *Gee*?" she asked, and he remembered that was the way that Alice B. Toklas pronounced "GI."

"You once knew me as Michel Bayard."

"Gertrude is dead," came the flat answer.

"I am very sad about that," he replied gently, "but it is you that I came to see."

The door swung open. Alice B. Toklas had changed almost not at all since he had last seen her. She was still frail, but rather more sharp-featured than he remembered. Her dark bangs were still strung along her forehead, and there was the demarcation line of black hair on her upper lip. She wore a fusty blue chiffon dress with maroon flowers, and there were food stains on the yoke. She was neat-looking but not immaculate.

Alice B. Toklas peered at him, and it seemed that she had shrunk. She was slightly stooped. "I remember you now, of course," she said with a sudden delightful smile that animated her face. "You brought the fresh perch when the Resistance man, Anatole, brought you to spend the night with us in Culoz, and you pretended to be a Frenchman! Then you came once again just before Gertrude died. Nineteen forty-three seems such a long time ago!"

She paused. "Forgive me for making you stand in the drafty hall. Please come in. You will find everything the same—except Picasso's portrait of Gertrude. It is exhibited in the entrance hall at the Metropolian Museum of Art in New York City." Her eyes were automatically drawn to the faded square on the wall where the portrait had hung.

"I shall put on the kettle," she said warmly, as if he was an old and trusted friend. "You would not refuse a cup of Darjeeling?" There was again the gamin smile. "I am going through an East Indian phase just now. Some of their curries are delightful. Please sit, I'll be back in a moment."

The large, high-ceilinged room appeared unchanged. The peculiar Japanese prints still hung in the entry hall, and the unframed monotone paintings and the large pink Picasso nude were in remembered places.

As Mitchell sat down on a cherrywood horsehair sofa, his eyes sought out the small canvas of yellow-green apples of which he was so fond, and he was overtaken with *déjà vu*. It seemed that Gertrude was only away on one of her customary walks with the tiny poodle, Basket; he fully expected to hear her heavy step on the stairs, accompanied by the sharp cries of the dog.

Alice B. Toklas came into the room with a black lacquered tea tray. "It's extraordinary, is it not?" she remarked casually.

"What?"

"Gertrude."

"Pardon?"

"She's been gone now for six years, yet she seems to be here still." She poured the tea. "You have noticed?"

Mitchell was suddenly very shy. He did not often think about the hereafter, and never discussed it; to cover the pause that was becoming awkward, he hurriedly took a sip of steaming tea and consequently burned his lip.

"I forgot to mention that it's very hot," she apologized.

"But it is also very *good*." He saw with some surprise that the *petits fours* on the small plate were covered with a casing of mold, which almost exactly matched the pistachio frosting. Obviously, she was losing her eyesight. "Have you been well?" he asked, and it suddenly occurred to him that without Gertrude, Alice B. Toklas was becoming an interesting personality in her own right; she no longer receded into the background.

"My arthritis troubles me during the cold winters here," she said matter-of-factly, "but I get away during the coldest weather to the Acqui Terme baths near Milan, which always seem to be beneficial."

"And friends keep you busy?" he asked politely.

She nodded and brushed her dark bangs back from her forehead. "Everyone comes—not in the great numbers of the old days, but I am not neglected." She paused. "I am also writing a book."

"About Gertrude?"

"Not exactly, although there are reminiscences." She paused somewhat dramatically. "It is a *cookbook*." She turned to him. "But enough of me, what about *you?* Gertrude and I were very curious if you ever found that young man whom you were searching for."

Mitchell was discomfited. He had conveniently forgotten about Jean Baptiste Faubert. In his mind's eye, he once again saw the beautiful Françoise, to whom he had made love so often during that AWOL sojourn in Paris during World War I.

Then his mind switched forward to the café in Plaisance-du-Gers. He had been under cover as Michel Bayard when he glimpsed the striking young man at the end of the bar— the striking young man with the Heron profile, who would have been the right age if Françoise had borne his child. That profile had haunted him for years.

After he had impersonated Herr Doktor Professor Schneider in Berlin in 1946, and again visited Paris, he had confided in Gertrude Stein, who made inquiries in Plaisance-du-Gers about the young man named Jean Baptiste Faubert.

Mitchell regarded Alice B. Toklas apologetically. "I'm sorry, my mind was a thousand miles away. I gave up the search for the boy a long time ago."

"Why?"

He looked at her in surprise. "I got to thinking that, if he turned out to be my son, what would happen then? He would have my blood, and nothing else."

"Perhaps. But would you not appreciate a long-lost father returning after so many years?" she asked. "It is something to think about. But on the other hand, if finding him is impossible, then you made a wise choice."

"But I did not drop by, Miss Toklas, to talk about Jean Baptiste Faubert. I wanted to find out how you were doing—"

"—without Gertrude?" Her voice was sharp.

Her tone unnerved him, and he wondered exactly why he had made the effort to come to V rue Christine after all. "No," he replied as gracefully as he could, "but to renew an acquaintance."

"So many come to worship at the shrine." Her voice was brusque.

Mitchell did not take her statement personally, because that was not the purpose of his visit. "That must be very difficult for you," he said with great feeling.

"Some bring poetry," she continued absently, "or a garland of flowers, or a book they've written, exactly as if Gertrude was alive. These people look at me curiously to ascertain whether I am still grieved." She set the cup into its saucer with an air of finality and frowned delicately. "Do you believe in the hereafter, Mitchell Heron?"

He was taken aback at the suddenness of her question. "Yes, I suppose so—don't you?"

"Gertrude thought that if a person did not accomplish a mission on earth, they never got another chance anywhere else. Life was a complete statement."

He regarded her intently. "I think that there are certain people—and certainly Gertrude Stein was one—who are immortal."

She seemed to withdraw into herself after that, and lighted a brown cigarette. She blew the smoke out of her nose with a sudden vengeance. "I do not know what to believe. I only know that she is here, and if she is here, death cannot be final." She peered at his plate. "You haven't eaten your *petits fours*," she said.

Hesitantly, he reached for one of the moldy bits of pastry and took a bite, which he swiftly followed with a sip of cold tea. "Did you bake these?"

She shook her head. "No. The oven is out of whack. Gertrude was always very clever about fixing things, but I . . ."

It was on the tip of his tongue to ask why she did not hire a repairman, and then it occurred to him that she might be very badly off financially. "I suppose"—he made his voice sound casual—"that museums would very much like to acquire these pictures?"

She threw him a quick glance through her sparse lashes. "Gertrude left the entire collection to me, of course, and the Stein heirs can do nothing—although they have tried, and will probably keep trying." She paused and frowned again. "They are thinking about the millions, which really do not interest me. As long as I have food . . ." She relighted the cigarette and puffed a moment before continuing. "I shall put on the kettle. The teapot is cold."

"Thank you, but not for me, Miss Toklas," Mitchell replied, thinking that he had been away from Charlotte long enough. "I must be going."

She raised her thick brows in surprise, as if it was unforgivable for a guest to leave without being dismissed.

"Oh?" It was as if she had come back from a long journey. She managed a small smile. "Please come to see me when you're again in Paris. I miss all the bright young men who used to come to see Gertrude."

It occurred to Mitchell as he shook her small, bony hand, that Alice B. Toklas was essentially a very lonely old woman. For a very long time he would remember her fleeting, ghostlike smile as she said adieu.

Downstairs, he looked in the open door of the bindery. "Hey, Etienne, it's time to go!"

The boy was beside him in a moment. "How did it go upstairs, monsieur?" He opened the door of the taxi.

"It was a strange interview," Mitchell replied, getting into the back seat.

"You are a journalist?"

"No, I meant the visit. Come to think of it, I don't know why I came."

Etienne started the car and headed out into traffic. "Rumor has it that the old lady is as poor as a church mouse, but will not part with so much as a pencil sketch. The sale of one Picasso would take care of her the rest of her life!" He shook his head. "We all have different values, *non*?"

Mitchell nodded. "Yes," he replied sadly. But he secretly applauded the lady who apparently never compromised, and whose spirit he admired. Then he thought of the boy with the Heron profile, whom he had all but forgotten since his last visit to Paris, and was troubled anew.

Whatever her shortcomings, Alice B. Toklas had given him a conscience once more.

The gleaming new blue bus pulled up before the Hotel Tricolor, and in the lobby the tour guide waved his large hands in the air, summoning the passengers, who apparently assembled more slowly than anticipated.

He was forty, short, and thick-waisted, and was perspiring profusely, although the temperature hovered only in the low seventies. He mopped a wide brow with a large white handkerchief, which he removed periodically from the pocket of his crumpled white suit. From time to time he peered at a manifest in his hand, as if trying unsuccessfully to decipher the names of his charges.

Charlotte stood back from the rest of the tourists, observing the scene with amusement. She turned to Mitchell. "What do you suppose an Italian is doing conducting a tour through the château country of France?"

"It's best not to know, dear." He laughed, pleased that she was amused and not annoyed, and picked up his camera case.

She whispered, "If that man drags out a crucifix and starts praying to the Blessed Virgin, this will surely seem like a scene out of a farcical movie of the nineteen thirties!"

Surprisingly, the man spoke with a cultured French accent that did not conform to his appearance. "I am Salvatore Reachi," he said pleasantly, thumping his chest; then he waved at the bus parked in front of the hotel. "And that is Gerda."

Charlotte winked good-naturedly at Mitchell and sputtered, "A bus called . . . Gerda?"

Mitchell laughed. "Why not? Europeans have a name for everything. I think it's sort of nice. Like calling our cars flivvers." Since Charlotte and he had been longtime friends before becoming lovers or husband and wife, they were easy companions and did not try each other's nerves. But, he mused, they had also never traveled extensively together, and sometimes strange things happened to relationships while on long journeys. Would they get along harmoniously on a trip where he would be distracted by that one miserable duty that he had to perform? He could not really be himself until his mission was accomplished. *Damn you, Pierre,* he cursed. *What have you involved me in this time?*

"What were you saying, dear?" Charlotte asked, removing their passports and the string of visas from her purse.

"Nothing," he muttered under his breath, and, aware of tour members lining up in front of Salvatore Reachi, held the camera in front of his chest in a pose typical of what a new bridegroom might assume. "Honey," he called in a voice loud enough that passersby in the street could not fail to hear, "I'd like to get a photograph of you coming out of the dining room. It's so picturesque."

She regarded him with surprise and smoothed the new pink sharkskin suit over her hips. "All right, but . . ." She turned sideways, with her right shoulder to the camera at what she felt was a slim angle, while he made a great fuss of focusing the lens.

After the flash went off, he held up his hand. "One more, just for safety—a cover shot."

She smiled self-consciously, and when the second bulb illuminated the entire west section of the lounge, she rubbed her eyes and sighed. "I didn't know you were such a photo buff, Mitch! But hereafter, dear, please concentrate on the scenery, because I'm not at all photogenic."

"Let me be the judge of that, honey," he admonished, then grinned happily. "You really look swell."

Charlotte did not in the least feel "swell," with twelve people staring at her. Even as much as Mitchell had traveled, he apparently still behaved like a tourist. He never displayed this sort of garrulousness at home, but there was even something touching about this new side of his personality.

Away from Enid, she concluded, Mitchell was apparently freed from the stereotype of behaving like the Successful Businessman. Here in Paris, he could be the uninhibited husband who made love to his wife with a surprising passion. She took his arm, resolving to be more considerate of his feelings; after all, this was a honeymoon trip, and she did not wish to stem his exuberance in or out of bed. Very clearly, she heard her mother's oft-repeated phrase: "Never be a millstone around a man's neck—particularly a husband."

Signor Reachi called the name Heron and brought Charlotte back to reality. Mitchell looked directly into his eyes as he handed him their papers, hoping for some reaction, but there was none; conclusion: Salvatore Reachi was not the missionary.

The travelers were shown into the front of the lounge, near the door to the street. Two older couples, probably retired, had obviously met the evening before, because they were complaining of the cost of the seven-course dinner at the George V Hotel down the street.

Signor Reachi, in the center of the group, raised plump, ringed hands, smiled, and checked his watch. "Since we are going to be together for the next five days until our tour ends in San Sebastian," he said in impeccable English which did not go with his Romanesque face, "when you will be on your own, I shall introduce everyone.

"I should like to present Miss Fava Dolin of Perth, Australia." He moved toward a tall middle-aged woman dressed in a svelte tweed suit with an orange scarf at her throat. Her shoulder-length blonde hair was too youthful for her brown, sunburned face, which was covered with a mass of tiny wrinkles. When she smiled, more lines formed underneath her bright blue eyes. Charlotte thought: *She's aptly named, because her face does look like a textured brown fava bean.* The relentless sun in some Outback sheep station had contributed to the leather look of her face.

"This is Grace and David Benjamin of Fayettville, Kansas." Signor Reachi indicated one of the older couples. "And old friends, Doris and Humphrey Hardesty of Babylon, Long Island, whom they have invited to tour with us."

The foursome seemed content in their newly found relationship, Mitchell thought, and dismissed them as possible contacts. So far only Fava Dolin seemed a possibility; she was mature, single, and looked like someone that Pierre Darlan might be forced to conscript at the last moment.

Signor Reachi paused beside a man of about forty, with dark hair and a Hitler mustache, who looked as if he might be a bank clerk on holiday. "This is André Gulot, of Johannesburg, South Africa, who is visiting France for the first time." The man smiled, rose from his seat, and bowed deeply twice. He reminded Charlotte of Charlie Chaplin; all that was missing was the cane!

"I should like you to meet Mrs. Henry Parsons, of Riverside, California," Signor Reachi said, as a plump, nondescript little woman with whiskey-brown hair and the air of a rather weary schoolteacher turned from the window and glanced over the group with a calm but authoritative air. She nodded pleasantly, and incongruously lighted a cigarette, which somehow did not go with either her personality or appearance. She was fussing with a Pekingese dog wearing a collar with the name Tibbetts spelled in rhinestones. The other false note was André Gulot's black hair, obviously dyed, and without the flawless technique of Felicia, Pierre's cosmetician.

Salvatore Reachi mopped his wet brow once more and restored the handkerchief to his breast pocket. "This is Betty and Ernest Blockton of Missoula, Montana." He nodded to a couple in their mid-thirties.

Betty was a typical housewife, the Harried Mother type, thought Charlotte, while Ernest was tall and rawboned with rusty red hair tinged with gray. "I'm in farm implements," he drawled, and Mitchell wondered why he identified his occupation, when none of the others had bothered to do so. Was an inexperienced operative trying to conveniently pigeonhole himself in everyone's mind and therefore divert attention?

"And last, but surely not least," Reachi was saying, "may I introduce Charlotte and Mitchell Heron from Enid, Oklahoma."

They nodded politely, acknowledging their fellow tourists, and Mitchell lighted a cigarette and glanced over the sightseers, not one of whom truly seemed interested in anyone other than themselves. *Pierre, you dog,* he thought savagely, *who in this miserable polyglot can be the missionary?* Truthfully, he must concentrate on the women, because obviously none of the men would be carrying a silver mirror. The Australian shepherdess seemed the most likely prospect.

Gerda, whose driver, Henri, seemed a sour specimen of the backwaters of some tiny French town, turned from the Champs Elysées down the avenue Montaigne and thence into the southwest portion of the city, through the Boulogne district, along the avenue Edouard Vaillant, and smoothly crossed the Seine at Pont de Sèvres.

Although sunlit and bright, the streets and quays looked gray and foreboding to Mitchell. *Here I am,* he thought, *with my new bride, in the most beautiful city in the world, and I can't enjoy myself because of the mission.*

Salvatore Reachi kept up a running commentary—via a hand-held microphone—that mostly consisted of clichés, and appeared disoriented from time to time as he peered through the windshield to get his bearings. Although the others seemed not to notice, it was obvious to Mitchell that their guide was woefully inexperienced.

Again he cursed Pierre, who had led him into this labyrinth. He belonged by himself, working alone. His forte was impersonating others, not playing himself—especially a middle-aged bridegroom. He glanced over the passengers: Fava Dolin, André Gulot, Betty and Ernest Blockton, Mrs. Henry Parsons (did she have a first name?), Grace and David Benjamin, and Doris and Humphrey Hardesty.

Frankly, none of the vacationers looked even slightly suspicious. Of course, that was the catch: one of these quite ordinary-appearing individuals held the key to the game, and whether he liked it or not, Mitchell Heron of Enid, Oklahoma, had to stem his impatience and wait for the person in question to make the first move.

The telephone rang in the Connecticut Avenue house, and Letty picked up the receiver somewhat impatiently. She was beating the whites of twenty-two eggs for an Angel Food cake, and was at that crucial point where the firmness of the mixture was tested by running a knife through the batter. She had sent the butler to the grocery store for some vanilla extract, and it was the maid's day off. "Yes, yes?" she said hurriedly.

"May I please speak with Mr. Luke Heron?" The cultivated voice was vaguely familiar.

"Luke Heron is in Tulsa, Oklahoma, and Luke Heron Three is in Korea. Which one did you mean?" She realized that she was not being clear, since the caller could not talk to either of them.

"I only spoke to the Tulsa operations a few moments ago, and the Mr. Luke Heron of which I speak was not present, but it was suggested that he might be reached in Washington, D.C. This is a friend from Saudi Arabia—"

"Oh," Letty replied warmly, "Muhammad Abn! This is Luke's mother speaking." They had met once when Bosely and Luke had brought him to the farm in Angel for a short visit. He was of the new school of Saudis, well educated, wise to the ways of the West, and had been an excellent host when Bosley and Luke had stayed at his house in Jeddah.

"How do you do, Madame Trenton?" he said. "I am in town for just two days to see the State Department on a hurried visit, and I wanted to touch base with your son."

The term "touch base" seemed incongruous in his Cambridge accent, Letty thought. She could see his face, bronze skin, intelligent eyes, and well-trimmed beard and mustache. He had been impeccably dressed in beautiful business suits at the farm, but when she saw him in her mind's eye, he was always standing on top of a sand dune, with the wind blowing out his burnoose—a dark silhouette before a striking sunset. . . . *How foolish*, she thought, *I'm romanticizing*.

"It's very true, Muhammad Abn, he may be en route. When must you leave?"

"Unfortunately, this evening. My father is not well, otherwise I'd stay on for a few days. If I do not see Luke, will you please pass along my regards? And I promise to write to him. The matter I have to discuss is not crucial at this time."

"Thank you so very much for calling, Muhammad Abn, and I will give your message to him. Where are you staying in town?"

"At a hotel known as the Statler. Thank you so much for your trouble, madame. Good-bye."

"Good-bye, Muhammad Abn." She hung up and ran the knife through the batter. No, it was not stiff enough, but soon she would have to add the vanilla, or it would be too late. She picked up the whisk again and began to whip the egg whites. If Muhammad's father was dying—and Luke had mentioned that he was in his nineties—his sons would inherit all those oil billions. Letty frowned, trying to remember if Muhammad was the eldest of the sixteen sons. She could not remember. Obviously, if he had power while his father was living, he would have even more influence when he died.

At that moment the butler came in, holding the bottle of

vanilla, and she smiled, forgetting about Saudi Arabia. "Just in the nick of time," she said.

Signor Reachi took the group to luncheon at the Alouette, a small café in Nevers, apparently a usual stop on the tour. Mrs. Parsons had become dizzy after a half-glass of Chablis, and retired to the bus. After the white fish *à la suprême* had been served, the proprietor summoned the guide to the telephone. Reachi came back with a smile and announced, "A new passenger, a Mr. Harry Stanton, will be along shortly—hopefully during dessert. He's a professor whose car has broken down, and wants to join us."

Ah, Mitchell thought, *now the plot thickens*. A late-arriving passenger, who just might have in his luggage a present for his wife, a silver mirror inscribed with the initial L.

But Mitchell's hopes were dashed when a bald man, with a slouch hat, holding a tiny grip in one hand and a rather large umbrella in the other, stumbled into the café as coffee was being served, and hesitantly introduced himself as Dr. Stanton. Mitchell doubted that he carried more than a change of clothing and a few toilet articles in his case.

Of all the passengers, he seemed the most unlikely prospect. In the first place, he was a fussy person with peculiar personal habits, like biting his upper lip and squinting every few moments through heavy pop-bottle glasses. No operative, thought Mitchell, would attract attention to himself with a series of such outrageous stage mannerisms.

As Gerda headed into the "Garden of France" and crossed the river Loire, over an ornate bridge, the spires of the Cathedral of Sainte Croix were pointed out by Salvatore Reachi. "I didn't know we were going to tour cathedrals too!" Charlotte exclaimed.

"Well"—Mitchell laughed—"we could hardly go through the Orléans district and not pay homage to the little Maid. The edifice isn't very imposing, if memory serves. If you like, we'll go for a walk while the others explore the turrets. According to the itinerary, we'll be visiting Chambord next, an enormous old castle known throughout the world."

"Never heard of it!" Charlotte replied. For some reason, she was feeling very uncomfortable. The passengers were an uninteresting lot, Signor Reachi was a loquacious bore, and she could not understand why Mitchell appeared interested in the group, and then also, he gawked at the countyside like a teenager on a first trip to France!

She would endure this strange journey because she loved him. But what was most peculiar of all was that she had the distinct impression that he was not trying to recapture an earlier period in his life, but that there was a *purpose* to the tour. She must be getting old, she mentally chastised herself, reading elements and emotions into this trip that did not exist.

André Gulot, who was seated behind them, tapped Mitchell on the shoulder. "My father said that the Château Chambord was very cold and drafty and smelled of dead mice when he visited the place as a small boy. But everyone who goes to France is not a tourist if he has not seen at least two or three of the great châteaux."

He paused, and his beady little eyes grew intense. "You are from Ok-la-homa? Such an interesting name! I know almost nothing of the States, except what I see in the cinemas, and we do not get many new films in Johannesburg. If it is convenient, perhaps we can sit at the same table for dinner, and you can relate something of your wonderful country."

Charlotte was not enamored of M. Gulot and pressed her leg against Mitchell's thigh insinuatingly, but he took no notice of her warning signal.

"Thank you, monsieur," Mitchell put in quickly, "we would be delighted to sup with you." This was the first contact that any of the passengers had made, and it was very possible indeed that the little Frenchman was his man.

Luke and Robert Desmond were going over the agenda for the monthly board of director's meeting at the Heron Building in Tulsa. "I want you to table that survey that's just been completed on the Gulf of Mexico offshore drilling project, Bob," Luke said.

"But why?" Robert Desmond stood up to his full height,

and, since he was wearing an elegant new dark gray pinstriped suit, looked considerably taller than he was. He was a hansome man who appealed more to women than to the masculine gender, which most usually worked to his advantage unless he had to deal with a roomful of men who resented his appearance. "There's oil there. Pennsoil knows it, and so do a lot of other companies."

"It's not a question of what's there or isn't there," Luke put in. "The question, as always, is money. As you damn well know, we don't have an extra two million lying around."

"Perhaps not now, but if we sell off some of those divisions to the independents that have not been producing, we can go ahead with obtaining the proper leases so that we can put an offshore rig out there."

"The men will be coming in shortly, and we haven't got time to argue, Bob. Table it until next month." Luke pushed the intercom. "Bernice, tell the gentlemen to come in, please."

Eight of the men were Heron employees who had come up through the ranks, but two, Danton Holmby and Jake Merchant, were from the outside, a millionaire banker and a millionaire florist respectively, and both were considered tough in their individual ways.

Bernice served coffee from a tray, just as she would serve club sandwiches from The Gingham Dog down the street at noon. She retired to the corner, opened her notebook, and raised her pencil in expectation.

Financial reports were passed around, and the morning was spent in going over figures. After lunch, each board member reported on his area of expertise, and it was only at four o'clock that Danton raised his hand. "As you know, I have a summer place in Weeks on the Intracoastal Waterway of Louisiana. I was down there a couple of weeks ago and heard through the grapevine that the Heron report had been completed. What's the story?"

"There is no story," Luke replied, giving Robert Desmond a quick look.

"Well, why wasn't it passed around with the other reports?" Jake asked.

"It's not quite ready," Luke replied smoothly. "Now let's turn over to British Heron—"

"British Heron be damned at the moment!" Danton expostulated, "I know that area down there, and why aren't we out there?"

Luke held up his hand. "Now, don't get hot under the collar, Dan," he said quickly. "Even if the survey gives us the go-ahead signal, we've still got to raise the money."

Danton lighted a cigarette nervously. "There's two divisions that we can dispose of right now," he said. "One is the trucking division that has lost money for four years, which an independent could operate successfully, and the other is the wildcat bit division, which only sells to cable tool outfits and is a real loser. My God, we've got divisions in Europe that are a disgrace to the modern age!"

Hearing Danton's outburst, Luke knew that Robert Desmond had put a bug in his ear prior to the meeting, and he was disheartened. "As all of you know, the trucking division was acquired when Heron took control of Desmond Oil from Bob's dad several years ago. I'd hate to dispose of it."

Jake gave a wry laugh. "You're not getting sentimental in your old age, are you, Luke?"

"That's a ridiculous statement." Luke looked at his watch. "Gentlemen, it is four-thirty, and I know that you have a plane to catch at five-fifteen, Dan, so let's move for an adjournment."

Robert Desmond stood up. "We'll continue the Vermillion Bay West and East Cote Blanche Bay survey next month. I move this meeting is adjourned."

When the men had gone, Luke turned to Robert Desmond. "I'll sell off the trucking division if that's what they want, but they can't touch the wildcat bit division. I won't part with that."

"But why, Luke? Hughes Tool Company has cornered the market with their platinum bit; only a few oldtime companies lease the Wildcat anymore. Why in the hell do you want to save it?"

"Because," Luke answered hotly, "my mother named that bit the Wildcat in 1904, that's why!"

8

The End of the Road

*The dinner was extremely boring at the Hotel d'Ambrosia in
Sancerre, with the exception of a magnificent biscuit-
shaped goat cheese.*

It seemed that André Gulot asked about every major town
in America, but nothing about Oklahoma. Charlotte asked
for another cup of the lukewarm but very strong demitasse
in order to stay awake. Her head was throbbing.

She could not understand Mitchell's preoccupation with
the little man. He was treating him with the attention of a
valued customer, and it was unnerving. At last André Gulot
arose and bowed and wished them good night.

The two older couples had enjoyed an early dinner and
disappeared, probably to one of the little sitting rooms,
where they could continue to rehash former times.

Fava Dolin was holding forth at the end of the bar in an
apparent attempt to pick up a rather skinny, unattractive
young man. Charlotte was amused and had to constrain
herself from taking Fava aside and saying: "My dear, your
technique is antiquated. It simply will not work. There is
one magic word that must, sooner or later, enter into the
conversation: *cash*—or, in this case, *francs*. If you continue
to simper and bat your eyelashes like a Pekingese, he'll
leave in a huff, and you'll go upstairs to your little white bed
alone."

Harry Stanton, still wearing his greatcoat and slouch hat,
and with his umbrella placed across the opposite plate to
ward off a seating companion, was sitting at a tiny table in

the corner of the dining room. He was making copious notes on what looked like yellow foolscap.

Mitchell's eyes gleamed because Mrs. Parsons, having avidly consumed a custard flan, was now plying her knitting needles while occasionally taking a sip of coffee. Seeing his look, she smiled and held up the piece of work: a little powder-blue coat for Tibbetts, who was probably raising hell upstairs in her room.

She finished the coffee and placed the knitting in a large bag, and as she passed Mitchell's table there was a menacing growl from the shopping bag. These old ladies with their whiskey-brown hair and their miserable mutts!

Later, he was reading *Paris Match* in the small, cramped room, when Charlotte came in from the hall dressed in a cerise robe which did nothing for her ample figure. "I don't mean to be critical, dear"—she sighed, keeping her voice even—"but whoever arranged this tour in Enid should be closed up for malpractice. The bath is not all that clean, to begin with, and the plumbing, I swear, is prewar—*First World War!*"

She removed her robe languidly, displaying the new beige satin nightgown that she knew was flattering to her figure, but Mitchell was looking out the window into the darkness, a strange, beguiling look on his face. "A penny for your thoughts," she said, knowing that he had not been listening to her complaint about the facilities.

He looked up in surprise. "Oh, my thoughts were a thousand miles away." He smiled and lied, "It's inventory time at the stores."

"But darling," she said in a little-girl voice, sitting down on the edge of his chair, "it's our honeymoon, and you have good people to take care of those things." She kissed him on the cheek. "Let's go to bed."

He looked at her out of corners of his eyes. He smiled. "What do you have in mind, wench?"

"Just what do you *think* I have in mind?" she murmured, and, bending down, kissed him full on the mouth.

While he undressed, she pushed back the covers of the bed and lay, arms akimbo on the white sheets, the beige satin nightgown half open, exposing a plump, rosy-tipped breast, which he kissed.

He turned out the bedside lamp, his mind still filled with the unlikely cast of characters, one of which was the villainess of the piece. He sighed, a soft sound which Charlotte took for passion, as she climbed adroitly over him.

"My dear, as you know, I am very much in love with you, but I'm really exhausted. Forgive me? Let's just cuddle."

"Oh, of course," she replied, bending down and kissing his cheek. "But I do wish you'd forget about inventories."

They lay in each other's arms, enjoying the warmth that their bodies created, and he was far, far away from her. She well knew that feeling, having lain in many uncaring arms in her lifetime.

The golden boys in the old days had always begrudged her desire for cuddling after they had satisfied themselves, and she had ended up near midnight lying on her side of the bed, while they snored loudly beside her. But Mitchell was distracted in another way. She had the strange feeling that it had something to do with this weird trip.

Signor Reachi, wearing the same crumpled white suit as the day before, was counting heads as Mitchell and Charlotte came into the dining room. "Ah," he said with a wide, friendly smile, checking his pocket watch and taking note that they were probably late because of their newlywed status. "Here you are! In twenty-five minutes we shall be leaving for the Château Cheverny. Then we shall visit the great hall at Château Chaumont and the magnificent formal gardens at Château Chenonceaux before having luncheon in Loches."

Mitchell and Charlotte had time only for cups of very bad coffee and stale croissants before being herded onto the bus. Everyone selected seats with care, avoiding those who had proven unsuitable companions the day before. Only Fava Dolin chose a seat by herself, across the aisle from Mitchell. She removed a bottle of cologne from her purse and proceeded to douse herself generously, until the heavy, cloying scent of gardenias permeated the bus. "Good morning," she said insinuatingly, in her peculiar Outback accent, as if she was very much aware of the reason that they had kept the rest of the group waiting.

Mitchell nodded pleasantly as she replaced the bottle of scent in her purse. He would not have been surprised if she had repaired her makeup with a silver mirror with the letter L emblazoned on the back. She did scrutinize her face, however, in a small compact mirror. He decided that no missionary would pass up such an opportunity, and dismissed her as a possible suspect.

Noting that Fava Bean was looking extremely well, Charlotte was observing her for an entirely different reason, and when she started to hum "Frère Jacques" in a low contralto, Charlotte wondered if Fava had not parted with a few francs, after all, and purchased the services of the thin, unattractive young man of the previous night. "If there is one perfume in the whole wide world that I cannot stand," she whispered to Mitchell, "it is gardenia. It always reminds me of the five-and-dime."

The smell brought back another sort of memory to Mitchell. He was back in Belle Trune's arms in her shack on the outskirts of Angel, a pilgrimage made every Friday night during the late thirties, when he had come back from France and was farming his mother's claim. This was years before she had opened the Red Bird Café and had regained respectability. But no one had any money during the depression, and he was certain that Belle, who charged two dollars for her favors, *had* purchased her perfume at Kress's in Enid.

Gerda was barely under way when both Mrs. Parsons in front and André Gulot in the rear opened the windows of the bus wide enough to allow the gentle, flowing winds rising up from the Loire to dilute the scent.

Mitchell nodded in agreement, and as the Château Chaumont was closed, the bus finally pulled into the pebbled driveway of the Château Chenonceaux and as Salvatore Reachi started his none-too-well-prepared spiel, Charlotte sighed. She would have preferred to sit in the bus and look at the perfectly beautiful flower garden, but she dutifully followed him.

Mitchell gave her a penetrating look. He cared not one damn about examining the château, but since none of the passengers appeared to be his contact, it was possible that a maid or a caretaker or someone encountered on the grounds might have been conscripted for the job. He dared not pass up any opportunity to complete his mission and leave this dreadful tour. "Very well." He made his voice sound regretful. "We won't be long, I'm certain—not with our itinerary."

The castle was built on parapets over the River Cher, which featured a flock of snow-white swans. Mitchell put his arm around Charlotte's waist and whispered, "Isn't it beautiful?"

She was touched. "Yes, it is extraordinary. It reminds me of a painting by one of the French masters."

As Signor Reachi summoned their attention again—he had taken to using a small whistle—Charlotte pressed Mitchell's arm. "I'd love to walk by the river and maybe have a picnic over there by those nut trees." When he did not respond, she went on carefully, "Maybe the next time that we come to France, we can rent a car and have a leisurely trip. . . ."

He wanted to shout: *Yes, yes, we'll leave the tour now; wave a merry good-bye to all these boring people; give the royal "finger" to Reachi; hike into town; pick up some bread and cheese and wine; rent a Mercedes and be back here in time for lunch!* Instead, he gritted his teeth and returned David Benjamin's wave. The old man was boring, but he might be the missionary. "I'm sure you'll enjoy the gardens," he said to him with an ingratiating smile.

Benjamin frowned fiercely. "Won't. Don't have a green thumb. Never did. The wife's the one who talks to roses."

Grace Benjamin twittered and shook her white head like a magpie. "Now, darlin', you make the Herons think I'm peculiar." As he helped her on the bus, she winked conspiratorially at Charlotte and rolled her eyes as if to say: *We must humor these men!*

Well, Mitchell thought, the Benjamins could safely be crossed off the list. It was highly unlikely that this dear old couple were operatives, unless, of course, like Charlotte and him, one of them had been conscripted by Pierre Darlan!

The sightseers could have only been gone fifteen minutes when the sky clouded up suddenly and a shower of cold rain pelted Gerda's roof, and Henri hunched down in his greatcoat, wishing he were home.

Twenty minutes later, Signor Reachi appeared under the great front arch of the château, making wide gestures and waving his hands frantically for Henri to bring the bus as close as possible to the entrance. Even then, Harry Stanton, whose umbrella, Charlotte observed, looked like an extension of his arm, was the only member of the group who escaped getting wet. He did not share his umbrella with either Fava Bean or Mrs. Parsons, both of whom looked like bedraggled chickens—but from different flocks.

Mitchell forced a grin. "After living here for so long, you'd have thought I'd have sense enough to bring a bumbershoot! These sudden spring rains can be drenching." Actually, he was furious. He had tramped up and down staircases, examined three dungeons, explored six towers, and crept in and out of the queen's chamber, without encountering a stranger, except an unfriendly housekeeper, who had kept out of the way.

Mitchell was disgruntled. Wouldn't it be just like Pierre the Perverse to have the contact planted as they got off the bus at the end of the tour in San Sebastian? Mentally he addressed the Frenchman: *You don't know it, old man, but you've screwed me long enough. This is my last mission! You can take Leary and all your cohorts and stuff 'em*. He wished fervently that he was back in his office, writing orders.

He tried to make his voice enthusiastiac for Charlotte. "That seventeenth-century solid brass fireplace was interesting, but on the whole, it wasn't worth climbing around all those staircases."

"I agree. Let's take off our wet coats, dear," she said in the tones of a concerned wife who cared nothing for seventeenth-century brass fireplaces. "Or we'll catch our deaths."

Even in the pouring rain, the formal gardens at Château

Chenonceaux, which were laid out somewhat like a baseball diamond, were exquisite, but when Henri could not bring the bus near enough for a closer inspection, Salvatore Reachi stood up apologetically. "Considering the weather, perhaps we should take the long way around to Loches. There is some marvelous scenery, and, who knows, perhaps we will be fortunate and be entertained by a rainbow if the rain stops."

That night was spent at the charming Inn of the Wild Horses at Chinon, after the group had viewed the Châteaux Blois and Amboise, the Cathedral of Saint Gatien at Tours, and the Châteaux Azay-le-Rideau between showers, after the vacationers had succeeded in retrieving rain apparel from their collections of luggage.

The Loire River had been crossed so many times, and Mitchell and Charlotte had climbed on and off the bus so often and were so weary and damp that the fine dinner of poached white fish lay untouched on the table.

Surprisingly, the other members of the tour—including the elderly Mrs. Parsons and the Benjamins and the Hardestys—ate with gusto. When Fava Dolin ordered a second helping of the mousse-au-chocolat, Charlotte became jaundiced and went to the suite and was joined by Mitchell after André Gulot offered to buy cognacs at a small café down the street.

"All of those old birds down there are as fresh as daisies, as Mother used to say," Charlotte remarked, coming in from the bath with hair wrapped in a towel, "when all I can think of is sleep! What time must we be up in the morning?"

Mitchell glanced at the itinerary. "Seven. We go back over the Loire to the Châteaux le Thoureil and Angers, luncheon at Les Ponts-de-Cé, and on to Saumur Castle. Then, believe it or not, we have the rest of the afternoon to explore the Anjou region."

"And gather pears, no doubt?" she retorted sarcastically, toweling her hair with quick, angry movements. She stopped suddenly and faced him. "Mitch, I have had enough! We are going to sleep until ten or eleven o'clock tomorrow morning, have a leisurely breakfast, rent a Citroën, and drive quietly back to Paris and civilization!"

"But darling," he protested feebly, surprised at her vehemence, "we *can't*."

"Why not? This charade that we've been enduring for the last few days has been a nightmare. Why not admit it? And we have this horrible weather to put up with as well! You've been pretending that you're having a great time, when I know you well enough to realize that you've been absolutely miserable." She finished drying her hair and demanded, "What's the point?"

He felt truly helpless. "It's just we've planned this trip so long, and it doesn't seem fair to throw in the sponge so early."

"*You* planned this trip, I had nothing to do with it," she replied angrily.

"But you went along with it, Charlotte!"

"Of course I went along with it, because I love you." Her anger was dying. "And truthfully," she admitted, "a tour of the romantic French châteaux did sound interesting back in drab little Enid, but why be so persistent? Why not admit that this entire trip has been intolerable? My God, Mitch, we all make mistakes! Write if off now!"

He slammed the door, and, once out in the hall, paced up and down in front of the steep, curving stair. Then, making a decision, he immediately went down to the public telephone in the foyer and called the emergency number that Pierre Darlan had reluctantly given him.

"*Oui?*" asked a feminine voice with a heavy Province of Gascony accent.

For a moment Mitchell was astounded, and then he smiled wryly. Whose voice had he expected? "This is Harold," he replied in French, "and I should like to speak to Gibson."

There was a long pause and he could hear the quite distinct sound of papers being shuffled, and he knew that the woman was surveying an alphabetical list of cover names and identifying data. "Where are you, Harold, in the Camargue?" she asked tentatively.

"No," he answered quickly, "at the Inn of the Wild Horses in Chinon."

There was another long pause. He could see a finger tracing the Château itinerary on a large map. He expected to be cut off any moment because the telephone system in this part of France was antiquated and famous for disruptions in service. "Hallo?" he said when he thought the line was dead.

"Hallo, Harold?" The voice was not so tentative now. "Call back in precisely five minutes." A loud click resounded in his ear.

At that moment Mr. Hardesty came into the foyer and held out his hand. Mitchell thought that his flushed face was perhaps due to Andre Gulot's cognac, a fact which his breath supported. "Sorry we haven't gotten to speak much, Heron," he said jovially, "but my wife, God bless 'er, never shuts up! She wasn't like that when she was young. Wonder what gets into women once the childbearing days are over?"

Mitchell was about to retort that his wife was still fertile and he didn't think that Charlotte, even if she reached a hundred and ten, would spout out strings of words like the machine gun that Mrs. Hardesty had become. However, this man could be the contact.

He cursed himself for trying to contact Pierre, because if he received the silver mirror now, he could leave the tour with good conscience. He smiled broadly. "I was hoping we could get together, Mr. Hardesty," he said with genuine feeling, and then went on guardedly, "I suspect we might have a lot in common."

"You're in farm equipment in Oklahoma?" was the quick reply, and with a sinking heart Mitchell knew that Mr. Hardesty was not his man. "No," he replied sadly, "I'm in furniture. Now," he continued brusquely, "would you please excuse me? I must make a telephone call."

Mr. Hardesty recoiled as if struck. He had planned to continue the conversation over another glass of Cognac, and he stamped into the bar.

"Hallo?" Mitchell was saying into the mouthpiece. "This is Harold again." There was a sputtering on the line, a garbled voice from far away that sounded German, and then a strange silence. A receiver was picked up and a sleepy voice answered.

"Gibson?"

"No," Leary's voice boomed, obviously fully awake. "Gibson is not here. This is Jacob."

A wave of relief washed over Mitchell to be talking to the boss himself. "The pudding is being spoiled," he said carefully. "The cook wants to quit because of a dispute with his wife, who is inexperienced in domestic matters. A replacement chef should be sent at once, or the dinner party will never come off." He felt rather proud of himself for the analogy.

"The cook must be retained at all cost," was the terse reply. "Chefs of his particular culinary art are impossible to hire on such short notice, even if the largest domestic agency in France is consulted." He paused. "I suggest that he have a talk with his wife and convince her to stay at least until after the dinner party is over."

"But—" Mitchell stammered.

"There are no *buts*!" The line went dead.

"Damn and double damn!" Mitchell muttered. Leary didn't give a shit what happened to his operatives once the objective was reached. He and Charlotte could be divorced, and it wouldn't matter to him. Just keep her on the job until he got that damned mirror! He went slowly up the stairs, his heart as heavy as his step.

There was nothing to do but to reveal himself to her—surely the most difficult trial of his life. How would he start? What would he say to make the unbelievable *believable*? And then a simple statement that Gertrude Stein had made years ago came back to him. Gertrude had said: *"The beginning. Always start at the beginning. . . ."*

It was two o'clock in the morning, and Charlotte still sat on the bed, watching Mitchell intently. He had been very scrupulous about telling her about the missions, deleting times and names, yet his impersonations of Michel Bayard and Herr Professor Schneider had taken place so long ago that he doubted details would be important, and Leary had not cautioned him to be discreet. Still, there was something that kept him from explaining all the complex elements of the story. And, of course, he had not told her exactly what assignment he was on at the present time; that was still *verboten*.

When he had finished, Charlotte lighted a cigarette and blew the smoke out in a long spiral. "Now," she said slowly, as if her voice were at the end of a long corridor and could only faintly be heard, "your wanderlust has finally been explained." She smiled with relief, and her face looked young again. "That was my only reservation about marrying you," she said finally.

He laughed. "You mean that you were afraid I'd take off into the wild blue yonder?"

"It had happened before!" she retorted, then held up her hand and went on quickly, "No, seriously, I went over and over your long 'vacations' in my mind. I thought for a while that you might be a periodic alcoholic, but that didn't seem to be the right pattern, and then it occurred to me that you might be shacking up with a girl somewhere, but that wasn't really logical. There would be no reason unless she was married, and you didn't seem like the type who would be content with only part of a pie."

She looked up suddenly and snubbed out the cigarette in a tray. "Then I told myself that I was just being suspicious. You were single, you had a business that was running smoothly, and there was no earthly reason why you should not take off now and again for a long vacation." She paused. "Tell me something. Remember when we ran into each other in the Statler Hotel elevator that time?"

He nodded. "I looked so disreputable that I'm sure you thought I was going to ask for a handout!"

She laughed. "It did occur to me. Had you just come back from France?"

"Yes, and I was bone-weary, unshaven, and still dressed in the cover clothes of Michel Bayard. That's why I made some feeble attempt to say that I'd been fishing or something."

"The Herons, God bless them all, were many things"— Charlotte looked very wise—"but never fishermen! Call it woman's intuition, but I had the strangest feeling that you were involved in something clandestine, and time has proven me right."

She lighted another cigarette, and glanced up nervously. "Tell me something, Mitch, why didn't you tell me about this before?"

"Good question," he replied, playing for time. "Oh, Pierre Darlan wanted me to come clean with you, but I was afraid—"

"Afraid? Good God, Mitch, I'm your wife!"

He nodded. "Not always. Sometimes you're the little Charlotte Dice that I grew up with—with poop in her pants." He grinned and then made a meaningful pause and could not look at her. "I suppose also, very truthfully, living alone for so long has taught me to be wary of giving a part of me away that no one knows about."

"Then it wasn't because you . . . didn't . . . trust me?"

He looked at her in amazement. "Trust didn't enter into it at all," he replied emotionally. "After all, you have a top priority clearance from the State Department."

"I do?" Now it was Charlotte's turn to be astounded. It seemed beyond belief, she mused, that the investigators had not discovered her attraction for the golden boys, but perhaps she had covered her tracks better than she had thought at the time. She snubbed the cigarette butt into the tray. "Now, with the nonsense of this trip out of the way, how can I help you?"

"Why, by just being the way . . . that . . . you . . . are!"

"I don't understand."

"We are Mr. and Mrs. Mitchell Heron from Enid, Oklahoma," he answered firmly. "That's who we actually are, so we don't need to be anyone else."

"But I want to assist you!"

He sighed, afraid of her attitude, and swallowed hard. "My dear"—he tried to be patient—"you must behave tomorrow exactly the way that you behaved today, yesterday, and the day before that—you must not change one iota." He sought for an analogy that she would understand.

"You took stage drama in high school. Remember what the word 'characterization' meant? That's what you must sustain now. Just be *you*."

"I don't know if I can do it!" she said fearfully.

He took her hand and smothered a retort about the Lord saving him from amateurs. "You will," he said gently. "I'll see to it."

"If I only knew what you were up against, I could react better."

Yeah, he thought, *and blow the whole thing?* Then, to distract her, he tightened his grip on her arm meaningfully. "In the meantime, darling, I suddenly feel rejuvenated. I want to make mad, passionate love to you." He raised his voice melodramatically. "I'll turn out the light, and you close your eyes and think of that beautiful young Frenchman Michel Bayard who labors so sweetly over you!"

"That's sounds absolutely decadent." She giggled.

"Or, of you prefer, you can sleep with that elegant old roué Herr Doktor Professor Schneider." He added slyly, "Which would you prefer?"

She appeared to give the matter great thought. "While the Germans are known to make love with wild passion, I think I would like a romantic *tour de force* tonight."

"Then," he said with a straight face as he climbed into bed, "I shall be myself." But nonetheless, he noticed that she still turned out the light.

Mitchell and Charlotte were legitimately late the next morning and did not even have time for coffee, and although Salvatore Reachi still smiled widely as they entered the bus, his expression was strained. It was obvious that he did not know how to treat middle-aged newlyweds.

Charlotte blushed as she saw the group waiting anxiously to begin the day's journey, but it was not from the embarrassment of being late, but because she felt everyone knew her secret. No one could possibly know—well, *one* obviously did—but none of the others could ascertain what Mitchell had told her the night before. *You've a guilty conscience, my girl*, she reprimanded herself.

But by the time that the bus was rolling through the

peaceful green hills and the orchards filled with fruit, the magic of the countryside held her in its grip and she was lost in the beauty of the great outdoors. Relaxed, she began to enjoy herself so much, and was in danger of exclaiming over every tree and bush, that Mitchell was forced to remind her in whispers to remember her calm demeanor of yore.

The group stopped at a tiny café at Ruffec at ten o'clock for croissants and coffee, because, Signor Reachi, explained luncheon would not be served until two in the afternoon at picturesque town called Coutras, at which time shopping was to be permitted, before Gerda crossed the Gironde River into Bordeaux, where they were to spend the night.

It was market day in Coutras, and the farmers had brought produce still wet with dew in from the hillsides and had set up stalls on one of the tiny, narrow streets. Yet, a block away, cars moved in traffic patterns understood only by the natives, and several buses of tourists were parked at a small shop that sold local pottery.

Charlotte and Mitchell stayed on the bus while Signor Reachi herded the other members of the group into the already crowded shop.

"I promise after all of this is over," Mitchell said quietly, "we'll have a good and proper honeymoon."

Charlotte gave him a penetrating look. "How can you be so calm, Mitch? Don't you sometimes have the feeling that you're sitting on a time bomb that might go off any moment?"

"Not exactly. One thing about these. . . . jobs," he explained, "even if one feels alone, there's always the knowledge that other people are out there somewhere who're on your side. These so-called 'missions' are very well put-together."

"I think you're over simplifying, Mitch. What about the *danger*?

He grinned sheepishly, "That's part of the 'kick'."

"The *kick*?"

"Of course. Why do you suppose people like me get mixed up in this sort of life?" He paused meaningfully. "I think I know what a criminal feels like who's 'on the lam'.

The blood flows a little differently, the adrenalin is higher and there's a sense of *awareness* that can be obtained no other way.''

"This feeling. . . . is it habit-forming?" Her voice was very low.

"I suppose it could be, if this was one's main occupation. Obviously, it's the sense of omnipresent excitement that appeals to something inside of me that I don't quite understand. Once I asked Pierre Darlan about this very peculiar quality that drew people to this field."

"And what was his explanation?"

"He didn't have any, but I have a feeling he didn't want to frighten me—an amateur, really—because I think it has to do with a 'criminal mind'."

He paused dramatically, "You see, Charlotte, essentially, it's the really old question of the good guys versus the bad guys, only I'm a good guy, and the bad guy is the criminal. Of course, from his point of view, don't forget, it's the other way around!"

She took his hand. "I wish I could help you, Mitch." she exclaimed. "I feel so useless. I've always been able to handle demanding jobs. At the Justice Department, I started out as a secretary and ended up in charge of a research division. If my parent's will hadn't required me to come back to Oklahoma to live, I'd have probably retired at the head of my group. But my job experience, as varied as it was, didn't prepare me for work of this kind."

"That's just it, Charlotte, this work doesn't require formal education or practical experience! It's a knack, a talent. I'm sorry that I involved you, that's all. I should have said *no* to the request, yet I knew that if they could have procured anyone else for this job, they'd have jumped at the chance."

"You see, dear in a strange way, all operatives are cast—just as actors are cast—in certain roles. You and I—well, we're cast as honeymooners. . . ."

Under his breath, Mitchell cursed Darlan, Leary, and the entire organization. Why had he agreed to this impossible mission in the first place? *Oh*, he thought, *why blame them*?

It all really boiled down to that damn Heron blood that made fools of wise men.

William had been at the piano all afternoon, but nothing creative was happening. He had played a number of runs, which usually started some inward impulse, but his brain was dead. He laughed wryly to himself. Always before there were tunes and musical phrases whirling around in his head, just waiting to be released as soon as his fingers hit the keys. Now, there was only emptiness. He was twenty-four years old, and had a mental block. He placed his head in his hands and cried as if his heart would break.

After a while, he stirred, and suddenly the world took shape again. There were no clouds outside; only the famous California sunshine. While depleted emotionally, he was relieved of tension. He had never understood why women always felt better after a 'good cry', which wasn't a cliche, after all, he decided. He did feel better! He looked down at the piano, and suddenly wished that he was back at Barrett University, so he could take a stroll down to the Red Bird Cafe and have some of Belle Trune's marvelous cherry pie.

He sat down at the small counter in the commissary, and ordered a chocolate malt from Barbara, the new waitress, a striking redhead, with huge green eyes and a figure that stirred his memory of a full-breasted girl named Nancy with whom he had gone to school in Willawa.

When she placed the tall, pale beige glass in front of him, she gave him a sidelong glance. "Are you an actor?" she asked, flashing a smile that showed her beautifully capped teeth advantageously.

He grinned, flattered that she obviously liked him. "No. I'm a composer."

"That's even better," she replied, and grew serious. "Most actors are stuck on themselves. What do you compose?"

"Music. I also write lyrics, sometimes. I'm working on an English picture."

Her eyes grew even wider. "You look like Tony Curtis, and I think he's dreamy. I'd love to act with him. You know, you look handsome enough to be a movie star. Dark eyes, wavy hair. . . ."

"Thank you." He was flattered. "Do you want to be an actress?"

"I *am* an actress." She corrected him. "This job is only temporary. I work with a little theatre group on Melrose. I'm rehearsing *Summer and Smoke*." She paused, "That's a play by Tennessee Williams."

"I know." he replied quietly, taking a sip of the malt, trying to hear her flat voice reciting difficult dialogue.

She leaned up against the counter, her breasts pushing through the white uniform in an openly provocative manner. "We open in two weeks. I'll give you tickets, if you'd like to come. . . ."

"I'm awfully busy," he answered, wondering what those fleshy mounds would feel like in his palms. Louisa had small breasts.

He liked Barbara and felt the same sort of attraction that she was obviously feeling toward him, but his iron bar remained flaccid. He had come once last night and again this morning, so he was not feeling sexual, yet there was something very erotic about this girl that could not be easily cast away.

"Well, let me know if you can make it," she said seriously, "and I'll leave tickets at the box office. By the way, have you. . . . written anything I might have heard?"

He colored. "I wrote 'The Cowboy Waltz.' "

Her green eyes opened even wider than before. "You *did*! Oh, I love the way Clement Story sings that song—and I'm not a fan of Western music, either." She frowned. "Didn't I read somewhere that you were part Indian or something?"

"I'm part Cherokee." He said, finishing the malt.

She sighed. "Maybe that's why I thought you were an actor. . . . you look like you could play a Western part."

He knew that she meant to be kind. "Thank you." He replied, in the same tones as if he were four years old and had been told to mind his manners. Obviously, her body was her winning point, not her brain.

She was flustered. "I'm ashamed to say that I don't know your name."

"William Nestor." He placed a bill on the counter and got up to leave.

"Mine's Barbara."

"I know."

"Don't forget to tell me if you can come to the play."

He grinned. "See you later."

As William went back to his office, he thought about Barbara's beautiful breasts. He would like to make out with her, and he knew she would not turn him down. But, how could he ever get away from Louisa long enough to even make the pitch?

9

The Contact

Gerda bravely labored over a steep, rolling hill and paused at the top of a promontory, as if gathering courage for the mountain ahead.

"Rest stop," Henri called, and bounded out of the bus in the direction of an ancient pink stucco inn, appropriately enough called Le Chapeau Rouge. In the far background, the Pic du Midi D'Ossau summit, located in France, but very near the Spanish border, was bathed in swirling yellow mist.

Mitchell took a deep breath of air, then sneezed. "My nasal passages are still stuffed up," he said, helping Charlotte out of the bus. "I haven't had such a bad cold in years." She looked at him sympathetically and gave him a fresh handkerchief from her purse.

The group, which had been traveling all morning, made good use of the primitive facilities of the inn. While Mitchell was waiting in line to use the *lavabo*, Henri turned to him and whispered, "There's a silversmith next to the inn who fashions unusual pieces. He's a Western movie fan and has designed and made a sterling saddle that's well worth seeing. Perhaps you should pay a visit before the others find the shop."

Mitchell, who wanted to use the bathroom very badly, was about to reply that he was not in the market for silver saddles, when it occurred to him that finally someone had made an overt move. Was Henri the missionary?

Mitchell left the washroom. None of the tour members

were about, so he ambled out of the lounge at the inn and found the cluttered shop next door quite empty. A large sign on the door read OPEN, so he pushed the door inward and entered.

In a huge glass cage at the rear of the store, the magnificent silver saddle was displayed advantageously on the back of a stuffed white horse, such as those bred in the marshes of the Camargue district of France.

He browsed for a few moments among the tables laden with silver jewelry and larger artifacts. He expected the smith to appear at any moment, because the merchandise was unprotected. It would be a simple matter to slip a money clip, a pair of earrings, or a key chain into a pocket.

"Hallo," he called, "hallo," but there was no answer. His voice sounded hollow and somewhat sinister in the empty shop. At once, his senses sharpened, and suddenly the atmosphere was charged with malevolence. It was as if he were on a mine-infested battlefield and one false step would be his last. He heard the ladies chattering outside; it would be only a few moments before they crowded into the shop in search of "that perfect little gift."

"Hallo!" he called urgently, and walked quickly to the back of the shop. His spine tingled. *There is danger here*, the inward voice whispered ominously. He looked behind the countertop where the cashbox rested.

The man had been dead for a very short time—possibly only minutes—because the blood was still dripping from his mouth and his staring, open eyes were not as yet fixed.

Instinctively, Mitchell whirled around, his eyes searching the shelves for a silver makeup mirror engraved with the letter L, but no such toilet items were displayed. He hurried to the door, quickly switched the OPEN sign to read SHUT, and closed the door firmly behind him.

Henri was nowhere to be seen, but Charlotte; Mrs, Parsons, with Tibbets in tow, a snarl contorting his pinched little face; Betty Blockton; Grace Benjamin; and Doris Hardesty were gathered in a little group, chattering anti-matedly while strolling toward the shop. Only Fava Dolin was missing.

Mitchell forced himself to saunter slowly toward the

women. "I was going to buy some trinkets"—he made his voice sound casual—"but the shop's closed. You'd think with the terrible French economy, these tradespeople would keep open, especially since this is a regular stop, but . . ." He shrugged his shoulders and turned toward the bus.

"Not to worry," Fava Dolin called, coming down the steps to the inn, "San Sebastian has some really good silver stuff, and I'm sure the price will be not so dear."

Did he detect a tone of triumph in her voice, or was it only his imagination?

Henri was already in position at the wheel as the group boarded the bus. When he saw Mitchell was empty-handed, his eyes grew wide. He glanced toward the inn; through the large-paned windows of the lounge, Salvatore Reachi could be seen talking to the proprietor.

Henri left the bus, and a few moments later was seen in the same window, pointing to his watch. Mitchell compared the broad gestures of the principals to a scene in a silent movie in which no one could identify the villain.

Mitchell held his breath as Reachi came out on the porch alone and took his usual front seat in the bus. A moment later, when Henri resumed his position at the wheel, his set jaw and bloodless white face told Mitchell that he had discovered the body.

Mitchell could not enjoy the spectacular scenery, with the shimmering white-capped waves of the Bay of Biscay on the right and the low, purple mountains on the left. All he could think about was the face of the smith surprised in death.

He had never failed in any of his missions, but, he reflected wryly, there was a first time for everything; also, not only had he been younger, and therefore more guileless, but the jobs themselves had been painstakingly planned by masters. The current operation had seemed to him hastily thrown together from the outset. Perhaps Pierre was getting old or losing his touch. . . .

"You're so silent," Charlotte whispered. "Anything wrong?"

He shrugged his shoulders. "I'm just tired. Didn't get

much sleep last night, remember?" He was pleased that she had the grace to blush.

Before Charlotte could give the smart retort which was on the tip of her tongue, the bus pulled to an abrupt stop and was immediately surrounded by soldiers. "Oh, my God!" she exclaimed, and pressed her face to the window.

"Keep quiet. This is the border," he ordered under his breath.

Salvatore Reachi turned to the group. "I'll find out what this means," he said, trying to keep his voice calm and not succeeding.

At that moment, Tibbetts, who had been dozing in his mistress's lap, awakened fully and started to bark viciously. "There, there," Mrs. Parsons soothed. "Nothing to worry about, sweets." And under her affectionate ministrations, the dog finally quieted.

Reachi stomped out of the bus and confronted the colonel who was obviously in charge of the cordon. A small, short-waisted man with white hair, he reminded Mitchell of the pet albino bantam rooster that his father had owned when he was a toddler on the claim in Angel. There was a flurry of Spanish, spoken so rapidly that Mitchell could understand only the word "confiscate."

Grace Benjamin, who was sitting with her husband, David, directly behind the driver, asked loudly, "Own-ree, what is the usual procedure?"

"I do not know," the driver replied with fear in his voice. "This has never happened before."

"My Lord!" exclaimed Doris Hardesty, patting her blue hair. "You'd think we were in one of the Iron Curtain countries. Look at those drawn bayonets."

Salvatore Reachi, nervously searching his pockets, finally remembered that he had logically placed the passports/visas in his inner pocket. He handed the packet to the colonel, who just as quickly gave them to his lieutenant, who methodically examined each one before passing them, one by one, back to the colonel. It was a ritual, Mitchell thought, that harked back to World War II movies, where strict military procedures were always observed. But on a mountaintop on the French/Spanish border, the routine would have appeared more comical had the consequences not semed so dire. He was thankful that he did not have the silver makeup mirror emblazoned with the letter L in his possession.

Ashen-faced, Salvatore Reachi returned to the bus, his hands making little helpless gestures. "I most humbly apologize to all of you, but the colonel has requested all luggage be opened—and your persons be searched."

Fava Dolin got up indignantly from her seat in the rear. "I have traveled all over the world and I've never run into such humiliation!" Angrily she brushed her shoulder-length hair back from her face. "I, for one, would not permit *any* man—soldier or civilian—to examine me!"

Charlotte smiled to herself. *Oh no?* she thought. *What about that boy at the bar last night? You had to pay him!* Aloud, she said, "I agree with Miss Dolin. We women should not be searched unless a woman . . ." Her voice trailed away when she saw that a female captain with short black hair and a lantern jaw was standing back from the soldiers that surrounded the bus.

"They've thought of everything, my dear," Mitchell whispered. "This is no small operation."

"But what can they be looking for?" Mrs. Parsons fretted, pulling the bulky blue coat around the dog's middle. "All this excitement may give Tibbetts a heart attack. I'd best give him an extra dose of digitalis." Flustered, she looked about the bus, and her eyes settled on Mitchell. "Mr. Heron, would you hold him for me? It won't take a moment."

Mitchell was not an animal lover, but he pitied the helpless old woman, so he rose up and went to her seat, where he placed one knee on the cushion and held out his arms for the dog, which snarled menacingly.

Mrs. Parsons winked at Mitchell and quickly rubbed some transparent liquid from a bottle on the back of his hand. Immediately the animal quieted and began to lick up the substance—smacking his lips rather indecently in the process, Mitchell thought.

"He's really quite gentle," Mrs. Parsons went on breathlessly, removing a vial from her purse, "and I don't

know why he's so upset over the soldiers. Perhaps he was a
member of the militia in his last incarnation." She twittered, "Dogs come back, you know, just like humans, and
sometimes we're interchanged. I've always wanted to be a
Pekingese! Hold his lips back, please, Mr. Heron, while I
manage the eyedropper. It should only take a moment.
Anyone can see that he likes and trusts you."

Lord deliver us from silly old women, Mitchell thought,
and dogs with faint hearts!

As if reading his mind, Mrs. Parsons threw him a long,
strange, and very penetrating look. She was trying to tell
him something. There was fear in her eyes. But it was not
until he was holding the dog and trying to open its mouth at
the same time that his elbow came into contact with an
oblong object beneath the dog's blue knitted coat.

Mitchell's body tensed for a moment as if from electric
shock, and as Mrs. Parsons applied the eyedropper to the
dog's lips he found himself saying quite calmly, "There,
Tibbetts, that's a good boy."

Mrs. Parsons looked at him gratefully, and he saw that
the apphrension had faded from her eyes. "I'll take him
now." She smiled. "And thank you for your assistance, Mr.
Heron." She opened the window. "Ah, that breeze will do
both Tibbetts and me good. . . . Ah . . ."

As Mitchell handed the dog back, he noticed that Mrs.
Parsons' face was not as old as he had at first imagined, and
he was now certain that the whiskey-brown hair piled so
sedately on the back of her head was the expert work of the
trusted Felicia, who had dyed his own hair to match that of
Herr Doktor Professor Schneider before the Berlin imperso-
nation mission.

But he prayed that Mrs. Parsons' bulky figure was not
aided and abetted by padding, which would be most difficult
to explain to the lady gendarme, who was now partitioning
off the back of the bus with army blankets.

"Fava Dolin," the captain said in a heavy accent,
"please?" She paused. "Ladies, when you have been
inspected, please assemble outside the bus."

The Australian rose stiffly to her feet and brushed the
long blonde hair from her cheek. Her eyes blazed, but she

was very self-possessed. "Before the Señora touches me, I wish to register an official complaint, Signor Reachi."

The captain held up the blanket for Fava Dolin, who glanced at her contemptuously before she passed through. Five minutes passed, and when she walked down the aisle of the bus, there was a glassy-eyed look about her. She had lost her dignity.

The guide flushed, and fresh perspiration broke out on his forehead. "Believe me, madame, if there was anything I could do," he replied apologetically, "I would have immediately done so."

A moment later, to Mitchell's horror, the colonel, who had seen Tibbetts's head out the window of the bus, walked up gravely. "My brother raises Pekingeses," he said with a thick Spanish accent. "They can be most temperamental. May I hold him?"

Mitchell dug his nails into his leg. The mission had just aborted. But the dog gave a particularly vicious yelp, and the colenel drew back quickly.

"Oh, I'm so sorry, sir!" Mrs. Parsons cried. "The poor thing hasn't been well, heart trouble."

"Yes, yes," the colonel agreed, trying to regain his composure. "They can be very . . . delicate." He nodded, turned on his heel, and went back to the soldiers.

Nothing in Mrs. Parsons' physical attitude changed, but Mitchell could almost hear repeated sighs of relief. But if one danger had passed, another remained.

The captain consulted the passport/visas in her hand. "Dolly Mae Parsons," she announced.

Charlotte nudged Mitchell. "With a name like Dolly Mae, no wonder she prefers to be called Mrs. Parsons!" But she noticed that he was not listening; underneath his relaxed pose, his body was so tense that she fancied she could hear his quick heartbeats. Something was happening, and she did not know what it was. . . .

Mrs. Parsons got up slowly, twittering to the dog, and arranged her bosom, looked around the bus quickly, and then as an afterthought thrust Tibbetts into Mitchell's lap. "He likes you," she said. "I won't be too long."

As Mitchell held the animal tightly, he received a small

bite in the tenderest section of his palm. Stemming the desire to hit the mutt sharply on his rear, he forced a smile and patted his head.

Charlotte saw the blood and had opened her mouth to speak when Mitchell threw her a warning look, and she closed her mouth firmly. A scene was being enacted, but not for her benefit. How strange to be involved in a situation that on the surface was perfectly normal, and yet so querulous underneath! There was some sort of relationship between Mrs. Parsons and her husband that had to do with the dog.

Mitchell drew in his breath. The pain was spreading out in circles now, but there was nothing he could do but endure the discomfort, although he was aware that Charlotte had a bottle of iodine in her purse. Soon Tibbetts was snoring peacefully, oblivious of the tension that held the bus in a tight, relentless grip.

Mrs. Parsons fluttered up the aisle and paused at Mitchell's seat. "Let me have the little dear," she said quickly. "I hope he hasn't been a problem."

"Not at all." Mitchell smiled graciously, but not until he lifted Tibbetts' full weight did he realize that the animal had been drugged; obviously, the small vial had held a substance other than digitalis.

Cooing and making a fuss over the dog, Mrs. Parsons joined Fava Dolin, who was leaning against the front fender of the bus, angrily smoking a cigarette. One by one, the other ladies, having been searched, became part of the group. Charlotte, who was last, threw Mitchell a questioning look as she came down the aisle and was helped out of the bus by Henri.

All the luggage had been opened, and the tourists looked on in morbid fascination as the soldiers held out their rifles and lifted up each article of clothing on the ends of their bayonets. It was, thought Charlotte, like an old World War II movie, where the Nazis were lining up patriots for extinction.

In the rear of the bus, the captain was replaced by the colonel, who called out loudly, "Mitchell Heron."

Mitchell brushed a smear of blood from his palm against

his trousers as he got up and went to the rear of the bus, relieved that he had nothing to hide.

"Please disrobe," the colonel demanded in a steely voice, and it was on the tip of Mitchell's tongue to retort that he was not wearing a robe, but he knew that he must not be flip. The colonel proceeded to press and squeeze each article of clothing given him, and went through Mitchell's wallet, but did not pay the slightest attention to folded papers. Mitchell knew then that names, dates, telephone numbers, or formulas were not wanted.

The colonel tapped and pressed the heels of the oxford shoes with his fingers, and, finding no false bottom, sighed. "Bend over, please," he said in English.

Mitchell felt a painless, expert probe, and it was then that he knew the colonel was a doctor, as was probably the female captain. For what could they be searching that could be contained in a metal rectal tube? Mitchell was aware of such devices, first developed by convicts to hold their contraband, because he had accommodated such a tube on entering and leaving France as Michel Bayard. He had later found out that he had brought a formula that the physicist Enrico Fermi had wanted double-checked by a noted metallurgist still living in occupied France.

There was a peculiar bemused expression on the colonel's face. His military bearing suddenly crumbled as he said in English, "You may dress, Mr. Heron." He paused, sighed audibly, and examined his manicure. "It grieves me that I have had to press this embarrassing procedure upon a relative of Clement Story."

Eyeing the colonel with misgivings, Mitchell slipped the boxer shorts over his thin hips. "I am gratified," he replied formally in Spanish, adjusting himself, "that my august cousin is so well known over here. It is my distinct pleasure to be connected in any way, however small, with the maestro." *You deserved that, you bastard,* he thought, *and I'll punch you in the face if you ask me to get his autograph.* He finished dressing as quickly as possible. He couldn't stand the man.

"My son loves 'The Cowboy Waltz,'" the colonel replied in a warm, fatherly tone of voice, still in English.

"So much so that he plays almost nothing else. I trust your cousin is well?"

"He certainly was the last time that I saw him," Mitchell said testily in Spanish. "Now, if you will excuse me, Doctor, I shall join the other . . . prisoners!"

"But—" said the colonel, holding up his hand, as if in self-defense.

Mitchell bowed. "Good day, Doctor."

"Harry Stanton," the colonel called as Mitchell left the bus and joined the other tour members outside. He had just lighted a cigarette when he heard a commotion inside the bus, and Henri shouting, "Stop him, stop him, stop him," in French, Spanish, and English.

The next thing Mitchell knew, Harry Stanton had left the bus and was running zigzag in expert military fashion up the small hill rising in back of the bus, using his umbrella as a balancer.

A shot rang out, and then another and another, as the soldiers scattered, some staying behind and others rushing after the escapee. The *rat-tat-tat-tat* of a submachine gun finally felled Stanton, who had reached the apex of the hill, within sight of freedom.

At once, the cocky little colonel was on the scene, giving directions in rapid-fire Spanish: Stanton's body was unceremoniously dragged from the incline and, after being searched, was covered with the army blankets brought from the bus; the luggage was closed up hastily and placed in the outside baggage compartment of the bus; the tourists were quickly herded on board; passports/visas were distributed; and the colonel saluted Reachi, who hissed under his breath to the driver, "Let's get the hell out of here!"

Henri pressed the starter, and the engine sprang to life. As the bus turned toward the highway, Mitchell looked out the back window of the bus in time to see the colonel hit Stanton's umbrella cane with his fist. He was rewarded with a shower of carbon nuggets, which fell out of the handle onto the blanket spread below.

Mitchell exchanged glances with Mrs. Parsons, who still held the apparently sleeping dog in her arms. They were safe for the time being. While the colonel was only interested in apprehending a diamond smuggler, Mitchell had a hunch that what Tibbetts carried under his blue coat was infinitely more valuable.

Two kilometers below, André Gulot asked to be let out of the bus, and, after retrieving his luggage, climbed into a waiting Mercedes with diplomatic license plates. Charlotte nudged Mitchell. "Wasn't he from South Africa?"

"So," Mitchell replied softly, "you're now able to put two and two together."

She was still perplexed. "So André was on to Stanton?"

"Probably not. Apparently, all he knew was that *someone* on board our Gerda was suspected of carrying diamonds; otherwise there would have been no point in searching everyone—and so intimately."

She threw him a long, hard look. "Don't complain. Just give thanks that you're not a woman!"

It was raining steadily when Gerda finally turned the corner that led into the busy intersection that marked downtown San Sebastian.

The passengers looked at each other, as if to say, *Can it be that, after what we've endured, we are nearing our destination at last?* Grace and David Benjamin and Doris and Humphrey Hardesty seemed to have weathered the incident best; they had not stopped chattering since the bus had left the soldiers.

Conversely, Betty and Ernest Blockton had not exchanged a word but were holding hands tightly. Mitchell could see Ernie back at the implement store in Missoula, entertaining the farmers with what they would surely regard as a tall story. Of course, Mitchell conceded, knowing how people in small towns were, he might not speak of his experiences on the trip at all, since it might be unwise to let his customers know that he was making enough profit for a tour of French châteaux!

Fava Dolin also had not spoken since the confrontation, and with her face in repose, Charlotte noticed that every line showed. There was also a new loneliness about her, and Charlotte threw a loving glance at Mitchell. Unless they had married, she might be on a bus tour alone like Fava Bean, hoping that the love of her life might be around the next corner.

Mrs. Parsons was trying to open her purse, disengage the band of her wristwatch, which had become entangled in Tibbetts' knitted coat, and remove a handkerchief from her pocket.

"Excuse me," Mitchell said to Charlotte. "Let me help the poor old thing." He smiled. "Let me hold the dog," he said helpfully, and picked up the snoring form; the drug apparently was still in effect. In the space of time that it took to place the hand mirror in his side pocket, Mrs. Parsons disengaged her wristband from the coat, opened her purse, and retrieved the handkerchief from her pocket. She looked up gratefully. "Oh, thank you, Mr. Heron, you've been a godsend."

Mitchell would have tipped his hat had he been wearing one, because he recognized the relief expressed in her eyes. He had felt the same way more than once during a mission. Her job was finished, and she was figuratively jumping up and down in ecstasy.

Gerda stopped under the huge brass porte cochère at the famous old Gothic landmark the Hotel San Lukas, three hours late—courtesy *l'affaire* Stanton/Gulot.

The moment that Henri opened the door and Salvatore Reachi emerged, a crowd of newspaper reporters surged forward, exclaiming all at once in rapid Spanish, "Was any passenger in danger during the heist?" "Were the diamonds cut or uncut?" and "When did you call in the police?"

Reachi held up his hands, and although the air was cool, he was perspiring heavily. "Just a moment," he shouted, and Mitchell was surprised to note that the guide's Spanish was as excellent as his English. "First of all, there was no 'heist.'" He moved into the hotel lobby, the reporters crowding around him. "Mr. Stanton was not a member of the original tour, but joined us in France when his auto apparently stalled. I did not call the police; the Spanish border patrol stopped the bus after we had left France. . . ."

Mitchell turned to Charlotte. "At least the signor is not a

fool; he has led the reporters away from us. Let's get out of here!" He paused a moment. "Oh, I almost forgot," he whispered. "I picked up a little gift for Aunt Letty. Didn't have time to have it wrapped. Would you put it in your purse, dear?" He gave her the silver makeup mirror with the engraved L.

Charlotte complied, giving him a curious look, but something told her not to make an issue of the incident, and she set her lips firmly together. So many strange adventures lay behind them that she had decided in Chinon that she would go along without question. She understood almost nothing of Mitchell's *modus operandi*, she wanted to keep it that way.

Now that the trip was over, and the passengers were free for the evening and not scheduled to meet again until the eight-o'clock flight back to Paris the next morning, a kind of sadness prevailed as they queued up in the aisle. It has been a strange group, Mitchell thought—not extremely friendly, yet a certain camaraderie had been established; they had all been brought together during what he would always remember as the Border Incident.

Exchanging pleasantries, the group assembled under the porte cochère, waiting for their luggage to be unloaded by bellhops not overly eager to dampen their maroon and blue uniforms. But the rain had turned into a light shower, and the sun was fighting to peer through fast-moving clouds.

A ragged newsboy, alert for new business, rushed up, waving a packet of newspapers, the front page of which featured a much younger photograph of Harry Stanton. The boy chirped in broken English; "Sou-ven-ir. Sou-ven-ir."

"Should I buy one for your scrapbook?" Charlotte asked, opening her purse.

"Please don't," Mitchell replied soberly. "I never save mementos."

"But *I* do!" she exclaimed, and purchased two papers. She opened one and translated the headline: "Diamond cache recovered," and then proceeded to read aloud the first two paragraphs of the story, by-lined by the famed journalist André Gulot. Mitchell was about to stop her, when he realized that she was behaving exactly as an ordinary tourist would behave, and he listened with interest as she read the list of people on the tour, lovingly pronouncing their own names.

"May I see the paper for a moment, please?" he asked.

"I didn't know you could read Spanish!" she exclaimed.

"Let's say it's not my second language," Mitchell replied, "but I can get by."

He had to see if the silversmith's body had been discovered, but there was nothing in the lead story to connect the murder with the diamond recovery, and a quick scan of other headlines revealed nothing. He sighed with relief. Perhaps the corpse was still lying behind the counter.

In his mind's eye, he could see a fat, mustachioed chief of police thumbing through reports and suddenly connecting the murder of the smith with the same tour that had turned up Harry Stanton. The incidents had nothing to do with one another, yet an inquiring mind might connect the two. . . . He did not want further investigation.

Suddenly there were cries of "Mummy! Mummy!" and Fava Dolin was surrounded by four children, ages two to nine. Amid hugs and kisses, one of the older boys asked excitedly, "Did they hold a gun on you?"

She threw back her blonde head and laughed. "Yes, but remember the soldiers were on our side!"

Charlotte exchanged glances with Mitchell and then burst out laughing. "Who would have guessed that she would turn out to be the Supreme Mother?"

"Which just goes to show, my dear, that things are seldom what they seem."

"I wonder where the Great Father is?" Charlotte asked, and as if in answer to her question, a tall redheaded man, who did not in the least look like a sheepherder, rushed through the crowd and took Fava Dolin in his arms. "Welcome home," he said emotionally.

"But . . ." Her voice was low, and there were tears in her eyes.

"I explained to the children this morning that you might still be on holiday, and might need more time to think, and it was possible that you wouldn't be on the bus. And then when we read in the late edition that your name was on the passenger list, we had some bad moments."

She smiled suddenly, and her face looked young. "By the time that I got to Labouheyre, I had made up my mind to come back to you and the children. I think, if we work at it, we can rebuild our marriage. But I don't want to live in Perth, and I won't be lost in a station in the Outback."

"Agreed," he said, and tenderly placed his arm around her waist.

Charlotte felt as if Mitchell and she had been indiscreet in listening to the emotional outpouring, and she took his arm. "Let's go inside," she said in a low voice.

Inside the cathedral-like lobby, the Benjamins, the Hardestys, and the Blocktons had been accosted by reporters, but Mrs. Parsons was nowhere to be seen. "Let's go into the dining room," Mitchell said under his breath. "We don't need any of this, and besides," he added with a grin, "Pierre would not approve."

"Oh, look!" Charlotte cried, pointing to a large placard, illustrated with the photograph of a beautiful woman.

FLAMINGO
World-Famous Impressionist
Appearing Nightly
Sans Souci Room

"I suppose," Mitchell sighed, "we had best make a reservation for the show tonight."

Charlotte looked at him askance. "I hate impressionists," she said slowly. "Let's enjoy some of the famous San Sebastian night life that I've heard so much about. Signor Reachi recommended the Club Afrique, which is supposed to be ever so decadent."

"I'm all for it," he replied unenthusiastically. "The early show here, and then on to the other place for the late show."

She grinned. "All right. I go with you, you go with me, right? I don't recall you being so diplomatic at home."

He squeezed her arm. "As Pierre says, 'Diplomacy is for fools.'"

10

The Narrow Road

The maître d' of the Sans Souci was extremely sorry, but Flamingo's nine-o'clock performance was sold out.

Mitchell counted to ten, made a difficult decision, and replied, "I am the cousin of Maestro Clement Story, who is looking for a night-club act to work with his orchestra in the States." As he expected, there was a quick gush of explosive Spanish. "Ah!" the maître d' exclaimed. "I shall seat you and your wife at the VIP table, courtesy of the hotel."

"We shall be delighted at this honor," Mitchell replied with a guilty feeling, "but only, of course, if we pay our own way." There were further outpourings, which he cut off with: "No, this I insist upon." He hung up and turned to Charlotte with an apologetic air. "This is the first time that I've used family strings to ask for a favor," he said. "I hope Clem will forgive me."

Charlotte gave him a strange look. "It's very important that we go tonight, isn't it?"

He nodded.

"Then," she replied softly, "I shall ask no more."

He smiled at her gratefully. "Do you suppose the makeup mirror will fit in the pocket of my tux?"

She laughed. "If it doesn't, I'll fix it so it will. Mother always taught me to bring three important items on a trip: needle and thread, a pair of shears, and an iron."

* * *

155

The nightclub, Sans Souci, might have been one of the top rooms in San Sebastian, but it had not been redecorated for many years, and, even in the dim red-neon-lighted foyer, looked old and forlorn—like a decrepit Washington D.C. dowager, Charlotte thought, in great need of a facelift.

Mitchell was dressed in a midnight-blue tuxedo, and Charlotte had altered the inside pocket in such a way that it could accommodate the mirror and still give him a flat-appearing chest. She wore a long orange wool sheath, a fifteen-year-old Hattie Carnegie that had cost fifteen hundred dollars. The dress was ideal for traveling, since it was not hung on a hanger but rolled on a tube.

The maître d', who greeted them with the reverence shown most usually for heads of states and movie stars, led them around tables that should have been set for six people but played host to eight, and down three separate tiers featuring banquettes, and finally found a ringside table for two.

Mitchell looked around the crowded room filled with tourists in gaudy formal attire. "I don't think another table could be crowded in here," he complained to Charlotte. "Let's hope there isn't a fire." He finally ordered a bottle of Mumms champagne from a harried waiter and noted with amusement that grotesque papier-mâché palm trees, which contained seedy-looking stuffed monkeys in the top fronds, ringed the dance floor. "Have you ever been in the Coconut Grove in the Ambassador Hotel in Los Angeles?"

When she shook her head, he continued, "The decor is similar, and this place, in the thirties when it was new, must have been very elegant. I'd like to see this room with all the lights on. I bet it looks like a musty, fusty, dusty, crusty heap."

"You *can* be descriptive!" she exclaimed. "I've never heard you use assonance before." She was about to continue when a strange whirring noise rent the smoke-filled air, to which the crowd responded with wild applause. Charlotte screamed with delight and pointed upward.

The tree monkeys were actually moving in a kind of slow dance. They stretched their scrawny little limbs, their bellies moved up and down, and their wrists whirled, while their little beady eyes rolled and glowed with pink neon.

"My God," Mitchell cried, clapping his hands along with the others, "they're *mechanized!*" He shook his head. "This whole performance is really obscene."

Charlotte took in the entire room at a glance. "And from the look of fascination in their eyes, most of this gang came to watch the monkeys. Flamingo better be good!"

Mitchell laughed, delighted with the antics of the animated animals. "I haven't seen anything so spectacular since Gargantua came to Enid with the Ringling Brothers and Barnum and Bailey circus!"

"They're in the same family," Charlotte replied, "so let's have a toast to Gargantua's cousins." When he raised his empty glass, she looked at him in surprise. "I thought you liked monkeys."

"I do, but I never drink on the job," he said. "But that doesn't mean that *you* can't get smashed."

She placed her glass firmly on the table. "Then I shan't drink, either. Let's order dinner."

The first course of stuffed oysters was exquisite, the meatball soup was good, the sautéed fish was poor, the pounded steak was bad, and the custard flan was not edible. "I'd have sent it all back," Mitchell said, "but I mustn't draw attention to us and make a scene."

He ordered coffee, which turned out to be superb, and they had two cups before the monkeys were turned off, the lights were lowered, and a drum fanfare reverberated throughout the packed room.

As the lights were turned off, the dance floor moved upward slowly until it was table-height. A moment of excitement buzzed through the crowd before a tiny lone spotlight was turned on a trim ankle and foot encased in a red sequined shoe, placed in such an unusual, twisted position that it was obvious the lady was lying upon the raised floor.

Slowly and sensuously, the pin spot moved up the shapely red-satin-clad leg and admirable thighs . . . to the exquisitely formed bosom, and finally rested on a face, in profile, of a lovely blonde venus with delicate eyebrows shaped like butterfly wings, dusky fringed eyes, and a carmined, pursed mouth. The effect was stunning.

She lay still for a long, precious moment, and as the tune of an Indian snake charmer was heard, played on a flute, the spotlight widened to include the entire voluptuous body slithering across the floor in a studied but abandoned manner, highly sexual in tone.

Then, with all eyes in the nightclub on the beautiful woman, the form suddenly flipped over and revealed a shocking change. Instead of the blonde venus, a horrible python writhed on the raised floor. So sudden was the transformation that the audience gave a simultaneous gasp: "*Ahhhhh . . .*" A moment later the form flipped over again, once more revealing the woman. "*Ahhhhh . . .*" Once more the voices of the crowd rose in appreciation.

"My God," Charlotte whispered. "It's the same *person*!"

Mitchell drummed his fingers on the table and whispered back, "I've never seen anything like this in my life!"

As the flute music quickened, the form began to twist in a series of bizarre contortions. It became apparent, to anyone who looked closely, that one half of the face, one half of the body, and one leg was dressed in red satin; while the other half of the face, body, and one leg comprised the scaled, silky body of the snake. The face, half woman, half reptile, was one of the most artful makeup creations that Mitchell had ever witnessed.

The fight now between the beauty and beast, woman and python, began in earnest. The eerie flute music was now joined by the single, primitive beat of a drum. The figure on the floor, taking cognizance of the change of mood and tempo, now raised slowly upward and twisted this way and that with the music, revealing the woman one moment and the python the next.

The music ceased; the form froze in a backward arabesque, the reptile on top of the woman. A single harpstring sounded once, twice, thrice, then began a feverish staccato beat, joined by the flute and the drum.

The fierce battle between good and evil was highlighted by an intense spotlight, which alternated flashes of brilliant red and green colors. The snake hissed and bared its fangs as the woman was subdued. Then with a sudden twist of the body, the woman was triumphant, but only for a moment. The snake bent over her as the legendary swan was supposed to have overpowered Leda.

The excitement of the audience was at a high point: all of them had forgotten they were watching a superbly choreographed single dancer simultaneously portraying two roles. Fascinated, Mitchell and Charlotte, scarcely breathing, leaned forward from their ringside seats, seeking a better view of the proceedings.

The harp became the focal instrument as the woman slowly strangled the snake. As the manipulations slowly wound down and down, the stage was lowered. When the female figure no longer moved, suddenly the music stopped.

After a moment of complete silence, the spell that had been so carefully woven was broken. But before the audience had time to applaud, the stage was filled with bare dancers in scant but brilliant feathered costumes. Full orchestral sounds boomed out suddenly, the stage was raised to maximum height, a dozen spotlights threw orange, magenta, and blue colors over the scene, highlighting the movements of the dancers spinning around and around in a circle.

All at once, the dancers moved together in a knot in the middle of the stage to the beat of a single drum. When the ensemble moved backward, a form was held aloft—the form of the snake which had consumed the body of the woman.

The spotlights were extinguished, the drumbeat stopped, and the audience applauded until finally the lights came up to reveal Flamingo standing up straight, turning the snake side of her body toward the crowd and taking a bow, then turning the female side of her body and taking another bow. The bows continued for several moments, then the form froze in an attitude of supplication, and the stage was lowered. The lights switched off and on; Flamingo had disappeared.

There was a sudden shifting of the crowd, the buzz of conversation, and a quick feeling of camaraderie as strangers exchanged comments from table to table. Charlotte was glassy-eyed from the performance, and Mitchell was emotionally drained. He arose. "I'll be back in a moment, dear," he said. "I'm going to the little boys' room."

Winding his way through the maze of tables, he took a long time to reach the rear of the room because the orchestra was drawing couples to the dance floor. At last he found his way to the corridor that led to the backstage area, where he expected a crowd of well-wishers lined up outside of Flamingo's dressing room, autograph books in hand. He was familiar with the routine from visiting Clem backstage.

But surprisingly, besides a few dancers in drooping feathers around the water-cooler, and a man adjusting a spotlight, the place was empty. He thought about the hollow sort of fame that Flamingo enjoyed; five minutes before, the crowd had been literally at her feet; now they were dancing to a modern orchestral beat and drinking champagne, and the goddess whom they had courted so vociferously was all but forgotten. In the grand scheme of things, it was something worth thinking about.

He knocked on the door with the faded star, which was opened by a harried little man who peered up at him through thick pop-bottle glasses. "Yes? Yes?" he asked nasally.

"I'm Mitchell Heron," he said, and then smilingly repeated one of the most used clichés in show business. "I would like an autograph for my mother, who's a great fan of Flamingo's."

"Come back in five minuts, Jorge." A light contralto voice with a heavy Spanish accent emanated from behind a large screen.

"Very well," the little man replied. "I'll bring back some coffee."

A head, half snake, half woman, appeared around the side of the screen. Close up, the heavily applied makeup did not appear as artful as under the strong spotlights, and in fact looked rather gross. There was no beauty whatsoever in the face; the loveliness that had struck the audience with such force was an illusion. "What is your mother's name?"

Mitchell thought for a moment before he replied, "Gibson."

"Ah, yes, Señor Heron, then you have something for me?"

It was when Mitchell was removing the makeup mirror from his inner pocket that he received the shock of his life. As the svelte form, dressed in a flowing black cape, strolled toward him and he got a good look at the face, it was obvious that under the layers of grease paint—Flamingo was a man.

Lopez, the travel manager at the Hotel San Lukas, was apologetic. The small airport was closed due to the heavy overcast, but he graciously offered to procure train tickets to Paris. "Don't you think that might be romantic, Señor Heron?" he asked, raising his generous eyebrows, thinking these people did not look like a particularly erotic couple, but one never knew about people who married in middle age. Of course, the most sensible arrangement was acquiring a young, nubile mistress instead of a wife like Mrs. Heron, who looked as if she might neigh and eat hay.

"Not the train," Mitchell replied quietly. He did not relish the idea of fitting his long, lean frame into an overnight berth. "But you might obtain a car for me, Señor Lopez. Hopefully some of the villages I once knew still retain some of their charm and hospitality."

"An excellent choice," Lopez said, mentally counting his commission, which would be considerable if he could convince Mitchell that the only way to travel through France was in a Rolls-Royce. And when he discovered that a Rolls-Royce was required, he positively burbled. "There are two available"—he checked his manifest—"a black convertible touring car and a white two-door hardtop." He made a bet with himself that the practical two-door would be the choice, and lost when Mrs. Heron selected the convertible. Ah, these crazy Americans!

Mitchell and Charlotte decided to have breakfast while the vehicle was being prepared for the journey, and went to a nearby restaurant.

"I'm certain that San Sebastian is absolutely beautiful when it's sunny," Charlotte remarked as they sat down in a back room, having refused to sit in the patio, "but it's so gloomy when it's bad. I, for one, will be glad to get back to France. . . ."

As she went on talking, Mitchell's attention was distracted by an attractive dark-haired lady sitting at a small single table a few feet away. There was something disturbingly familiar about her, and then it occurred to him that she was the erstwhile Mrs. Parsons, but with hair restored to its normal color and a makeup complete with eyebrows and lips.

She could be no more than thirty, he decided, and was perhaps even younger. Even her figure had changed. She was svelte in a foundation garment that lifted those areas that needed to be lifted and constricted those areas that needed to be constricted.

There was one organizational rule that was never broken: no operative ever recognized or spoke to another operative while performing a job. Many senseless deaths had occurred because of a casual greeting or other unintentional acknowledgement in public.

For instance, Pierre, who loved to spread horror tales, had told about an incident that occurred on the streets of Paris during the Occupation. A horribly beaten Englishwoman escaped from a passing car and begged an acquaintance, who happened to be passing, for assistance. When he answered, also in English, that he was "on duty," he was arrested by the Gestapo and put to death—but not before he was tortured and broken, giving the Nazis a list of names that put an entire network in the Low Countries out of commission for months.

When the woman glanced in Mitchell's direction, he stared straight ahead, but to his surprise she waved gaily, took a sip of water, got up, and came forward.

"Who is she?" Charlotte asked, slightly perturbed, "an old 'ghost'?"

He smiled at her term for former lovers and said under his breath, "Show no surprise and act naturally." Apparently, "Mrs. Parsons" was not breaking cover, but he would have to wait for her to make the first move.

The woman extended her hand. "Mitchell Heron," she

gushed, "I don't suppose that you'll remember me, but I'm Monica Fredricks, a friend of Letty's."

"Of course!" he exclaimed in a delighted tone of voice. "How nice to see you!" The woman obviously had a reason for making the contact. "Won't you sit down?"

"Thank you."

"By the way, Monica, this is Charlotte, my wife of a year."

"Oh, how do you do, my dear," the woman said breathlessly. "What a catch you've made!"

"It's very nice to meet any friend of the Herons," Charlotte replied graciously, thinking the woman was extremely familiar. "Did we meet in Angel?"

"No, I think not," she replied quickly. "I knew Letty in Washington."

"Then that's where we've met." Charlotte beamed. "I lived there for many years."

"How interesting," the woman said, and then turned swiftly to Mitchell. "I take my first trip abroad and keep running into people I know." She was flushed and enthusiastic. "For instance, I ran into dear old Mr. Jacob's wife—what's her name?—and she was full of news, as usual. Her husband was very happy because his latest operation—he's had so many—was a complete success."

She clicked her tongue in the best gossipy manner, before continuing hurriedly, "With him recovered, the surgeon can go on that long-planned vacation."

"Did she mention the Gibsons? They were great friends, if I remember."

She pursed her lips. "No, she talked about so many people, but I don't recall her mentioning the Gibsons." She rose up breathlessly. "Now, if you'll excuse me, I must run. When you see Letty, do give her my love." She turned to Charlotte. "Watch him carefully, my dear, he's a treasure!" And she was off, trailing a cloud of Patou perfume.

"I swear I remember her from somewhere." Charlotte said slowly. "I forgot to ask her if she was ever a hostess for the USO during the war."

Mitchell smiled. It was highly unlikely that the woman had ever been in Washington, D.C. But, he was happy to know that Leary was concerned that he should know that the operation was a success and that it was all right to continue the honeymoon without calling the special number in France. The woman was certainly a skillful operator, but of her two impersonations, Mitchell preferred the quiet, underplayed mouse, Mrs. Parsons.

The fighting had quieted along the 38th parallel due, as scuttlebut attested, to renewed armistice talks. Luke Three had been out in the field with the lieutenant for sixteen days, delivering dispatches that could have been more quickly and more easily carried by helicopter.

His superior, who felt exactly the same way and was extremely vocal about it, had given him Sunday off. "Go get yourself a piece of ass," he advised, "which is what Ah'm gonna do if Ah can arrange it. Ah've been trying to get into one of them army nurses, but the last time, she had the rag on, so maybe this is my lucky night!" And, looking around, and seeing he was unobserved, went into the officer's latrine. Evidently, Luke Three mused, his body hair had not grown back sufficiently to take showers with the other officers.

Luke Three waited until dark, then climbed into the jeep and headed out of the compound. He gave the password to the sentry who nodded and said: "Hell, you going out again?"

"Yeah," Luke Three replied, placing his hand into his blouse, "you want to see my orders?"

"Ain't they same as always?"

"Yeah."

"Go on, then. Watch out for snipers."

Luke Three heaved a sigh of relief. One thing good about this job, going in and out of the compound so often, he was seldom questioned. Everyone knew that Lieutenant James Foxwood Elliott IV had a nasty temper and a vile tongue. No one liked to cross him, least of all the sentries to whom he was most abusive. They would have turned him in if they dared, but it was rumored that he had friends in high places. Besides, it was a crappy job in a crappy war. What really mattered when it was all said and done?

Luke Three knew the road to Witch's Village like the back of his hand. The moonlight was so bright, that he could see the ruts in the road. There was no fog lingering over the distant round hills and the sky was clear of night planes, which had been a nuisance as recently as last week.

T'am's sweet face swam before his eyes. As he neared the village, his heartbeats increased to the point where his temples were pounding so heavily that the sound of the jeep's engine was muffled. He was rigid in his pants, and he thought, *you're a grown man, Luke Three, you've never even been to bed with this girl, and yet it's like you were sixteen years old!*

Nothing in his life had prepared him for this moment; yet he had loved many women and had surely been loved back—but was that *love* or was what he felt for T'am *love*? What was true and what was false? Was grown-up life continually mixed with emotions that could not be comfortably classified?

His heart sank as he reached the village: no kerosene lanterns were glowing anywhere and no music—Korean or American—was issuing forth from the Joy House. He parked in front of T'am's house, automatically turned off the jeep's motor, switched off the dull green camouflaged headlights, and slumped over the steering wheel.

Obviously, some catastrophe had befallen the village causing everyone to leave. Perhaps an epidemic of some sort had broken out. If the Army or the Marines had closed the Joy House, word would have spread like wildfire among the men.

Then suddenly, his nose flared and picked up a whiff of incense—that special never-to-be-forgotten odor connected with T'am's house. At that moment the door opened and a tiny, flickering sliver of light from a tallow candle fell into the shape of a crescent over the street. A small form was silhouetted as the door swung open.

"Hello!" Luke cried, delighted that the house was still occupied. "This is Luke, first class Gyrene in second class jeep."

"Howdy?" Do'm exclaimed. "No Coke? No church key? No family? Everything gone?"

"What mean?" Luke asked, the skin on his face growing taunt with fear.

"Boxes full up, see?" Do'm opened the door. "It fifteenth, seventh moon? Astrologer say get the hell out?" He grinned impishly. "We move Hour of Boar to Reed Pond?" He paused, and listened for a far off chant and nodded. "They come?" He said, bowed formally and opened the door wide. He placed the candle beside the door. "We sit?"

Perplexed, Luke Three joined Do'm on the bare floor, which was none-the-less still slightly warm from the heat beneath. The mood was ghostly, and the atmosphere very different from the first time that Luke Three had come to Witches Village.

Through the open door, down the slight incline of hill in back of the village, came several figures in native attire each carrying a lighted taper. A very old man, wearing a blue, embroidered robe, and a sort of top hat with a wide brim of black horsehair, identical to the ones that Luke Three had seen many men wear, entered the room first.

Do'm rose and bowed deeply and spoke solemnly in Korean. He turned to Luke Three and made a delicate gesture with his hands toward the old man. "This is Mr. Pak." He said, for once not closing his sentence with a question mark.

Do'm waved to Luke Three. "This first class Gyrene, with second class jeep."

Luke Three bowed to the old man, because it seemed the logical thing to do and the elder bowed in return and replied in English strongly accented with Japanese. "Welcome to the house of P'yon."

Mr. Pak's tone was not unfriendly, but there was an air of reserve about him that Luke Three could not classify and he felt out of place. He suddenly realized that he had been in Korea for almost a year, yet he knew almost nothing of the culture of the country.

Somehow, and quite stupidly, he had assumed that the smiling faces that he had seen in the war-torn villages represented the entire population. It occurred to him that the soldiers, and that most certainly included himself, only saw what they wanted to see.

Ashamed, he got up awkwardly. "I am intruding," he said, with as much dignity as he could muster, "and I apologize."

"Although an unexpected guest, you are most certainly welcome to take part in an important family ritual." Mr. Pak said.

"I beg your pardon?" Luke Three replied.

"Please sit," Mr. Pak answered effortlessly. "Only today, the ancestor tablets have been smuggled down from the North. The old home was not safe under bombardment. I, as the headman of the village, have been asked to transport these precious tablets to a new house just built on the Pond of Reeds over the hill."

He adjusted his spectacles, and went on somberly. "This house is under bad influences, so we have been advised to move at this special hour of the month. If you will accompany us, we shall have a feast—not a feast in our eyes—but something to eat—once we have placed the ancestors in their niche." He looked up. "What is your name."

"Luke Heron."

"Ah," the old man smiled. "There were, I believe four important men in the book that you call a Bible. Matthew, Mark, Luke and John." He frowned. "Were they brothers?"

"No," Luke Three replied, "they were disciples of Christ."

The old man smiled again. "Yes, now it comes back to me. In my youth we had a missionary from England in Seoul where I was born and she spoke about these men who followed Christ."

He bowed again. "Now, we must start. It is the middle Hour of the Boar . . . ten o'clock your time." He picked up a small stone square on which characters had been chiseled, which he held in his left hand, and with the lighted taper in his right hand, turned toward the door.

One by one, the villagers entered, picked up a stone tablet and then stood shoulder to shoulder with their backs to the wall. The last one in the procession was T'am and when she picked up the tablet, she glanced shyly at Luke Three, apparently not at all surprised to see him. In the flickering candle light, she looked more beautiful than ever.

The villagers filed out of the door again, and Mr. Pak handed Luke Three a small stone Buddah. "You may join us as we go to the new house," he said with great dignity.

Luke Three and Do'm rose in unison, as if they had been rehearsed. Luke Three bowed. "Mr. Pak, may I please be excused? I must return to my outfit."

A look of sadness crossed over the old man's face. "I understand." He paused, as if trying to find the proper words. "You are not like the other soldiers," he said finally, "During the Japanese occupation of my country, before nineteen-forty-five, I was employed as an interpreter of three languages and met many people. It was said that I could look in a face and tell the history of that person. What I see in your face. . . . you are an old soul, and your karma rests in this country."

"I don't know what you mean, Mr. Pak."

He nodded. "Someday you will."

Luke Three handed the statue of Buddah to Mr. Pak, who presented it to Do'm. They went into the street.

The villagers had formed a circle. With their hand-held tapers lighting their solemn faces, it seemed to Luke Three that he had stepped back a hundred years in time. He found himself bowing and when he looked up again, the villagers with Mr. Pak leading the parade, were walking single file up the hill.

It was a long time before Luke Three climbed into the jeep. He was experiencing a variety of emotions. This ritual that he had witnessed—which had seemed so bizarre before—now did not seem out of place. It was he who did not belong. . . .

11

Sky High

Mitchell and Charlotte had ordered the car for six a.m., in order to appreciate a drive over the curving road that bordered the Mediterranean Sea from Monte Carlo to Cannes.

"But darling," Charlotte had said, "you won't get to see very much, negotiating all those hairpin turns!"

He had laughed. "But I'll get to see the views on the way back, because *you'll* be driving!"

While the car was being brought up to the entrance of the Hotel Fleur de Lis, Charlotte looked in the lobby mirror. Certainly she had not lost any weight on the trip, but she did look chic, she thought, in her red-and-white polka-dot dress, with a skirt wide enough to actually make her waist look small. Mitchell looked rather like a sea captain with his white trousers, navy-blue coat, and billed cap.

He came up behind her and looked over her shoulder in the mirror. "Enjoying the view? I've enough scrambled eggs on my cap to feed an army." He laughed. "I look like some old geezer who was decorated by the Czar. I'll be right back. What can be keeping the driver?"

He went to the cobblestoned entrance of the hotel. Dawn was breaking on the far horizon, and the sky was mixed with violent reds and yellows—but not the muted oranges that flooded the Oklahoma skies every morning. A janitor was polishing the brass double front door, and a cleaning lady was on her hands and knees, swabbing the cobblestoned terrace, where tables were later spread for luncheon, then cleared for tea.

The car valet was nowhere to be seen, and as Mitchell came forward to the driveway, the cleaning lady turned, and he caught the shape of her extraordinary profile out of the corner of his eyes.

He caught his breath. No, of course it could not be; memory had played a trick on his brain. He sauntered to the unwashed section of the terrace and lighted a cigarette, stealing a glance in her direction. She was like a robot: her gray head was bent down, and she was making wide, expert swipes with the cloth, each time covering more and more room. "It is a lovely morning," he said quietly in French, heart beating very fast.

"It is indeed, monsieur, as always," she replied, continuing her work, glancing up quickly so as not to be rude, but not really looking at him.

His mind flashed back thirty-four years to the Paris of 1918, and he was holding Françoise's hand as they strolled along the Left Bank. He was wearing cast-off clothes purchased from a junk dealer, because he had burned his army uniform when he had gone AWOL. Hardly believing his good luck at meeting a girl, he kept looking at her striking profile as they walked, to be certain that she was still by his side.

In the many years since they had parted, after that glorious but brief affair, her profile always came up before his face when he thought about Paris. Was it the same profile that he was seeing now as the woman turned and rinsed the cloth in the pail of water?

What had Pierre Darlan said in one of those grueling sessions about disguise? It had to do with the bone structure of the human face. Then he remembered: the little Frenchman had smoothed his generous mustaches with the tips of his fingers and had exclaimed: "*Mon cher*, the face falls with age, cheeks sag, hollows appear under the eyes, the chin becomes infirm, the neck hangs in folds, the eyebrows go gray. Only two things do not change: one is the color of the eyes, and the other is the profile."

It was on the tip of his tongue to say something more, but

at that moment Charlotte called out, "Mitch, where are you? The car's ready. The valet couldn't find you."

He turned and strode toward her. "I was just watching the sunrise, and I guess I got carried away."

She shrugged. "Not as pretty as the ones we have in Angel."

"Do me a favor? If you'll drive this morning, I'll drive back this afternoon."

"Of course," she replied as the valet opened the doors of the white Rolls-Royce.

He had to think, which he could not do if he had to keep his eyes on the hairpin turns on the road. He was still shaken by Françoise's—or the janitoress with Françoise's profile. What should he do, when she held all the answers to the questions that had bothered him for so many years?

He thought of his precious visits to Gertrude Stein and Alice B. Toklas in his quest for Jean Baptiste Faubert. Françoise could tell him if that man was their son. . . . But what of Charlotte, who was now driving so skillfully over the high mountain road from which could be seen the blue Mediterranean below? What would his new bride, who now knew about his secret missions, say if she knew that he might have an illegitimate son?

He smiled ironically. For a respected, upright, forthright member of the Chamber of Commerce in Enid, Oklahoma, and both the cousin of a famous bandleader and the nephew of a millionaire dowager, his past read like what his English friends would call a penny dreadful—a sleazy dime novel. Still, he decided, he owed it to himself to meet Françoise— if, indeed, it was she—face to face!

Charlotte pulled over to the side of the road. "I'm dizzy." She laughed. "This road is more curvaceous than Marilyn Monroe!"

Mitchell grinned. "Perhaps, but not nearly so interesting."

"I didn't know that you liked the blonde sexpot type."

With his thoughts on Françoise, he felt guilty; she had been reddish blonde, curvaceous, and a sexpot. Then he thought of the old scrubwoman, and his eyes suddenly teared. "Look," he said, to distract Charlotte's attention, "see the spires of the old château? I'm told the chapel inside is entirely made of glass."

"Really? Well, personally, I don't care if I never see another château, chapel, church, or cathedral!" She paused, and they lighted cigarettes. "Shall we get out of car and walk?" she asked.

"Not unless you want to," he replied.

"In that case, no. You seem so distracted today—as if you were still on the . . . mission. It's finished, isn't it? You don't have to report or anything, do you?"

He shook his head. "No. Everything's copacetic. It's just that after a job I feel—well, sort of disjointed, up in the air, lonely. It's difficult to explain."

Charlotte snubbed out her cigarette in the ashtray and repaired her lipstick in the windshield mirror.

"One of my bosses calls this condition the postpartum blues," he explained ruefully. "It goes away after a few days. But in the meantime I guess you'll just have to put up with it. I'm sorry."

"It's no big deal. If I were in your boots, Mitch, I'd be a quivering mass of jelly. As a New York friend of mine would say, 'You're entitled.'" She started the engine and moved onto the empty road, which had straightened out somewhat over a kind of bare plateau; but the ocean could still be seen shimmering in the far distance. "Will you ever be able to talk about the 'diamond caper'?"

He gave her a swift look. "Of course I can discuss it, but, aside from our mutual experience on the bus, unfortunately I don't know any details that weren't published in the Spanish press, and that was precious little."

She kept her eyes on the road. "But I thought—"

He gave a dry, wry laugh. "Charlotte, my sweet," he said seriously, "my job had nothing to do with the 'diamond caper,' as you call it."

"It *didn't*?"

"No, that was just a coincidence—one of those crappy chance bits of business that can drive operatives up the wall and onto the ceiling. We are trained to be on the lookout for scams that may complicate a mission.

"In this case, I had one fairly simple job to perform, and

I was as surprised as anyone at the police cordon—which, I might add, *could* have been connected with my work. I had some bad moments until Harry Stanton was revealed as the diamond smuggler; then I knew that we were home free."

"*We?* You mean you and me?"

"No."

"Then there was someone else on the bus—in this thing with you?" she asked hesitantly.

"Yes."

"You've awakened my curiosity."

"Sorry, I didn't mean to."

"Then I won't ask any more questions."

"That would be a good idea." He paused. "But there is something that I'd like to tell you about." He drew in his breath. "An incident that happned when I was just a kid in military service in World War One."

The road had become complicated again, and Charlotte slowed down in order to take the curves more smoothly. "If it has anything to do with romance," she put in gently, "please don't continue, because I have no intention of reciprocating by swapping stories of my love life before we married."

Mitchell cleared his throat. "I agree that's infantile. But there is a very good reason why I want to confide in you. As always with me, nothing is ever simple or uncomplicated." And very haltingly, with many pauses while he tried to select exactly the right words, he told her about Françoise and Jean Baptiste Faubert.

They had reached Antibes, and Charlotte drew up before a tiny sidewalk café. "They used to have the most marvelous croissants here," she said, "and good American coffee." When they were seated under the wings of a spreading oak tree, separated from the other diners by a wrought-iron rail, she continued in a low voice, "So you think this cleaning lady may be Françoise?"

Mitchell nodded. "I could be wrong. Memory can hardly be reliable after such a long passage of time." He ordered pastry and coffee from the overly patronizing waiter, who had been hovering about, brushing imaginary crumbs from tablecloths, then went on quickly. "Pierre Darlan, who is interested in all sorts of surveys and statistics, says that if twenty people see a traffic accident and are interviewed immediately afterward, fifteen will tell the same story. If one day lapses, only five will agree on what happened, and if a week goes by, there'll be twenty different versions of the accident. So after thirty-four years I'm probably wrong. What should I do?"

She paused while the waiter served the food in his nauseating, self-effacing manner, waved him away, took a sip of coffee, and grimaced. "Damn, it's not the same at all!" Then she added philosophically, "Which just goes to prove that nothing ever really remains the same. Nothing is forever—which is exactly the reason that I believe you have no alternative but to speak to this woman."

Mitchell was waiting at the service entrance of the Fleur de Lis hotel at seven o'clock in the morning. He nervously bit his fingernails—a habit broken at fourteen—as he watched the day-shift employees arrive and the night shift depart. He swore under his breath; it was just his luck that Françoise had left early.

He had turned to retrace his steps to the suite when he saw her pause in the doorway. She was wearing a gray cloth coat and had carelessly thrust on her head a floppy black beret such as artists wore prior to World War I.

She lighted a cigarette, threw her head back, and deeply inhaled quickly, as if the smoke were a rare essence. It was the one gesture with which he was familiar. For a moment he panicked. Nagging thoughts, which he had kept conveniently in the back of his mind, now rushed into consciousness, and he grew dizzy. Why disrupt her life again? Was it fair to bring back a relationship that had been ended so many years before?

For the first time, he was conscious of his meticulously tailored white shantung suit and the expensive bench-made arrow-tipped brown-and-white shoes. The only addition required to resemble Paul Henreid in the old film *Casablanca*, he thought humorlessly, was a white panama hat!

Why in the hell hadn't he worn something more casual that would not peg him as a ne'er-do-well? Had he, with some hidden psychological quirk, purposefully overdressed so that the contrast between their stations in life would be more marked?

How could he introduce himself to this shabbily dressed creature whom fortune had obviously ignored? The smiling face of the bowing waiter at the sidewalk café in Antibes, came up before his eyes; it would be a disgrace to appear like that to her, a patronizing figure from her past.

He turned away, but the face of Alice B. Toklas came up before his eyes, and he heard her words: *"Would you not appreciate a long-lost father returning after so many years?"* No, having come thus far, he could not go away without finding out if he had a son.

Then, so that he would not change his mind, he forcibly turned his body to the doorway and abruptly said, *"Bonjour,* Françoise. It is Mitchell Heron."

She glanced up at him, the cigarette dangling from the side of her mouth, and there was no expression whatsoever on her face. Although her complexion was chalky from not being exposed to the sun, the wrinkles could not hide the fact that she was indeed the woman that he had loved as a boy. The squat body had once been lithe and beautiful, the breasts firm and rosy-tipped, the legs pink and white.

"Bonjour, Mitch," she said without a smile, conversationally.

He looked at her incredulously. "After all this time, you aren't surprised to see me?"

She glanced sideways, a trace of a smile on her lips. "I was indeed astonished to see you . . . and your . . . wife check into the hotel." Her voice was flat, so devoid of emotion that she might have been speaking about the weather. "I was not positive, of course, that the elegant gentleman was the Mitch I once knew, but there was something about the angle of your shoulders . . ." She ground out the cigarette with the toe of her heavy shoe. "But curiosity got the better of me, and I asked the concierge your name."

"Then you knew it was me when I spoke to you the other morning?"

Oui."

"Can we walk a bit?"

"Certainly."

He politely escorted her through the small garden in the rear of the hotel, and politely took her elbow as they climbed the steps to the street. She looked up at him. "Although my legs are stiff, I am not yet to the point where I need assistance." It was a statement with no underlying bitterness. "When I do, I shall use a cane." She laughed hollowly.

Once more he felt guilty, because they were the same age, and yet she was an old woman with nothing, and he had so much of everything.

She must have read his thoughts, because she said, "You look well, Mitch." But she did not look at him but turned so that the beret hid her face. He could not reply in kind, because she was wan and pale and looked ten years older than he. Suddenly there was an unexplained burning in his chest. "Let us stroll through the park across the street," he said.

Her eyes were wide and questioning. "You will be seen with me there?"

He frowned. "Of course."

"How could you explain my presence to an employee of the hotel?"

He frowned again, irked that she was pursuing this line of thought. "I do not explain anything to anyone"—his voice was sharp—"least of all to a servant."

"But I am a servant."

"Not in that sense," he replied quickly, at odds on how to play this current role. On assignment, his characterization would have been worked out to the last nuance. But, as in the experience on the motorbus, he was finding that playing himself was the most difficult of all. They had crossed the street, and the park was deserted except for a young man doing military exercises and an old flower woman picking over her basket of mauve blooms that reminded Mitchell of English heather.

"What about your . . . wife?"

"I am here with her permission," he replied, and when

they came to an iron seat fringed with tall orange flowers he asked, "Shall we sit?"

"If you like." She sat down and made a little ritual of removing the beret and running her hands through her hair, which slightly loosened the gray wings on either side of her face. There was something studied about the performance, as if she were saying, "Here, look at my face and see what changes time has wrought."

Curiously, he found that he did not know how to start a proper conversation. He racked his brain for something to say. In the days of their love affair, she had modeled for artists; that was all that he really knew about her. They could not have exchanged very much information. It occurred to him that she must also know very little about him. Truthfully, their days together had been spent in each other's arms.

Before the pause could become awkward, she took a cigarette from her pocket and held it while he found a match. "*Merci*," she said languidly, and there was another short pause while she repeated the habit of bringing her head back and inhaling in that erratic way. "I have always wondered what happened to my Marine," she continued with a slow smile that only pointed up the difference, somehow, between the way she used to look and the way that she looked now. "I assumed that he went back to—was it Ok-la-hom-a?"

He flushed. It was the first time that anyone had ever referred to him in the third person. But in a way, he supposed, he was no more that Marine now than she was the girl with whom he had fallen in love in 1918. "I did not go back for a very long time. I stayed over here and worked for a glass factory. I sold figurines from house to house."

Her fingers caressed his fine shantung sleeve. "You have done well in this selling business?"

He shook his head. "No, I did not do well. I did not become a success until a few years ago, when I went back home and opened a furniture store."

"Oh?" She smiled politely, taking another puff from the cigarette. Apparently, she did not intend voluntarily to reveal anything about herself.

He was becoming more and more ill-at-ease; no matter what they had shared thirty-four years ago, they were two strangers trying to make small talk. He kept his voice low and gentle. "I assume you are married?"

With a sort of finality, she snubbed out the cigarette with the toe of her shoe, but she did not look at him. "Yes. My first husband worked for the railroad. He died of coaldust in the lungs." Her voice was so unemotional that she could have said in the same tone: "Yes, I go to Mass on Sundays."

She rubbed her right knee. "There are pains this morning." She paused. "My second husband played a violin in a cabaret band. He was knifed in the chest one night after work." She continued to rub her knee. "I have worked always, as I did when I knew you. . . ."

His face flamed at the memory of their weeks together. He remembered now that he had not one sou in his pocket when they met in Paris, two days after he had left his regiment at Château Thierry. Françoise had paid for bread and wine and cheese. In the intervening years, when he had thought about those days, he envisioned her glorious body in bed—open for him to enter any time that he wished.

". . . after I could no longer figure model," she was saying in her understated manner, "I posed for head-and-shoulder pieces. Then, when I was no longer in demand, I became an *au pair* girl, cleaning houses for people for a few francs and board and room. I sold flowers to tourists on street corners for a time before going to work for the Hotel Fleur de Lis."

Only now, looking at her rough, red hands, did Mitchell remember that she had cooked their meals on the gas ring in the room. Because he was afraid of being arrested as a deserter by the Military Police, she had gone alone every day to the fishmonger and the baker and the greengrocer. And when she returned, he was always waiting for her in bed, certain, with the arrogance of youth, that she had been counting the moments until she could join him. . . .

He remembered now that once or twice, when there were no sous in the sugar bowl, she had accepted a modeling job. He was embarrassed to recall that he had questioned her severely about the artist who had painted her in the nude, insisting quite angrily that her body was his property alone. Oh, how foolishly he had behaved! He had given her nothing except—perhaps—a son. . . .

She had stopped rubbing her knee. "Your wife looks very healthy," she said conversationally. "Are you happy, Mitch?"

Her question took him by surprise. "I—I think so. I am only recently married for the first time." He colored. "In fact, this is my honeymoon!"

It was her turn to look surprised. "I do not suppose I should ask the question, but I will. Why did you wait so long?"

He contemplated the answer for a moment. If he were on assignment, and able to use any technique whatsoever, he would probably say, "Because of you," which would probably elicit the right response. She would be on the defensive, vulnerable to attack, leaving an opening for him to launch into the real reason for the meeting. But he could not trick this sad little woman.

"I waited because I was always too busy for marriage." He paused, and then went on quickly, "That's not strictly true. To be totally honest with you, Françoise, I was too selfish to get seriously involved. I grew up with Charlotte, and when we were brought together later in life, it was easier to marry her than not." He had never before placed his thoughts into words, but he knew what he had said was the truth.

Françoise gave him a penetrating look, then arranged her purse over her arm, preparatory to getting up from the bench. He knew that he must ask the crucial question now. "Did you have children?" he asked casually, offering her a cigarette to further delay the departure, then providing a lighted match.

"Yes." She hesitantly puffed on the white shaft. "A girl." She replaced the beret on her head at a rather rakish angle for a middle-aged woman, and smiled wanly at him. He saw that her teeth were as white and evenly spaced as he remembered. She got up slowly from the bench. "I must leave now." She held out her hand awkwardly. "*Adieu*, Mitch."

He nodded his head. "*Adieu*, Françoise."

She walked with great difficulty up the path. His eyes burned; it would not be very long before she would need a cane.

It had been an exciting week for Mitchell and Charlotte. Now that he was no longer plagued by his past, and the mission had been successfully completed, he was able to relax and enjoy himself. Charlotte, seeing him so happy, responded in kind. They went to the beach every day, ate picnic lunches, had dinner in tiny restaurants that specialized in the cuisine of the area, and for amusement occasionally gambled in the casino, wearing evening clothes as if they had never worn any other attire. It was a delightful, sophisticated world, yet they longed to be home.

On the last night in Monte Carlo, Mitchell left Charlotte at the tables, where she was concentrating on roulette, and went out on the broad stone terrace that overlooked the Mediterranean Sea. He lighted his new demijohn pipe and smoked, watching the lights shimmering over the quay. Yachts, illuminated by strings of white bulbs, sparkled over the water, which reflected the ambience in waving light shadows. It was one of the most beautiful sights that he had ever seen, and he gazed intently at the view, commiting the scene to memory.

"At last we are free to speak," a familiar voice said.

Startled, he turned abruptly and looked into the face of the woman whom he knew both as Mrs. Parsons and Mrs. Fredricks. Now she was a vivacious redhead, dressed in a white floating gown that hid her girth. She wore only a trace of makeup, and he noticed that she was very attractive. He held out his hand. "How do you do."

"How do you do, Mr. Heron. My name is Sharp, Helena Sharp, but I'm not really." She laughed gaily, showing her white, even teeth that reminded him slightly of Françoise. "Are you on vacation also?"

He nodded. "I'm on my actual honeymoon."

"Then Charlotte is your real wife?" She laughed. "As

you know, in our business one can't be certain of anything. She's a nice lady, and I hope that you'll be happy."

"Thank you. Aren't you glad that the mission is over?"

"Yes, thank God, free of messy Spanish border patrols, slick diamond smugglers, and pesky dogs!"

His face was filled with admiration for her. The few female operatives he had met were glacial creatures, more suited to boardrooms than fieldwork. But this woman had showed him two perfect creations, both entirely different from this person, who was obviously herself. "I think I've just performed my last job. My life is complicated enough now as it is."

She gave him a hard look. "Yes, let us all have fewer complications. My first really terrifying moment was when I was called to be searched. The guard was so thorough, I was scared to death they'd frisk that miserable Tibbetts and find the mirror. I will never, *ever* work with an animal again!"

"Did you know that he bit me?"

She nodded. "And for that I'm sorry, but he bit me too, twice, once on each arm. We hated each other with a passion, you know. I was scared to death that he would bite the colonel, and then the fat would have been in the fire." She smiled wryly. "There were a few bad moments there.

"In the first place, I didn't have time to make friends with the mutt. My contact simply thrust him into my arms two minutes before I arrived at the hotel, and I had to pretend that he was my most precious possession! Thank God I could knock him out now and then with a sleeping potion. I was sure he would make friends with one of the guards and the job would blow up in my face!"

She sighed, and frowned. "It was sad about the silversmith, but he was a new recruit and failed to recognize Henri. He would not give him the makeup mirror, and pulled a gun. For some reason, the smith thought Henri was the enemy and threatened to notify the hotel manager."

She paused. "Henri was a fast draw and he only meant to give a flesh wound, but the smith leapt at him and the bullet went through his heart. I am thankful for two things: first, the gun had a good silencer; and secondly, Henri found the mirror displayed—would you believe?—on the shelf in plain sight. Sometimes this is a dirty business, Mr. Heron."

She turned from the sea view. "I should allow you to return to your wife." She held out her hand once more. "It was a pleasure seeing you again, Mitchell Heron. I shall always remember the experience that we shared. Good-bye."

"Good-bye, Helena Sharp," he said, then added as an afterthought, "Please give my regards to 'Gibson' when you see him."

A stricken look came over her face, "Oh, you didn't know? Pierre Darlan died of a heart attack the day we started the château tour."

The express train to Paris left at eight a.m., and Mitchell and Charlotte arose at five, performed morning duties, packed luggage, and were the first to be seated when the dining room downstairs opened at six-thirty.

Mitchell had looked about the public rooms on the lower floor in the hope of seeing Françoise, but she was nowhere to be seen. The previous day, with Charlotte's permission, he had withdrawn two hundred thousand francs from the bank, which he had placed in a packet to give to her. It was the least he could do, he felt, and Charlotte had agreed with him.

No amount of money would compensate her for the actions of that callous young Marine, but she might be able to raise her standard of living. He would have left the packet for her in the manager's office, but the amount was in loose francs. He had learned a long time ago that money could disappear quicker than any other commodity; he would place the packet in her hands himself.

A few moments before seven, he excused himself from the table. "Order more coffee for me, please?" he asked Charlotte, who nodded and waved him on his mission.

He waited inconspicuously under a tree near the service entrance as he had before, and watched the employees leave and enter, until Françoise appeared, talking animatedly to another woman. Mitchell waited until they parted, but as he came forward, packet in hand, another man appeared by her side. *"Bonjour, Maman,"* he said, and as he turned, Mitchell was face to face with Jean Baptiste Faubert.

Françoise was in the midst of lighting a cigarette when she saw the two men staring at each other. The pent-up hysteria of thirty-four years poured forth; her face crumpled and she began to cry; long, agonizing sobs shook her body.

"Maman," Jean Baptiste soothed, taking her in his arms, *"Maman . . ."*

Mitchell's heart beat very fast as he looked at the face of the man with the Heron nose. Jean Baptiste had matured since he had seen him sitting at the bar of the Golden Apple in Plaisance-du-Gers, He was still extremely handsome—better-looking, actually, than any of the Heron boys—but there were lines around his mouth and under his eyes, and the downy appearance of his face had disappeared and he was tanned a dark brown.

At last Françoise quieted. "I hoped this meeting would never come," she said in a strained and unnatural voice. But before she could continue, the men looked at each other and there was a strange moment of recognition. There were many emotions that flitted across Jean Baptiste's face: hurt, anger, suspicion—and then he cleared his throat and said to Mitchell, "There is much talking to be done between you and me. Can it be now?"

When Mitchell could trust his voice, he replied, "Come upstairs."

Jean Baptiste turned to Françoise. "I will look in on you tonight, as usual, *Maman.*"

She held out her hand to him, and her face twisted. "But, there is so much you must know. . . ."

"Let us find out for ourselves." he replied gruffly.

Inside the lobby, Mitchell asked him to stand by the lift. "I shall be back in a moment . . . Jean Baptiste." How strange the name sounded coming from his lips, even though he gave the words the correct French pronunciation! He went into the dining room, as if stepping on air, and paused at the table.

"What kept you so long, dear?" Charlotte said, wiping her mouth with a napkin, preparatory to rising.

"Charlotte," Mitchell exclaimed, "cancel the train reservations! We are going to stay on for a while. I have found my son!"

William Nestor awakened when a hand made butterfly circles on his back. He turned and took Louisa in his arms. "Just because my iron bar is ready," he said playfully, trying not to breathe into her face, because he had not brushed his teeth, "is no sign that *I'm* ready! What time did I get in last night?"

"Eleven, I think. I was about to send out the vigilantes."

"Pardon me?" He kissed her ear.

"Don't start anything that you can't finish," she said succinctly, pleased that the blackout curtains were still at the windows, making the room dark. She did not look her best at seven a.m. "Now about the vigilantes. They were a sort of posse—"

"What's a *posse*?"

She gave him a long look. "You're the Indian in the family and should know these things. Vigilantes and posses are what they used to send out after bad people—and sometimes good people like Indians. Anyway, I was getting worried. How is it coming?"

"Fine, I think. Oh, we have a new title for the picture. It's now called *Colin's Girl*, which I don't like. I swear, Louisa, this is a crazy business. You never know from day to day.

"Anyway, they gave me a tiny recording studio with a small screen and a piano and a projection booth, and a man to rewind the bits and pieces of the film that I'm timing with a stopwatch. You see, every character has separate identification music that's whenever they're on the screen. If you're a good composer, the audience isn't aware of the music itself, just the mood it creates."

"It sounds very complicated, Billy." She ran her fingers lightly over his shoulder.

"Cut that out!" he exclaimed playfully. "Anyway, themes can be used all sorts of ways to establish a character's mental state, or sometimes even inanimate objects have themes. Tara, the plantation house in *Gone with the Wind*, for instance, had a theme, and so did Twelve

Oaks, a neighboring property. Scarlett, Rhett, Melanie, Ashley—all major characters—had theirs, too. In *Colin's Girl*, I've written a theme for a cat."

"A *cat*?"

"Yes. He has a very important part in the picture. He lives in the slum where the story takes place, and I want him to be sort of an observer—like the audience—and I think that the theme will do the trick." He laughed. "I keep calling the cat a 'he'—the camera never really gets that close—because I've given him a very masculine motif."

"How can music be really masculine or feminine?" she asked, her fingertips still busy on his shoulder.

"Easy. Violins, harps, the celeste would certainly be classed as feminine, while woodwinds would be masculine."

"The oboe?"

"Depending on the key."

"The glockenspiel?"

He laughed. "Definitely masculine." He sighed. "You've done your devil work. You're really the Flame of Willawa!"

She giggled. "It's been a long time since you've called me that, Billy."

"Somehow it's fitting this morning." He took her in his arms, and as he looked down into her face, the toothpaste forgotten, she sighed gently and opened herself to his full embrace.

It was a very long interval before William's climax approached, and Louisa expertly gauged herself to be ready at the same instant. In the beginning of their relationship, when he was so young and the experience was still so new, their bodily contact would be over almost the moment it had started.

Although he was ready again almost at once, and the second and third times were always more satisfying for her, he often had to leave early. The farm was two miles from her house in town, and his parents had decreed that he be in bed by nine p.m. If he had homework to do, he would leave immediately after dark.

She had taught herself to respond to him in a mental way

during shorter times with him. She loved the feel of his adolescent body over hers. Other women were forced to fantasize about such moments as this, but, she thought happily, there was no need to conjure up the face of a college boy or the kid down the street, because she had her lover right here in her arms.

She would rub his smooth back, as she was doing now, and as his frantic movements increased, when he could not stay his ardor and was forced to labor for that supreme delight that no other could approach, she would experience, in those precious moments, something very akin complete fulfillment. Only after he had left her bed, when she was empty and hollow, would she feel alone and abandoned.

Only on prayer-meeting nights—Wednesdays—and gospel-reading nights—Sundays—was he allowed to arrive home late. On those two nights, they would enjoy each other's bodies for two hours. Now, of course, he was an experienced lover, always vigilant—and she smiled at the word—for her pleasure, and he never spent too quickly. Feeling his climax approaching, she rose up to meet his expert thrusts.

After it was over, they lay, as always, in each other's arms. "I think we're doing it too much, Lou," he said when his heartbeat returned to normal. "With my schedule, I seem to get tired very quickly, although the days seem awfully short. I get so interested in the picture that time doesn't mean anything anymore." He kissed her on the cheek. "I've got to get up, the limo will be waiting. Do you want to come out to the studio for lunch?" He got up and opened the blackout curtains, and sunlight flooded into the room.

She turned away from the glare, knowing that her face was red and splotchy and her hair awry. "Not if we must eat in that dreary commissary." She smoothed her hair back and rose up on an elbow as he went into the bathroom. "Tell you what," she called, "I'll bring lunch and we can eat on the back lot."

"You never get tired of those old sets, do you?" He appeared in the doorway with lather on his face and a razor in his hand.

She laughed. "The lunch will be good, I assure you. How about some of Chasen's fabulous chili?"

"Sounds good to me, but it's still not as good as Belle Trune's."

"And some lemon pie from Dick Webster's shop on La Cienga."

He disappeared again into the bathroom, and she got up quickly, wiped her face dry of cold cream, put on lipstick, touched her brows with a brown pencil, and slipped on a peach chiffon negligee, so that, when he came into the bedroom after his shower, she would look appealing as he kissed her cheek. She must keep her hold over him, or all would be lost.

12

Strange Reunion

The French that Jean Baptiste spoke, filled with argot slang, was sometimes difficult for Mitchell to follow, and the boy knew no English.

"Always," Jean Baptiste announced with conviction, his finely sculptured face animated and dramatic-looking, "I knew that I was different. My father"—he looked up apologetically—"my *step*father tried with great difficulty to be a companion to me as a boy, but we had nothing in common, and mother was always withdrawn in those days, worrying about money, because we were very poor."

Mitchell and Jean Baptiste sat opposite each other in big overstuffed chairs in the Heron suite, and it seemed that the boy could not take his eyes from his newly found father's face. He smoked one brown cigarette after another, yet his hands were steady; he had lost his earlier nervousness.

He possessed a natural poise, and although his rough clothes contrasted sharply with the luxurious furnishings in the room, he seemed unaware of the difference, which impressed Mitchell, who also had been blessed with self-assurance at the same age. In a strange way, the boy seemed a part of the room and did not look out of place. All of these things Mitchell noticed as the conversation progressed into the morning.

"I was a strange boy," Jean Baptiste went on slowly, "as I am a strange man. My stepfather died when I was twelve, of black lungs from work in the railroad mines in the

188

north, and we moved back to Paris. One day, Mother talked to me in a very serious way."

He smiled, showing his white teeth, and suddenly looked very much a Heron. "Already my short pants were bulged out in front, and since I was on the edge of becoming a man, Mother presented me with long trousers and said, 'There is something that I feel you have known in your heart for a long time.' And then she told me that Faubert was not my father.

"I was only twelve, but fifty inside, and I nodded like an old man. I felt such excitement that I cannot tell you what it was like—except I did not have this same glorious feeling again until Liberation Day."

He coughed to recover his composure, and opened his eyes wide so that the rims could contain the sudden moisture. "When I asked Mother what the name of my father was, she answered that she remembered only that it was the name of a bird, and that, like your namesake, you had flown away in the night."

He made a little, empty gesture which looked rather like a benediction. "That was the only time that she spoke of you, and when I asked her about it later, she just shrugged and said that it was not important to remember things that happened so long ago when she was young and foolish."

"Jean Baptiste," Mitchell said, his voice deeper than usual because he was trying to mask his emotion, "when I know you better, I will tell about those days during World War One, my war, when your mother and I were in love." He sought an analogy. "You remember how it was when you were a *maquis*, a mountain boy, during World War Two, your war?"

"But how did you know that I was a *maquis*?" Jean Baptiste looked as if he had been struck. "Only a few know about that, not even Mother! It was a confidential thing that we did—performing our sabotages and then going back into the hills. Then, too, later, at the end, we went into villages and prepared the townspeople for the German pull-out. . . ."

"Yes, Jean Baptiste, I knew you existed as a person even then." Mitchell related the experience in Plaisance-du-

Gers—of seeing him at the bar in The Golden Apple and noticing the resemblance at once.

"But, Papa," Jean Baptiste exclaimed, "what were you, an American, doing in the province of Gascony during Occupation?"

Mitchell had hardly heard the question. The boy had called him *Papa!* How odd to hear the term come so easily from someone he did not really know. "Again, I will tell you one day. There is so much information to exchange."

Charlotte had luncheon sent upstairs at noon, then went to see a lovely French film, *Beauty and the Devil,* with Gérard Philippe. Then she went shopping at several quaint stores, had dinner sent upstairs at seven, then ate alone in the dining room.

She discovered to her delight that another Philippe film, the romantic *Devil in the Flesh,* with Micheline Presle, which she remembered seeing in Washington in 1949, was being reissued and was playing at a cinema around the corner from the hotel. *Well, Charlotte, my girl,* she thought in a lonely frame of mind, *why not see two Devilish films in one day!*

Seated in the comforting darkness of the theater, she upbraided herself for not having a handkerchief in her purse. She had forgotten that the plot dealt with an older woman in love with a young man. Philippe looked very much like a Marine whom she had been sleeping with at the time that the picture was originally released. Big Jack, as she had called him for obvious reasons, had looked gorgeous in uniform but was quite selfish in bed—the failing of most young men.

She did not often think of those foolish days when she had catered to so many undeserving young men, but the film brought back so many memories that she found she could not keep her eyes dry. At the sad conclusion, when the lovers parted, dissolved in tears again, she stayed in the comforting darkness during a newsreel before venturing out into the lighted street.

She took in great lungfuls of fresh air, and it seemed as if she could smell the sea. This was the first time that she had really cried in years, and the most wonderful part of all was that she was going back to a man whom she truly loved. She felt absolutely marvelous.

When Charlotte quietly let herself into the suite at nine-thirty and went to bed, father and son were still talking.

The sharp clang of the telephone rang, and Mitchell groggily reached for the receiver, dropped it on the bed, and cursed. He had been dreaming about his childhood in Angel, and Belle Trune, of all people. "Yes?" he said into the mouthpiece.

"*Bonjour, monsieur,*" the hotel operator said cheerfully. "The time is eight."

"*Merci.*" He hung up the telephone and lounged back on the pillow. In his dream, he had been pushing Belle Trune on the swings in the playground at the school in Angel, waiting for her to pump higher and higher, so that her dress would spread out in the wind and he could peek at her floursack bloomers.

He smiled fondly at the recollection; they had both been eight or nine years old and innocent. It was only after he had come back from France and started to farm that they had become intimate—and then only on Friday nights at two bucks a throw. Belle had been in love with him and had hinted about marriage, which would have been the mismatch of the century! What would have happened if they had married and had a son?

He was shaken out of his reverie. *A son*? He sat straight up in bed. But he had a son, Jean Baptiste. He had a son who called him Papa! A son, he remembered now, who would shortly be coming for breakfast!

He bounded out of bed, feeling very invigorated, and awakened Charlotte in the process. He kissed her on the cheek. "Get up, my dear, and get beautiful. Your stepson is arriving in half an hour for coffee and a croissant."

"What's he like?" she asked, fluffing out her hair.

"You'll see." He paused. "I think that I'd like him even if he wasn't my son. But he looks more like Luke, rather than me, at the same age."

"Is he coming alone?" Charlotte asked, removing the cold cream from her face with a huck towel.

Mitchell gazed at her in surprise. "I suppose so."

"He's not married?"

"He didn't mention a wife."

She began to comb her hair with quick, brisk strokes. "Is he coming over before work? What does he do?"

Mitchell gave her a long look. "Do you know, I didn't ask him."

"Well, my God, Mitch," she exclaimed dramatically, "you talked all day and half the night! What did you discuss?"

"Oh," he replied vaguely, "you know—things."

"As long as I live, I'll never understand the workings of the male mind." She laughed. "If that had been the first meeting between a mother and a daughter after thirty-four years, you can bet your bottom dollar that they'd know *everything* about each other." She paused. "Did you tell him about Enid and the furniture stores?"

He looked at her sheepishly. "I . . . don't think so. When we knocked off last night, I think I had only gotten up to the place in family history where Luke bought Aunt Letty that pink Caddie that she drove all during the World War Two. . . ."

"I never even knew about that!" she replied, sensing a juicy story. "I was away in Washington all during those years." And, she almost added, sleeping with the golden boys. "How did it come about?"

"The car was the last off the assembly line after war was declared, and Luke, as usual, had put off replacing her old one—you know how tight he is. Anyway, it was a custom paint job for some rich old lady who died before it could be delivered. Luke told Aunt Letty that he'd have it painted, and she asked him what shade it was, and he told her it was Shocking Pink, and she told him that she'd love to drive it around Angel because it was time to shake everyone up a bit—or words to that effect." He paused. "We've got to get crackin', as your dad used to say. Charlotte, don't dawdle," he reprimanded gently. "He'll be here soon." He went into the bathroom and lathered his face with shaving cream.

"But it's *you*, dear, who are dawdling, Mitch!" she called. "By the way, are we going to have breakfast sent up?"

"No, we'll eat downstairs." He paused. "Oh, damn!"

"Cut yourself?"

"No. I just remembered. Françoise works here. It might not be a good idea to eat in the dining room, after all. The French can be funny about such things. I wouldn't want Jean Baptiste to feel uncomfortable. You know how holier-than-thou French waiters can be!"

"Then let's eat at that little sidewalk café down the street. The concierge told me—" She was interrupted by the clang of the telephone bell. "I'll get it," she called above the insistent ringing.

"Hallo?" She paused and her face flushed. "Oh, Jean Baptiste! I am your father's wife, Charlotte. Yes, we'll meet you at L'Auberge for breakfast in five minutes." She hung up slowly, deciding that Jean Baptiste had a most intriguing voice. He also had manners: he had sense enough to use the telephone instead of barging into the suite unannounced.

The Auberge was situated on the incline of a slightly rolling hill, with a sweep of several kilometers of countryside dropping away to the right. Built of round, brown stones, the place had once been a small inn, but now its tiny rooms were devoted to kitchens, pantries, a pastry shop, and two dining halls. The stone terrace was built partly over the hill and extended to the actual sidewalk, where Jean Baptiste was sitting as Mitchell and Charlotte came up the incline.

Dressed in a three-piece blue pinstriped suit and a scarlet faille tie, Jean Baptiste looked, Mitchell thought, as if he had come from a wedding where he had served as best man. "*Bonjour*, Jean Baptiste," he said.

"*Bonjour, Papa!*" They hugged, as Frenchmen do in the tradition of the country.

At the word "Papa," Charlotte almost burst into a peal of laughter. She could scarcely keep a straight face. It seemed a preposterous, if correct, form of address. She had never thought of Mitchell as a domesticated male, and when he introduced her as his new bride she was taken by surprise when Jean Baptiste ignored her outstretched hand and with great bravado resoundingly kissed her on one cheek and then the other.

Charlotte laughed. "I'm beginning to like the Gallic touch!" she said to Mitchell in English, then turned to Jean Baptiste and, trying to make him feel at ease, explained in French: "In my country, women must be content with the pressing of a man's lips on one cheek—if they are fortunate—but in your delightful and romantic country, two kisses are always administered."

Jean Baptiste smiled widely at her quaint expressions. "It is a tradition that is not only coveted but promoted," he said with a twinkle in his eye.

Ah, my boy, Charlotte thought, *you also have wit! The other Heron men are rather dull.* "You must excuse my French," she replied quickly, liking him tremendously. "It is little more than high school—*gymnasium*—and I don't speak it enough not to be laughable."

"Actually, the old way is charming," Jean Baptiste answered with a smile.

"How gallant you are!" Charlotte exclaimed, and then said to Mitchell in English, "You could pick up some pointers from this boy!" She examined the plates of food on other tables. "The brioches look heavenly. That's what I'll have."

When the huge individual puffs of richly browned dough were brought to the table, along with a plate of butter, Charlotte smiled nostalgically at Jean Baptiste. "My mother—who was a country woman—baked all of her life, and the Dice specialty was a delicious light bread called Sally Lunn—"

"Are you sure that you want to tell that particular story?" Mitchell asked apprehensively in English.

"I'll clean it up," she replied, then continued in French. "But on Mama's first visit to France, after oil was discovered on the farm, she fell in love with the brioches. She promptly came home and, using the Sally Lunn recipe, created the distinctly brioche shape. 'It's the same thing really, except that little *knob* on the top!' "

The men laughed hollowly, and Charlotte realized that the story lost something in translation, because her mother had actually used the word "teat" instead of "knob."

They fell to eating then, and when Charlotte had consumed the first brioche, loaded with sweet butter, she asked, "Are you married, Jean Baptiste?"

He turned red at her pointed question, and even in his state of discomfiture was very handsome. "At eighteen, when the blood was hot, I married, but at twenty . . . she ran away with another man. That was thirteen years ago, and since we were never divorced, I am still married." He paused. "Do you know, I do not know how to address you."

Charlotte appeared startled and looked at Mitchell for assistance; obviously, Jean Baptiste was thinking of Françoise. "Why not just call me Charlotte?" she replied simply. She certainly would not be comfortable referred to in any of the various forms of "mother"!

"My only desire is to be respectful," he answered soberly.

"Besides," she answered with a warm smile, "I love the French pronunciation of Charlotte, which is, of course, Char*lot*!" She finished the second brioche, reached for another, thought of her waistline, shook her head, and took a sip of coffee instead. "What do you do, Jean? By the way, may I call you Jean and dispense with the Baptiste?"

He nodded. "Certainly. Now, what was your inquiry?"

"What do you do?"

He looked blankly from Mitchell to Charlotte. "*Pardon?*"

Mitchell smiled. "Your occupation?"

"Oh, I see, Papa, what do I *do*? I work in a varnish factory three days a week."

"My God!" Mtichell exclaimed, and went on in such a rush of words that Charlotte could barely understand him. "That is most interesting! Your grandpapa was a deluxe cabinetmaker, and, very early in this century, designed beautiful furniture that is still prized by the owners. Two or three pieces repose in museums. I myself, in a small way, although I am not a craftsman, have carried on the tradition—but, of course, not on a grand scale."

"But then, Papa," Jean replied incredulously, "even in our occupations we are similarly connected!"

There were tears in Charlotte's eyes. "Oh, Mitch," she said winsomely, "I wish our dear Sam, Born-Before-Sunrise, was sitting at this table."

"Yes," Mitch replied. "Wouldn't he be having a wonderful time?" He spoke to Jean. "We have been speaking about a Cherokee Indian—"

"Cowboys in white hats and red Indians?" Jean asked. "Like in the USA Western movies?"

Mitch smiled indulgently. "No," he said, but he thought of some of the tales the old settlers told about the opening of the Cherokee Strip, when there were indeed cowboys and Indians. "No, this was an Indian who became a famous medical doctor, but he kept what I suppose one could call his 'mystic ways.'"

Mitchell rubbed his eyes. He could see Sam in his white turban ministering to the ill. "You see, Jean, he would have an explanation of how we met after all these years and had so much in common—even similar occupations. He would say that we had tapped into some great force out there in the universe and that we were destined to meet and to become friends."

Charlotte nodded. "Sam always said that nothing was left to chance, that there was a plan to everything."

"I too believe that," Jean replied seriously. "Certainly us coming together in this strange manner . . ."

"What do you do in the factory?" Mitchell asked. "Are you on the line?"

Jean shook his head. "No, Papa, only when I came to the company, before I went to the university to take a course in chemistry." He paused, and smiled proudly. "Now I work in the laboratory. The chemical composition of lacquers and varnishes must be controlled very strictly."

"Yes, I am aware of that very thing. My father had developed a varnish that has yet to be duplicated. It was a formula that he had come across, I think, in a mysterious way, because he never told anyone about the composition. Barrels arrived at a storehouse in Enid every few months, from some place in San Francisco, I think. I never inquired, because in those days I was young and not interested in varnishes, only how blue were the eyes of a girl!"

He paused, his eyes filled with memory. "One thing I do seem to remember was a terrible smell, and it seems to me that it was very sticky and took a long time to dry. . . ."

Jean leaned forward eagerly. "What was the color, Papa?"

"The most beautiful shade of deep brown, lustrous and almost transparent. The varnish gave the furniture . . . depth."

"Ah." Jean took an intake of breath, and his face was like a beacon of light. "I'll wager it was the sap from the Chinese ginkgo tree!" he exclaimed with excitement. "It is not used anymore because it's so difficult to work because of the extended drying time and the gases that accumulate. Since the Communist takeover in China, none can be exported. But it seems to me that the tree also grows in India and Tibet."

Mitchell chuckled. "If this is the secret of those varnishes, no wonder your grandpapa kept everything to himself. In those early days, people in Oklahoma had never seen a Chinaman, and the Orient meant slopy eyes, incense, and opium!"

He stirred and, looking about, discovered that they were the only party left in th café and the waiters were setting the tables for luncheon. "Time has gotten away from us again," he said to Jean, and then turned to Charlotte. "You see how it is? There is so much to say."

"Well," Charlotte put in brightly in English, "I'd say that one way to solve the current problem would be to invite Jean to come to Enid and see everything for himself!"

Mitchell gave her a long look. "Do you *know* what you're saying?"

"Yes, I do." Her voice was firm.

"We shall see," he said, "we shall see."

Mitchell and Charlotte had flown to Washington after their flight from Paris, London, and New York, and cashed in the airline tickets to Oklahoma City that Pierre had provided. "It distresses me," he said, "that the organization isn't paying for the entire trip, but we should drop off for a few days at the Heron Connecticut Avenue house so you can see some of your old friends."

"I can do that in twenty-four hours," she quipped, "but I do think it's a good idea for us to become Americanized again after going through what we did in Europe, don't you?"

He nodded. It seemed so long ago that they had taken the châteaux motorbus tour, but not enough time had elasped that the trip had taken on an air of romanticism.

At National Airport in Washington, he had just given the baggage checks to a Sky Cap and told him to bring the luggage to the sidewalk entrance, when he glimpsed a familiar figure in the lobby, which was joined by another familiar figure.

"Oh, look, Mitch, there's that nice Mrs. Parsons from Riverside, California. Fancy meeting her here! Let's go say hello." Before he could stop her, Charlotte had rushed over to the woman and cried, "We meet again, what a nice surprise!"

The dumpy Mrs. Parsons, *née* Helena Sharp, with every whiskey brown hair in place, smiled and cooed and allowed herself to be patted and kissed and showed none of the surprise that she also must have been feeling. She was indeed a cool operator.

Mitchell shook her hand, his eyes full of amusement. "How nice to see you again, Mrs. P." And to test her response, he looked about quizzically, before he asked, "Where is Tibbetts?"

She squinted up at him, every inch the tweedy busybody that she was impersonating, and deftly removed a handkerchief from her purse and made little bird noises as she dabbed her nose. "His little heart just gave out." she said, then added as an afterthought, "He's buried in San Sebastian." She turned to her companion, H.L. Leary. "I'd like you to meet my husband, Mr. Parsons."

As they shook hands, Mitchell saw that Leary had aged; he had probably taken Pierre Darlan's death very badly. "Well," Mrs. Parsons was saying, "we must be going." She smiled and kissed Charlotte on the cheek and shook hands with Mitchell. "As they say in French," she said airily, "*au revoir*." Leary said something about how nice it was to have met them, and then they disappeared in the crowded lobby.

Mitchell felt a pang of regret. Helena Sharp was off on another adventure, while he had played out his last mission. He would go home to the Heron Furniture Company in Enid, Oklahoma, but he would never quite be the same man again.

They met the Sky Cap, who had found a taxi, and after giving the Connecticut Avenue address they lounged comfortably in the back seat. As the encounter with Leary faded from his mind, Mitchell became more content with the knowledge that never again would he be on the sort of dangerous journey that Mrs. Parsons was embarking upon. He knew Leary well enough to know that he would not be accompanying her to the plane if he were not fearful for her safety.

He turned to Charlotte, appreciating her presence in the cab. "You know, dear, it's an extraordinary thing, but I'm more at home with you on this last leg of the journey than ever before." He pressed her hand. "With what we've endured lately, I've found that you're not put together with flour-and-water paste."

"What lovely compliments, dear." She kissed his cheek. "I might very well say the same thing! I married the one man that I thought I knew. After all, Mitch, we used to make mudpies together when we were four. But during the last few months I've discovered that you are a completely different person."

"I hope I've not disappointed you."

"*Au contraire!*" She laughed. "My God, Mitch, it's as difficult to get away from speaking French as it was becoming acccustomed to it!" She paused. "I've got to watch myself, because I hate people who scatter their conversations with foreign phrases. I think it's pretentious."

"*Oui, ma chérie.*"

She broke into a peal of laughter. "Do you know, my new husband is much more fun than the old one?"

"You know all about me now—all of the stories have come together."

As the taxi pulled into the long drive that led by the huge house set back in an acre of lawn, two men in business suits held up their hands, blocking the passage. The cabby immediately pulled over to the curb.

"What's the problem, driver?" Mitch asked, concerned.

"It's a limousine, sir, and those look like bodyguards. Are you sure this is the right address?"

Mitchell laughed. "I'm certain."

At that moment, three black cars, two Chevrolets with a Caddie limousine in between, sped down the drive, and Charlotte glimpsed a pink hat. "Oh," she cried, "it's Mamie Eisenhower."

The cabby turned to look at his passengers before continuing up the drive, and Mitchell said with great amusement, "No, driver, we aren't anyone important!" He winked at Charlotte. "In fact, we're the new maid and butler."

The cabby, who had been driving in Washington too long to be fooled, shot back, "In that case, I'll drop you at the service entrance." But he stopped at the front portico.

Letty, wearing a blue flowered-silk dress, was still waving a lace handkerchief after the disappearing limousine. And when she recognized the occupants of the taxi, her face broke into smiles.

"Well," she cried, "if this isn't a nice surprise!" She hugged and kissed them both and told the butler to pay off the cab and bring the luggage up to the Bluebird Room.

"The Bluebird Room?" Charlotte asked, squeezing Letty's hand.

"Formerly Bosley's study," she replied nostalgically, "and it was once George Story's bedroom, too, so now it's a guest suite in red, white, and blue chintz with flying birds." She paused. "I must say you're both looking well."

"Thank you, Aunt Letty," Mitchell said. "If we had known you were in residence—"

"In residence?" Letty laughed. "That sounds like the queen. Strangely enough, I hadn't planned to come back to Washington ever again." She waved her finger at them.

"That's another thing that I've learned, and that is *never* to say never, because surely you'll do exactly what you said that you'd never do!

"Now, where was I? Oh, yes, well since I've turned Republican again—another point of what I was just saying—Mamie Eisenhower has talked me into heading a program to help the elderly, and Luke, bless him, was nice enough to lend me the *Blue Heron* to make traveling easier. That's the only thing about growing older that I don't like; it's more difficult to get from place to place." Her eyes lighted up. "When are you two going back to Enid?"

"On Thursday, probably," Mitchell said, "but if more people are coming in on you, we can leave earlier."

"Oh, land sakes, no," Letty replied airily, "but I just thought you might like to keep me company in the blue bird." She glanced at him. "It would save commercial air fare."

"Do you know I've never been in it?" Mitchell grinned.

"Well, you're the only member of the family who hasn't, then. What say?"

"Oh, Mitch, let's do it!" Charlotte exclaimed.

"I'm all for it."

Letty took his arm, and winked at Charlotte. "Let's sit outside a while in the summerhouse and enjoy the good weather."

"Are you warm enough, Aunt Letty? Would you like a shawl?" he asked politely.

"My dear Mitch," she exclaimed, raising her thin eyebrows, "I may look like a fragile old lady, which I am, but I have not been cold this afternoon, I am not cold now, nor do I expect to get cold, and if I did I would certainly not wear a shawl!"

He laughed and squeezed her arm. "Have I told you lately that I love you?"

She grinned crookedly. "No, but I expect to be told more often now that you're back from traipsing all over Europe!"

When they reached the Victorian summerhouse, she bade them sit under the shade of the crisscrossed arbor hung with grapevines, then pushed the buzzer under the table. "I assume that you'd like refreshments?"

"Some cognac, please," Mitch requested.

Letty glanced at him sideways. "You may have what you like, but Charlotte and I will have tea." She gave the order to the butler and leaned forward on the table. "The funny thing is, it never occurs to me to have tea at four o'clock in Angel."

She frowned. "But Washington has always affected me very strangely. Here, I seem to be someone else. Mamie and I were talking about this very thing this afternoon. She and the General are home bodies in Gettysburg, and yet when they're on display, there's a formality that's quite awesome. . . . The Trumans are very informal in Independence, and will be again if he loses the election, which I think he will! But, I have a feeling the Hoovers ran a tight ship in Stanford."

The butler brought the tea service and Mitchell's Cognac, and when Letty asked Charlotte to preside, she looked over the teapot. "Do you know, Aunt Letty, this is the first time I've poured since that time at Evalyn Walsh McLean's when I gave Alice Roosevelt Longworth a leaky cup and spoiled her dress, remember?"

"I wasn't there, but it was all over town that, with your dad being a Republican senator and all, you were getting back at the Roosevelts." Letty smiled crookedly. "You weren't, were you?"

Charlotte shook her head. "Alice has always been a Republican, so it wasn't that, but it was the most embarrassing moment of my life, and Alice, as you know, has a sharp tongue. I remember she said something to the effect that if I stayed out of cocktail bars and paid attention to the finer things in life, I wouldn't be so gauche. And she reminded me that I had ruined her red Chinese silk dress."

"What did you say to that, dear?" Mitchell asked roguishly.

"I reminded her that if the dress was *real* Chinese silk, it would launder beautifully! Aunt Letty, what were the White House Roosevelts like?"

Letty pursed her lips in remembrance. "Bosley and I were invited to a picnic at Val-Kill Cottage once at Hyde Park during the war, and were served hot dogs and finger food on paper plates. Lord knows Eleanor was friendly enough, and even showed us the big house, but throughout it all—well, Charlotte, it was kind of what your mother would have called 'hoity-toity.' "

Letty took a sip of tea. "But that might have been only our reactions. People do react to opposite emotions. Don't you find that you're different people in different surroundings?"

Mitchell exchanged glances with Charlotte. "That's very true," he agreed, and then because the day was so pleasant, and the air was so warm, and the summerhouse held all the charm of another century, he went on very quietly, "Aunt Letty, Charlotte and I had planned to invite you for dinner one evening during the week per month we spend in Angel, and butter you up for a private discussion.

"But, since we've been talking about how the environment changes our lives, I think the present time is very apropos. Do you agree, Charlotte?" When she nodded, he went on gently, "I've just made a very important discovery. But before I tell you about that, I must go back a very long way—to World War One, in fact. . . ."

Surprisingly, he did not find it difficult to tell this sympathetic woman about his affair with Françoise. Indeed, it seemed that he was speaking about two other people that he had known long ago. "Then," he continued gently, "the years pass, as they do in the movies, with the pages of a calendar falling off a wall, until it's nineteen-fifty-two and Charlotte and I are enjoying ourselves in this lovely hotel in Monte Carlo, when very early one morning I see this charlady. . . ."

Letty looked at him tenderly. "It was Françoise, wasn't it?"

"Yes. It was the most peculiar thing, Aunt Letty. I didn't feel anything but compassion. And I was abashed to see her like that, but strangely enough, she wasn't at all embarrassed."

The most difficult aspect of this so-called confession, he had realized from the beginning, was that he could not talk about that mission in France during the war. He could not reveal that he had suspected that Jean was either Luke's or his son when he had first glimpsed his Heron profile at The Golden Apple in Plaisance-du-Gers.

Mitchell went on slowly. "So after Françoise and I conversed, I decided to leave her some money, and as I waited for her to come out the side entrance of the hotel that morning, there was a young man waiting for her. . . ."

Letty looked at him with an expression that he had never seen before on her face, compassionate and yet shrewd. "Françoise had a baby, Mitch, and this young man was your son—am I right?"

He nodded. "Oh, Aunt Letty, I wish you could meet him! He's a great guy."

"Well," she replied lightly, "he is a Heron, isn't he? Seriously, though, Mitch, of course, he must come to this country. There's no question about it!"

"That's what I've been telling him," Charlotte rejoined, "but he's still not convinced."

Mitchell hunched his shoulders. "I'm thinking about what a trip of this sort would do to him. He doesn't speak English, and his views are, naturally, Gallic. All he knows of Americans are the tourists, which are hardly typical. I don't think it's fair, confronting the boy with hordes of people he doesn't know. We're a strange lot, Aunt Letty."

She set the fragile teacup down with a sort of finality. "There are several things that you must get straight, Mitch. For one thing, stop calling Jean a boy; he's a grown-up man of thirty-three. Secondly, he can always learn English. With all of the problems that our family has encountered over the years, and are still encountering, for that matter, no one can certainly condemn you for having a son out of wedlock in nineteen-nineteen!"

"Then you think that I should bring him over?"

"Not *bring* him, Mitch; he's not a child. *Invite* him. Have you considered the possibility that he may be perfectly happy over there and may want no part of your life? *You must never assume anything*—that's a Heron weakness, if I say so myself." She dabbed at her nose with a lavender-smelling handkerchief. "Did you perchance tell him of your connection with the Heron Oil Company?"

Mitchell thought a moment before replying, "No, there

was so much personal material to cover on both sides that I didn't get around to speaking much about relatives."

Letty smiled. "Good! Then he knows nothing of the family holdings. Now, the factory where he works must have holidays. Send him a round-trip air ticket, pick him up in Oklahoma City, and drive him to Angel to the homestead, where I will make him feel part of the family."

"Thank you, Aunt Letty, for your offer of hospitality," Mitchell replied softly, "but naturally I'll want him to stay with Charlotte and myself in Enid."

Letty held up a finger. "Of course, in due time, but not for the first few days. Give him time to see how simply we live in a small town." She dabbed at her nose with the handkerchief. "You must not spoil this man, Mitch. Jean has lived thirty-three years in comparative poverty, because, very frankly, you did not marry his mother, and who knows, even if you had, could you have supported them selling figurines from door to door? Be realistic. There is no point letting him know that there is wealth connected with the Heron name."

Mitchell stared at an Aunt Letty that he had never known before, and was amused. "After all this time, you are finally admitting that we are not one of the ten neediest families?"

She laughed self-consciously. "Don't make fun of me, Mitch. I was brought up to know the value of a dollar. And"—she looked kindly at Charlotte—"as your mother would say, we never lived 'high on the hog.' "

"Yes," Charlotte agreed, "but remember, my parents were not educated, and they spent a lot of money unwisely. And they were also prejudiced people. Remember, I still have seven years before I will inherit the money I should have had when Daddy died. If I had a fatal heart attack tomorrow, the Angel library would get the whole kit and kaboodle. There's such a thing as being too tight-fisted, and if Mitch wants to help Jean, I think he should."

"I agree," Letty put in quickly. "There's no quarrel with that, only I don't think it fair to introduce him too quickly to a way of living that he knows nothing about. Remember what happened to Luke Three, and how money turned his head? It took a long time for him to come to his senses. We don't want Jean to become a playboy."

"But that's romanticizing the whole story, Aunt Letty!" Mitch exclaimed.

"Perhaps I'm not using the right new slang, but you know what I mean, Mitchell Heron! Now," she continued crisply, "it's getting rather chilly. Charlotte dear, would you fetch my shawl?"

13

The Genius

William worked feverishly over the motion-picture score.

He asked Joe, the projectionist, to run the ending title again, made another calculation on the stopwatch, and threw his pencil in the air. "Whoopee!" he shouted, and waved to the porthole in the rear of the room. "You can go home, Joe," he called happily. "It's finished!"

He poured a cupful of coffee from the Thermos that Louisa had brought from the commissary earlier, lighted a cigarette, and puffed amateurishly. He had just taken up smoking, which he found relaxing between frantic sessions bent over the music sheets.

He hoped that Nicol and Harry would like his concept for the picture. They had stopped by the little studio only twice in the last six weeks, and then only to shake his hand and welcome him belatedly to the "team." Everything with those two, he reflected was "teamwork."

All of the music for the film had been completed; only the jukebox number remained to be written, and he had purposely waited until the score was completed so that his mind would be freer.

Finally he came up with a loud, jazzy instrumental piece to replace the sentimental song that had been recorded by the full orchestra in London. The film was such a documentary of basic human emotion, photographed in sharp black-and-white, that the only time the characters escaped the drabness of the slum was Lisa's twentieth birthday, celebrated at the employees' club at the mill where Colin worked.

The jazzy piece would be very effective, he thought, because the next scene took place outside of the club, where Colin kissed Lisa for the first time. He felt there should be no music at all, only their heartbeats becoming louder and louder, continuing into the next scene, which took place in the bedroom, and which, Nicol had indicated, would have to be considerably cut because of censorship problems.

Nicol and Harry ambled out of William Nestor's bungalow after hearing him play the themes on the piano and walked toward the Prop Department in silence. At last Nicol clicked his tongue and said, "I think we should give the boy his head. Since Universal doesn't do this kind of picture, no one understands what we're up against. The front office couldn't care less about a story that takes place in a Liverpool slum, and frankly, I don't either, but it's got good performances, even if the characters don't wear makeup, and it's certainly real, and I like the idea that the picture's not overloaded with a lot of music. He uses it sparingly. I like the themes. What do you think?"

Harry shrugged his shoulders and lighted a cigar. "I'm with you, Nicol. This is the kind of little picture that they used to bring into the Little Carnegie theater in New york and play for six months, building word-of-mouth. It won't do for general release, and it shouldn't be paired with a big color film. Sneak it around, open it in a few selected theaters, and see what happens.

"It didn't cost anything to acquire—it was among a package some executive got talked into purchasing one dark, drunken night—so what have we got to lose? William's music—or rather lack of it—is just fine. I think it gives importance to the picture. And you know something else?"

"Don't keep me in suspense!" Harry replied dryly.

"It's the first time that a cat has its own theme music!"

William finished the orchestrations early one morning, after having worked all night, and when the copier brought them in a week later, a recording date was set up for a Monday morning.

Louisa brought him to the studio as usual, and when she wanted to stay, he shook his head. "This is the first time that I've conducted, outside of playing around at a few rehearsals with Mr. Story's band, and I've got to concentrate on what I'm doing. The timing is going to be a bitch!"

He cupped her chin with his hand and said lightly, "And I don't need the Flame of Willawa around to take my mind off my work."

The members of the studio orchestra were taking their places as William came onto the recording sound stage. He tested his earphones and glanced up at the booth where the engineers plied their trade. He nodded and mouthed, "Good morning."

When the members of the orchestra were seated, he tapped the podium with his baton. "Good morning, ladies and gentlemen," he said with a shy smile. "I'm certain that all of you remember that morning several months ago, when I visited this studio for the first time and got so carried away by the music I stood up and shouted, 'Bravo, bravo,' and spoiled the recording."

There was a deep silence, and it occurred to him that they did not know whether to laugh or not, so he grinned from ear to ear and shouted, "Well, I'm back!"

They laughed, and he knew he was home free. "I ask you to be patient with me," he said. "You're all fabulous musicians with far more experience than I have, and you've been through many recording sessions. I haven't. I haven't written very much music, as you see, so it's not going to take two weeks to fit the music to the picture. This isn't a long job for all of you, and it's a little picture, but I expect all of you to do a big job." He paused. "Now, let's rehearse a bit. There's a tricky run by the oboe. . . ."

Nicol and Harry stood beside a sky drop at the side of the stage and listened for a few moments; then they left quickly before the red light flashed on indicating that the recording session had started. "You've got to hand it to the kid," Nicol said. "Those musicians will play their hearts out for him. How could they resist an approach like that?"

"Yeah," Harry replied, and grinned. "Don't it just break you up?"

"Don't be a smartass. You know what I mean—he didn't go in there and crack a whip like some of the big New York composers do and make a spectacle of himself."

"No." Harry sighed. "He used the Okie approach, humble pie."

"And what would you know about humble pie?"

Harry laughed. "Not much, but I was born in Oklahoma City!"

The Fox Pomona Theater, a venerable, ornate movie palace that had featured vaudeville in the late 1920s, was chosen for the first unpublicized showing of *Colins Girl*, and the front and side marquee featured SNEAK PREVIEW in large letters.

Just before the end of the current feature, *Meet Danny Wilson*, starring Frank Sinatra and Shelley Winters, William Nestor and Louisa Tarbell joined the studio brass in a roped-off section of the old loge section of the plush old theater located thirty miles east of Los Angeles.

In the lobby, bored publicity men, having sat through the film once at the studio, were cooling their heels, having set up a cardboard station with preview cards and pencils, in order that the audience could conveniently make their feelings known after the picture was over. The studio limousines were lined up by the side entrance, their drivers having already started a crap game by the old stage door.

Immediately after the end title of *Meet Danny Wilson* had faded from the screen, the manager's voice boomed through the loudspeakers. "Ladies and gentlemen, the Fox Pomona Theatre is proud to present our preview attraction."

But when the title *Colin's Girl* flashed on the screen, there was a disappointed murmur from the audience. A man in a side row called out, "Another Limey stinker!" The audience laughed, and William hunched down in his seat.

Nicol Herbert turned to Harry Leinsinger and muttered, "This is the wrong audience for the film! What in the hell did they expect, C. B. De Mille's *The Greatest Show on Earth*?"

The crowd was restless throughout the main titles underscored by William's plaintive oboe solo. But by the time that the opening establishing shot faded in, of the ominous factory belching smoke against a white sky, the audience had quieted somewhat. And when the whistle blew and hundreds of exhausted workers swarmed out of the building, there was comparative silence: Mexicans in the theater knew all about factories.

William grew more confident as the film was unspooled to increasing attention. Nichol Herbert, who held the "fader box" on his lap, from which the sound could be regulated, actually had to turn the volume down because there was no noise in the auditorium. Harry Leinsinger noted that no one had walked out of the theater, nor had anyone coughed in the last half hour. "Jesus, Nicol," he whispered, "they actually like it!"

Louisa was spellbound. The film was harsh and uncompromising, and so real she could sense the cold as Lisa shivered under her shabby cloth coat, and feel the cinders falling, covering everyone with black snow.

When the shy Colin, photographed from the unusual vantage point of the cat on the hearth, finally took Lisa in his arms, and the tabby turned to the camera and licked his paws, Louisa sighed. It was a lovely moment, made memorable, she thought, because of the lack of music; there was nothing to intrude upon the tender emotions that were being displayed on the screen.

What was happening to Colin and Lisa was *real*, and when William brought in a variation of the cat's theme to end the shot, providing a logical transition into the next scene, the audience chuckled appreciatively. Only her Billy Boy would think of using a French horn for the cat's theme!

A wave of apprehension ran through the audience during the employees' social club scene, and the tension built as Colin pushed the button on the jukebox and seemed as surprised as the audience when the jazz music burst forth. How disturbing it was to break the mood that Colin was trying to create with Lisa, but how like this awkward, bumbling boy to hit the wrong button!

William knew in that moment that his instincts about the

scene were right, but he was not happy with the music, which did not seem to hit the right emotional plane.

At the end of the film, when Lisa prays over Colin's grave, with the factory workers gathered in front of the moldy old seventeenth-century tombstones scattered around the moss-covered church, sniffles could be heard throughout the audience.

And the last shot of the bereft, forgotten tabby, looking up expectantly at the sky—with the French horn theme fading gently away, until all that could be heard was the wind whistling through the bare branches of the trees— brought a simultaneous clap of thunder from the audience. The applause continued vociferously through the silent ending titles, and when the lights came up in the auditorium, both William and Louisa were crying.

An hour later, Nicol Herbert, Harry Leinsinger, and the publicity men gathered in the manager's office and riffled through the stacks of preview cards. "Listen to this one, boys," Nicol read. " 'Deserves an Academy Award.' "

"How about this?" Harry laughed. " 'Best Limey picture since *Hamlet*.' We know who wrote that."

" 'More pictures should have this kind of music,' " Nicol read from the last card. "Christ, don't let Nestor read that— or that shrew who manages him—or he'll expect more for the next picture." He glanced at the theater manager. "Got the tally yet?"

The man nodded. "Two hundred and seventy-five 'excellent,' a hundred and eighty-four 'good,' forty 'fair.' Five complained that they couldn't understand the dialogue, which isn't bad at all. We always get complaints on the foreign pictures."

The manager coughed. "By the way, a hundred and four didn't like the title." He picked up a card he had placed aside and handed it to Nicol. "Read this!"

Nicol glanced at the comment, leaned back in his chair, and laughed, "Listen: 'Loved the picture, hated the title. I'm English and know how to pronounce Colin correctly, but I bet Americans will call it COLON!' I think she's right. We'll have to come up with a new title." He lighted a long cigar. "But that's minor. I can't wait for the top brass to see these cards."

"Why wait?" Harry asked impatiently, "I'm going to call Hedda Hopper right now."

The publicity man looked at his watch, "She put tomorrow's column to bed hours ago."

"Well, *she's* not in bed!" retorted Harry. "You know how she likes to get a scoop ahead of Louella."

The publicity man raised his eyebrows. "I know we're all excited about the response tonight," he said dryly, "but I honestly feel that this isn't going to be the biggest news ever to hit Hollywood."

"Maybe not," Nicol replied softly, "but it's going to rock the studio. This little programmer that we picked up for peanuts in a big package of films, is going to be the big 'sleeper hit' of the year or my name isn't Nicol Herbert!" And he wondered why everyone laughed so loudly, until he remembered that his father's name was Cohen.

"Someone's on the wire from Kansas City," Phoebe called from the tiny reception room, "but the line is very bad. Shall I have him call back?"

"No, I'll take it." Having experience with country telephone lines that were frequently in various states of disorder, William was accustomed to garbled conversation. He picked up the telephone. "Hello, Mr. Story."

"How did you know it was me?" Clement's voice sounded as if he were in South Africa.

William laughed. "You're the only person I know in Kansas City except a reporter on the *Star*, and I doubt that he'd be calling me. How are you, sir?"

"When are you going to cut the 'Mr.' and 'sir' crap, Billy?" Knowing he wouldn't get an answer to his question, Clement went on quickly. "So the studio has given you a personal secretary, something I never had when I was working there." His voice was filled with excitement. "Congratulations."

"Pardon?"

"Oh, on the secretary too, of course, but what I meant was: congratulations on the beautiful review of *Colin's Girl* in *Weekly Variety*, although the title's a dog. And don't tell me that you don't read the trade papers? It was a ritual when I was in Los Angeles. I always read *The Hollywood Reporter* and *Daily Variety* on the john every morning. If a picture I'd made got a bad notice, I'd be constipated for days!"

William laughed, then paused before he went on in a tightly controlled voice, "I was pleased that the critics liked my contribution to the picture, but I didn't really have that much to do with it, Mr. Story. After all, it was completely finished when I looked at it."

"As usual, you're too modest. I understand the original score was an atrocity by Sir Hilary Metcalf."

"There was nothing really wrong with the score, sir; it was just that it didn't fit the subject matter. Actually, Sir Hilary did me the greatest favor, because I don't think I'd have known exactly what the film needed if I hadn't heard his full-blown work first. Then I knew what *not* to do."

"I see your point," Clement answered soberly, thinking that William was becoming more mature about the way that he looked at life. "How's Louisa?"

"Fine, enjoying Hollywood. How's Mrs. Story?"

"Enjoying Kansas City." He paused. "I was wondering when you'll have some free time? I'm going to be doing the Ed Sullivan show again, and I want a special arrangement of 'High Noon.' "

William was stunned. "But . . . sir," he stammered, "that's Tex Ritter's song."

"It's not his song," Clement defended. "Ned Washington wrote the lyrics, and Dmitri Tiomkin wrote the music."

"I know that," William replied icily, "but Mr. Ritter's voice was used on the movie soundtrack."

"Of course"—Clement was defensive—"but that doesn't mean that no one else can sing it, Billy Boy!"

William swallowed hard. "How would you like it, Mr. Story, if Tex Ritter recorded his version of 'The Cowboy Waltz'?"

"Well"—Clement laughed—"he doesn't have the right voice for it, for one thing."

William was very angry. "It's a matter of principle as

well as artistry, Mr. Story. Do you think you have the right voice for 'High Noon'?"

There was a long pause before Clement answered. "You mean you won't do the arrangement for me, is that it?"

Tears filled William's eyes. The last thing in the world he wanted to do was quarrel with his mentor. Before he could open his mouth to speak, the line went dead. He hung up slowly and then went to the window that overlooked the lot.

"Did your call come through okay, Mr. Nestor?" Phoebe asked.

"No," he replied. "There was trouble on the line."

"What was that all about?" Sarah asked, coming in from the bedroom, drying her nails in the air.

"Nothing."

"Don't you dare tell me 'Nothing,' Clement Story!" she exclaimed. "Your face looks as black as an Oklahoma tornado."

"I just asked someone for a favor, that's all."

"Which, I take it, was refused?"

"That goddam snot-nosed kid would still be playing for choir groups in Willawa if it wasn't for me!"

She looked at him, wide-eyed. "You mean Billy Nestor turned you down? That's strange; you're his idol." She touched her thumbnail to her tongue, found it was still wet from the polish, and began to wave her arms again. "He must have got a swelled head out there in Hollywood. He's always been solicitous and sweet."

"Well, the little bastard isn't solicitous and sweet now!" Clement fumed.

"What did you want him to do?" Sarah asked, finding a smudge on her right forefinger.

"Max called, and Ed Sullivan has booked me again. I want a new arrangement for 'High Noon,' that's all."

"But that's Tex's song!"

"Oh, Christ, not you too, Sarah!"

"But Clem, you can't go on television singing a song that's closely identified with a competitor."

He glared at her. "Tex and I have never been competitors in our entire lives. I do not sing Western tunes."

She placed her hands on her hips. "Oh, no—well, the two songs that are connected with your voice are 'The Cowboy Waltz' and 'The Old Chisholm Trail,' and you can hardly get more Western than that."

"Why in the hell is everyone against me all of a sudden?" He picked up his coat and stamped out of the room. When he came back four hours later, his step was unsteady and his breath smelled of scotch whiskey. Sarah turned her face to the wall and pretended to be asleep.

It seemed to take hours for him to undress and climb into bed, and he fell against furniture twice. She felt guilty, because on those few occasions during their long marriage when he had drunk too much, she had always looked after him.

Always before, his intoxication had resulted quite accidentally, at a party where fresh drinks were constantly being pressed into his hand, or when he had drunk alcohol on an empty stomach. He was always remorseful afterward, and had always joked that he really could not drink because of his "Indian blood."

But tonight, willfully and spitefully, he had purposely set out on a drinking spree, and under those conditions she could not help him get undressed and into bed. If he was going to play the Bad Boy, she would not encourage him by playing the Earth Mother.

Louisa placed a collect call to Max Rabinovich at the MCA office in Chicago. "He's on another line," a hurried voice said, "but I'll find out if he'll accept your call. What did you say your name was?"

Louisa tapped her foot on the tiled breakfast-room floor. "This is Louisa Tarbell, manager for William Nestor."

"Where is this call originating from?" the voice asked plaintively.

Louisa, who had never forgotten her twelve years in the schoolroom, almost blurted, "Young lady, never end your sentences with prepositions," but she held herself back and said, "Hollywood, California, United States of America."

Louisa's sarcasm was lost on the girl, who left her tapping her foot for exactly two minutes by the kitchen clock. "Hello, Lou." Max's abrasive voice came on the line. "I don't appreciate collect calls. Now, I'm busy. What's up?"

She quelled her anger at being dressed down, replied calmly, "As you may know, Max, William's at Universal, but I'm not happy about what's been going on moneywise."

"I read the trades, Lou," Max put in dryly. "Billy Boy has finished *Colin's Girl*, and the studio thinks its gonna be a hit, right? Don't try to tell me my business. I have clients at the studio, you know."

"Well, yes. . . ."

"What you may not know is, as of ten o'clock last night, the title's been changed to *Suspension in Time*." He paused, and she knew that he was lighting a Havana.

"But that's the second title change, Max! It's already been shown to reviewers as *Colin's Girl*. Isn't that confusing?"

"No, dear lady, the studio just sends out telegrams giving the critics the change of title. This happens all the time."

"But what about the general public?"

"There hasn't been any publicity yet, so that's no problem. Now, what's yours?"

Rebuffed, she adopted a more gentle tone. "William did the picture for the same money as Corny brought him in to do *Maidie Loves Norman*."

"So, now that they think the picture may be up for Academy nominations, they want to sign him to a term contract, right?"

"Yes, and I'm a manager, not an agent."

"So . . ."

Her toe stopped tapping, and she swallowed painfully. He was making it very difficult for her. "Max, you're the best agent I know, and—"

"Probably the *only* agent you know!"

She reddened with anger. He was one of the most exasperating men she had ever met, and although they did not really get along, they both had ignored the personality conflict because of William and had years ago drawn a tacit truce. If she had to grovel, she would grovel. "Would you take on William as a client?"

Max was puffing so swiftly on the cigar that she could hear him breathing hard. "I'll let you know. It's not that I don't like the kid, or I don't think he's talented, but we're dealing with protocol of the highest order. I've represented Clem for twenty-five years, and I don't want a conflict of interest. If he tells me to go ahead, I'll call you back—collect."

He hung up, convinced more than ever that women in the executive side of show business were a pain in the ass. Because of their sex, they had to be mealy-mouthed and ladylike while negotiating contracts, and couldn't use the sort of language that usually brought results. He shouted for his secretary to place a call to Clement Story in Kansas City.

When the call came through, the voice was fuzzy. "Are you sick, Clem? You sound awful."

"No, I'm fine."

Max laughed. "Thank God. If I didn't know you better, I'd say you've been drinking. Anyway, something interesting has come up, and before I take any action at all, I need your thoughts."

"Well, this is a . . . switch, Max," Clement replied, his voice thick. "Do you remember when you asked . . . my advice last? It was in nineteen-thirty-three, when you asked me what kind of . . . a wife I thought Rachel would make."

"Yeah," Max replied, "and you told me it would be the biggest mistake of my life if I didn't marry her. Well, you were right." He paused. "Why I called is this: William Nestor's picture is apparently going to take off like *Gangbusters*."

"I'm not surprised," Clement answered grudgingly. "I saw a preview here in K.C. It's dynamite. The kid has really come up with an inventive piece of work—as usual."

"The studio wants to put him under contract."

"I'm not surprised. It'll be a slow death, though." Clement cleared his throat and sounded more lucid.

"I'm not so sure, Clem; if he gets a nomination, they won't dare give him crap. And Louisa told me that he likes the freedom of the medium, thinks he's found his niche, and all that crap." He puffed his cigar for a moment. "You wouldn't mind, then, if I handled him?"

There was a long pause, and then Clement cleared his throat again. "No, I'm the guy that discovered the kid, remember? Go ahead, take him on. I just don't understand why you felt my permission was needed, that's all."

"Well, after all, Clem," Max answered defensively, "you spent a lot of money educating him, and he was supposed to go to work for you full time."

"Yeah, that's true, but I knew all along that I couldn't keep him—and didn't want to—if he had real talent. I was happy to do what I could for a mixed-blood Cherokee. He's more than paid me back by writing 'The Cowboy Waltz.' We're not speaking at the moment, but that doesn't make any difference."

"May I ask why, or is it personal?"

"Hell no, it's not personal!" Clement said angrily. "The little bastard won't do a new arrangement of 'High Noon' for me for Ed Sullivan's *Toast of the Town* show, because he doesn't think—now get this—that I should follow Tex Ritter's version!"

There was a pause; then Max replied quietly, "He's right, you know. You can't sing his song on a national TV show! What are you trying to prove?"

"Nothing. I just want to sing the song, that's all!"

"If that's it, then get it out of your system by including it in your regular repertoire, don't slap the man's face in public."

"Why in hell is everyone against me on this?" Clement exclaimed angrily. "I'm going to do the number, and that's that!"

"Have you spoken to Sullivan about this?"

"No, the booking is several weeks away. He'll be on the horn soon. He's always been flexible."

There was a long sigh at the other end of the line. Max hung up, and Clement was left holding a dead line.

"Get me Ed Sullivan on the line," Max shouted to his secretary, "but first call Nicol Herbert at the studio."

He snubbed out his cigar and when his intercom buzzed, picked up the telephone again. "Nicol, Max Rabinovich, and I just wanted you to know that I'm representing William Nestor."

"Oh, Christ," Nicol muttered.

"What was that?"

"Nothing."

"I understand from Lou that you want him under wraps?"

"Well—we have been thinking about giving him a break . . ."

Max laughed. "*You* giving *him* a break? Who's kidding who? If he gets nominated, he can write his own ticket. Every studio in town will be after him, so it behooves you to work out a contract now. I'm amenable, he's amenable."

"We're thinking about a straight seven-year pact—"

"Look," Max said, cradling the receiver against his ear and shoulder so that he could have his hands free to remove the wrapper from a Havana. "You screwed the kid once with the money on *Maidie Loves Norman*, which was supposed to be one song, and he agreed to do both a song and the score for *Suspension in Time*."

"How'd you hear about the title change? It was just decided last night."

"I've got spies. Want me to tell you what you had for dinner last night and the name of the waiter? Anyway, you can forget about a seven-year pact. I want a three-picture deal, each assignment to follow the next by only six weeks, so that the kid can get a little rest between jobs but not really goof off. The pictures must be quality—A product, no B's—strictly star vehicles, and after you come up with some property ideas, then we'll talk money."

"But . . ." Nicol stammered, "what if he doesn't get a nomination?"

"You're not going to be stuck with a nonentity; that kid has talent up his ass. Sooner or later he'll not only get a nomination, but an Oscar, too."

"I don't know." Nicol replied hesitantly, beginning to perspire. "Let me talk it over with the brass and the Legal Department. . . ."

"Let me know. I'll give you twenty-four hours."

"Forty-eight?"

"No. Do you want me to go to Metro or Warner's?"

"All right. Twenty-four hours, then. And Max?"

"What?"

"You're a tough son-of-a-bitch!"

"But lovable." Max hung up, then called Louisa Tarbell to tell her that the deal was in the bag—only money had to be worked out advantageously.

Nicol Herbert explained to William and Louisa that *Suspension in Time,* would open in Los Angeles for one week on December 21, 1952, in order to qualify for Academy Award consideration, but would not be released in major cities until February 1953.

Nicol was jubilant as he waved his ever-present cigar. "It's the front office's opinion that *Suspension* may get a nomination in three categories—best actor, best art direction, and best musical score—and they're putting money behind a campaign."

William refrained from asking more about the "front office," since he knew none of those people; the top executives were only names to him. He felt closer to the uniformed gateman, who waved to him every morning as the limousine drove on the lot, and waved to him in the evening.

But he respected the big executives' opinions. "I'm pleased that they're going to spend money on me," he said modestly, "but I don't think I have a chance for a nomination."

Nicol was taken aback. "What do you mean?"

"Have you seen *High Noon*?"

"Ya, it's a tight little picture."

"With a touch of genius!" William exclaimed. "It's the only picture that I can remember where the plot is forwarded by a song. Ned Washington's lyrics are an integral part of the picture; they actually explain the action."

"So?"

"You'd have to be a musician to know how difficult that assignment was. My work on *Suspension* pales in comparison, and then too, there's that wonderful dry, sardonic voice of Tex Ritter, singing all the way through the picture, and

Dmitri Tiomkin's dramatic score, and Gary Cooper's great, craggy face—"

"Oh, God, William," Nicol exploded, "Cooper's just lucky to get the part at his age, Ritter is a has-been, and Tiomkin should stick to swashbucklers. You're a shoo-in for a nomination."

William smiled sadly. "I only hope to God that you're right!"

Louisa had found a beautifully furnished house on Sunset Plaza Drive, above Sunset Strip, and at five o'clock one evening she arrived at William's office and announced, "You are now the proud owner of a new 1953 white Cadillac. You can afford it, Billy," she said, "and besides, now that you're under contract to the studio, I've been getting some flak about the limousine and driver. They're getting uppity, and I had to park in the employees' parking lot. . . ."

"That's nice," he replied distractedly, because he had been listening to her diatribe with only one ear, having been thinking about a strange musical beat that had been going around and around in his brain all day.

"Nice?" she repeated. "To hell with them!"

He looked at her askance. It was the first time that he had ever heard her swear.

The musical phrase running around in his head had a strange beat, a sort of *thump, thump, thump*, that he thought might be effective.

After she had left, he sat down at the piano, and suddenly the erratic beat that had been plaguing him turned into sus-*thump*-pen-*thump*-shun-*thump*. In the heat of creativity, he worked the rest of the afternoon and then asked Phoebe to fill his Thermos bottle with hot coffee from the commissary before she went home at five o'clock.

The next morning he asked Phoebe to call Nicol and Harry and ask them to drop by his studio at their convenience sometime before lunch. And when they arrived at ten-thirty, he asked them to sit down while he played a number.

They sat transfixed, confronted with this new sound,

thump, thump, thump. Then he whirled around on the piano stool and, with wide eyes, asked, "What do you think?"

Nicol laughed condescendingly. "Whaddah mean?"

"The tune?"

"Is this just something you composed at the moment?" Harry asked.

"Do you like the beat?" William pressed on. "Doesn't it make you want to get up in the middle of the room and strut your stuff?"

"No," Nicol answered.

William turned to Harry. "How about you?"

Harry shrugged his shoulders. "It's sort of African."

William clapped his hands in delight. "It's supposed to be; that's the point. This is the new number for the jukebox sequence in *Suspension in Time.*"

Nicol got up angrily. "What do you mean, the *new* number? We've got the music already recorded. It's already on the soundtrack! There is no way that it can be changed." He lighted a cigar angrily. "Jesus Christ, I thought by this time that you'd have picked up a little technical knowhow. It can't be changed. The jukebox number that we already have is great."

"You changed the entire musical score for *Is This Enough?*"

"But that was dire necessity."

"Just listen to the lyrics, please?" William asked plaintively.

"Why?" Nicol shouted angrily. "The film is going to stand as it is!"

Please?" William begged. "It'll only take a second."

Nicol rolled his eyes. "Oh, God, why did I get into this business? Deliver me!" He exchanged glances with Harry, who nodded, then he plumped down in the chair. "All right, as a favor to you, we'll listen, but for God sakes hurry it up; we're due at eleven-thirty at the Smoke House for lunch."

William whirled around and faced the piano. "Now, I don't have the voice for this kind of song. In fact, I don't have a voice, period. Think of a very hoarse-type voice, like the singer had laryngitis—well, a voice like Louis Armstrong has, okay?" He sang:

> *"There is no future,*
> *There is no past.*
> *There is just you and me,*
> *Together at last.*

> *"Time has suspended us*
> *For just one hour.*
> *Let us make use of it,*
> *For just one hour. . . ."*

Then he started the chords that represented heartbeats, and sang:

"SUS-PEN-SHON! SUS-PEN-SHON!"

When William finished, Nicol exchanged glances with Harry. "Je-sus," he said in awe, "I've got goosebumps."

"That *thump, thump, thump* even had these tired old feet drumming on the carpet." Harry laughed. "It's a terrific number, Nicol."

William whirled around on the stool and faced them. "Is it a deal? I record the song for the jukebox sequence?"

Nicol fidgeted in his chair and stared at his cigar, which had gone out. "I'll have to get front-office approval. It's going to cost them money." He got up. "But I'll see if I can shake them up a little by visiting the publicity office first, talk up this new approach, and if we can maybe get a hit record out of it . . ." He paused. "I'll let you know, Willie."

"My name is William," he replied, "and don't you forget it."

"Sorry," Nicol apologized, and when they were outside he took Harry's arm. "He's a sensitive bastard."

"Yeah, but he's entitled. He's got talent. I feel entirely different about the picture now. I really feel we've got something to sell, if we can get them to okay this new song."

"It's in the bag, Harry," Nicol replied smugly. "I didn't tell you, and I certainly didn't let on to William—after all, I've got to keep him under my thumb—but I was going to go in this morning and tell him he had to write something different for the jukebox sequence." He grinned. "The head of the studio hated that jazz music. He said it dated the picture!"

William's only studio contacts were Nicol Herbert and Harry Leinsinger. He had the distinct impression that everyone else on the lot regarded him as either a musical upstart or a hick from the sticks—or perhaps a combination of the two.

Not being a Hollywood person, he had no invitations to parties, conferences over coffee and Danish, or interviews in the newspapers. But he was content as long as he had an office, a piano, and the use of a projectionist when he needed to run a film.

Corny, who was recovering from a slight stroke suffered playing tennis at the Racquet Club in Palm Springs, clomped in on his crutches one day, and after listening to William's tale of woe, shook his head. "Why bitch? The paycheck comes in every week. Don't worry, you'll get an assignment soon. The front office don't want to give you a potboiler. If you get an Oscar nomination, you'll get an important picture. Just be thankful you're not working on trash.

"And," he cautioned further, "make use of your time. Pick up some old films in the vaults. You can learn a lot by screening features and studying how other composers treated serious subjects."

His eyes shone, and an odd tone crept into his voice. "I worked on a lot of goodies in the old days which they now say only nostalgia buffs are interested in watching." He paused and tried to keep his hand from shaking. "Take a look at my big musicals. Some of them are still fun to watch. Although I didn't have anything to do with it, my personal favorite is Deanna Durbin's *100 Men and a Girl*. It was made in 1937 with Stokowski conducting; it's a treat. Then, when you get bored, be titillated by the sex 'n' sand color movies."

The old man got up with difficulty from the chair, waved gaily, and limped out on his crutches. William felt sad, watching him stumble down the path toward the Music Department, because he had the feeling that Corny would never return to the studio, and he thought that Corny knew that he was saying good-bye.

He was right. A week later, the old man died of a heart attack.

14

Morning Glory

There were twelve people at Ray Cornwallis's funeral at Forest Lawn in Glendale.

No one made an appearance from the studio except William, who still did not consider himself an employee. Louisa heard Corny's stony-faced wife tell the only reporter present, Louella Parsons' legman, that the reason there was such a poor turnout was that the service was "private," but she pressed a long list of Corny's credits and a biography into his hand.

The legman was not stupid; no one in Hollywood went to funerals: it was not considered chic, and besides, looking at a friend or co-worker laid out, however opulently, was a reminder that no one—publicity stories to the contrary— was immortal.

That afternoon, when Nicol Herbert asked William why he was looking so gloomy and was told he had just returned from Forest Lawn, he waved his cigar. "Ya, I'd planned to go all right, but something came up."

Seeing William's look of disbelief, he went on gently, "You've just had your first Hollywood lesson. Frankly, no one but you liked the old fart. He'd outlived his usefulness here at the studio, because he'd lost touch with music when he was in the service. When he returned, he didn't have sense enough to retire."

Nicol paused. "Besides, wise families don't even have funerals anymore, because it's always the same. I suppose Ethel thought every star in town would be there in furs and jewels." He set his jaw. "I bet there were tons of flowers, though."

"Yes," William replied grimly. "How many were there, Lou?"

"Seventy-eight pieces. You could barely see the bronze casket—or the minister, as far as that goes."

Nicol pulled his shoulders back. "I sent the white cross of China mums."

"Which one?" William asked smugly.

"How many were there, for Christ's sakes?"

"Four."

Nicol looked uncomfortable only for a moment, then brightened. "There was a certain male star—big in the thirties—who must remain nameless," he related with relish, "because he was probably one of your heartthrobs, Louisa. Anyway, he moved to an extremely wealthy community back East to get away from Hollywood and drank himself to death. He was quite a"—he looked at Louisa and changed the name he was going to use—"ladies" man, and I suppose he bedded every lady who owned a Rolls-Royce.

"Anyway, his liver finally gave out and he died. And do you know what? Not one of his lovers showed, but they sent their maids and butlers." He paused meaningfully. "So, here in Hollywood, it's sad when only the Little People show."

William frowned. "Little People?"

Nicol smiled grimly. "I'm not talking about midgets or dwarfs, Billy. I mean hairdressers and wardrobe men and grips and gaffers."

"I think that's rather sweet," Louisa said, almost forgiving him for suggesting that she was old enough to have movie heartthrobs in the 1930s, although, of course, she had. She loved Hollywood tales, and when she heard the name of her favorite columnist, Hedda Hopper, mentioned, she leaned forward in order not to miss a word.

"Her real name is Elda Furry, you know. Anyway, she's a pretty good dame in my book," Nicol was saying. "She once told me that she wanted her body to be rushed to the airport and carted back to her home town in Pennsylvania post-haste. She said, 'Who would come to pay respects to an old broad whom everyone disrespects?' She laughed when she said it, but she's right."

Letty had a severe head cold, so she stayed in bed in the house on Connecticut Avenue that Sunday. When the butler discovered that Clement Story was to appear on the *Toast of the Town* television show, he carted his portable television set up to the master bedroom and tuned in the set, with the rabbit ears pointed toward the Capitol. "Wouldn't you know it would be headed toward the Hill?" he cracked.

Letty smiled wanly. "I feel badly to take your set away," she said, wiping her nose with a handkerchief. "You must, of course, come up and watch the show with me."

"No, thank you, ma'am, but I'll watch it in the maid's room." He averted his eyes, and Letty wondered exactly how much time he spent in that area of the house.

She turned on the set a few moments before eight o'clock; then, when Ed Sullivan appeared, looking very uncomfortable in front of the camera, and announced the guests on the program, she discovered that Clement was number four in the lineup. He had always been in the star spot before.

She yawned through a popular singing act, an acrobatic team from Yugoslavia, and a modern dance team, before Clement's name was announced. The camera picked him up, standing with his back to the audience, which Letty thought was a clever touch. He turned slowly to the audience, his guitar poised very high on his chest, as if he were going to play a classical instrument.

A gauze curtain opened behind him, revealing the Cherokee Swing Orchestra, and he began to sing, "*Do not forsake me, oh, my darlin', on this our wedding day. . . .*"

Letty sat up in bed. Why was Clem singing Tex Ritter's song? The orchestra was backing him strongly, but he was not singing well. He had always seemed very much at home on camera, but tonight he fidgeted with his shoulder strap, and during the second verse began to sway somewhat erratically to the music, something that he would have horsewhipped a singer with his band for doing.

Then, as he launched into the chorus and was obviously straining his voice, he seemed so pleased with himself that she knew he was drunk. Only someone with an unrealistic perception of what was happening could display such a self-satisfied look. Clement thought that he was right with the world, when he was very wrong with the world.

Letty began to cry into her handkerchief. On the small screen, Clement took a short bow and the camera switched to Sullivan, who, it seemed, hastily introduced the next act.

Letty asked the long-distance operator for Clement's number in Kansas City, and was told that the line was busy and to call later. When she finally got through at nine-thirty, Sarah's voice was under strict control, and Letty could tell that she had been crying.

"Everyone advised him not to do the number, Mother Trenton," Sarah said slowly. "And the reason the orchestration was so lousy, Billy Nestor refused to do it! And, in a way, I can't blame him, Clem's too big of a star to follow in another star's footsteps. . . ."

"I'm surprised that Mr. Sullivan let him sing it!" Letty exclaimed.

"Well, Max called him, and since Clem hasn't had a hit since 'The Cowboy Waltz,' Sullivan said if he wanted to do it, to go ahead—and, as everyone in the country has seen, he did. Do you have a cold?"

"Yes, but not a bad one." She paused. "I just wanted to call to let you know I saw the show, Sarah. Take care, hear?"

"Good night, Mother Trenton," Sarah said and hung up the receiver.

"How peculiar!" Letty said aloud. "She's never called me 'Mother Trenton' before!" Was it because Sarah wanted to separate her from Clem in her mind's eye? Was it because by not thinking about Clem as being her son by George Story, she was preserving their friendship by not calling attention to his drinking?

"Oh, what's the matter with me?" Letty said aloud. "I'm not thinking straight. It must be the cold medicine."

There was a knock on the door and the butler entered and unplugged the television set. "Mr. Clem was just fine." He beamed. "But I thought he looked a little peaked."

"Yes," Letty replied, "I thought so, too."

William Nestor took Corny's advice to heart, and after a few weeks had screened most of the musicals that the studio had produced over the years—from short subjects made by the big bands in the 1930s and '40s (including two with Clement Story and his Cherokee Swing Band, which were not very good), to a couple of features starring Marlene Dietrich; all of Deanna Durbin's pictures; and popular wartime films featuring the Andrews Sisters, Gloria Jean, Donald O'Connor, and Peggy Ryan.

During this interval of inactivity, he would have preferred to stay at the house on Sunset Plaza Drive and acquire a suntan poolside, but Nicol shook his head. "Nah, you gotta come in every day to qualify as an employee. I promise we'll have something for you soon. If you get bored, order a comfortable couch for the reception room and screw Phoebe."

William could not tell him that, no matter how tired he was, he had to perform every night for Louisa, and then sometimes she was at him in the mornings also. Even if Phoebe interested him sexually, which she did not, his iron bar would stay docilely wrapped away in his underpants.

One morning when Louisa drove the white Cadillac into the space in front of the studio gate, in order to turn around so that William could alight before she rushed out into the Lankershim Boulevard traffic, the gateman waved for her to come through the crossing. He tipped his hat. "Good morning, Mr. Nestor," he said with a wide Irish smile. "Good morning, Miss Tarbell."

"Why, good morning, Felix," William replied, surprised at the form of address, because the gateman had always called him by his first name before.

Felix was still smiling. "You've been assigned parking on the lot, next to the Prop Department," he said, waving them through the gate.

But that was only the first surprise. The door of his office now held a brass plate engraved with his name, and Phoebe opened the door with a proud look on her face. She waved at a huge basket of English heather, a large bowl of fresh fruit, and a demijohn of champagne.

William gingerly picked up the card, which he read in a glance, then turned with misty eyes to Louisa. "All these presents are from Nicol and Harry, congratulating me on my Academy nomination for *Suspension in Time*."

Patricia Anne was waiting in the tiny lobby of the private airstrip at the field in Philadelphia as the *Blue Heron* DC-6, made a perfect landing. Seeing the plane, with the famous Heron in flight on its tail, always caused her heart to flutter.

Normally, she did not think of her family as celebrities; it was only when she came face to face with the Heron logo, or saw a newspaper photograph of her Uncle Luke opening a new service station, or watched a television show where her dad appeared, that she remembered that her maiden name caused eyebrows to rise. She supposed that marrying a man named Larson had cut the umbilical cord as far as the name was concerned.

As pilot John Carrier and co-pilot Robert Ives—nick-named Currier and Ives—appeared in the hatch, a newspaper photographer ran out on the field and held up his camera, and caught a shot of Letty being helped down the steps. She wore a black picture hat and a black dress with white collar and cuffs. She paused a moment and spoke to the man, who was taking notes, then continued toward the lobby, making sparing use of a silver-handled ebony walking stick such as Patricia Anne had seen Washington dowagers sport on walks in the park.

Patricia Anne took the frail form in her arms and hugged her. "Grandma, you look terrific!" she exclaimed joyfully. "You look absolutely smashing."

"That was the idea," Letty replied smugly.

"Just like you just stepped out of *Vogue*."

Letty smiled crookedly. "Better than *The Poultry Journal*, which is my usual style! Now, be careful of my makeup," she cautioned. "There may be another photographer around somewhere. My, you look spiffy in that blue crepe, Patricia."

"Thank you, but what was all the fuss about? And why the interview?"

"Oh, I talked to the reporter by telephone early this morning before I left Angel. I just gave the photographer my address so that he could send the shots along if they turned out really well. My beauty consultant says that a big hat frames the face, and that black is very slimming, and that a white collar reflects light up into the face so that the wrinkles don't show so badly. Don't .look so startled, Patricia. And please close your mouth, dear, you're showing too much teeth. How do you like my new image?"

"But," Patricia Anne protested, "what is all this about, Grandma? Interviews, pictures, images?"

"If I am going to head up this new organization to help the elderly, I can't go around wearing a J.C. Penny's house dress and my hair in a finger wave! Mamie says that I must always look chic. You see, dear, many older folk just let themselves go to pot."

She threw her a quick look. "Perhaps that's really the wrong word in today's culture, I should've said 'seed.' Anyway, there's no reason in God's world why senior citizens should be shuffled aside. I'm going to call attention to their plight and make everyone aware of the many ways that we neglect the elderly." She paused. "Somehow I've got to pull myself together and be an inspiration to the older folk."

They were well on their way into Chester County, and as the afternoon wore on, they both enjoyed the countryside. "It's almost like Oklahoma in a way," Letty said. Then she lowered her voice. "You haven't mentioned Lars."

"I know." Patricia Anne sighed. "Because there is nothing new, Grandma. He seems to be getting better—at least his trips are farther apart now."

Letty stared at her. "He's going on *trips* now?"

Patricia Anne smiled. "Doctor Sam used to call them 'experiences,' but Lars calls them 'trips,' which is really what they are—'trips into the world of the nether mind.'"

"Dear Sam," Letty said sadly, "If he only knew what his research had brought about, he would be quite stunned."

"I don't think so, Grandma, he knew that he had discovered something miraculous, and he cautioned again and again in his notes that the amounts of the mushroom compound must be carefully controlled. Only, Lars doesn't think that he knew how powerful the drug really was, nor that it could perhaps not be eliminated by the body."

"You mean to say, Patricia, that it is stored? Where?"

"That's just it, they don't quite know. It may be in the bones. But it looks like anyone taking the compound in any quantity at all will have the same problem. Lars says that only time will tell. The drug may lose it's potency after a while."

"How long has it been since he first took the . . . medicine?"

Patricia's eyes filled with tears. "About six years."

"How much?"

"All told, not more than would fit on about six pinheads."

Letty was shocked, "*Pinheads?* But that's almost nothing?"

Patricia nodded, "I know."

"But I can't understand it," Letty remonstrated. "Remember, I was with George Story when Sam gave him the capsules, and I administered them myself to Sam on his instructions." Her tone was very grave. "Those capsules contained a great deal of the mushroom compound!"

"I know, Grandma, I know, but these men were *dying* from terminal illnesses, and the capsules started them on that last trip, and, don't you see, it didn't matter if the substance remained in their bodies or not. But when you are well and take the drug, the first several trips are very mild, and controllable to some extent, but then, because the material builds up in the body, each new trip enhances—"

Letty set her lips together firmly. "When we leave the Eisenhowers, I want to go back to Washington with you and visit Lars. It's been so long since I've seen him."

"I wish you wouldn't, Grandma."

"Is he that ill?"

"Oh, no, he's not emaciated. In fact, outside of being pale, he looks wonderful, and he's had a very great deal of bed rest. It's just that he really doesn't want to see anyone now." Her voice was very low, and Letty had to lean forward to hear. "You see, he never knows when he's going on one of those trips, and it's not very nice to see."

"Convulsions?"

"Oh, no, nothing like that." Patricia paused. "It's like he's having a nightmare."

"Let us pray that dear Sam, who was so spiritual and such a mystic, will be able to help him from the Other Side."

Patricia sighed gently. "Grandma, Lars is a scientist. He's an atheist. For him, there is no Other Side."

"But you believe in God, don't you?"

". . . Yes."

"And you pray?"

". . . Yes."

"Then Sam will know."

Letty looked at the road. "I've been talking so much, I haven't been watching where we're going. I think we should have turned back there at Parkersburg. Pull over, dear, and I'll ask that motorcycle policeman."

"But, he's giving a ticket, Grandma!"

"That doesn't make him tongue-tied does it?"

They pulled over, and Letty summoned her nicest voice. "Officer, are we on the right way to Gettysburg?"

He nodded. "Keep right ahead. It's at Lancaster that you veer southwest and go over the Susquehanna River to York. It's not far from there."

"On, thank you, officer."

"You're welcome, madam."

"Every time someone calls me 'madam,' I flinch," Letty giggled. "If I live to be a hundred, Leona Barrett's face always comes up before my eyes." She adjusted her white collar. "You know, dear, that there's not many women who've had business dealings with a madam."

"Grandma!" Patricia Anne was shocked. "What do you mean?"

The car passed from Chester into Lancaster County, and Letty waved to some children who had just climbed down the steps of an old-fashioned school bus.

"I think it's as good a time as any to tell the story. I know that you can keep your mouth closed. You're like your cousin Mitch in that regard. Anyway, it's time that the younger generation knew some of the facts about how the family fortune was made." She laughed. "This is one story that Sam, Born-Before-Sunrise, didn't tell in his autobiography, although he knew it, I'm sure.

"When the banks wouldn't loan money to bring in the Discovery Well in 1903, I went to Leona Barrett, who loaned me five thousand dollars, and I gave her a big chunk of stock."

"Does the rest of the family know?" Patricia Anne asked, her face quite red.

"Your Uncle Luke, of course, but I don't think anyone else does outside the top executives of Heron Oil."

"What happened to Leona Barrett, Grandma?"

"Oh, she closed The Widows just after statehood, went to New York, married a millionaire named Holden Elder, and became quite famous, I believe, as a patron of the arts."

"And what happened to her stock?"

"That's where the Lord, or fate or whatever you want to call it, comes in, and suddenly all of the blackbirds are back in the pie." Letty smiled crookedly. "Leona founded the Barrett Conservatory of Music with the dividends, and when she died some years ago, all of the stock was left to Barrett. So you see, she gave everything back to Angel."

"That's an extraordinary story, Grandma."

"Well, there's more. Leona was essentially a good woman, and she performed one other very great service for our family. As long as I'm in a confiding mood, I might as well tell you that she was responsible for your father's career in music."

"*What*?" Patricia Anne stared at Letty.

"Please keep your eye on the road, young lady! After your dad got back from the First World War, where he had played piano for—oh, dear, I can see her face, but I can't remember her name, it'll come to me in a minute. Anyway, she entertained at the front."

"Elsie Janis?"

Letty smiled her thanks. "Yes, she sang and did monologues. Anyway, your dad ran into her in New York, and she took him to one of Leona's salons and she introduced him to Lester Mainwaring, who booked him into the nightclubs in all of his hotels. That was the beginning. Your dad was practically a baby when she closed The Widows, and he never knew that Leona was Mrs. Holden Elder. But she knew who he was, and, of course, he was extraordinarily talented, and it wasn't as if she were pushing an amateur."

"I assume that you and she kept in touch over the years?" Patricia Anne asked.

"No. Only three times. Once I telephoned to thank her for her efforts for your dad, and then late one night when George Story lay dying, she made the trip to see him."

"What did they talk about, Grandma?"

"I don't know"—Letty smiled sadly—"because I wasn't in the room. The last time I saw her was at his funeral."

"That must have caused a stir!"

The skin on Letty's face tightened with remembrance. "No, she came all in black with a veil down around her face."

They had long since passed York and Hanover and were nearing Oxford, when Patricia Anne stopped for gas at a Heron station. They were greeted by a pleasant young brown-haired man in a blue uniform trimmed in white piping, with the famous blue heron logo on his breast above the machine-embroidered name "Bob."

"It was Luke Three who suggested changing the uniform," Letty revealed. "It used to be white trimmed in blue, but after working at the station in Angel and getting his trousers and shirt dirty all the time, he suggested the colors be switched."

"Aft'noon." Bob said with a wide grin as he touched his forefinger to his eyebrow in a friendly salute.

"He's certainly solicitous," Patricia Anne remarked.

Letty nodded. "He better be. Paragraph four, in the manual, details greeting procedure."

"Fill me up with the Heron Supreme, please," Patricia Anne said.

Letty examined the outside of the station. "Four demerits if he doesn't ask if you want the oil checked," she whispered.

"May I look under the hood, ma'am?"

Patricia nodded and gave her grandmother a questioning look.

"If he doesn't ask about the tires, that's another two demerits."

"Water and oil are fine, ma'am," Bob said, wiping the windshield.

"If he ogles your legs," Letty added, "that's three demerits."

"Do you use 28 pressure in the tires, ma'am?"

Patricia Anne laughed. "Yes."

"Excuse me," Letty said. "I'll check the ladies' bathroom—two demerits if there is no toilet tissue, two demerits for water on the floor, and five demerits if there's a problem with the commode."

"How many for a dirty mirror?"

"One!" Letty replied, getting out of the car. When she returned, she was smiling. "Young man, you run a tight ship."

"What do you mean, ma'am?"

"I haven't found any infractions of the Heron Code."

His manner changed immediately and he became extremely businesslike. "You're a scout?" he asked incredulously.

She laughed. "No, Bob, I am not a headhunter. The company is not hiring little old ladies to do a man's job!" She handed him a gold credit card.

He glanced at the name and turned beet-red. "It's a very great honor to make your acquaintance, Mrs. Trenton," he said. "Wait till I tell my grandmother who came into the station today. She'll never believe me, although she's a great admirer of yours. She's eighty, and very concerned about what's going to become of people her age."

"You can tell her for me, Bob, that people of our generation are entitled by the Constitution of the United States to live with dignity. I'm on my way to a meeting with the President's Lady to discuss a program to be brought up before Congress." Her voice took on an evangelistic fervor. "We hope to instigate senior citizen's clubs in every city in every state."

He paused, still red in the face. "How many demerits would it be to get you to sign something to prove that Luke Heron's mother was here?"

"I'll autograph anything you have—but a check!"

He returned from his desk with a Heron memo pad that read: DO IT RIGHT THE FIRST TIME!

"What's your grandmother's name?"

"Lavenia."

Letty wrote in her spidery, Spencerian hand:

For Lavenia:
 Who has the same name as the original Luke's mother.
Letty Heron Story Trenton

They had driven through Gettysburg, and Letty peered through the window of the roadster. "The house is over there," she said, "and if it wasn't so late, and Mamie was expecting us for dinner, we'd stop and I'd show you Cemetery Ridge, where President Lincoln delivered his address. You can see part of the battleground from the upstairs bedroom."

Patricia drove slowly. "You do get a feeling of history here, don't you, Grandma?"

"Yes, and it's different from Oklahoma, which only became a state in 1907—but here, life was going on way before the War between the States."

"Why, the house is brick!" Patricia exclaimed. "I naturally thought it would be clapboard like our farm. It's quite small."

"Oh, they're going to be adding two wings and all sorts of improvements soon, so that by the time his presidency is over, they'll have a place to settle down."

"Do you think the President will be here this weekend?"

"I very much doubt it. Mamie said not to count on it; she only came down this morning herself."

As they came down the road, a pleasant young man in a business suit saluted. Patricia stopped the car, and Letty rolled down the window.

"Your names, please?" he asked politely.

Letty introduced herself, and then added, "This is my granddaughter, Patricia Anne Story Hanson."

"You may proceed," he said gravely, and Patricia put the car in gear.

Twice more they were stopped en route to the house, and each time the same information was exchanged, and then Patricia left the car with another man to park, and as they came up to the house, a familiar figure dressed in a simple powder-blue dress was standing in the front doorway.

"Goodness!" Mamie Eisenhower exclaimed. "I'm glad you've arrived a little early." She gave a merry laugh. "I was afraid you'd lost your way."

Patricia noticed that there was a touch of gray in the famous bangs strung across her forehead, and she had not realized Mamie's eyes were blue. She was also much prettier than she photographed.

"So good to see you again, Letty," Mamie Eisenhower said in her soft accent, which was a combination of Midwestern twang and Rocky Mountain crispness.

"I'd like to present my granddaughter, Patricia Hanson," Letty said softly.

Mamie Eisenhower shook Patricia's hand firmly. "Welcome to Gettysburg, and this house, such as it is." Seeing Patricia's look of awe, she went on in an informal, conversational tone, "I've told your grandmother all about it, but, goodness, we're going to enlarge the kitchen"—she led them into the parlor—"so we can have room for a long table and chairs, and a big fireplace and modern appliances. . . ."

By the time Mamie Eisenhower showed them the wide, sweeping meadows where the battle of Gettysburg had been fought, Patricia had overcome her shyness and was chatting animatedly about how wonderful it must be to be a part of such a historical area of the country. Mamie winked at

Letty; the trick of talking for five minutes had worked: Patricia was herself again.

"You're in the bedroom at the top of the stairs on the second floor," Mamie Eisenhower said. "Please bear with us. The next time you come, hopefully, we'll have the remodeling done and everything will be hunky-dory. Would you like to rest a bit, Letty? I know the drive was tiring."

"No, I'm fine, Mamie. If it's all right, we'll freshen up and be right down."

Letty, dressed in a red-and-blue plaid wool dress and wearing a blue stocking cap, and Patricia Anne, dressed in a gray sharkskin skirt and pink blouse, went for a short walk in the gathering dusk. They sadly viewed several of the Civil War plaques scattered over the old battlefield, and returned to the brick farmhouse in a thoughtful frame of mind to the smell of chicken frying.

Mamie turned from the stove. "It's very informal tonight," she said.

"Good, a welcome change of pace," Letty replied, removing her stocking cap and fluffing out her white hair.

When Mamie had set the food on the table, she called upstairs that it was time for supper, and it was only then that Letty noticed the table was set for four.

Steps resounded on the stair, and a moment later the 34th President of the United States appeared in the kitchen doorway, rubbing his hands together. "Do I smell chicken, Miss Mamie?" he asked with a slow smile, and kissed her cheek.

"Indeed you do!" She laughed, then turned to her guests. Immediately Dwight Eisenhower held out his hand. "It's very good of you to come to see us, Mrs. Trenton," he said with a disarming smile.

"It is my pleasure, Mr. President," Letty answered warmly. "Patricia Anne Hanson, I should like to introduce you to President Eisenhower. Mr. President, this is my granddaughter, and"—she smiled—"whatever the feminine is for 'chauffeur.'"

Patricia Anne felt a warm hand grasp her own, and she was so flustered that she almost curtsied. "Shall we?" The

President waved toward the table. "Are there place cards?" he asked.

"Goodness, no," the First Lady replied, wiping her hands on her apron, "we have too much protocol in Washington to be bothered here at the farm. Being in the service for so long and moving all over the world, and being in so many camps, we love informality at home."

They sat down at the table and bowed their heads. "O Father, bless this house and this food," the President said simply, "and these guests, and give us the pleasure of your divine guidance." Then he handed the plate of fried chicken to Letty.

During dinner, the President's presence filled the room as he spoke in an amusing way of his once becoming lost in Foggy Bottom. And to Letty, who had known so many Presidents, Dwight Eisenhower seemed to be the most human. At sixty-three, his grandfatherly appearance was deceiving, she thought, because he seemed the embodiment of youth when he spoke about his years of military service and his happy marriage. "I swear," he said, "Miss Mamie would follow me to the ends of the earth."

"I have!" she retorted with an explosive laugh.

Immediately after coffee was served, the President excused himself. "There is a great deal of reading that must be done tonight," he said, "that won't wait until tomorrow."

After his footsteps died away on the stairs, Letty turned to Mamie Eisenhower. "I didn't know the President was coming this weekend."

"Goodness! Neither did I!" Mamie Eisenhower exclaimed. "But he said the White House was lonely and it was worth coming down, if only for one night. It's so peaceful here, don't you think?"

As the First Lady arose from the table, Patricia Anne stood up. "Mrs. Eisenhower, please let me clean the table and do the dishes."

Mamie Eisenhower smiled. "You're a very sweet girl. I'm going to accept your offer only because your grandmother and I have such a long program to outline. Thank you."

As Patricia Anne filled the sink with hot water and added flakes of soap, she thought how interesting it would be at a future cocktail party to say, "I remember when I was doing the dishes at President Eisenhower's farm at Gettysburg. . . ."

Clement Story dialed the number from a phone booth in the lobby of the Wyandotte Hotel in Kansas City. "Pat?" he said distinctly into the mouthpiece. "I got your message to call from my telephone answering service." His tone was urgent. "Lars isn't worse, is he?"

"Oh, no, Daddy, the news is *good* for a change. Guess what? I am now secretary/associate to the chairman, or, in this case, chairlady of the Senior Citizens of America League."

"Well, that is good news, I'm certain, but what does Lars think about you going to work? You don't need money, do you?"

"No, Daddy, no. Lars is all for it, and I'm certainly not doing it for the money, but Grandma thinks I'll be smashing."

"What has she to do with it?"

"You haven't heard? Why, she's the new chairlady."

"Well, my God," Clement cried, "what does she want to get mixed up in politics at her age for, I wonder?"

"Oh, it's not a political job, it's a presidential appointment."

"But isn't that political?"

She laughed. "No. She's going to suggest programs not only for the older Republicans but the older Democrats too, Daddy. Everyone! I hope to be her right hand."

Clement's voice was worried. "Mama always tries to do too much as it is, but there's no stopping her once she's made up her mind. Maybe you can make her take it easier." He paused, and lighted a cigarette. "Won't this take you away from the hospital a very great deal?"

"Not really, Daddy. Her job wouldn't be full time. I think they mostly need her to be a spokeswoman. After all, the President is sixty-two, and he would hardly allow an eighty-two-year-old woman to take over a really strenuous job, nor would Mrs. Eisenhower, who's fifty-six."

"I wish Mother would take these things up with the family before she makes decisions like this," Clement complained.

"Well, you know Grandma!" she paused. "How's Mom?"

"Fine. I've got to run now, baby. Let's keep in touch, and give my best to Lars."

He hung up, then took the elevator up to room 2008 and opened the door with his key. "Hi, sweetie," he said.

The woman, dressed in an ivory satin slip, was turning down the bed. "What kept you so long?"

"I had to return my daughter's call from Washington, just a social thing." He glanced appreciatively at her slim figure. "You look absolutely gorgeous, Marthene."

She laughed and struck a pose, hands on hips, blonde head down, mascaraed eyes with long, upswept lashes cast provocatively upwards, and wiggled her amble bosom. "If this works for Marilyn Monroe, it should work for me."

"I know that you work for me," he said, "and you don't need to sing 'Diamonds Are a Girl's Best Friend,' either!"

He took her in his arms and kissed her. "Oh," she said, "you feel scratchy. You're much nicer without clothes."

"So are you, sweetie. Get bare for daddy, will you?"

When she languidly pulled the satin slip over her shoulders and fluffed out her long shoulder-length hair, she was nude. He pulled the heavy drapery across the window, which threw the room into semidarkness. By the time she had stretched out on the bed, he had quickly removed his shirt and trousers, and then, holding his stomach in as far as he could and throwing back his shoulders, he looked down at her, running his eyes over her soft white body, hoping to arouse himself by the sight of so much naked flesh.

"Take off your shorts," she said invitingly, "and come in, the water's fine."

He blanched. That was a phrase that Sarah often used! He was hesitant to follow Marthene's instructions, because he was feeling nothing inside. He quickly slid the material down his thighs and legs and climbed on the bed, and took her in his arms and kissed her deeply.

Although the touch of her lips was very agreeable, and he was pressed tightly against her body, he still felt nothing. He kissed her again, more deeply this time, and brushed her hair back from her face, the way he always caressed Sarah. He drew his hand back guiltily and began to stroke her back.

"I think it would be wonderful to just hold you in my arms today."

"You know how I love to cuddle," she whispered in his ear, and, bringing her body close to his, she began to sway with wanton motions, up and down, around and around, and then up and down again, shuddering deliciously.

The feel of her body was so new and fresh and different to him—almost like an alien thing—that it disturbed him that she brought forth no reaction. He felt embarrassed and suddenly shy. He clicked his teeth. "Damn, sweetie, I forgot." He made a show of looking at his wristwatch. "I've got to call my agent in Chicago, I want to catch him at the office."

He bounded out of bed and gave Max Rabinovich's number to the hotel operator. The call came through quickly, and he sat on the side of the bed with his back to Marthene.

"So what's new, baby doll?" Max croaked. "Excuse this voice, I've been shouting clear across the Atlantic all afternoon. Those damned lines are so crackly, I'd swear I was in a henhouse! How did the gig in Atlantic City go? Sold out as usual, I suppose?"

Marthene's hand had crept around his thigh and was now resting on his groin. "Not quite." Clement did not want to dwell on the concert. Her hand was now actively engaged, but her attempts were futile. "Anything new?"

"No, not at this end," Max replied gruffly. "It was you who placed the call. What's on your mind?"

"Just checking in, that's all."

Max laughed. "Well, this isn't Central Casting, you know. It's five o'clock, and I want to get the hell out of here, so good-bye, so long, and amen!"

There was a giant pop in Clement's ear as Max hung up,

leaving his ear ringing. He looked over his shoulder and laughed. "Unhand me, wench, I've got to go. Important meeting."

"It didn't sound very important to me, daddy." She pouted.

"Well, it is!" He swiftly put on his clothes, then bent down and kissed her on the lips. "I'm sorry, sweetie, I completely forgot. . . ."

"It's okay, lover," she said with a half-smile, "but just because . . . nothing happened . . . doesn't mean . . ."

"I know," he said, placing a fifty-dollar bill on the television set, and thought: *When we used to pay for it as kids, we always placed the two dollars on the bureau.*

"Why are you smiling?"

"Nothing. Private joke." He waved. "I'll call you," he said at the door.

"I have a sexy girlfriend named Sally," Marthene said, stretching out full length on the bed. "Maybe next time, if we both tried, we could get it up for you."

His face flaming, Clement closed the door gently, fighting the impulse to turn and hit the carved wood with his fists until his knuckles bled.

Instead, he walked very carefully down the hall to the elevator, and, once in the lobby, headed for the tavern.

The barkeep used to be a trumpet player with Henry Busse's orchestra before he lost his lip. "Hi, Mac," he said airily, "how about a double scotch?"

15

Moment of Triumph

The Pantages Theatre on Hollywood Boulevard was ablaze with klieg lights.

It was still light, yet the long line of limousines snaked slowly around the block, finally depositing their glittering occupants on the red carpet, on each side of which had been erected high bleachers to accommodate the fans.

William Nestor in a new midnight-blue tuxedo, and with his blue-black hair slicked back with brilliantine, and Louisa Tarbell in a pale mauve bugle-beaded dress and a white fox fur, with her auburn-rinsed hair swept up in a swirl on the top of her head, were situated in the limousine behind Cecil B. De Mille.

They waited patiently for the furor to die down after the famous seventy-two-year-old director/producer stepped out on the red carpet, waving to the crowd, his bald head reflecting the lights in the overhead marquee, which announced:

25TH ANNUAL ACADEMY AWARDS

A blue-uniformed page assisted Louisa from the limousine, and she was met with a battery of flashbulbs. It was the supreme moment of her life, being photographed for posterity. She smiled prettily, seeing the picture—a half page—in *Life* Magazine.

A moment later, she was crushed to hear a photographer say, "Damn, I thought that was Shirley Booth!"

A cohort flipped back, "No, she's in New York. Who's the kid with this old broad?"

Her face flaming, Louisa turned to William. "Take my arm," she hissed, and as he did so, there were wild screams from the bleachers. He looked up at the fans, face beaming, until he saw that all eyes were on Anthony Quinn, behind him, who had been nominated as best supporting actor for *Viva Zapata*.

William nodded to Louisa, who had regained her poise. "Shall we go in?" he asked, politely. They were soon swallowed up in the crowded lobby, ignored by a radio emcee, microphone in hand, describing the sights while waiting for Lana Turner, who had been nominated as best actress for *The Bad and The Beautiful*.

Once they were seated in the plush auditorium, with William in a convenient aisle seat—as were other nominees, so that the stage could be reached more easily if their names were announced as winners—the embarrassing entrance in front of the theater was soon forgotten as Louisa pointed out the stars in attendance.

Two hours before the telecast, the Baptist minister, Reverend Clyde Menzies, drove to the Nestor farm two miles from town. A tall, corpulent man of fifty, he found Mrs. Nestor coming in from the henhouse, carrying eggs in her Mother Hubbard apron. Even though it was rather cool, she had thrust her dusty feet into a pair of faded old mules, and he could see that she wore nothing but a thin cotton dress under the apron.

"Howdy, Reverend," she said without smiling, and then turned her head and called, "Finney, get yourself up here. We've got company."

He noticed that her gaunt face was very pale and that her body was very thin. "How are you?" he asked.

"Ailin' a bit," she replied. "Come on in the house. We's about to sit down for supper." She held the screen door open for him, and they came into a bare living room, with a 1934 calendar picture of Jesus kneeling in the Garden of Gesthemene on the wall. Flies were buzzing around unwashed dishes piled in the iron sink.

"I'm going to fry up some hen fruits," she said weakly, "and we also got biscuits and gravy, and I think there's some ham left. You can stay, if you're a mind to." She brushed her brown-gray hair back from her temples.

Reverend Menzies swallowed the lump in his throat. "Clara fixed supper before I came over, but thank you, anyway."

"Fin-ney," she called again, "come in!"

Finney Nestor loped in the back door, wiping his hands on his overalls, which were two sizes too small for his big frame. He managed a pucker meant for a smile, and shook hands with Reverend Menzies. "Won't you sit a spell?"

The minister took a straight, narrow pressed-wood-back chair, and prepared himself for the ordeal ahead, trying to ignore the smell of rancid grease coming from the kitchen as Mrs. Nestor fried the eggs. "You folks know what's happening tonight, don't you?"

Mrs. Nestor paused in the kitchen doorway, holding the smoking frying pan in her right hand and pulling a stray hair out of her eyes with her left. "Jean Lightfoot said something the other day in the grocery store about Billy being on that television thing tonight. Are they going to give him a medal for his music?"

Reverend Menzies cleared his throat. "Well, we *hope* so! He's been nominated for an award from the Academy of Motion Picture Arts and Sciences in Hollywood." He paused, and selected his words carefully so that the Nestors would understand what he meant. "He wrote the music for a picture called *Suspension in Time*. I know that you don't go to movies, but it played locally."

Mrs. Nestor pushed the eggs to the side of the pan and placed two small pieces of ham in the fat, then stood at the Propane stove and watched the meat fry as if preparing supper were all that was on her mind.

The minister nodded. "It's a very important award."

Finney Nestor's eyes narrowed. "Does this mean he'll make more money?" he asked, joining his wife at the table.

"Conceivably." Reverend Menzies blinked because the room was rapidly filling with smoke. "But that's not the most important point. It's his growth as an artist that's crucial."

Mrs. Nestor looked up quizzically. "Reverend Menzies, I know we don't belong to your flock, but you're a religious messenger anyway, and we'd be pleased if you'd ask the blessing in the name of your Baptist Lord."

Reverend Menzies bowed his head.

"We hold hands when we pray in the Church of the Redeemer," she reminded him with a slightly superior air.

"Oh, yes, of course. I had forgotten." He had also conveniently forgotten that they also spoke in tongues and occasionally handled snakes while in the throes of receiving the Holy Spirit. He sat down at the table and grasped their hands, and said a far more elaborate and emotional prayer than he did at home over the evening meal.

After the Nestors had echoed his "amen" and started to eat, Reverend Menzies cleared his throat again before going on with his memorized appeal, hoping that he had left nothing out. "As you know, I feel, in a very small way, that I was a stepping stone to William's success—"

"That's true," Mrs. Nestor broke in. "If you hadn't let William practice on the pipe organ in your church, he would've never amounted to anything."

Reverend Menzies flushed. "Well, that's not entirely true, Mrs. Nestor, the boy was born with natural, God-given talent."

"Yep," Finney Nestor agreed. "He shore didn't git it from the Mrs. or me." He paused, fork in the air. "That's why it's so hard for us to face the fact that he's working for the devil."

Not wishing to pursue this line of thought, Reverend Menzies paused and then continued. "He had a great deal of help, not only from the Lord and myself, but also from Louisa Tarbell, who, don't forget, brought him to the attention of Clement Story!"

Mrs. Nestor cleaned her plate with a bit of biscuit. "That was the only time in my whole life that my Cherokee background meant anything at all. Clement Story wouldn't have spit on Billy if he wasn't a mixed-blood."

"Be that as it may," Reverend Menzies said, realizing

the conversation was not proceeding the way that he had planned, "Mr. Story enabled him to graduate from the Barrett Conservatory of Music in Angel, and start his career in the music business. 'The Cowboy Waltz' was a good song."

Finney Nestor nodded. "It did have a kind of lilt to it," he said begrudgingly. "Although the words didn't seem to mean much."

"Nevertheless, you have every reason to be proud of Billy," the minister said convincingly, and then went on quickly, "That's why I think you should come uptown with me and see him on television this evening."

Mrs. Nestor dropped her fork. "Why, no one in Willawa has anything to show it on," she said, flushing.

"Herman Crane has placed a television set in the window of his hardware store and an antenna on the roof pointed toward the reception tower in Tulsa. Andy Washington has contributed folding chairs from his mortuary, and quite a crowd is expected to show up. After all, he's a hometown boy."

Seeing the look of longing in Mrs. Nestor's eyes, Reverend Menzies launched into the closing argument, exactly the way that he wound up a sermon in church. "Naturally, the townspeople are proud not only of William, who's gone on to the hall of fame"—he hoped he wasn't overdoing it—"but his mother and father as well. Everyone will be very disappointed if you don't show up to see Billy in his moment of glory."

He paused and sought to assess their faces before giving the *pièce de résistance*. "After all, folks," he announced proudly, "the whole world is watching."

Mrs. Nestor looked at him in wonder. "The *whole world*?"

"Well, practically."

Mrs. Nestor turned to her husband. "Granted, Fin, that it may be the devil working the air waves, just like he does the radio, but this is a chance to see Billy, and I think we should take it."

Finney Nestor frowned and pursed his lips. "I don't want

to be seen by a lot of people. Neither one of us has any proper clothes."

Reverend Menzies stood up quickly. "I'll park at the curb." Knowing that he must not permit them to think, he went on, "Hop in the car, and we'll go." He looked at his wristwatch. "Come on, we don't want to miss anything."

On the short ride into Willawa, Reverend Menzies kept up a running conversation to place the Nestors at ease, and when he pulled up at Crane's Hardware Store, forty people were sitting in folding chairs in front of the television set in the window, and twenty-five children were seated cross-legged on the sidewalk, staring up at the screen.

"Why, the picture's so small!" Finney Nestor exclaimed.

"That's true," Reverend Menzies admitted, "but there's three seats right up in front. Come on."

"Hurry," Herman Crane shouted, adjusting the big speaker in front of the window, "the show's already begun!"

Caught up in the excitement, Reverend Menzies ushered the Nestors to the seats that Herman had reserved, just as Cecil B. De Mille's limousine pulled up at the curb in front of the Pantages Theatre.

Everyone's eyes were fixed on the small screen, and when William appeared there was prolonged applause from the oldsters and whistles and shouts from the children. Seeing William, as if he was standing before them in a bank of lights, Mrs. Nestor began to cry, and when she glanced at her husband, tears were also streaming down his face. "I just can't believe we're here in Oklahoma," Finney Nestor said, "watching our Billy Boy in California."

In the Pentages Theatre, there was an expectant hush as the lights dimmed. Maestro Johnny Green lifted his baton, and William settled back for the overture, heartbeats quickening as he heard the *thump, thump, thump* of *Suspension* worked expertly by the arranger into the medley of themes from nominated scores.

The huge velvet curtain swung back, revealing the glittering set, which included a giant television screen, and the crowd burst into a spontaneous roar of approval.

William was dazzled; he laughed at the emcee's jokes, applauded the musical numbers, waited patiently for the television commercials, which were not shown to the theater audience, and responded appropriately to the many comings and goings onstage.

The rest of the evening went by in a blur; he was conscious of awards being presented; of long, short, pertinent, or amusing acceptance speeches being given; of film clips being shown on the giant television screen on stage; of nominated songs being sung; of mentally going over his acceptance speech; and of Louisa twice complaining that the bugle beads on her dress was cutting into her derriere.

But when the moment for the nominees for the best score of a dramatic or comedy motion picture was announced, and he heard his name mentioned, he was half out of his seat before he felt Louisa's restraining hand on the sleeve of his tuxedo. The envelope was opened, and Dmitri Tiomkin's name was announced for *High Noon*.

William grasped Louisa's hand tightly, and his throat caught. He had lost the Academy Award, but he had lost to a genius. And he found himself laughing along with the others when the little Russian gave the most memorable acceptance speech of the evening. He beamed.

Clement watched the awards from his easy chair in Kansas City, a tall scotch in his hand. "Johnny's doing a good job," he said to Sarah. "Do you know how many music cues he's got to have up his sleeve? Remember, he doesn't know who's going to win in any category, so the orchestra had to rehearse all of the themes for the nominated pictures. It's a job I wouldn't relish."

He took a pull from the glass. "I bet Johnny has an enormous pile of lead sheets. The moment the envelopes are opened and the winners are announced, he has to cue the orchestra to play the right theme as the nominees get to the stage, which I'm told is like the last mile at Sing Sing—the longest walk in the world."

Sarah watched the awards with building excitement until Tiomkin's name was announced, and then she exclaimed,

"Oh, damn!" She glanced at Clement, whose face was impassive. "Aren't you going to say anything?"

He took a long gulp of scotch. "Why should I?"

"But don't you feel a sense of pride about your discovery?"

"No."

He remained silent for the rest of the evening, and when *The Greatest Show on Earth* was announced as best picture, she applauded.

Sarah was so engrossed in the proceedings that it was not until she turned off the television set that she saw that Clem was nodding in his big chair. She stopped for a moment to look at his craggy face. "Come on, honey," she said quietly, not finding it within herself to be angry at his having too much to drink again, "let's go to bed." With difficulty, she helped him up from the chair and then, watchful that he did not fall, guided him carefully into the bedroom, her eyes full of tears.

Letty, not having a television set, had driven to Enid to watch the telecast at Mitchell's and Charlotte's house, next to the Garber mansion. "Let's dress formally," her hostess had said over the telephone. "I think it would be fun, and we'll pretend we're in Hollywood with William."

Letty had agreed. "I'll wear my lavender lace. It's an 'old woman's' dress, but it's the prettiest thing I have, and if I look like Whistler's Mother, well, I look like Whistler's Mother!"

"I'm going to wear a chiffon dress that the French call a 'shift,'" Charlotte replied. "I got it at a nifty little shop in Nice. It cost a fortune, Letty, but it makes my waistline look 'misty.' I've gained so much weight that I need all the camouflaging I can get!"

Letty laughed, but she approved of Charlotte's deportment; she was turning out to be a superb hostess for Mitchell. Fontine would have been justly proud of her offspring, who, she had once confided, lived a wanton life in Washington, D.C. If that had been so—and Letty could scarcely believe Fontine's stories about the young boys—

she had drastically changed since coming back to Oklahoma.

In lieu of a sitdown dinner, which would conflict with the presentation, Charlotte served a delicious buffet, which they consumed on little knee-high tables that Letty thought were wonderful. She made a mental note to have her dinner in the same manner when she purchased a television set "after they got it perfected." Everything is so good," Letty said, wiping her lips daintily with a damask napkin, one of a dozen that she had once given Fontine.

Charlotte grinned. "Thank you, but these are just old country recipes."

"Would you call beef Stroganoff country?" Mitchell asked.

"Well, sort of. Isn't it rather like creamed hamburger?"

Letty cleared her throat. "Well, I suppose, in a way. Isn't it time for the show?"

Mitchell turned on the set to the outside interviews, just in time to see Cecil B. De Mille alight from his limousine. Letty sighed. "I'll never forget his *The Ten Commandments*—the silent version, I mean. Your mother and I saw it right here in Enid, and it was fabulous. I thought there was too much crepe hair on the men, and Moses' wig was a little long, but it was an enthralling spectacle. . . . Oh, look, isn't that Louisa Tarbell?"

Charlotte adjusted her glasses. "I do believe it is, but what is a woman her age doing wearing *bugle beads*? And she's grinning like a Cheshire cat! Are those her own teeth?"

"Well, William looks awfully grown-up in his tux," Letty put in. "He's looking very handsome. In a way, he resembles George Story, don't you think, Mitch?"

"A little, perhaps. He seems to photograph more Indian than he looks in person."

"Oh," Charlotte cried, "there's the overture. Does anyone want anything before the show starts? Good, we'll just relax and enjoy the show."

Letty thought that even the commercials were entertaining, and when the funny little Hungarian received the award instead of William, she clicked her teeth.

"Yes, it is a pity," Mitchell said, "but he's young, and he'll be in the running again."

Letty's eyes stung with tears when Gary Cooper won as best actor for *High Noon*. He was her favorite, even over Clark Gable.

When Mitchell switched off the set, Letty wiped her eyes. "It was a beautiful show, and when it comes down to it, I guess I'll have to spring for a set. I don't like to impose upon you two when I have to invite myself over when Clement's on audio-video."

Mitchell laughed. "It isn't as if you can't afford it, Aunt Letty."

"It has nothing to do with money, Mitch," she cried hotly. "It's just I've been waiting until they've got all the kinks out!"

Patricia had rented a television set for Lars, especially for the Academy Awards telecast, but occasionally a doctor or nurse would drop by to see who had won what, until she hung a Quarantine sign on the door, which fooled no one but made the point that they did not want to be disturbed.

Lars had not had a trip for eight days, and he was feeling so good that when Louisa and William were shown getting out of the limousine, he turned to Patricia with a devilish look in his eye. "Do you suppose they're sleeping together?"

"Who?"

"William Nestor and Louisa Tarbell."

"I'd never thought about it before." She frowned. "I rather doubt it, though."

"Did Trilby sleep with Svengali?" he asked.

"Probably. If so, his hold over her was more than hypnotic. What a peculiar question."

"Not necessarily. Remember"—he laughed—"I'm a peculiar person."

"But Billy and Lou?" She frowned again, trying to picture them together and watch the telecast at the same time and succeeding in neither. "Oh, that's nice, Anthony Quinn won an Oscar for *Viva Zapata!* If so, he has an Oedipus complex, and she likes boys."

"Like Charlotte Dice," Lars put in with a wave of his hand.

"*Used to!* Don't be nasty, dear," Patricia retorted. "Obviously, she reformed before she married cousin Mitch. They seem to be perfectly happy, and apparently had a wingding of a time on their three-month European honeymoon." She paused and stared at the tube, and gasped as Shirley Booth, cut in remote from New York, almost stumbled on her long dress coming up the stage steps to accept her award as best actress for *Come Back, Little Sheba*.

She turned off the set and adjusted his pillows. "Not many surprises this year, but I'm sorry that Billy didn't win for *Suspension in Time*, because the music made the picture. I surely liked the beat to 'Suspension.'" She snapped her fingers and sang, *thump, thump, thump*.

"Which reminds me, Pat, I forgot to tell you that your mother called yesterday."

"Really? What did she have to say?"

"It was a professional call."

"What does that mean? You can't talk about it? She knows you can't practice from a hospital bed. I love her, but—"

He raised his eyebrows. "You might as well know. Your dad, it seems, is having a problem. He's been drinking a great deal, and she has a feeling that he may be having a love affair."

"Dad?" Patricia burst out laughing. "Mother's out of her mind. He's never even permitted anyone in the band to take more than a social drink and as far as marijuana is concerned, if one reefer is found in one locker, the man's fined and then fired if there's a second offense. Mother must be going through change of life."

"No, Pat, but your dad is!"

"What do you mean?"

He smiled wryly. "Who do you think put the 'men' in menopause?"

"I know you've been feeling wonderful lately," Patricia Anne said with a laugh, "but must you make those terrible jokes?"

"Actually, I'm quite serious. Men do go through a midlife climacteric, just as women do, but some sail through with no problems and others have a hell of a time."

He sat up in bed, and Patricia Anne was pleased because he looked very much the professional; the indecisive look that he had held so long was gone. *Oh, thank God,* she thought, *he's getting better!*

"Letty would probably call it 'the itch,'" he continued. "But even old-fashioned wives had sense enough to look the other way when their husbands began to dye their hair, start to exercise to get rid of the paunch, make remarks on how young they felt inside, and look at young girls half their age."

"But," Patricia Anne exclaimed, "doesn't that complex come about when middle-aged men begin to feel they are failures? Dad has led a fabulous life, has pots of money, a loving wife, a beautiful home, a couple of cars, is sought and admired—and don't forget he had a fabulous hit record in 'The Cowboy Waltz.'"

"You've hit the nail precisely on the head, my dear. What better time in life to wonder if he can ever top himself? Can he continue to have it all? Can there ever be another 'Cowboy Waltz'?"

"I see what you mean." Her voice was strained. "I was beginning to think that you meant he was going through a glandular thing."

"He is, that's what at the root of all evil. Women lose estrogen at menopause; men lose testosterone. I told her to have doctor Forbes in K.C. send him to a gland man. A series of hormone shots and a few B-1's to help his energy level, and I think he'll pull out of the dumps in fine shape.

"She was a bit dubious about this treatment, which isn't widely known yet, until I explained that this was one of the endocrine theories that Dr. Sam, Born-Before-Sunrise, noted in the research papers that I inherited. He's still A-Number-One in her book."

Patricia Anne kissed Lars on the forehead, nose, and lips. "Have I told you today that you are a magnificent doctor and a terrific lover?"

He grinned widely. "Shouldn't that be the other way around?"

Bella Chenovick took the peach pie out of the oven, then made her way slowly out to the back porch of the farmhouse and adjusted the twenty-five-foot pole upon which rested the television antenna. She looked up to be sure the long needle was pointing from Angel toward Enid, as the installation man had recommended.

She felt strange, doing what she felt was "man's work," but Torgo, God bless him, was confined to a wheelchair with arthritis, and Gerald, the male nurse, was so prissy he wouldn't soil his hands with what he called "field work."

She looked out over the prosperous farm with its hundred acres in winter wheat and the forty acres of peach trees and the twenty acres that surrounded the house. It was a far cry from the desolate, rolling prairie that Torgo had claimed during the Cherokee Strip Land Rush back in '93. But now they were old, and the farm was difficult to run with just two hired men, and life was not like it used to be when she could play the piano and Torgo the violin.

She sighed gently, because she was not one to look back unduly. She brushed a piece of lint from her red "good calling" dress trimmed in white lace, with an embroidered blue apron that she had brought from Prague as a young girl, which she only wore for special occasions. True, the sides had been let out several times as she grew fat around her middle, but the material was still good.

She had put on the dress for good luck. She had prayed every night since she had heard that William Nestor was up for that Oscar award that they gave out every year out in Hollywood.

Suspension in Time had played for two weeks at the Blue Moon Theatre on Main Street in Angel, and she had gone twice, once with Torgo, when she had to whisper what was happening on the screen, and once again alone, so that she could enjoy the picture by herself. The music was real good, she thought, only that peculiar thumping song on the jukebox had given her the willies.

She checked the peach pie to make sure the bottom crust

was browning, then went into the living room and pushed Torgo's wheelchair nearer the television set. "Where's Gerald?" she asked.

Torgo grunted and nodded his head toward the bathroom door, and switched on the television set. "Isn't it time for Belle Trune to show up?"

"Yes." Bella nodded. "But she has to do the dishes at the Red Bird Café before she comes over; otherwise she'd get there at five in the morning facing all those truckers and no dishes." At that moment, there was a knock on the door. "Speak of the devil," she said, and admitted Belle Trune, and they kissed each other on the cheek.

"I'm lucky tonight having two belles!" Torgo quipped and pushed out his face to be kissed. "Sit down," he ordered. "The show's about to begin." He peered at the tube. "Isn't that Billy?"

"Where? Where?" Gerald cried, coming out of the bathroom and combing his hair.

"That handsome young Indian boy," Belle said.

"Is that his mother?" Gerald said. "She doesn't look old enough."

"No," Belle Trune said, "that's his business manager."

Gerald rolled his eyes heavenward. "A *female* business manager?"

"Why not?" Torgo cried. "If they'd had such things when I was young, I'd have had one too!"

"Over my dead body," Bella said. "Oh, lookee, isn't that Lana Turner?"

"Yes," Gerald said, "doesn't she look heavenly? And those furs!"

"And that Anthony Quinn," Belle Trune said dreamily, "he could put his shoes under my bed anytime."

"Yes," Bella replied through tight lips. Although she had known Belle Trune since babyhood, they had only been fast friends for ten years. There was a long period when they did not speak. During the depression, Belle Trune had entertained men for money in her shack on the outskirts of town.

She had been ostracized then, but when the war brought prosperity to Angel, and the Herons reopened the refinery and the airplane factories in Wichita employed thousands of men, Belle had started the Red Bird Café, with money not from her ill-gotten gains, but borrowed from Letty Heron. From that day forward, she had become respectable, and the town forgave her. And Bella had also forgiven her for calling her a "bohunk" on Main Street in 1936.

"There's Tony Curtis!" Gerald exclaimed. "And Janet Leigh, and Gloria Grahame—I hope she wins for *The Bad and the Beautiful*."

When the curtains of the Pantages Theatre opened, "Bella announced, "Now, let's be quiet, I don't want to hear a peep out of any of you, and that goes for you too, Gerald." She took her rosary out of her blue apron pocket and began to pray.

When the music nominations were announced, Bella swelled with pride, but when Dmitri Tiomkin's name was announced she gasp out loud, dropped her beads, and fanned her face with a handkerchief. Gerald brought her a glass of water.

When Tiomkin began his acceptance speech, Torgo turned to Bella. "He speaks worse English than we did when we came over on the boat sixty years ago!" And to everyone's astonishment, he turned off the set. "Gerald, I'm tired, put me to bed."

Bella switched on the set. "I swear you're getting cantankerous in your old age, Torgo. What about us watching the rest of the show?"

"Don't know why," he replied. "As far as I'm concerned, it was over the minute that our Billy lost that little figurine."

William and Louisa stood in the shoulder-to-shoulder crowd outside the Pantages Theatre, waiting for their limousine, listening to the voice on the loudspeaker drone on: *"Miss Parsons' car, Mr. Gable's car, Mr. Brando's car, Mr. Douglas's car, Miss Hutton's car . . ."*

"I don't know why we can't go to the post-Oscar party." Louisa complained. "We never get invited anywhere, and this is your one chance to be seen. . . ."

"Miss Crawford's car. . . ."

"It is *your* one chance to be seen, Lou. I simply don't

want to go. I'll have the driver drop me off at the house and take you."

"Mr. De Mille's car. . . ."

"I can't go alone," she protested. "But if you're not there, everyone will think that you're a sore loser."

"Mr. Nestor's car. . . ."

"But you and I, and our friends, will know that's not true," he replied quietly, escorting her to the curb, where their limousine was slowly inching its way up the boulevard in a long line of other impressive vehicles. "I've said all along that *High Noon* would win. Tiomkin and Washington deserved that award, the same way that Alfred Newman won the Oscar for the score of the musical *With a Song in My Heart.* Lou," he went on with great conviction, "some things are preordained."

The crowd lining Hollywood Boulevard was thinning out now. Oscar losers, who had been smiling and waving to the fans left in the bleachers in front of the theater a moment before, were now sitting back in rented limousines, opening flasks and downing bourbon and vodka in preparation for the grand entrance at studio-sponsored parties at the luxury hotels in Beverly Hills.

Oscar winners, in other limousines, were toasting each other with ice-filled glasses of liquor prepared by the drivers, and deciding whether to celebrate the occasion by getting drunk or maintain the dignity that their new awards presaged.

The valet opened the door of the Nestor limousine, and after William and Louisa were situated in the back seat, the driver, a young extra player, asked, "Which party, sir?"

"None," William replied, stony-faced. "Take us home, please."

"Can't we just drop by the Beverly Hills Hotel long enough to get some food," Louisa wheedled, "and say hello to Nicol Herbert and Harry Leinsinger?"

"As I said before, Lou,"—he looked her in the eye— "please go on without me. In all the crowd, no one will miss me. If they do, you can say I'm at the bar or in the john. There will be hundreds of people milling about."

"But I can't go alone!" She glanced at him out of the

corners of her blue-mascaraed eyes. "Besides, I'm hungry."

They were nearing Hollywood Boulevard and La Brea Avenue, and William picked up the intercom. "Driver," he said, "please go around the block and park at Hugo's Hot Dog Stand."

"Yes, sir."

Louisa was dumbfounded and remained silent as the limousine pulled over to the curb. The driver helped Louisa alight; then William climbed out of the back seat and escorted her into the small, brightly illuminated place.

A couple in denims, a blonde teenager, and two Hollywood High School seniors, all of whom had been seated in the bleachers in front of the Pantages Theatre, looked askance as the lady in a mauve bugle-beaded evening dress, with white fox furs, and the young man in midnight-blue tuxedo ordered chili dogs with onions, mustard, and sweet pickles.

Louisa discovered a letter with a Willawa, Oklahoma, postmark in the mail a few days later. There were a few lines scrawled on a piece of yellow foolscap:

April 9, 1953

Dear son:

This is your pappy, Finney Nestor, writing to you from the farm. We went agin the Lords wishes and saw you in front of the hardware store. Yore ma said she ain't never seen enny thing like it. We did'nt unner stand why you werent good enough to get that thing they was handing out. Yore ma has to have her gall bladder cut out or the doctor says she won't have a chance. It's gonna cost a lot of mony but we told him we would get it all from you who got plenty. Please send 800 dollar by return mail.

Pap

P.S. Who was that lady we seen you with?

At first Louisa laughed, because she had been away from Willawa for so long that she had forgotten that people like the Nestors still existed. In her present life, it seemed impossible that she had once also held a narrow viewpoint. Thank God she had been saved by her college education, and had been able to be malleable and grow with William.

She glanced in the living-room mirror, somehow expecting to see the faded, stoop-shouldered woman with dishwater hair, dressed in nondescript clothing, that she had once been, instead of the svelte, elegant, auburn-haired stranger who was gazing back at her now.

She placed a person-to-person telephone call to Dr. Frank Lambert in Willawa, and was told that Mrs. Nestor did indeed require a gall bladder operation, and if there were no complications, the fee would be five hundred dollars. She wrote a short note in her spidery handwriting to Finney Nestor, saying William would pay the bill, which would be forwarded by the hospital.

She was already sending the Nestors a hundred and fifty dollars a month, and even that she considered blackmail. They did not deserve another red cent.

16

The Game

The road along the 38th parallel had been repaired for the fourth time in six months but was still in a deteriorated condition.

Lieutenant James Foxwood Elliott IV strode out of the quonset hut and addressed Sergeant Luke Heron III in a confidential manner. "Ah don't care how ya do it, but Ah want to spend the night in Witcha's Village."

Luke Three was delighted at the opportunity of seeing T'am. "Sir," he replied seriously, "I think I should draw your attention to the fact that I've been having carburetor troubles, and I just checked the motor pool and there's not another jeep available."

The lieutenant appeared to study the matter in some depth. "We'll just have to chance it, Sarge. I gotta get this damn packet over to the Lower Headquarters. With your mechanical background, I'm sure you can get us through." He winked, and laughed under his breath, anticipating the evening that lay before him. He had a plan.

The terrain had been battered with mortar fire since Luke Three had made the trip six weeks ago with the lieutenant and another officer. They had not been able to stop at Witch's Village, and the other three times that he had made the trip, he had led a convoy of trucks, so he had not seen T'am in eight months. She might have left for her grandmother's village or gone to work in the black market. He packed a sack with provisions he had collected.

He was realistic enough to realize that their meetings

might have made no impression upon the girl, and it was possible that she might not even remember him. But he was also romantic enough to hold a glimmer of hope that all would be the same as before.

T'am was the first woman he had ever met, except for Darlene Trune, for whom he felt a twinge of deep affection. With Darlene, those feelings had been satisfied in the various conveyances in which they had made love in Angel. He felt slightly guilty that he had never formally gone to bed with her.

But his behavior as a teenager did not embarrass him now, as he looked back over his various conquests in Europe. First on the list was the beautiful if delicate Ardith, the daughter of Sir Eric Huxley-Drummond, head of Heron British. It was only later that he discovered that she bedded all of the field men, probably because of a necessity to prove superiority. What was the opposite of the Don Juan complex? Ardith, he was certain, was not merely promiscuous, because she did not possess that need to dominate in bed; it was a matter of pride with her that she only went to bed with executives. She had taught him to be wary of well-educated pieces of fluff who might have ulterior motives for turning down the bedcovers.

Next was Hedvig, the prostitute he had met in a nightclub called the Hague in Rotterdam, who had been impressed with his cleanliness and the fact that he was circumcised, which most European men were not. She had taught him that sudden encounters on a purely sexual basis could be both satisfying and rather sweet.

How could he ever forget Jolene Fertig, the Belgian countess in whose hunting lodge Robert Desmond and he had spent the night? She was middle-aged, redheaded, broke, a lousy cook, believed that life was "pre-ordained," had sung "Lili Marlene" in German, and then had crawled into bed with him and used him as he had used Hedvig. She had taught him to beware of the predatory female out for her own pleasure.

And then, of course, there was Linda Roman, whom he had met at a reception at the American Embassy. A blonde, outdoorsy type, she had called him Cowpoke and Lukey.

Anger swelled up in his breast; he still looked back upon that six-month episode as the most humiliating period of his life. They had traveled to the Greek Isles on board her parents' yacht, the *Saratoga*, sleeping together every night but keeping up the facade of just being "friends" during the daytime. He became weary of going back to his stateroom every morning in the wee hours, exhausted and with an empty feeling in his stomach, as if he had not had enough to eat for dinner. This was his one experience with the lifestyle of alcoholic millionaires who have nothing better to do than give endless parties. Linda had taught him not to fall for every beautiful girl with a gleam in her eye who would cast him out of her life at an inopportune moment.

So far, that was his repertoire of women; surely not a great number, but each was a learning experience.

"What in hell are ya thinking about, Sarge?" The lieutenant's laconic voice interrupted Luke Three's musing. "You've almost driven off the road twice! Am Ah goin' to haf to get me a new driver?"

Luke thought: *I wish to hell you would!* Aloud he replied, "Oh, no, sir, I guess I must have been dreaming, or maybe the heat is getting to me."

They had early chow at the MASH unit and then set out on the road again, and it was three o'clock before the jeep turned down a bend in the road and they saw Witch's Village cradled in the arms of two small, rolling hills. The place looked deserted, and there was not even a ragamuffin in the street.

The pink door was battered, as if a truck had skidded off the street, and the window paper had been torn from the frame and patched with what appeared to be an old GI raincoat. Luke Three pulled up in a cloud of dust, and the lieutenant knocked loudly on the pink door, and, when there was no answer, flattened his hands and made slapping noises. Finally the door opened an inch, and the fat madam peeked out. "What want?"

"Whadda mean, 'what want'?" The lieutenant yelled. "What in the hell do you think?" He paused and removed his cap. "Doncha remember me? Jimmy."

Her brow furrowed as she tried to recall his face or his

name or the incident that had brought him to her door. Luke Three was highly amused to think that out of all the soldiers that had passed under those infamous arches since that last encounter, the lieutenant actually believed that she would remember him.

Suddenly the madam grinned, disappeared for a moment, and returned with a razor, which she held up to his face. "Jimmy?"

The lieutenant glanced furtively at Luke Three, who was paying elaborate attention to the communications packet, and, thinking he was unobserved, murmured, "Ah got some chocolate."

The madam laughed. "Come in? Short time, five smackeroos? Long time, ten smackeroos? All night, twenty smackeroos?"

The lieutenant waved a Hershey bar and a twenty-dollar bill in her face, and winked at Luke Three. "Ya come and get me in the morning, heah?"

"Yes, sir." Luke Three waited until the broken pink door closed, then parked the jeep in the little alley space beside T'am's house, and scratched at the window. The door opened, and Do'm appeared.

Luke Three smiled. "Remember first-class Gyrene, second-class jeep?"

Do'm grinned, and his eyes disappeared in his face. "Howdy. You come, I open Coke?"

"Is sister T'am home?" He gave him the sack of provisions.

"She workee mountain patch, gather reed. You see her. I lead you, not far, not near. You take me Stateside as shoeshine boy?"

Do'm wiped his bare feet carefully and put on an oversized pair of GI boots and a Marine cap and ran out into the street. "Come," he shouted, and slowed his pace to a trot so that Luke Three could keep up with him. He led him up a well-worn path behind the village, and through a grove of trees that had been partially burned by firebombs.

Beyond a small sweet-potato patch tended by an old man in a wide straw hat, a small, muddy-looking pond was situated. As Luke Three and Do'm drew nearer, two women up to their ankles in water were picking tall reeds, which were then tied into huge bundles by a third woman.

Luke Three was taken aback by the beauty of the scene. It was difficult to believe that there was a war being fought nearby, or that these women were of the present age. This little valley seemed untouched, and since it was protected from the winds, the vegetation was lush and green.

The silence of the place was broken by the boy's shout—a rapid phrase in Korean and then, "Lookee, lookee, first-class Gyrene in second-class jeep."

He saw that the woman bundling the reeds was T'am, and he wondered if she would remember him with affection as she spoke to one of the women picking stalks. They came out of the water as Luke Three drew nearer, and carefully dried off their feet and removed the wide hats. They were both wearing blue padded jackets, with trousers folded up to their knees.

During all the months that Luke Three had dreamed of T'am, he thought his memory of her complete, but when they were face to face he discovered that she was far more beautiful than he remembered: her complexion was flawless, her eyes were larger and less slanted, and she was less robust. She was, he thought, probably very much like those delicate china figurines that Uncle Mitch had once told him he had sold in France between the two wars.

He bowed slightly, and the women bobbed up and down gracefully in return, an inborn gesture that was both polite and touching.

"Welcome back to this neck of the woods," T'am said seriously, looking down in deference before she glanced up into his face.

He smiled at her American slang. "I'm pleased to see you again, T'am." He repeated her name lovingly, and his pronounciation caused her to smile in return.

"Sir . . . Luke," she said formally, drawing herself up to her full height, "I present for introduction my momma, Jhonga, who has escaped from the North."

The mother was as beautiful as the daughter, he saw, only tiny, fine lines—like the crackle finish of an ancient vase—lined her face. There was suffering in her eyes. She smiled brightly, and some of the pain vanished. "Glad to meet you, sir," she said, and he realized that she must have worked once in the house of an Englishman, because she spoke with the same sort of Oxford accent as Robert Desmond. He found the contrast between face and voice charming, if incongruous.

Jhonga came forward immediately in a very businesslike way. "We have simple dinner," she said. "You stay?"

"If I may."

"Yesss." She pointed to a series of small grass huts by the side of the pond. "Factory," she said, "and eating and sleeping too. All children home." She counted on her fingers. "Number One, Two, Three girls." She looked up into his face and lowered her voice. "Friend at Joy House short time, long time, all night?"

Luke cleared his throat uncomfortably. "All night," he said gravely.

Jhonga nodded. Experience had taught her the ways of soldiers. Most went to the Joy Houses; some, like this straight-eyed boy, did not. "You have wife, yesss?" she asked plaintively, and when he shook his head, she laughed, showing a row of perfect teeth. "What wrong?"

He was confused; it was a question that had never been asked of him before. "Nothing," he replied carefully. "I am a very part-ic-u-lar man."

She frowned. "What is this 'part-ic-u-lar' word?"

He tried to think of a simple term that she could understand. Finally he said, "I want a very special woman."

"Ah." She nodded, seemingly relieved that nothing was wrong with him physically. "I too am part-ic-u-lar. My husband was famous poet." Her eyes grew misty. "Japanese Government was angry at his poems, which talked of freedoms and . . . free . . . thinking. Ten years ago, he put in street with pigs and—rifle shot." She paused a moment to regain control of her emotions. "No money left, fine house gone. My amah told me how to make reed baskets."

She brightened. "We work, no need to work in black market." She reached into her jacket pocket and brought forth a small book bound in green kidskin. "My husband's words are always with me." She paused. "We have bar-be-cued sweet potatoes soon." She turned to T'am. "Momma speak. T'am speak?" She made a little gesture and went back to the field.

The girl smoothed her hair back from her face and looked directly into his eyes. "Momma likes you; she no speak to strangers in town." She paused. "Do'm thinks you married guy with no kids. He told Momma you come back and take him Stateside."

She glanced down at her chapped hands, which she hid behind her back. "He no understand. First GI come to village, laugh and say he take Do'm home as shoeshine boy in Phil-a-delph-ia. He get killed. Every GI since, Do'm want to go and be shoeshine boy for."

Luke Three was touched at her naivety. Obviously a passing remark was taken seriously; he must watch his language. Her eyes were wide and honest, and she was so serious and . . . He sought the right word. *Feminine*—yes, that was it; there was a certain delicacy in her movements.

He contrasted T'am's demeanor with the other women who had played an important role in his sexual education, but none of them had this sort of . . . simplicity, except perhaps Hedvig. He was shocked at the mental comparison between these two very different females. Hedvig was a whore, yet in many ways she was more of a lady, more subtly feminine, that all of the others put together—except T'am.

Yet he could not be certain that other soldiers before him had not taken T'am sexually. It had not mattered with the others if they had gone to bed with dozens of men, but somehow he could not bear the thought that T'am was impure. *Impure*? Why had that word popped into his brain? He had never used that term regarding a woman before.

She was looking at him as if she expected an answer, and as he had been distracted, he had to think back to her words. "Oh, yes, Do'm. I do not need one small boy," he said kindly. "I have no one to take care of him."

"No marry?"

He shook his head. "You?"

"No find guy. Long time ago, when Daddy alive, I eight year old and he fix me up to marry son of high-class vase painter, but Daddy murdered; painter die; war come; many GI get off boat, carry candy, bubble gum, white cigarette; many Chinese turn Commie. Old ways go; no one trust own grandmama." She began to talk very quickly, very nervously. "Now T'am eighteen year old, no husband, no way procure husband in fighting war. Korean guys have nothing, work hard after war to procure wife. Only many GI's say love me, take me Stateside."

Luke Three thought that he was going to be physically ill. It was the same wartime story that had not changed since biblical days: soldiers promising marriage for a one-night affair, then leaving to go into battle and be killed, or, if they were spared, to go on to the next village and more promises of marriage to more virgins. In this new light, he rather admired the lieutenant for going to the Joy Houses, where he paid for the delights that an experienced woman could provide. It was only the young kids, he thought, not yet dry behind the ears, or old veterans out for a thrill, who despoiled the young virgins. . . .

She was looking at him curiously again. He swallowed and asked very gently, "You have First Class Dogface or Gyrene guy?"

She was aghast and shook her head violently. "No! Not T'am." Then tears came into her eyes. "My sister"—her voice choked and she could not go on for a moment—"sister has . . . Gyrene guy . . . come soon . . . take her Stateside." She looked at the sun and nodded. "Time for breakfast—no, wrong word. Dinner?"

He followed her to the largest of the grass huts pondside, and followed her example and sat on a grass mat on the floor, upon which rested an earthen bowl of roasted sweet potatoes, each pierced by a whittled stick, individual bowls of green tea, and a box of graham crackers. The ancestor tablets were displayed on the wall, and the Buddah rested on a small stool.

Hearing a commotion outside the door, Luke Three got to his feet. One by one, each member of the family came into the room, led by Jhonga. She introduced T'am's sisters, who had names that Luke Three could not pronounce, but the last girl, who had combed her hair down around her shoulders American style, smiled and said, "Call me Sally."

Do'm was next, followed by the man whom Luke Three had seen in the field earlier, whom Jhonga introduced as "Po Po"—"Uncle," a friend who had lost his wife and children in the war. The man nodded politely but he did not smile, and at a sudden command everyone sat down on the mat, and it occurred to Luke Three that this man had taken over as head of the family.

The group ate the sweet potatoes on the sticks first, a pan of vegetables and then Jhonga served small bowls of red rice. The bark tea bowls were replenished, and then Sally took a small Hershey bar from a knapsack and, while everyone watched intently, broke the chocolate into small pieces, which she placed on a porcelain plate. This was obviously a rare treat, and they all smacked their lips, moving the morsels around on their tongues with expressions of delight.

At that moment there was the sharp cry of a baby, and Sally got up immediately and rearranged some coverings on a mat. She picked up the baby, who had a pink ribbon tied in her quite luxuriant growth of dark hair, and, bringing the child to the dinner mat, fed her a few grains of rice. "Baby name Ginger," she said happily.

"How old?" Luke Three asked.

Sally counted on her fingers. "Eighteen moons—months."

Luke looked at the baby girl with the admiration expected, and was shocked to discover that her eyes were straight, with only the suggestion of a fold of skin at the inward corners, and the complexion was stark white.

Sally handed the baby to Jhonga. "I show picture of daddy," she said, and going once more to the knapsack, she brought out an old pro kit that had been used, a handful of change, a set of car keys, and a photograph taken in a booth such as those set up at sideshow carnivals. "As soon as red

tape over, he come back, see Ginger first time, take she, me
Stateside."

She handed the photograph to Luke Three. With great
shock, he looked down into the smiling face of Rich
Halprin.

Luke Three shared a small hut with the man known as Po
Po, and Do'm, but he had difficulty going to sleep. He kept
seeing Hal's face smiling up at him from the photograph,
and then he saw the calm expression on his face as he lay in
the dugout with his body blown away from the chest down.
How could he tell Sally that Hal was never coming back?
How could he say that Hal had never known there was a
baby, or that it would not have mattered to him if he had
known, and that he had no intention of taking her back to
America? He could see her waiting patiently for years, with
this strange-looking mixed-blood child.

He was overcome with revulsion until he realized that
Uncle Clem was a mixed-blood. He turned over on his side
and pondered the strange rites of mankind and the thousands
of mixtures of blood that could occur throughout the world.

Halprin, he thought, *wherever you are, you're a son-of-
a-bitch for not caring enough for Sally to wear a condom,
but caring enough for yourself to take a pro in case she had
a disease*. If there was a way that he could have the baby
shipped home to Hal's family, he would do so at once. Then
slowly, very slowly, sleep softened his thoughts, and in his
dream, he was making love to T'am, moving delightfully
within her, and taking pride because she was uttering little
animal cries of joy. . . .

Luke Three awakened instantly when the hut was
illuminated by the sun. So as not to awaken Po Po or Do'm,
he got up quietly and adjusted his fatigues, then stealthily
crept out of the door. He stretched his frame and smothered
a yawn; then he drew back in surprise: T'am was heating
gruel over charcoal, and she smiled and pointed to a bowl of
warm water.

She handed him an old but clean olive-drab army towel,

and when he had washed his face and combed his hair, she motioned him to a mat, where she served the *congee*.

When he had finished breakfast, she indicated that she would accompany him to the village. When they were out of earshot of the sleeping family, she said, "T'am see eyes when Luke look at picture. You know Rich Halprin?"

He did not know whether to tell her the truth or not. Finally he decided that he could not lie. "Story is sad," he said, trying to find words that she would understand. "Rich Halprin is dead." He decided not to tell her more.

She turned away from him a moment, then resumed the walk. "T'am know he dead."

"How?"

She touched her breast. "Inside. Rich Halprin come back long ago if alive."

He was almost moved to tears by her trust. "You tell Sally?"

She shook her head. "No, tell Uncle. He say dead to her." They had left the grove of trees and were going down the main street of Witch's Village. "When Luke come back?" she asked.

"Not easy," he replied. "One moon-month, maybe."

"T'am be in reed village, not in this place." She glanced at the pink door across the street from the town house. "Big fight. Much drinky, too much soft touch."

She held out her hand, and he found himself awkwardly shaking it, and he grinned and quickly bent down and kissed her cheek, then turned away and knocked on the pink door.

Instead of the madam opening the door as he expected, the lieutenant appeared, sober, neatly dressed, face shaven and faintly smelling of gardenia perfume. "Ah jest had to teach the bitch a lesson," he whispered, and opened the door wide so that Luke Three could see inside: strange, muffled sounds were emanating from the dark interior.

Luke Three blinked twice as his eyes became adjusted to the gloom. He could not believe his eyes. Struggling to get loose, the fat madam was strapped to a bamboo chair, a gag in her mouth. Around the chair were long snippets of hair. She had been shaven completely bald.

* * *

Letty and Patricia Anne arrived at the television station in Omaha fifteen minutes early.

"I hate to leave the cab out there with its meter running, Grandma, but I don't know what else to do. Your next show is in forty-five minutes across town, and I'm afraid there won't be time to call another taxi."

"It can't be helped. Do I look all right?"

"Fantastic, Grandma," Patricia Anne said, admiring Letty's black skirt, red chiffon blouse, and silver upswept hairdo.

"I haven't got too much makeup on?" Letty asked. "I don't want to look like a kewpie doll, but on the other hand, I must have enough base to cover my liver-spots."

Patricia Anne laughed. "It's very subtle. By the way, the man at the hotel said that Miss Fairfax, who's going to interview you on the news show, is a pioneer in local television and is quite well liked."

"Well, in that case," Letty replied, "I'll remember to say something nice."

At that moment a young man came through the swinging doors and greeted them warmly. "My name is Dwight Leeds, and I'm producer of the show. We are most pleased to have you aboard, Mrs. Trenton."

"Thank you. This is my granddaughter, Mrs. Hanson. Can she come into the studio?"

He smiled. "Certainly. I'll find her a chair somewhere." He led them down a long corridor and into a large room with a beige sofa, a red leather chair, and a coffee table placed against a blue-painted wall. "Oh-oh," Dwight said, adjusting his enormous hornrimmed glasses. "This will never do. Mrs. Trenton, you're supposed to be seated on the red chair, and with your outfit, you'll be lost on camera."

He looked around frantically and finally found a pale blue chair in the corner, and while he made the exchange he explained, "Pale blue shows up as white on camera, so your red blouse will look great."

Letty whispered to Patricia Anne, "Make a note, dear, to call the television stations a day or so before I do a show, and find out what the color scheme of the set is going to be. This nice young man fixed everything today, but we might not to be so lucky in the future." She raised her eyebrows. "I don't want to fade into the furniture."

Drucilla Fairfax, a steely-eyed stick of a lady with peroxided hair, wearing a navy suit with a pale gray blouse, held out her hand to be shaken, but did not smile. While she greeted Letty and Patricia Anne, her eyes were roving over the studio, as if trying to find an employee who was causing an infraction of rules.

"You'll have five minutes only, Mrs. Trenton," Drucilla Fairfax said icily, "so I do hope that you have an opening and closing statement. The last question that I will ask will be: 'To what can senior citizens look forward in the future?' Please stay seated for my wrap-up of the news until the red light goes out on the camera. Please call me Drucilla. Shall we take our places?"

Dwight guided Letty to the blue chair and fastened a microphone on a cord around her neck, vainly trying to hide it in the folds of red chiffon; then he stepped back, lights flooded the set, the director of the show held up three fingers, then two, then one, and pointed at Drucilla Fairfax.

A startling change came over her face the moment the red light on the camera flashed on. Gone was the hard veneer. She smiled sweetly. "Good morning, everyone," she said warmly. "Welcome to the Morning Show. Our very special guest today is a lady whom I've long admired. She comes from one of the most influential families in America, and I'm delighted that she can take time out of her hectic schedule as head of the Senior Citizens of America Group to be with us today. May I introduce Letty Heron Trenton. Welcome to the show, Letty."

"I'm so glad to be here, Drucilla, but before another thing is said, I want you to know that you're a much beloved lady hereabouts."

Letty could only assume that Drucilla Fairfax's expression of delighted surprise was real as she burbled, "Thank you. Now, would you give us your formula for being an active member of the community?"

As Letty gave her usual pitch, with just enough humor and just enough serious advice, she knew that the show was going to be special. Drucilla Fairfax came in with the right questions at the right time, and after her sign-off, when the red light was switched off, she kissed Letty on the cheek. "Come back any time, my dear, you were charming."

Later in the cab, when Letty removed the red chiffon blouse, revealing a plain pink blouse underneath—not having time to change between shows—she sighed and addressed Patricia Anne. "There must be a moral in there somewhere connected with Drucilla Fairfax. I suppose she was expecting a senile old coot who'd talk about her grandchildren!"

"You're so good on television, Grandma, that you should really have your own show," Patricia Anne said admiringly.

Letty laughed. "No, thank you." She paused. "We're to be in St. Paul for two days. Would you change the hotel reservation to a suite with a kitchen? I want to do a bit of cooking. I've had my mouth set for an Angel cake!"

The huge platform containing the Heron rig had been constructed of steel and concrete at a small inlet on Vermillion Bay, a short distance from Weeks, Louisiana, then gently towed to the offshore drilling site, eight miles beyond Tigre Point.

Luke and Jeanette flew on a commercial airline to New Orleans and took the shuttle to Morgan City, where they boarded a helicopter that would fly over the rig. "Isn't this exciting, Jeanette?" Luke said with more enthusiasm than she had heard him use in months, as they circled the platform floating on the dark blue-green waters below.

"Just thrilling," she replied laconically. "It would be far more thrilling, though, if we were in our own plane."

"You're not going to keep hitting me with *that*, are you?" he groused. "You know that Mama has the *Blue Heron* all this week. You can't expect a woman her age, making all those personal appearances to take a commercial airline, can you?"

"A woman her age," Jeanette replied succinctly, "should be home in Angel, and not gallivanting around the country making a fool of herself on television."

"I believe you're jealous!" he exclaimed.

"I am not!" she retorted. "Only it's embarrassing, when we're all Democrats—"

"Aha!" He nodded. "So that's it! May I remind you that Herons only turned Democratic before Roosevelt's fourth term, because Bosley had known Truman since his haberdashery days in Kansas City?"

"Yes, I remember," she answered dryly, "and I was never at home with the Republican women's groups. It was only when I joined the Democratic Ladies Club that I felt useful. Then when my own mother-in-law—"

"I wish you wouldn't keep harping on that, Jeanette," he said crossly. "She's really representing the government on the senior citizens issue, and that has no party demarcation lines. Her position is actually apolitical."

"Of course it is, I'm not stupid! It's just that she's photographed with Mamie Eisenhower all the time. Just this week in *Time*, for instance, there they are at some shindig in Washington. Really, Mamie is nothing but an army wife, and I'll never forget that photograph of her with her shoes off, rubbing her feet after the inauguration. Absolutely no class."

"I never realized before," Luke replied, "that you're a snob, Jeanette."

"I am *not*. But I know my place."

"Your place," he answered grimly, "is watching what's going on down there. Look, they're raising the Heron flag on the rig, that means that the platform is in place and drilling will start tomorrow. It's taken the men three weeks to weld the platform to the pilasters sunk in the bottom of the bay. Tomorrow we'll take the boat out there with a photographer as they start putting up the rig."

"You can go, dear, I'm going to have my hair done. Remember you promised to take me dancing at the Blue Room of the Roosevelt Hotel for our anniversary tomorrow. Didn't Clem appear there in the old days, before he got too uppity for showroom dates?"

Luke sighed. "He was there for two weeks twice a year, but as far as being uppity, he's now become so famous that he only does concerts. He doesn't have to spend those terrible hours playing for middle-aged dancers anymore. I should think you'd be happy to have a living legend for a brother-in-law."

"Well, I've never heard him give you credit for 'The Cowboy Waltz.'"

"Why should I get credit?"

"If you hadn't drug him out to Willawa to meet Louisa Tarbell, he'd never have discovered William Nestor."

"Oh, my God, Jeanette, how far-fetched can you get? You know damn well Louisa wrote a letter to me in care of Heron Oil, and I just happened to draw Clem's attention to it!" He turned to the pilot. "Let's go back to Morgan City," he said, "but I'll want your services later in the week, because the photographer will be wanting to take some pictures of the platform and the partially constructed rig from up here."

He turned to Jeanette. "I wish you'd come with me tomorrow. They have a miniature city down there with a complete kitchen, deluxe dormitory, recreational facilities, a small movie theater, a library."

"All the comforts of home. I think that's very sweet."

"I don't appreciate your sarcasm, Jeanette. After all, those Canucks will be spending seven days straight on the platform, which means two weeks a month there and two weeks at home. They'd go nuts if they didn't have great facilities."

"For what those Canucks are being paid, Luke, it seems to me that they could rough it."

Luke ignored his wife and turned to the pilot. "Before we leave, would you swing around once more? If that isn't the most beautiful sight I've ever seen, I'll eat my hat."

"You're not wearing one, dear," Jeanette interjected, and glanced below at the strange sight of the man-made island that seemed, as they dropped nearer, to be the size of a city block.

"I do have a suggestion," she said. "It's all so bare down there. Why don't you bring in a few trees in big containers? If those men have to be out there for long stretches, they can't stay indoors all the time when they're off shift. It seems to me that a couple of park benches under the trees would give some relief from the monotonous scenery."

"My God, Jeanette," he cried, "I think that's a great idea. I wonder why the architect didn't think about that?"

"Because"—she smiled tightly—"the architect is not a woman!"

When an article in depth appeared about the Heron offshore drilling concept in *The Petroleum World* three months later, the piece was illustrated with several photographs of the facilities, including a shot of dormitories with flowered drapery and matching bedspreads, which Jeanette had also suggested. But the largest picture of all was of a pensive driller posed on a park bench placed on artifical turf, reading a newspaper in the shade of a date-palm tree, with the caption: *Roustabout Terence O'Reilly is really living the life of Reilly on Heron Oil's first offshore drilling rig, off Tigre Point in the Gulf of Mexico.*

"Well, Luke"—Jeanette sniffed after examining the photo layout—"I should think that you'd give credit where credit is due. After all, those men would still be sleeping in a dormitory with venetian blinds and no bedspreads and no place to sit outside, let alone enjoying green trees, if it wasn't for me!"

"Oh, pipe down," Luke replied sourly. "The next thing I know, you'll be harassing me to put you on the payroll as a consultant." He paused. "And furthermore, if you'd take the time to read the goddam article, you'd see your name mentioned on page two!"

17

The Yearning

The moonlight illuminated the road so brightly that it could have been late afternoon.

Luke Three had stolen out of the compound after lights out, passed the sentry, and made his way to the jeep, which he had parked a half a mile away under a bayberry tree.

Lieutenant James Foxwood Elliot IV had been given a transfer to Pusan, far to the south, and to Luke Three's disgust, he was assigned to continue as driver. He had heard the lieutenant tell the CO: "That Okie is the best driver in Korea—of course, outside your own, Colonel!" He had almost retched. It was bad enough to be assigned to a battle zone without fighting per se, but to be stuck with a miserable excuse for a man, and a superior at that, was almost more than he could bear. He prayed every night that the peace talks would prove fruitful. Besides, to his surprise, he was homesick for Angel.

He started the jeep's motor and pulled onto the road. It was the height of irony, he thought, that repairs had been made, and since there had been no new bombings by the Chinese Commies in the last three months, the road was in excellent condition. If luck was with him, he would reach Witch's Village by eleven.

As he rounded the grove of trees that protected the village from the winds, he saw no lights ahead, nor were there any musical recordings being played, unusual for the Joy House at this time of night.

He was filled with dread; the place was deserted, and the

few houses looked abandoned. The pink door was swinging idly in the wind, and there was nothing except the smell of Lysol emanating from the musty interior. Pieces of straw mattresses lay about, and when he looked across the street he saw gaping holes where paper had been stretched across the windows of T'am's house. *Oh, dear God,* he prayed, *let the family be safe!* Although he had only been to the reed pond once, lead by Do'm in daytime, he picked his way carefully to the little path behind the village, impeded somewhat by briars and brambles that stuck to his fatigues.

When he reached the top of the hill and loped down the path to the clearing, he saw the huts were still there, although the quiet was disturbing. Someone had once written that "silence was deafening," and he had thought it a ridiculous quote. Now he knew the truth of the statement; silence *was* deafening!

He slowed down his steps as he reached the largest hut, where food was normally served. He did not have the power to call out or make his presence felt. What if the family had been routed out? It was not possible that they could ever be traced. He paused at the door of the big hut; were his senses playing tricks on him, or did he smell the odor of that special bark tea that he had enjoyed on his previous visits?

"Hello, hello, Do'm, T'am," he called. "It's first class Gyrene in second class jeep."

The door was flung open and the smell of burning kerosene poured into his face. Po Po stood on the threshold, his face grave as he bowed slowly and waved Luke Three into the room.

The entire family sat in a circle, men on one side, women on the other, illuminated by two large lanterns hung from the ceiling poles; each member held a basket at some stage of weaving. Do'm stood up and cried, "You come back"— his voice cracked, but he went bravely on—"to take me to Phil-a-delph-ia as shoeshine boy?" His face beamed with pleasure, but there was a new set to his jaw; he was losing his baby fat. Do'm was becoming a man.

Jhonga stood up, her face expressionless, and Luke Three knew that something was wrong; the family had never before been so subdued. She bowed low and ceremoniously.

"Pleased to see you, Luke." She smiled slightly, because she knew that she had pronounced his name correctly.

Sally stood up and bowed and sat down again, followed by the younger sisters, whose names Luke Three could not pronounce, and lastly T'am stood, and she was very nervous. Her hands shook as she also bowed low. The atmosphere was charged with electricity.

Luke Three bowed solemnly. "I glad to find you here. Village is gone away." For some reason he was filled with both joy and doubt, a combination of emotions that was new to him.

Po Po gave a swift command in Korean to Do'm, who ran out the back door; then he waved Luke Three to be seated, not next to T'am but beside Jhonga, who poured a bowl of bark tea for him.

There was a strained and awkward silence; the girls stared at the baskets they held, but T'am, Jhonga, and the uncle sat with folded hands, their eyes fixed seemingly on an identical spot on the opposite wall. Luke Three was mystified by this strange behavior. He sipped his tea, and the room was so quiet that the contact of the bowl with his lips could be heard.

At last the door opened and Do'm entered, leading an elderly man by the hand. It was only after he was in the room that Luke Three realized that he was blind. The man was in his early sixties and almost bald, but he wore a thin gray mustache that hung down over the corners of his mouth. He greeted the group in Korean and then turned instinctively to Luke Three. "Good evening," he said in perfect English. "You may call me Bobby, which is what my English employer called me when I was chauffeur for a banker in Hong Kong."

Luke Three did not find it advisable to ask how a blind man had driven a car; obviously his infirmity had begun since his sojourn in Hong Kong. "It is good to hear my native tongue as it should be spoken, Bobby."

"I understand perfectly," the man replied. "It is a pity that you do not all speak the same language. These people's English is made up mostly of GI slang, which is unfortunate. That is why I was asked to be present tonight, because there are many important things to be said on each side and there must be no misunderstanding." He paused. "Also, this conversation must be carried on with dignity and tact, and not in half-understood phrases."

Bobby sat down on the mat, and a cup of tea was poured, and he performed a small ritual of appreciation before he cleared his throat as a signal that the conversation was to begin.

Luke Three was as mystified as ever now that the interpreter had been summoned, and when the Po Po spoke slowly and earnestly for a very long time, it became apparent that this was a family conference of some importance.

Bobby turned to Luke Three and spoke formally. "This is the fourth time that you have been kind enough to grace this household with your commanding presence. It is a tradition of our village that goes back many generations to question most deeply the intentions of one who creates such a vivid impression upon a younger member of the family."

Luke Three blinked at the man. He could understand his words perfectly well, but the meaning was not clear. "What does this mean?" he whispered to Bobby.

The interpreter turned sideways and murmured, "When a young man visits a family so often, it means that he's interested in the one of the daughters. The uncle wants to know if your intentions are honorable."

Luke Three's palms began to perspire as he continued in a barely audible voice. "I don't know how you're going to word this, Bobby, but I came to say good-bye for now. I'm being transferred to Pusan. I want to see more of T'am, we haven't been together very much, but I don't know if I'll be back soon."

Bobby translated carefully, seeking the facial expression appropriate to the context of the statement, and the uncle replied in a quick, sharp voice.

"In essence, he says," Bobby repeated informally, "that you've already seen much more of her than you would have in similar circumstances had not war disrupted the country. Traditionally we Koreans protect the young females of our families, and marriages are arranged. The uncle is trying to do the right thing for this family, who've lost all the male members who normally take care of such matters with the help of a go-between." He paused. "It all boils down to whether you want to marry T'am or not."

Luke Three paused. "In my country, Bobby, as you may know, there's a period of engagement, where both parties get to know each other. Then, after a period of time, the couple decide if they want to marry. I'm very much attracted to T'am, as I think, she is . . . to me."

Bobby translated quickly, and there was a polite but emphatic burst of Korean from the uncle. "He says that since you are leaving for the south, and the family must remain in the north, it seems that it is best to remember each other only with pleasure."

He paused dramatically. "He goes on to say that the family would very much like to have a photograph of you in full-dress uniform to place in the family chest."

Luke Three looked about the smoke-filled room at the impassive faces. T'am's eyes were downcast in supplication, but there was a tear on her cheek. *Oh, how he wanted to take her in his arms and protect her from all the enemies in the world!* "More than anything, Bobby, I want this relationship to continue. There must be in Korean literature a love story about two people who were separated by conditions beyond their control, that would illustrate my dilemma?"

Bobby's eyes grew bright. "Yes, there are many such tales, but I don't think it is a wise tactic to bring up such a story." He glanced at Sally. "You must remember, Sergeant, that the family has already suffered a great deal. This girl was alone in the house when Private Halprin made many promises, after which he made love to her. He promised marriage, and then ran away. What is Sally to do with the baby? She belongs to no particular race and will join many outcasts who have white fathers, after peace comes."

Luke Three considered the situation carefully. He must be honest with himself as never before. He was certainly infatuated with T'am, as he had been infatuated with Darlene Trune, yet, even with a satisfying sexual relationship, he had known from the beginning that he could not spend the rest of his life with her. Could he take T'am back to Angel?

During his musings, the uncle had been speaking, and Bobby cleared his throat meaningfully. "He wants to know what work you perform when you're not serving your country."

"You may tell him that I . . ." Luke Three paused. The name Heron meant nothing in this part of the world. Something inside of him said not to mention the family holdings. "I work in a petrol station," he finished.

"That is certainly respectable," Bobby conceded. "The uncle was afraid that you were mixed up in the black market."

Luke Three smiled. "You may tell him that there's no black market in my country." It was this sort of point of view, he realized, that was so difficult; it was not only that T'am was of another race, but her entire outlook on life was opposite to his own.

Also, deep in his mind was the unalterable belief that he could not marry a woman to whom he had not made love. He glanced at T'am again. *Oh, how he wanted to hold her tightly, and press his body into her own!*

Bobby translated the uncle's reply. "It seems that the winds of fate, as the Buddha would have said, have separated two people, perhaps in a judicious manner. It might be that you were meant to go back to your own country and marry a woman of your race, and that T'am is destined to remain at the pond of reeds and wait for the right native man to take her away from this place."

Tears stung the back of Luke Three's eyes. With such a prospect in mind, he knew that he must see T'am again. "Tell Po Po, Bobby, that my intentions are totally honorable, and that, to show my feeling for T'am, I will leave a sum of money to help the family over financial difficulties."

He took a deep breath and continued. "This war is nearing an end; it is only a matter of time until peace comes—within a matter of months, or at the most a year. If I am shipped home without returning here, I will come back at once. If I die, I will leave in my will a certain amount of money for T'am—the same sum that my wife would have received had I been married. All that I ask is that she wait for me."

After Bobby had translated Luke Three's words, the atmosphere in the room changed subtly. The pungent fumes from the kerosene lanterns, mixed with incense, still hung in the air, but it was as if his statement had lent dignity to the occasion. Before the uncle could reply, T'am looked into Luke Three's eyes. "I wait," she said, then frowned while she found the right word from her limited English vocabulary. "I proud to wait."

"It is settled, then," Bobby said.

Luke Three lowered his voice. "May I ask what you do here, Bobby?"

"Since I came from Hong Kong, I've been cured of tuberculosis, and I now pack the baskets these people make and sell to the townspeople. It's not a good business, but what is there left to do in a place as wartorn as my country?"

"You speak so well. While I am gone, if I give you money, will you teach T'am English? Then when I return, at least we'll be able to speak what's on our minds and not be forced to communicate in GI slang."

He paused. "I must go back to the base now. No one knows that I've left." He reached into his wallet, thankful that he had just received his pay. He extracted all of the bills, which he handed to Bobby. "This is all the money I have with me, but it may make conditions a little easier until I return."

Bobby translated very quickly, and suddenly the tension was broken with shouts in both English and Korean, and there were laughter and feelings of good will, and they all were on their feet and Luke Three was surrounded by family members. It was as if a momentous decision had been made and all sides were in agreement on the outcome of the negotiations.

Jhonga took his arm. "You are good Gyrene," she said seriously, and he had to swallow his laughter. If there was one term, even if he used it himself, that was repugnant to him, it was "Gyrene."

Bobby said, "Since, in a way, I have acted as go-between, T'am and I will accompany you to the jeep." And when Do'm made a move in their direction, he waved him back.

Po Po and the rest of the family followed Luke Three, T'am, and Bobby as far as the pond, good-byes were said, and they stood by the hut and waved farewell. The moonlight was even brighter than earlier, and when Bobby assumed the lead, Luke Three reached out and took T'am's hand, and, touching each other, they walked up the incline by the grove of bay trees.

Luke Three in all of his years had never experienced the tender, subtle delight in the closeness of their bodies. There was no need to speak because their mental communication was at a high peak of excitement. He did not want the walk to end.

When they reached the jeep, Bobby suddenly became involved with examining the surface of the moon, and Luke Three took T'am in his arms. He brought his face down to hers, and they touched lips. She did not know how to kiss! His body was tense, and, embarrassed, he drew back from her and kissed her tenderly on the cheek.

With perfect timing, Bobby turned and held out his hand. "There is an expression in your country, 'God go with you.' We have a similar saying, 'The Buddha will strew your path with flowers.' "

"I think both are appropriate," Luke Three said soberly. He raised T'am's right hand to his lips and kissed the palm. Then he got into the jeep, started the motor, and turned the vehicle on the road back to base camp. He did not drive in a straight line, because the road ahead was suddenly blurred.

Mitchell opened the short letter from Jean, which was very difficult to read because the writing was so very poor and Jean had used a pen with a scratchy head. At last, Mitchell figured out that Jean had accepted the invitation to come to the United States as his guest for "the American holiday, 4 July," when the paint factory would give him one week's vacation.

"Well," Charlotte said with a wry laugh, pouring glasses

of sherry before a dinner of beef stew, "that gives us time to prepare the family for the appearance of your long-lost son."

Mitchell nodded. "Yes, although I don't know why I should feel apprehensive about it whatsoever. We're all grown up, and the Korean war has sobered everyone further. Remember how naive we were during World War II?" He took a sip of wine. "Each generation seems to have its war, and yet no one has the guts to say ENOUGH, ENOUGH; they just go on killing each other with finer and more expensive weapons."

"Which reminds me," Charlotte said, "has anyone heard from Luke Three?"

"Not since he wrote me that very funny letter about being assigned as driver to some cornball lieutenant. That's what I mean about this new war. It's all so casual. In the first war, we damn well knew we were fighting the Huns, and in the second one, we had Hitler's mustache, Mussolini's bald pate, and Tojo's slopy eyes indelibly written on our brains, and we fought like hell. But today, does a Chinese Communist look any different than a Korean? Who can tel the difference?"

"Of course you're right, Mitch, and what is Luke Three really fighting for, anyway?" Charlotte poured another glass of sherry. "The American Way Of Life for those people in Southeast Asia? She shuddered. "Thank God I'm not in politics. But I swear to you that if a woman were to run for president on an antiwar platform, she'd win by a landslide."

He grinned. "You may very well be right. I migh mention it to Aunt Letty. She'd cop the nomination for sure if all of her senior citizens would vote for her!"

Charlotte held up a scarlet claw. "Now, don't make fun o Letty; she's got more spunk at her age than anyone I know After all these years, she's become a national symbol— which privately she was to us all along. She's a survivor Mitch. She founded the town of Angel, established an international oil company, buried three husbands, reared a famous composer—"

"And," Mitch put in, draining his glass, "don't forge

she made the humble blue Heron bird one of the most famous logos in the world."

"And all the time," Charlotte interjected with a laugh, "she kept an immaculate house, taught a Sunday-school class, and even managed to whip up an Angel cake now and then!" She paused and grew serious. "By the way, now that we're on the subject of Letty, did you ever find out what was in that makeup mirror with the letter L that you had such a hell of a time getting into Spain on that motorbus tour through the château country?"

Mitchell shook his head sadly. "No, and with Pierre dead, I don't suppose I'll ever find out. He was my contact. Always before, he showed up sooner or later and brought me up to date. But now that my name has been dropped from the list, I don't suppose we'll ever find out. Not that it's all that important. I did a job, and that was it; nothing else mattered at the time, or matters now."

"But aren't you just the slightest bit interested?"

"Not really." He threw her a penetrating look. "That's why men are more fitted for these jobs than women. We don't have a natural curiosity."

"I'm not sure that I agree with your statement," she replied coldly.

"Be that as it may, it's right on the button, which, if my olfactory senses aren't steering me wrong, is not the case with dinner."

"Oh my God, the stew!" Charlotte cried and ran into the kitchen, only to return a few moments later. She stood in the doorway. "The only change in menu is that our Oklahoma Mulligan has now become, through very artful self-basting, a superb dark French *ragout*!"

Lars Hanson had been home from the hospital for five months, and Patricia Anne had been able to stay home at the cottage in Chevy Chase, Maryland, now that Letty was back at the farm, preparing for Christmas.

He had lost the weight that he had accumulated in the hospital, was back on strenuous exercise, and looked brown and healthy, and had not been on a trip for six months. "I think the drug has finally been eliminated by my system,

Pat. Either that, or the enzymes have rendered it impotent. What's so maddening is that it will take years to discover how these hallucinatory compounds control the brain. And we may never find out."

"Shall we continue your paper?" she asked, picking up her notebook and pencil. "We left off when you performed the first experiments with the mushroom compound."

"No," Lars replied, "I don't think I'll work today. I'm mentally tired. I'll finish the book I'm reading, a fascinating account of the exploits of a South African jouralist named André Gulot. Apparently the book was a bestseller in Europe, and this translation is doing fine in this country. It would make a super-duper-pooper movie, because it's supposed to be filled with a lot of secret stuff. He's now on the trail of diamond smugglers on a motorbus tour through France."

"Have fun, dear, I'm going to the supermarket. How about a mushroom omelet for lunch, with a side dish of ambrosia?"

Lars nodded and picked up the book, and when Patricia Anne returned an hour later, he was staring out the window. "Honey," he said thoughtfully, frowning and turning toward her and looking very much like a professor in class, "didn't Mitchell and Charlotte visit the French Riviera on their honeymoon?"

She began to unpack the groceries. "Yes, but I don't think they had much fun, because they never mention the trip."

"Do you suppose that they could have been on that trip with Gulot? It included a tour of the famous châteaux."

"Mitchell and Charlotte on a motorbus tour? Highly unlikely. After all, he lived in France, and she's no stranger over there. If they wanted to see those places, they'd have rented a car."

"But what if they had a *purpose*?"

"What do you mean, Lars? None of this is making sense." She broke four eggs in a small mixing bowl, added a pinch of salt and pepper, a half ounce of water, and some chopped mushrooms. "Charlotte may seem very 'down home,' and in many ways she is, but she was reared with a silver spoon in her mouth, and she's always lived well and traveled a good deal—the Grand Tour and all of that.''

Lars picked up the book. "Let me read you this paragraph:

"Among the potpourri of passengers were three older couples—provincial types—a vivacious blonde lady from Australia; a plump little woman, by the unlikely name of Dolly Mae Parsons, from Riverside, California, with an ill-tempered Pekingese dog; middle-aged honeymooners from Enid, Oklahoma; and the man that I was pursuing, Harry Stanton, who, as it turned out, carried the rough diamonds in his umbrella cane. . . .''

Patricia Anne stood frozen with the mixing bowl in her hands. "How many middle-aged honeymoon couples from Enid could there be mixed in among the tourists?"

"That was my feeling also," he replied thoughtfully, "but not only that; they were searched by border police, and it became a famous scandal."

Patricia Anne began to beat the eggs rhythmically with a wire whisk. "Charlotte still has enough of the hometown girl in her not to regard this as a high point of their trip, and yet she never mentioned the motorbus tour at all. She told me about losing money at the casino in Monte Carlo, but not a word about this diamond-smuggling business."

Lars nodded and shrugged his shoulders, suddenly losing his professorish image. "Not only that, but in the last chapter Gulot relates the story of three people on a journey who are responsible for bringing a mysterious article out of France into Spain. I'm just getting into this part of the book, but it sounds like that woman with the dog and the honeymoon couple. . . .''

"Fancy that, Clyde!" Charlotte exclaimed, signing her name on the slip of paper. "A package from my husband's niece."

"It's a book, Mrs. Heron," the postman said. "Maybe it's an early Christmas gift."

"Well, if it is, Clyde, we'll have to get her something in return. We've never exchanged gifts before."

When Mitchell came home for lunch, sitting on his plate was the package. "Why didn't you open it, dear?"

"It was addressed to you."

"That's never stopped you before!" He laughed.

She grinned. "Just because I sleep with you, is no sign—"

"Charlotte," he interupted, "it's a book by André Gulot."

"Who?"

"Remember that man on the château tour who turned out to be a journalist?" He flipped over to the flyleaf. "Humm, Lars says to read the marked paragraphs on pages two hundred and ten and four hundred and eleven." He read aloud the descriptions of the passengers on the motorbus. The accounting of the diamond search was so authentic that the skin on his face tightened with remembrance. "I'm afraid to look at the next section," he said.

"Go on, I'll pour some coffee."

"A glass of sherry would be more appropriate," he replied with a strained half-smile. When she returned with the glasses, he gave a cryptic toast. "To André Gulot, a journalist who can't keep his mouth shut."

Mitchell cleared his throat and read in a strong voice:

"Looking back over my thirty years as a respected member of the Fourth Estate, I would list as favorite stories my coverage of the Nazis marching into Paris; the exposé of the deluting of the French wines; the election of General de Gaulle; and Willy Messerschmitt's becoming an advisor to the Spanish Government. . . ."

He took another sip of sherry. "It gets better," he said, and resumed reading:

"One fascinating story that is yet to be told, however, has all of the elements of a detective story that would spur the imagination of that great Agatha Christie detective, Hercule Poirot. The elements of the plot concern such diverse ingredients as the smuggling into Spain of a toilet article formed of a special metal shield that contained radioactive material to be used in cancer cure research; an unsuspecting Oklahoma yokel and his fat wife; and a woman with a vicious dog—but that and other stories must be reserved for the second edition of my exploits in the journalistic field."

"That little bastard!" Charlotte expounded. "Calling me fat and you a yokel, I mean *really*!"

Mitchell gave her a long look. "As usual," he said sourly, "being a woman, you've overlooked the most important point. At last you and I know what the mission was all about."

She looked at him blankly. "What do you mean?"

"You weren't listening carefully enough, apparently, Charlotte. The makeup mirror that I acquired and passed on was that—how did he put it?—'a toilet article formed of a special metal shield.' "

"Ah, the cancer research material. We might have been blown to bits if it was radioactive."

"Hardly, my dear. There might have been other adverse effects, such as severe burns; our hair might have fallen out and our teeth turned black—"

"I must say you paint a rosy picture," she said and then frowned. "But how *did* you get the makeup mirror?"

He gave her a long, searching look. "Oh, I just picked it up, that's all."

"In other words, you're not going to tell me. Right?"

"Right." Mitchell laughed. "But I'll tell you anything else you want to know. Since that damned Gulot practically spilled the beans, there's no harm in your knowing."

"Your contact? Who did you give the mirror to?"

He smiled. "You mean 'to whom did I give the mirror'?"

"Oh, grammar be damned! Don't keep me in suspense."

"Flamingo."

Charlotte's mouth dropped open. "That gorgeous creature was an operative? Will wonders never cease?"

"Not only that," Mitchell answered blithely, "but that gorgeous creature was . . . a man."

Charlotte held up her hand. "Don't tell me any more. Don't disillusion me."

"Well, the most shocking thing about the entire trip was when I found the silversmith murdered in his shop."

Charlotte got up quickly. "You're making this all up. None of it ever happened. We never went on the château trip. We never met any of those people. We don't know anything about strange men with diamonds in their unbrellas." She picked up her glass of sherry and raised it a bit drunkenly. "Here's to that maggot André Gulot. Damn, I can't think of a good French curse."

"May he rot in a shroud." Mitchell tipped his glass.

"Yes," Charlotte cried, "may he rot in a shroud."

They downed the last of the sherry, and on the way to the dining room Mitchell paused at the radio. "Let's have some soft dinner music," he said.

But blaring forth from the speaker was the voice of a Louis Armstrong-type singer belting, "SUS-PEN-SHUN! SUS-PEN-SHUN!" Mitchell switched off the radio. "Damn, you can't go anywhere anymore that you don't hear that song!"

"I don't like it either, Mitch, the beat is too primitive for my taste, but every time I hear it, I also hear the shekels ringing the cash register for Billy Nestor."

"Only one thing has me upset, Charlotte."

She laughed, dishing out the Swiss steak. "Billy making a lot of money?"

"No, no," he replied quietly. "Why was it necessary to smuggle out the radioactive stuff with us? It could have been shipped out in numerous ways, instead of all that intrigue, five or six people involved, a senseless killing. Why didn't the French government conduct the research? We would not steal from them, we would have sent specialists to work with their doctors. No, my dear, this was Pierre's last great master plan, and there's much more to it than perhaps even André Gulot knows."

H. L. Leary ran his hand over his white butch haircut and looked glumly at the desk opposite. Pierre had been dead for over a year, and yet very often he would glance up and expect him to be sitting there, smoothing those magnificent mustaches.

Perhaps it was time to retire to the California desert, while there was still time to enjoy the latter part of his life. Pierre had dreamed of spending his last days at his farmhouse in Normandie and had never made it—he had suffered that last, massive heart attack right across the room.

Leary had heard that the mineral waters in Desert Hot Springs could do wonders for an aching body, and at the moment he had a variety of sore muscles. He had taken up golf again. . . .

The blue telephone jangled. That meant his boss. "Yes, sir?"

The voice at the other end of the line was filled with fury, an emotion not often indulged in by his superior. "There's a new book on the market by that crappy French journalist Gulot, that blows the lid off that French château motorbus operation. The son-of-a-bitch blabs practically the whole goddam caper.

"All the reader has to do, H.L., is put two and two together. Not only does he talk about that cancer research, but practically reveals how we smuggled it out of France into Spain; only he gives the impression we were stealing the radioactive material from the French!"

"Oh, Christ, then we're sitting on an international incident. Have the frog authorities been on the horn?"

"And how!" The voice was weary but edged in bitterness. "A little knowledge can be very harmful in the wrong hands, particularly a newspaperman out to prove that he has the greatest balls since Casanova!"

"But what did you tell the French?" Leary asked, afraid of the answer.

"I had to square with them. I didn't go into details on exactly how we managed to get it away from the Soviets, through operatives in Poland and Germany into France, but at least they know that it wasn't developed in one of their own clinics."

Leary nodded. "This doesn't help Eisenhower in dealing with the Russkies, knowing we stole classified cancer research data out from under their red noses!"

"Well, that's only part of it," his superior continued hotly. "That damned Gulot screwed us up as well. He doesn't name names, but describes that furniture dealer and his wife from Enid, Oklahoma, to a T."

"That's unfortunate for the Herons," Leary replied sadly, "but I've already removed his name from our files. In fact, he knows that the château job was his last."

"What really gets me, though, is his very accurate description of our dear Mrs. Parsons. Helena Sharp will never again be able to use that cover, and she was so good as that sweet little old lady—"

"But, my God," Leary cried, standing up straight at his desk, "I've placed her on a current mission."

"Why didn't you tell me?" his superior demanded.

"I sent the stuff by messenger. It should be en route. I only gave her the assignment two days ago."

"Get her off the job right now!"

"I can't," Leary shouted into the receiver. "She's on a flight from Lima, Peru, to Valparaiso, Chile!"

"Who's her contact?"

"She doesn't have one until she gets to Tulcahuano, where she meets Valdez."

"Get in touch immediately and have him tell her to drop the Mrs. Parsons disguise. She can finish the mission as herself, but we'll have to fly in her real passport and visas."

Leary groaned. "We've never used her as Helena Sharp. Damn. That mission on the cruise ship to Hawaii would have been perfect for her, and would have been fun, too. She's gone from one assignment to another this past year with no vacation between." He paused thoughtfully. "I really hate for her to use her real identity on the Chilean job. How many people will read that book?"

"Who knows?" his superior cried. "If only one of the wrong crowd reads it, her life is in danger."

"All right, I'll make the necessary contacts. I wish I had that frong journalist here in this office!" He gritted his teeth. "What can we do about classified information being printed by unscrupulous people?"

His superior gave a nasty laugh. "Or even 'scrupulous,' for that matter. Nothing. Ignore it, unless our own State Department leaks to the press; then we go to the President. We can't do anything about Gulot's book, which I understand was printed in both French and English versions at the same time." He paused. "We might scare the hell out of him and prevent that sequel where he promises to blow the lid off more classified secret stuff."

Mitchell was reading the sports pages of the *Enid Morning News* at the breakfast table, and Charlotte was immersed in the second-page news, when she gave a little cry. "Oh, Mitch, remember Mrs. Parsons?"

He did not look up from the paper. "Yes," he replied absently, "what about her?"

"She's dead."

"What?"

"According to this little squib at the bottom of the second page, she and a man named Valdez were killed in a traffic accident in Tulcahuano, Chile, yesterday."

Mitchell put down the newspaper and stared into space. He could see fussy Mrs. Parsons, the scatterbrained Mrs. Fredricks, and the charming Helena Sharp. "God bless her," he said solemnly. "May she rest in peace." Then his eyes filled with tears. "God damn them!" he said savagely.

"Why, Mitch, what's wrong?"

He brushed his hands over his eyes. "You know most of the story," he said, "but there's no harm, I guess, in your knowing that it was Mrs. Parsons who gave me the makeup mirror."

Charlotte clicked her tongue. "But how, when, where?"

"It was concealed in dear little Tibbetts' blue coat."

"Imagine that! She paused. "Well, it's sad that she had to meet her death in a foreign country. She was from Riverside, California, wasn't she?"

"No!" Mitchell cried. "Mrs. Parsons was only one of her disguises. She was young and pretty. Don't you realize, Charlotte, that she was on a mission and the opposition killed her in cold blood?"

It was raining very lightly as the commercial airliner set down on the field outside Oklahoma City. "Damn," Charlotte cried, patting her beige raincoat, "wouldn't you know the weather would be bad for Jean? Oklahoma is so green and pretty this year with an early summer and plenty of moisture, and all he's going to see is fog the entire way to

Angel. Oh, look, Mitch, there he is! Wave so he will see you!"

Mitchell held up his hand as Jean stood for a moment in the door of the airliner; then he clutched Charlotte's arm. Coming down the steps directly in back of Jean was Françoise.

18

The Past Is Close

"My God!" Mitchell exclaimed. *"What is she doing here?"*

"As mother used to say," Charlotte replied, "this is not the end of the world."

"Papa!" Jean cried, running up to Mitchell and throwing his arms around his shoulders. "It is a great pleasure seeing you again." He turned his Heron profile to Charlotte, then kissed her on both cheeks. He wore a cheap pinstriped wool suit that was nonetheless flattering to his slim frame, as the cut accentuated his small waist.

He removed his billed cap, such as workmen wear, and wiped his brow with his hand. "Since this is my first trip out of France, and the way was very long, I knew that you would not mind if I reached into savings and traded my first-class ticket into two small-class ones, so I could bring a chaperon."

"Of course not," Mitchell replied, turning to Françoise, who had just come in the door from the airstrip, supporting herself on a cane. *"Bonjour,"* he said evenly. "Françoise, I should like you to meet my wife, Charlotte."

"Welcome to Oklahoma," Charlotte said evenly and held out her hand, which Françoise shook nervously. She was dressed in a new cheap brown tweed coat, and her large brown beret hid her best feature, which was her eyes.

"I did not know if I should attempt the trip," Françoise said, "but the hotel said I could take a holiday."

"Oh, the sights we have seen!" Jean was enthusiastic,

and he looked very handsome, very boyish as he described the mountains and the valleys and the plains glimpsed from the plane.

Charlotte glanced out of the huge window as an airliner came in for a landing. She felt drained of emotion, and yet the day was far from over. She loved Mitchell, and he loved her, yet one could not ignore the solid fact that even if what he and Françoise had shared so many years ago was long over, their son still stood between them. She thought of her parents, Fontine and John Dice—"Fourteen" and "Jaundice"—and silently asked, *What should I do?* And it seemed that she heard her mother's voice: *Why, you just be as nice as you can be, hear?*

"After we collect the luggage," Mitchell was saying, "shall we have something to eat? Are you hungry?"

"No, no, Papa, we had something on the plane. *Maman*, do you want some chocolate?"

"No, no," Françoise replied quickly, glancing fearfully at her son.

It occurred to Charlotte, in that revealing moment, that for the first time on the trip, Françoise had realized that this journey was not a holiday at all, and that her presence might prove to be a disrupting factor. However beautiful and desirable she might have been as a young girl, Françoise probably had not been very intelligent, and her mind had not improved over the years. Her anxious eyes seemed to inquire: *What am I doing here?*

With two small pieces of luggage in the trunk of the Chrysler, and with Jean and Françoise installed comfortably in the rear seat, Charlotte talked about the history of the area and the Land Rushes, and when Mitchell drove past the capital building, she pointed out the oil wells on the grounds.

"Ah, Papa, will you stop the car so that I can take a photo?"

It was on the tip of Mitchell's tongue to say that since it was such a gray day, it would be best to stop at a curio shop where color postcards could be purchased, but he felt Charlotte's knee against his and he pulled over to the curb. Finally Jean located a small Brownie box camera in his suitcase, and called, "*Maman,* come and pose against the derricks." And when she demurred, he insisted.

She got out of the car and stood self-consciously on the curb and smiled soulfully for the camera.

As they drove through Guthrie, Mitchell automatically turned to go down the street to the furniture store, and then thought better of it; he did not want to give the impression of largesse. Charlotte pointed to the beautifully preserved red sandstone houses on either side of brick streets. "The stone is from a local quarry," she explained, "and the red cement block houses are of the same substance, only pulverized."

"Ah, look," Françoise exclaimed, "the trees come together in a canopy overhead!"

"Guthrie was the first capital city of Oklahoma," Mitchell said, "and in nineteen hundred and seven, on this actual street, a young Indian maiden was 'married' to a white man in a ceremony uniting Indian Territory with the new state."

"Mitchell, don't you think you should telephone Aunt Letty," Charlotte said in English, "and let her know the time of our arrival?"

He threw her a quick look. "Yes," he replied grimly, "I suppose it would be the polite thing to do."

"Not only polite, dear, but *mandatory*!" Charlotte retorted.

Letty had her hands in buttermilk biscuit dough when Hattie answered the telephone. "It's Mitch, calling from Guthrie."

"He probably only wants to let us know when they'll be here. Just take the message."

"No!" Hattie exclaimed. "He says he must talk to you."

"Very well, then." Letty washed her hands quickly but did not take time to clean the sticky dough from between her fingers. "Yes?" she said into the mouthpiece.

Mitchell's voice was strained as he chose his words carefully, knowing that there were probably other people on the line. "I hate to impose on you further, Aunt Letty, but as it turned out, Jean's mother came with him."

"What?"

"Yes, and we should be there in about an hour and a half."

Letty placed the receiver in its cradle, washed her hands again, and started to cut out biscuits. "Hattie," she called, "would you put some fresh flowers in the guest bedroom upstairs, please?"

"What?" Hattie called from the living room.

Letty raised her voice. "Please turn off the television!" It was bad enough, she reflected, to listen to soap operas on the radio, but at least housework could be done at the same time, but with television, you'd lose the plot if you didn't watch. . . .

Hattie came into the kitchen with the oil mop to indicate that she had been dusting the hardwood floors. She pursed her thin mouth. "I swear you're getting childish," she whined. "Just like you told me, I put the boy in the new downstairs suite, so he'll have a bathroom all to hisself. And men don't need flowers."

Letty sighed. "Hattie, I'm not getting senile. The upstairs bedroom is to be used by the boy's *mother.*"

Hattie's mouth dropped open. "You mean to say that he had the gall to bring that woman here?"

"I don't know the circumstances, but Mitch called to prepare us."

"Prepare us?" Hattie sucked her false teeth. "What is this world coming to, Letty? Here we got Mitch and his new bride and Mitch and his old bride under the same roof."

"They were never married, Hattie."

"I *know* that, but it sure sounds better!"

"Besides," Letty replied hotly, "they won't be under the same roof at all. Charlotte and Mitch will be staying in Enid."

"And that's another thing. Why should they be putting us out, practically running a hotel, when the Dice mansion is empty. Jean and his mother could stay over there."

Letty placed the last biscuit on the cookie sheet and started to brush the tops with melted butter. "It was my idea, so don't be getting uppity, Hattie. I want him—them—to see how ordinary families live over here."

"There's nothing ordinary about this family!" Hattie retorted. "The younger generation's a bunch of screwballs, if you ask me."

"Hattie," Lettie said sharply, "no one has asked you, now will you please get on with your work?" She set the tray of biscuits on the kitchen counter, checked the fried chicken in the stove warmer, and made sure the pot of boiling potatoes was ready to fire, then went into the dining room to see that Hattie had used the good china to set the table.

Since everything was in readiness, Letty poured herself a cup of coffee and sat down in the living room to go over the mail. "Nothing but circulars and bills," she muttered and was about to set aside the stack when she saw Luke Three's APO number in the left-hand corner of an envelope. *What a pleasure*, she thought, because he seldom wrote. She read the message once, and then again:

Dear Grandma:

You're the only one that I can write to about something that's happened to me. I don't want to get personal, but I don't know how to avoid it, because I've got to discuss a very private matter. As you know, Darlene Trune wanted to marry me before she finally hooked Bobby Baker, and there have been a few other girlfriends over the years, but I had never really been in love with any of them—that is, enough to get married.

Letty's hand shook, because she had a flash of intuition of what was to come.

This is where the difficult part comes in, Grandma, because I've really fallen in love for the first time. I feel that you'll understand my problem better than anyone else, because you married a mixed-blood Cherokee. . . . Although you never had cause to mention it to me, you must have had to overcome conventions when you married him.

George Story's face came to mind, the way that he had looked the first day that they had met at the Saturday

Merchant's Drawing on Main Street in Angel: coal-black hair, porcelain-blue eyes . . . And once more she felt the pull of his sexuality.

Those first years were not easy, even though he was educated and had great social standing as a Cherokee tribal lawyer. But together they had weathered prejudice. But those were simpler days, and the Indians, although some people failed to recognize the fact, were truly the original Americans—but an Asian girl was something else again!

> Her name is T'am—can't pronounce her last name—and she's nineteen years old and speaks a little English. She comes from a fine Korean family, who don't have much now, but before the war they had a fine house with a tile roof and servants.
>
> I'm going to start the red tape, so that we can be married. It won't be easy because, as you know, the government doesn't want servicemen to marry native girls. But, Grandma, I'm not a Heron for nothing, and I'll prevail.
>
> I'm counting on you to start preparing the family for my bride.
>
> My love,
> Luke T.

A tear escaped her lashes and fell on the letter, obliterating his signature.

"Well, what are you doing in here, mooning?" Hattie said, coming downstairs and polishing the railing at the same time.

"If it's any of your business, Hattie," Letty replied crossly, "I was just reading my mail. I must say you're in a bad mood today. You haven't had a pleasant word for anyone. Sit down and have a cup of coffee to calm your nerves before the guests arrive." She paused. "And furthermore, watch your manners with Jean and his mother."

"What's her name?"

"Françoise."

"I can't even pronounce it!"

"Hattie, do you want your walking papers?"

There was a long pause. "No, ma'am."

"Then calm down. I want no more grousing."

"Letty?"

"Yes."

"When I was a young girl—"

"But you're not young, and neither am I, so let's not ruminate." Letty smiled in spite of herself. "Come on, Hattie," she said kindly, "pour yourself a cup of coffee and freshen mine up, then sit down and plan what we'll serve for breakfast tomorrow morning."

Mitchell had pulled off the country road onto the highway, where the flat fields on either side contained only golden stubble after the wheat had been harvested.

"You don't see many farmhouses, Papa."

"That's true. Every hundred and sixty acres used to have a house and barn, but farmers have to work several sections of land today to make money. Many families have moved to the city to work in factories. Then, too, soldiers and sailors came back from the war and decided not to follow in their fathers' footsteps."

"Oh, look," Françoise cried, "there is a fire."

"Don't be alarmed," Charlotte answered quietly. "The farmers are burning the stubble from the wheat fields. The ashes, when plowed into the ground, make fine fertilizer."

"There is the town called Enid, where I live," Mitchell said, indicating a few buildings on the horizon. "To show you how flat our land is, Jean, Enid is thirty miles away. To the left is Covington, to the right, Garber. In between—over there—where you can see the water tower and the granary, is Angel."

Charlotte turned around in her seat and faced Jean and Françoise. "There is a touching story about how the town got its name in eighteen ninety-three. My father said that your Great-Aunt Letty, whom you'll meet shortly, had given part of her claim for a God's Acre to bury several of the men—including your Uncle Luke—who had been killed in the rush for free land."

Charlotte was warming to her subject, happy to be practicing her French. "The minister had just said a few words over the graves, and since he was a man of God, and apparently not very practical, and had arrived on the scene after all the land was claimed, Letty gave him land for a church and parsonage. Someone suggested opening a general store and a post office, which in those pioneer days was all that was needed to form a town, and the minister pointed up into the sky, which was filled with a huge cloud that looked like something from heaven. Letty said, 'If a town is to spring up here, let it be called Angel.' And it was!"

Françoise clapped her hands like a young girl. "That is beautiful!" she exclaimed. "Just like a romance story."

It was then that whatever resentment Charlotte had felt toward her ebbed away, and she smiled kindly. "Yes, it is like a romance, isn't it?"

Mitchell took the section road that ran beside the town. "I have quite a pretty sight to show you," he said, and he pointed to the left at the acres of peach trees filled with ripening fruit.

"It looks like it goes on forever," Françoise said gently. "The people who own this giant orchard must be very wealthy indeed."

"Yes," Mitchell agreed, and, seeing that the fruit stand was open, added, "In fact, I shall introduce you to the owner's wife." He parked the car in front of the stand and climbed out of the car. "Good afternoon, Bella," he called. "The peaches surely smell good this year. A bumper crop?"

The plump little woman nodded, turned from sorting peaches, wiped her hands on a towel, and smiled from ear to ear. "It's good to see you, Mitch. How's Charlotte?"

"Fine," he replied, noticing that she looked very haggard. "Why not come out to the car and say hello. How's Torgo?"

Bella shook her head and rearranged several red and yellow peaches in the lugs on display. "Not well at all. He's in such pain from the arthritis, and it's such a trial to get him in and out of the car, even with the help of Gerald, the nurse, that he won't go to Mass anymore."

She sighed. "And the young priests today aren't like they used to be, and don't bother coming over much. Of course, when you get our age, Mitch, we're not very interesting to have around. Do you want some peaches? I have some real ripe ones that'll have to be used by tomorrow."

"Just enough for breakfast."

She filled a sack full of plump fruit for him, and then slowly went out the side door of the stand to the car. "Hello, Charlotte. My, you look as pretty as a picture." She handed her the peaches.

"So do you, Bella." Charlotte had the next phrase planned. "I'd like you to meet some friends of mine from France. This is Jean and Françoise Faubert." She turned. "And this is Bella Chenovick."

"Sorry I don't know any French," Bella said, "but I greet you both the same."

Both Jean and Françoise said very carefully, "How do you do," in English.

Bella went back to the stand and returned a moment later with a jar of peach preserves, which she handed to the smiling Françoise. "From my hands to yours," she said solemnly, "to those who have come from across the sea."

Mitchell translated quickly, and when Françoise spoke he translated: "She says in reply that you are as generous as your disposition is good!"

Bella laughed. "Thank God she said 'disposition' and not 'waist.' The woman has tact."

And when Mitchell translated, both Jean and Françoise joined in the merriment. "We'll take off, Bella."

"Give dear Letty my love," she said, and waved her red apron as they left.

"That lady selling peaches, Papa, owns the orchards?"

Mitchell smiled. "Yes, and is a millionaire many times over, not only from the peaches, which are shipped all over the United States, but also from oil wells."

"This is a wonderful and strange country." Françoise remarked quietly, looking at the glistening jar of golden and pink fruit that she held in her hand.

Bella watched the Chrysler disappear in a cloud of dust. Letty had told her the story of Jean Baptiste. He was a fine-looking man, she decided, and wasn't it wonderful that father and son were together at last? She and Torgo had no

children, and what families had been left in Prague had not
been in touch for many years, and had never visited
America. It was good to see that for certain people, like
Mitchell and Charlotte, there was a happy ending, after all.

She looked up into the sky to see if the dark rainclouds
were coming up from Oklahoma City like the weatherman
said on the radio, but the sky was still blue. She was tired. It
had been a profitable day. She had sold seventy-five lugs of
ripe peaches ready for canning, and twenty-three pints of
preserves, not counting two quarts that she had given away.
She looked at the platinum-and-diamond watch on her wrist
and decided to stay open one more hour.

A fly buzzed over a dark spot on a fat peach in a display
lug, and as she reached over to turn the spot so that it would
not show, she felt the first throb in her breast. She clutched
the side of the stand with both hands as the second and third
pains shot through her body like bullets. She gasped for
breath, to be prepared for the next jolt, which never came.
Very gracefully, as if in slow motion, she fell in the dust at
the foot of the fruit stand.

The moment that Letty heard the car in the driveway, she
ran her hand over her upswept hairdo and smoothed out a
wrinkle on the rose-colored crepe de chine dress that she
had worn on many television shows. She hoped that she was
not overdressed, but how often, she thought, did one greet a
great-nephew that one had never met?

By the time that she had reached the front porch, Mitchell
and Charlotte were coming up the walk, and after they had
kissed, Mitchell introduced Jean and Françoise. Letty was
somewhat overwhelmed when Jean kissed her on both
cheeks; then she stood back and looked at him. "There is no
question," she said. "that this boy is a Heron, with that
nose!"

Mitchell translated, and Jean laughed; then he introduced
his mother, who looked very flustered and embarrassed as
she awkwardly held out her hand with the jar of peach
preserves.

"I see that you stopped by Bella's." Letty smiled and

thought, *Darn, I am overdressed*. Aloud she said, "I am so happy to see you, my dear."

And while Mitchell translated, Letty mused: *This woman, with the delicate prematurely aged skin, trying to look genteel in tweeds, could be my grandniece if she had married Mitchell*. There was something wistful about Françoise, as if she had been defeated by life itself.

"I'm sorry now that I never learned French," Letty said regretfully. "It was always something that I was going to pick up and never did."

"Mine is getting a brush-up, I can tell you." Charlotte rolled her eyes. "I'm even remembering idioms."

Letty held the door open. "Charlotte, would you show Françoise to the guest room upstairs, and Mitch, would you take Jean to Muhammad Abn's suite?" She checked herself and explained, "We've always called the new addition by that name, because Bosley had it built when Muhammed and his entourage visited us, just before Saudi Arabia came into World War II. Oh, those days were filled with excitement."

Charlotte turned on the stairs and looked down at Letty. "You mean there hasn't been much excitement lately?"

Letty laughed, thinking of Luke Three's T'am and Mitchell's Jean and Françoise. "It's just different, Charlotte, more human, I guess you'd say." The telephone rang, and she called, "Hattie, dear, please get that, will you? Charlotte, when you come down, there's just one thing I want you to do. Would you mix the honey-butter for the biscuits just like your mother used to do?"

Hattie came quickly into the foyer, and tears were streaming down her plain old face. "Oh, Letty, they just found Bella out by the fruit stand, and she's—dead!"

It was seven-thirty in the evening, and the twenty-five thousand seats in Hollywood Bowl were almost filled for the benefit for South Korean refugees.

The first part of the evening was to be devoted to opera and symphonic music with Alfred Wallenstein conducting the Los Angles Symphony Orchestra, and after intermission Clement Story was to head his Cherokee Swing Orchestra, which was to play for the popular singing stars of screen, stage, television, and radio, who had been rehearsing all afternoon under Tracy Newcomb's baton.

William Nestor and Louisa Tarbell, seated in a box in the very social, blue-book section, directly in front of the apron that fronted the enormous shell, had come early and brought box suppers of fried chicken, Beluga caviar, and Mumms champagne to be consumed before the concert began.

William was dressed in the latest style for men: a dark charcoal suit with a pink silk tie and matching handkerchief, and Louisa wore a navy-and-white polka-dotted dress with a wide skirt that spilled over the canvas director's chairs where they sat. Pushed back on her shoulders was the wide collar of a fully let-out sable coat, which was too warm for the July weather, but which she refused to leave at home. She looked up into the dark sky covered with stars, and the two enormous spotlights that shone up into the heavens, and sighed.

Spreading a cracker with the black caviar, she suddenly giggled. "Billy, are you thinking the same thing that I am?"

He grinned. "That we're a long way from Willawa?"

She looked around at the boxes filling with the Who's Who crowd, and nodded. "I sometimes have to pinch myself that I'm still not teaching school and you're not a student." She looked toward the orchestra, which was filtering in from the doors in the side of the shell, and listened as the musicians began to warm up their instruments. She was peacefully content, actually serene in this atmosphere where she felt very much at home.

The musicians were in their places, the lights were lowered, and the crowd quieted. Alfred Wallenstein appeared at the side door; the audience applauded and continued to applaud as he shook the concertmaster's hand. He bowed formally and picked up his baton. There was a moment of silence; then the first strains of the overture to *Tannhaüser* wafted out from the shell, filling the vast reaches of Hollywood Bowl with glorious sound.

"Who's the first star on the program?" Louisa whispered.

"Helen Traubel singing the *Liebiestod* from *Tristan and*

Isolde, I think," William whispered back. "She can't read music, you know. Wallenstein has to follow her!"

Helen Traubel was indeed the first on the program. Dressed in a violet-and-white flowered dress and wearing a white fox cape, she was warmly greeted by the audience, and a chill ran down William's spine as her voice soared in the halls of Wagner. For an encore, she sang the "Ave Maria," which surprised William, who had thought she might have rehearsed something from *Götterdämmerung*. Of course, he conceded, the "Ave Maria" was easier!

He placed his head back and listened to the remainder of the classical concert, relaxed and inspired. Then, all too soon, the lights came up for intermission, which called for more Mumms champagne, which Louisa had kept cold in a small icechest. They raised their glasses in a toast.

At that moment a photographer, scanning the crowd, singled them out. "Would you pose, please, Mr. Nestor?"

"Of course." Making certain that his tie was straight and his handkerchief flat in his breast pocket, he turned to the camera and smiled.

"One more, please? A cover shot. Thank you."

A few moments later another photographer asked for a picture, but this time with Louisa. He very carefully asked for the spelling of their names.

"How does it feel to be famous?" William asked. "Does it make your heart flutter?"

"What a question!" Louisa exclaimed. "We're the same people—inside—that we were in Willawa."

"Yes." he laughed. "Only the outside has been changed considerably."

"Hi, Billy!" a familiar voice called, and William looked up at Tracy Newcomb, who was coming up the aisle from the side entrance. He bent over the box and said in a low tone, "Have you seen Clem?" His voice was urgent.

"Why, no," William replied. "Isn't he here?"

"No, he was supposed to show a half hour ago to get ready. He's to conduct tonight." He leaned Clement's guitar against the apron of the stage in a prearranged position where it could be easily found.

"Is Sarah with him?" William asked.

"No, she's still in K.C." He brightened. "If you're in a party mood, we're meeting in the front room at Chasen's as soon as the concert's over."

"Thank you, Tracy," William replied. "Let's play it by ear, huh?"

Louisa poured the last of the champagne, but William only made a show of sipping. What had happened to Clem?

At last the lights were lowered in the enormous half-moon seating section and the stage lights came up, and there was an enormous burst of applause as the conductor appeared at the side door of the shell and made his way to the front of the stage. Most of the audience was too far away to see that it was Tracy Newcomb who was taking the bows.

The first star on the popular program was Bing Crosby, who sang a medley of his hits, including "Blue Skies," "If I Had My Way," and "An Irish Lullaby." He finished to a huge ovation.

Rosemary Clooney was singing when Louisa finally found her glasses and looked at the program. "Clem's on next," she whispered, and although William had never been in a Catholic church, he solemnly crossed himself.

"You've got it backwards." Louisa smiled. "You made the sign of the cross like the Greek Orthodox do."

"I imagine it's just as effective," he whispered back as Rosemary Clooney took her bows, glanced offstage, and, from the way that she swung into the next song, William knew that the encore was unscheduled. She was playing for time. She finished, bowed, and had left the stage, when the *clump, clump, clump* music was heard, which was the introduction to "The Cowboy Waltz." William sighed with relief. "He's here!" he said triumphantly.

The spotlight found Clement, dressed in evening clothes, at the side door of the shell. He waved to the crowd and walked very carefully toward the apron of the stage, instead of ambling as he usually did, which fit the casual lyrics of the song. He bent down to pick up the guitar, which was so close that William could have touched it, saw Louisa first, and waved, then saw William and waved again.

"He's *drunk*!" Louisa exclaimed in a stage whisper.

"Oh, Lordy"—a term that she had not used since her days in Willawa.

Clement retrieved the guitar, which he waved in the air, and sauntered to middle stage, while Tracy kept the *thump, thumps* rolling.

He paused, finally found the shoulder strap, which he awkwardly placed over his head, while grimacing, waving, and clowning for the benefit of the fans in the cheap rear seats, who applauded and shouted approval. But there was only silence from box seats down front, where a photographer callously went from party to party, taking bets on whether Clement would finish the song.

> *College frats in sheepskin chaps . . .*

Clement cleared his throat, then went on.

> *Shootin' irons stuck down,*
> *In holsters, brown 'n'*
> *Fuzzy from the dew . . .*

His voice smoothed out, and William thought: *He's going to do it, he's going to be fine.*

Clement went on more confidently with the second verse, and the third, and then started on the chorus:

> *Teenage cats in sheepskin chaps,*
> *College frats in Stetson hats,*
> *Three-piece suits in roun'-tip boots,*
> *All sippin' malts, discussin' faults,*
> *And doin' the cowboy, doin' the cowboy . . .*

The orchestra crept in for the last line:

> *Yes, doin' the COWBOY WALTZ.*

There was applause that seemed to build and build and ricochet from one side of the bowl to the other, and William sighed; the old Clement Story luck was holding out. But he was confident too soon, because, instead of bowing and then going to the orchestra and taking up his baton, Clement had walked down to the edge of the apron again to the microphone, and held up his hands for silence.

"Folks." He was weaving slightly now and he grabbed the microphone base for support. "I just know . . . that you love 'The Cowboy Waltz' just as much as I do. And I'm pleased to see in the audience tonight an old buddy of mine. . . ."

William thought: *Oh, no, this can't be happening, please God* . . .

Clement was holding on to the microphone with both hands now. ". . . a boy . . . a half-breed Cherokee Indian like I am, whom I discovered way back in—" He grinned foolishly. "Can't think of the damned town at the moment. Anyway, I found this little twerp playing an organ in a church. . . ."

The audience laughed. Clement was enough of a showman, William thought, to pull off this maudlin scene, if he played strictly for laughs and got offstage after a big punchline. As long as he gave a performance, his fans would rally round.

Louisa was dumb struck. Clement's routine was out of a nightmare in which William and she were unwillingly involved. "Get off while you can, Clem!" she prayed out loud.

Clement was waving his hands in the air. ". . . As I said, he's right down here in a box seat with his dish of a manager. Hi, Louisa! Billy, come on up and meet the folks out there!"

William turned a stark, white face to Louisa. "What am I going to do?" he whispered, panic-stricken.

"There's nothing you can do but be introduced!" she hissed back. "There's twenty-five thousand people here, Billy. Get up there and get him off somehow."

Clement's voice took on the tones of a carnival barker: "Ladies and gent'men, may I present . . . for your edification . . . the talented William Nestor, who . . . composed the music and . . . wrote the lyrics for . . . 'The Cowbay Waltz' and who's also the composer-lyricist for 'Suspension.' Billy baby, get your ass up here and take a bow!"

Tracy Newcomb, realizing the alarming situation, cued the orchestra into the *thump, thump, thump* "Suspension" music as William ran up the front steps to the apron of the stage while a new segment of the crowd—the teenage element—applauded, stomped, and whistled.

Oh, God in heaven, William prayed, *you've been good to me so far, please help me now!* As if in answer to his entreaty, like an actor, he suddenly knew how to play the scene. He embraced Clement, and then looked out over the huge audience lost in the dimness of the half-moon-shaped tiers scooped out of the hillside.

"Thank you, Clem," he said with a wide smile that he hoped was not too artificial-looking, mentally thanking Tracy for continuing the SUS-PEN-SHON music in the background. "And thank you, folks, for that beautiful reception."

He went on quickly, "Now you've met Clem, and you've met me, but you haven't met our conductor for this evening, Mr. Tracy Newcomb and the Cherokee Swing Orchestra!"

Tracy bowed and, as the applause rang out, brought the members of the orchestra to their feet for an ovation. William raised his hands, and in the silence that followed went on in an intimate voice, just above a whisper, which the microphone picked up exactly. "Just one more thing, folks. You've met all of us, but we haven't met any of you. Do us a favor, please, and light a match or a cigarette lighter in front of your faces, so that we can see you!"

Tracy, struck with the drama that William was creating, cued the orchestra to play "Red Sails in the Sunset," while there was a giant stir among the audience. A moment later, those on stage were treated to the unforgettable sight of twenty-five thousand pinpoints of light that turned the far reaches of the Hollywood Bowl into a shimmering, glimmering sea of faces.

William turned to the orchestra and made a sign to Tracy, who knew immediately how to end the moment. He made a rising sign to the orchestra, sat down at the piano, and when the musicians stood up, he carried the melody himself on the keyboard as William and the orchestra applauded the audience.

William took the benumbed Clement's shoulder and whispered, "Bow, dammit, bow."

William and Clement simultaneously bowed with the orchestra, the stage manager turned off the apron and shell lights, and William supported Clement offstage in the darkness, as the announcer quickly introduced the next act.

Clement shook off William's arm backstage. "Lemme alone!" he shouted furiously. "I introduced you, punk, and whadda do? Screw up the whole act!"

"You fool," Max Rabinovich snapped. "He just saved your ass!"

"Oh, yeah?" Clement raised his fist and whirled around drunkenly, missed Max's jaw, lost his balance, tumbled off the riser, and fell in a crumpled heap six feet to the ground.

"Jesus!" Max cried. "Somebody call an ambulance."

19

The Red Moon

The small brick hospital with the high iron railing and the locked gates was located on a side street in Mission Hills, a remote section of the vast San Fernando Valley.

Clement's three-hundred-dollar-a-day room was located on the third floor and looked out on a back alley. He was strapped in bed, and his left arm was mounted in a plaster cast suspended from pulleys in the ceiling. He was being fed from a tube placed in his nose that ran down into his stomach, and there were two needles in his arm, attached to bottles hanging from a steel support.

The plump, big-boned night nurse bustled into the room with a bowl of flowers, which she placed, not too gently, with the thirteen other arrangements on a large shelf which had been brought in for that purpose. She indicated the form on the bed with a nod of her dyed blonde head, and mouthed the words "Out".

The day nurse, a smaller and daintier edition of the night nurse, closed the romance magazine with a snap. "The doctor wants him to have a shot every four hours, Madge, and watch those IV's in his arm. How he pulled them out of his arm last night, I'll never know, considering that truss he's in, but he did. As you know, they get antsy right after they've been cast."

Madge looked at her wristwatch. "I'm five minutes early."

"Want a cup of coffee?

"If I have another cup, Grace, I'll faint. My kidneys are

floating as it is." She glanced at Clement's face. "I loved to dance to his music in the 'forties. Gee whiz, could he lay on the shmaltz! I never dreamed he was a boozer."

Grace shrugged. "After working in a place like this, I wouldn't be surprised if the President of the United States was brought in screaming and yelling with the DT's!" She got up and stretched her back. "Do you suppose it's the pressure of fame?"

Madge frowned. "That may be part of it. I've worked at a lot of funny farms, and I think all those famous people on booze and pills are the most insecure people in the world. You and I know there's going to be a paycheck at the end of the week, they don't. An actor always thinks he'll never be asked to do another picture, and I suppose old-timers like Clement Story think their career could always be over tomorrow."

"But all that money!" Grace said, eyes glittering. "To live in a mansion and have servants and big cars and sign autographs—what an exciting life to lead!"

"You've been reading too many romances," Madge said not unkindly. "Now, let me take over, you go home to Charlie."

"Oh, Madge, he keeps calling for his wife. Is she coming in?"

"Probably, after the drugs wear off, about the sixth day, when the physical craving stops, but the pyschological craving is still bad, the doctor will ask her to come in. She's Indian, you know, same as him, but Sarah certainly isn't an Indian name."

"But he keeps asking for *Marthene*!"

Madge rolled her eyes. "He can afford a mistress or two!"

"Or even maybe *three*!" Clement cried. "My God, don't you broads have anything else to do but gossip about your patients?" He laughed at their stricken faces. "It's all right, I have a tough hide. Grace, get the hell out, and take *True Confessions* with you!"

When she scurried out of the room, he turned a wry eye on Madge. "Get me a glass of fresh water; send all those flowers to the Children's hospital over on Vermont Avenue in Hollywood; remove these restraints for a minute and massage my wrists; take my temperature by *mouth*; call the doctor and see if I can have some roast beef for dinner; rent me a television set; and bring me all the latest editions of the newspapers."

As she turned to the door, he called, "And, Madge, if I ever hear you discussing my love life again, I'll have you fired!"

A half hour later, Clement was half sitting up in bed, having adjusted his cast, reading about his so-called accident at the Hollywood Bowl. One newspaper reported that he had collapsed from exhaustion—a story obviously planted by Max—and another capsuled his life like an obituary and commented that "he has lately been showing signs of strain" and that his performance at the benefit was "somewhat more boisterous than usual."

When Madge showed the maintenance man where to place the television set, Clement looked at her sternly. "I want a cup of black coffee with two cubes of sugar."

"But Mr. Story—"

"Don't 'Mr. Story' me, Madge, there's nothing wrong with my right hand—that's the hand I drink coffee with, you know. Indians are not left-handed!" As she ran to the kitchen, he laughed and turned the page of the newspaper and stopped smiling when he saw the photograph of William and Louisa, two columns wide, toasting each other with champagne at Hollywood Bowl. The two-column headline, read:

MONIED COMPOSER SUED BY DESTITUTE PARENTS

The caption under the photograph read: *William Nestor, 25, composer of the rock hit "Sus-pen-shun" and "The Cowboy Waltz," with business manager Louisa Tarbell, 44, in happier days*.

Clement gritted his teeth. The accompanying story omitted nothing in tracing William's career and revealed the lawsuit for maintenance was instigated by Mr. and Mrs. Nestor of Willawa, Oklahoma.

The second newspaper did not feature a photograph, but related in the last paragraph of the story, that "only last night, bandleader Clement Story had paid tribute to the young man and had introduced him from the stage of the Hollywood Bowl."

Clement rubbed his head. The night had whirled by so quickly that all he could remember was standing on the apron of the stage, looking at thousands of lights flickering from the audience. He did not remember William, what he sang, or the fall backstage.

At that moment, the doctor came into the room, followed by Madge, and looked aghast at the newspaper-strewn bed. He was a tall, commanding individual with a shock of gray hair and a huge nose, which, at the moment, was pointed into the air.

"Good evening, Mr. Story," he said with a guarded smile, as Madge gathered the newspapers. "Turn over, please, it's time for a hypo." He deftly inserted the needle, pressed the plunger, and as Clement sank into oblivion a few moments later, the doctor retied the restraints and turned angrily to the nurse.

"I've never seen such insubordination in my life, Madge! What do you mean letting a patient browbeat you into submission? I've already laid down the rules in this case. He was admitted here not only for the fractures, but more importantly to be *dried out*!

"He's a mess physically, badly dehydrated, and probably needs an enema. He's to be kept under sedation, allowed no visitors, and don't forget to keep those IV's going. You've handled celebrities before. And I don't care if Clement Story was your girlhood idol, keep your equilibrium!"

She was near tears. "Yes, doctor, it's just that—"

"I know," he said in a kinder tone. "His orchestra played for my high school prom. I'll never forget the way he sang 'Red Sails in the Sunset.' "

Max was on the telephone to Louisa. "I thought I told you to take care of William's parents."

"I have been taking care of them, Max." She was still in bed, with a covering of cold cream, which she had added after William had left for the studio. "He paid for his mother's gall bladder operation and they've been cashing their hundred-and-fifty-dollar monthly checks."

"No wonder they're suing!" Max shouted. "That's chicken feed. When we first talked about this, years ago, I told you to keep paying them off. William is making good money. He's had two hit records, the studio contract is not too restricting, plus a couple of the summer music festivals in Europe want him to conduct."

"Conduct what?"

"Some light classical programs, which will be good for his image—if he can live down this current mess. I'll put an attorney on this and we'll make an out-of-court settlement."

"But his family are nothing but trash!"

"Watch your language, Lou, trash means different things to different people. My suggestion is that he buy that farm that they've been sharecropping."

"But, Max, they'd never make a go of it, his pap—father is a lazy good-for-nothing, and his mother has been browbeaten for so long she doesn't know her first name—"

"Louisa, will you kindly listen? The farm is actually a good investment; there may be tax credits and that sort of thing. But he'll be helping his parents, who may not deserve it but they haven't got a pot to piss in, and then the publicity will be wonderful.

"In about six months," he continued, as his imagination took over, "we'll do a press release about him going home to the farm, recapturing his dreams as a boy, shaking hands with the old church choir, walking through the cornfields. I know it's a lot of malarky, but we can turn this bad publicity to our advantage."

"All right, Max," Louisa admitted, "I see your point, but it still goes against my grain to cater to those people."

Max paused. "It's William's money, isn't it?"

"Yes."

"And they're his parents, aren't they?"

"Yes."

"And it's his career, isn't it?"

"Yes."

"And you're his business manager?"

"Yes."
"Then fuck off!"

Three hundred people attended Bella Chenovick's funeral at the small Catholic church in Perry, Oklahoma. After the church was filled with mourners, the priest called Eb Peterson, the undertaker, to borrow folding chairs, which were placed on the lawn outside. Then he asked the choirmaster to ask the soloist to stand in the vestibule, so that the music could be heard by those friends outside.

Letty, Mitchell, Charlotte, Jean, Françoise, and Belle Trune sat in the same front pew. It was the first funeral mass that Letty had ever attended, and she felt strange and out-of-place at the standings and kneelings and sittings that took place during the service, and at the unopened bronze casket in the front of the church.

Eighty percent of those who attended the service were Protestant, and Letty knew most of gathering. Belle had played the organ for dozens of weddings and funerals before arthritis claimed her hands and she could no longer hit the right notes. In the early pioneer days, she had played the piano at the Methodist Church in Angel in defiance of Catholic belief. But in those early days, she felt it was her contribution to the community, and not one word was ever spoken against her.

Letty lost count of the floral tributes after eighty-four, but she knew that the big basket of red roses was from Clement, because Sarah had called and said that he could not get a plane from California in time, and would she order the flowers and have the card read: *Could not come. In memory of my first piano teacher.*

Torgo, Letty was told, was too ill to attend the mass, even with the help of Gerald, and as the strange words were being said, Letty thought of Bella, whom she had met September 16, 1893, her first friend in the Territory. She was grieved beyond tears, and after the service, when some of the ladies asked her about the Senior Citizens of America group, Letty nodded wanly and said that she would be in touch.

Bella was buried in the cemetery at Perry, to the

consternation of many of her friends, who thought that she would naturally be laid to rest in God's Acres at Angel, until it was explained that she could not be placed in "unconsecrated" ground. At the conclusion of the graveside service, Letty noticed that the mason had chiseled an "h" for the "k" in Chenovick, on the tombstone. It seemed, she thought, a comment on what the world was experiencing in the nineteen-fifties.

She had ridden with Mitchell and the others, but asked Belle Trune, who had closed the Red Bird Café for the day and added a new rinse to her auburn hair, if she could ride back to Angel in her car. And, silent with grief, Belle had taken a dusty old road until they had reached the wilderness of the country, and then she and Letty had held each other in their arms and cried.

Then they dried their tears and spoke lovingly of their friend, and it seemed as they told stories about Bella's generosity and her peculiarities, their grief lifted and the stories became humorous and touching at the same time.

"I'll never forget the time that Fontine Dice called Bella a 'Bohunk' to her face on Main Street." Letty smiled.

"And what did Bella say?"

"She forgave her on the spot, because this was in the days before either Fontine or John could read and write, and Bella knew that Fontine, bless her was so dumb she thought Bohunk was a country in Europe!"

Belle Trune nodded. "I had forgotten that we used to call them that. You know, Letty, there are so few of the old settlers left, it occurred to me the other day that when they're all gone, who will people talk about?"

"Why," Letty said, "they'll just keep on talking. No one is a true legend until they're dead!"

Letty arrived home before Mitchell brought Jean and Françoise, to find Hattie, who had only gone through the fifth grade, laboriously writing the last of four telephone messages. "I swear," she said, "this place is getting to be like Grand Central Station. Everyone and their dog has called." She held out the notepad. "First, Jeanette said to tell you not to worry, that everything's okay, but that Luke has the shingles and can't travel, and was supposed to meet Muhammad Abn in Paris, and to call Tulsa."

She cleared her throat. "A government man of some sort called about Luke Three and some Korean girl, and said to call back at your convenience." She rubbed her long, thin neck, trying to make out her own writing. "Oh, yes, your television appearance in Minneapolis on the fourth of next month has been called off because they've canceled the Public Service part of the show." She sucked her teeth and furrowed her brow. "And Patricia Anne just hung up. She and Lars would like to come here for a week or two this summer if it's okay with you. He's doing a lot better and wants to finish his book, and if every day gets to be like today, you're going to need a full-time secretary, because I can't do everything."

Letty sighed. "Thank you, Hattie. Things are hectic, I know. Nothing is simple anymore, it seems. Everyone in the family's in turmoil, and some days I don't know whether I'm coming or going!"

"The coffee's on," Hattie said. 'I'm going to have a cup. How about you?"

"No, I'm in the mood for tea."

Hattie grimaced. "Wouldn't you just know it? You're getting difficult too in your old age, Letty."

"Yes, I suppose I am."

Hattie paused at the kitchen door. "There's one bright spot of news, though. Oh, on top of everything else, the telephone system is finally getting around to putting in dial phones. The conversion is going to take six weeks."

"Poor Nellie Drack," Letty said softly. "She'll have to retire at last."

"Yeah," Hattie replied dryly, "Poor, deaf old Nellie. Imagine having to retire at sixty-nine!"

Letty gave her a long look. "There are times when I don't appreciate your sarcasm," she replied.

"I hope," Hattie said with a flourish, "that this isn't one of them. You're getting to be as soft as a marshmallow. You need someone like me to keep things stirred up, and, speaking of stirring things up, if you'll make an Angel cake, I'll make the icing."

Letty laughed. "That's a good idea, Hattie. You know, cooking has saved my sanity many times, and I surely have a lot to think about today."

After the funeral, Mitchell moved Jean and Françoise to the Federal Restoration mansion next to the Heron clapboard, where they would have the run of the house, and when Letty brought half the Angel cake over in the latter part of the day, she found Françoise on her hands and knees, scrubbing the kitchen floor.

Charlotte shook her head. "She told me not to take offense, because she had a lot to think about and that she always thought better when she was working. Actually, Aunt Letty," she apologized, "the floor was not really that bad."

"I don't know how you feel about it, Charlotte, but Françoise is a good woman, and it may not be the conventional American way for a wife to entertain . . . a mistress." She had difficulty saying the word. "But life deals different blows, and we all pay the piper one way or the other."

Charlotte put her arm around Letty. "You're closer to me than my own mother, Aunt Letty. You've been an inspiration because you've always rolled with the punches. I admire your spunk."

"Why, thank you, dear." Letty smiled indulgently. "I'm going to need a great deal of that spunk this next year. The family is changing—branching out. I wouldn't be at all surprised if I'll be the only member left in Angel."

She paused. "I've been so worried about Clem, and I couldn't talk to anyone. Luke has his own problems with Heron Oil, and he and Clem have never really understood each other. Since babies, they've looked at life differently. I suppose Clem's Indian blood has led him to follow a different drummer."

She brushed a hand over her heart. "I might as well be frank, Charlotte, Clem's had a drinking problem for a long time. He would have been to Bella's funeral—come from the ends of the earth to be here—but his agent, Max, called to say that he became intoxicated and fell and broke his left arm. It was a godsend, really, because they put him in a hospital that specializes in . . . helping people"—she could not say the word 'alcoholic'—"like him."

Mitchell came into the kitchen from the garage. "What's all this whispering about?" he said lightly.

Letty smiled. "Oh, just rehashing family secrets, that's all. What's up?"

"What's up is that I'm going to take Jean over to the cabinet shop in Enid. No one will be there this late in the day, and I want to show him around. We'll be back by dinnertime. What are we having?"

Charlotte shrugged her shoulders. "Françoise is preparing the main dish. All I know is that it contains chicken and red wine. She's down in the cellar now, selecting the stock. She won't use a good vintage for cooking."

When Mitchell left, she took Letty's arm. "The peculiar part of it is that Françoise and I have developed a—I guess you could call it a friendship. At first it was an 'armed truce' sort of thing, but she's really extraordinary."

She paused, and it was difficult to go on, but she rallied. "I'm going to do something unorthodox by Angel's standards, Aunt Letty. I'm going to buy her a little apartment near the hotel where she works. Ordinarily, she'd never accept this, but I told her that Mitch and I will be coming over to Monte Carlo once in a while, and it would be cheaper if we had a *pied à terre* where we could put up. You know that the French are very practical people. She agreed." She paused a moment. "I've thought it over, and I really don't regard this as 'conscience money.' I'm doing this because I want to do it, and I have the money."

Letty laughed softly. "You sounded like your mother then, Charlotte."

"Did I? Well, maybe we have more in common than I thought!"

Then the telephone rang and when Charlotte answered, she called, "Aunt Letty, it's for you. Luke. One thing we're going to miss is Nellie looking all over hell's half acre to find someone. With the dial system, we can say good-bye to personal service."

"Yes, that's true, Charlotte, but just think, for the first time in our lives we'll be able to have a private conversation. What a joy." She paused. "But on the other hand, I'll kind of miss all those people listening in, because our 'grapevine' will be cut off overnight!" She picked up the receiver. "Hello, Luke, how are you feeling?"

"Mama, I know that this is a helluva time to ask a favor, but I'm due in Paris on the nineteenth to meet Muhammad Abn to sign some papers on six oil rigs for the Saudis. His father finally died and he's in charge, being the eldest son. I can't make the trip because of this skin condition. Travel only aggravates it, and the welts are all over my back and stomach. Can you go to Paris with Robert Desmond?"

"Why, Luke dear, why do you want me to go? I don't know anything about the company anymore, since Bosley passed away. Robert has all the facts and figures at his fingertips."

"Of course he does, Mama, but Muhammad Abn *knows* you, and after all, you're head of the family."

"But Muhammad Abn won't want to deal with a *woman*, Luke!"

He laughed softly. "He knows you practically brought the Discovery Well in by yourself in nineteen and three, Mama. He understands *tradition*."

"Well, of course I'll go if you think it's the right thing to do, Luke. Yes, yes, good-bye, dear." Letty hung up and turned to Charlotte. "Talk about the world changing. Do you know where I'll be on the nineteenth of this month?"

"No, where?"

"At the George Cinq hotel in Paris, France!"

Heron Cabinet Shop Number One was located on North Broadway in Enid, almost at the edge of town, and Mitchell opened the door to the warehouse with pride.

"Oh, Papa!" Jean exclaimed, looking at the finished pieces in various stages of packing for shipment. "You must have a very good business!"

Mitchell conceded that orders were very satisfactory, but he did not mention the similar facility in Guthrie or the plant in Tulsa that had made the furniture for the Tulsa Tower Hotel. He led him into the shop, and a light came into Jean's eyes as he ran his hands over the modern equipment.

"We still do everything by hand at my factory," he said, "but with tools like these"—he pointed to the electric routers, drills, and lathes—"we could increase our business one hundred percent." Then he paused. "But of course, then we would be idle, because there are not that many orders." He looked about the huge room. "Where is the finishing shop?" he asked.

"Through there." Mitchell indicated a padded double door. "But before we enter, we must put on these." He picked up two white coats.

"It is like a laboratory!" Jean exclaimed, and when they came into the warehouse-sized room, he looked in wonder at the plastic-covered windows, padded doors and floors covered with felt, and the giant compressors. "There is no dust here!" he cried jubilantly.

"How do you prevent dust particles from alighting on the wet varnishes at home, Jean?"

He laughed. "You may not believe this, Papa, but we pray very much!" He looked about expectantly. "Where are the finishes?"

"Come into the adjoining room."

Jean's eyes grew wide as he glanced at the heavy steel shelving that held five-gallon containers of various varnishes, shellacs, and lacquers. "Every color of the rainbow," he said with awe; then he followed Mitchell into the sanding room and rubbed his hands over a cherrywood headboard. "The color is very nice, Papa, but there is no depth in the finish."

He paused. "You must obtain some of the Chinese ginkgo from the varnish trees. The Communists will not let it out of Mainland China, but it can still be exported from India. It is very difficult to work with, and must dry by itself overnight, and the odor is so strong no man can take it for very long, but the finish is extraordinarily beautiful."

"Jean, there is something that I have been meaning to ask you, but I don't know quite how to put it. Now that you have seen the way that we live here in Oklahoma, and my store, and this facility—and there is still much to be seen in this regard—what would you think of emigrating to this country and working for me?"

Jean ran his hand along a mahogany tabletop and did not look up immediately, and when he finally turned to Mitchell, his eyes were misty. "I had in the back of my mind that you would invite me here, and I have long pondered what I would say. I love you, Papa, and to have found you at last is the triumph of my life so far, but I am French and you are American, and our ways of life are not similar. . . ."

He fought to place words in proper sequence. "I should remain where I am. One day soon I will marry. I want my children to grow up in France to be near their *grand'mère.*" He paused. "What I would like to do, however, is to change my name legally to Heron—a proud family of which I want to be a part—if that would not be an embarrassment to you?"

Mitchell shook his head. He was very moved, and when he could trust his voice, he replied, "It is also my wish." He took a long breath. "What I would also like is to be responsible, in part, for the education of your children.

"We are approaching the Jet Age, and there is no reason that I must always stay here in Enid, or that you must always stay in such an expensive place as Monte Carlo. You can visit, and Charlotte and I can visit, and the children, who will be bilingual, can travel back and forth between your country and mine, so that they will have two heritages."

"That is a good plan, Papa, but you understand that I must be independent, no?" He made a little, helpless gesture. "I guess that you could say that I am the 'black sheep' of the family."

Mitchell laughed. "Funny you should say that, Jean. I was the original 'black sheep'—and sometimes I think that I still am!" He sighed. "We Herons are a strange lot. We look at life differently than most people—but in the end, remember, son, that we always win!"

When they returned to the Federal Restoration mansion in Angel, Letty informed Mitchell that Torgo had passed away in his sleep. "He just couldn't live without his Bella, I guess," she said sadly, "and in the summer, when the peach trees are in bloom, I'll miss them most of all. . . ."

20
_____

Journey Into Light

Paris had never been more beautiful.

Letty took a short walk down the Champs Elyseés, supported by the new gold-tipped cane that she had purchased at the shop in the George V Hotel. When Robert Desmond had offered to escort her, she had declined with a smile. "Forgive me, Bob," she had said kindly, "but this may be my last journey to Paris, and I want to walk and browse in the shops and gawk at the people on the street and just be a pesky old woman. Do you understand?"

And he had laughed. "Be back by luncheon, or I'll send the gendarmes after you!"

As she strolled down the wide boulevards, and became a little drunk with the very smell of the city, which was different from any other city, she thought of the family at home. Each member seemed enmeshed in difficulty at the moment, but as she thought of all that had happened to her over the past eighty-three years, it was plain that she had surmounted great difficulties also. The current generation's problems were different only because the times were different, and she came back to the hotel from her stroll, feeling tired physically but strengthened mentally.

That afternoon Robert accompanied her to the House of Dior and sat patiently by her side while the models paraded up and down. Most of the designs were for younger women, but she finally selected three suits: a navy-blue trimmed in pink grosgrain ribbon, an off-white with a shirred skirt, and a mauve taffeta that was dressy enough for a reception at the White House.

The very elegant saleslady, who was *not* dressed by Dior, Letty noticed, asked when she could come for a fitting of the "costumes." Letty laughed. "They are costumes, I guess, Bob, because I'll certainly never wear them in Angel."

Then she had discreetly turned away while the elegant saleslady who did not wear Diors discussed the price of the outfits with Robert Desmond. "I don't want to know how much anything costs," she said. "If I do, I won't enjoy being in Paris at all!"

Sharply at ten o'clock the next morning, Robert knocked at the door of Abn's suite. "What is that old saying about 'if Muhammad does not come to the mountain, the mountain must come to Muhammad'?"

"I think you have it turned around, Bob," she retorted with a smile. "I'm trying to think of all the things you told me on the plane. And I've been practicing my greetings in Fawzi. I hope I won't embarrass you."

He laughed. "You very probably know more about drilling procedures than Abn does! And just slur your tongue over the foreign phrases."

The door was opened by a dark-skinned young man in a brown business suit. "Good morning," he said pleasantly. "Would you have coffee?"

"Yes, thank you," Robert Desmond replied.

"Please sit," the young man said. "The son of Muhammad will join you very shortly."

The suite was decorated with white brocade walls, beige velvet-covered gilt furniture, and the crystal chandelier was so clean that the hundreds of prisms reflected sections of the room, which was brilliantly lighted. On the floor between two enormous couches, a blue-and-green Persian carpet had been laid over the plush blue carpeting of the suite. It was one of the most beautiful rooms that Letty had ever seen, and she felt vaguely uncomfortable in her burgundy silk dress.

They had only touched the delicate cups to their lips

when the door to the bedroom opened and Muhammad Abn swept into the room. He was dressed in a flowing white burnoose, and behind him could be seen a retinue of men similarly attired. He had not aged in years; his face was still handsome and his beard expertly groomed as always; but his deportment had changed.

This was the first time that either Robert or Letty had ever seen him in native attire. He closed the door, and they were alone.

Muhammad Abn bowed slightly. "*is-salaam 'alaykum*," he said.

Robert Desmond bowed. "*wa-'alaykum is-salaam*," he replied.

Muhanmad Abn turned to Letty, and the same ceremony was repeated, but when Letty added, "*sabaah il-khayr*," which was the equivalent of "good morning," he beamed.

"Please sit down," Muhammad Abn said graciously.

"May I offer my profound sympathy at the passing of your beloved father," Robert said gravely. "He was a great man."

Muhammad nodded. "Yes, he was, but that is not to say that he was not, at times, shall we say, quite difficult?"

His Cambridge accent did not seem so pronounced as Letty remembered, and she wondered if it was because he did not have many opportunities to speak English.

Muhammad's eyes sparkled. "I must do things a bit differently, now that my father has joined Allah. I must give up some of my Western habits and take on the responsibilities of what has become my large family. Death changes many things, as you know, Madame Trenton. It was a sad day in my life when I heard of your husband's passing. He was the first man who spoke to me about petroleum in a layman's language that I could understand."

He smoothed his beard in a delicate, habitual gesture. "I am sorry that Luke could not be with us to enjoy Paris. He telephoned yesterday and described his condition. My father was stricken from time to time with this malady, which I understand is caused by stress."

"Really?" Letty exclaimed. "I had no idea! If there was

anyone in the world that I would think would be less bothered by tension, it is Luke."

Muhammad Abn frowned slightly. "I would think a mother might not be aware of certain pressures . . ."

Letty was not offended. She smiled. "Yes, I'm quite certain that you're right."

Muhammad opened a large tin on the coffee table and offered sweetmeats. "Perhaps these are not to the Western taste, but I brought them from home." He paused. "They were made personally by . . . my . . . wife."

It was a very kind gesture, Letty thought, for him to mention his wife, because she was aware that this was a breach of etiquette in his own country. She took a bite of the honeyed morsel, which had been coated with ground nuts. "It is delicious," she said. "She who made this is very accomplished."

"Thank you," Muhammad Abn replied, and she knew that he was pleased. He removed six small packages from a drawer in the coffee table. "From my father's collection of small, worthless artifacts, I have brought these things for you to open in Angel."

Letty removed from her purse a small box. "This is for you, Muhammad Abn, and should it not suit your taste, please exchange it for something more appropriate. The shop is located downstairs."

He was delighted. "Shall I be impolite and open it now?" He was like a small boy with an unopened toy.

"Please do," Letty replied, saying a prayer that she had been led to the right gift.

His eyes grew large as he removed the platinum watch engraved with the figure of Mickey Mouse. "The hands!" he cried. "The hands tell the time! It is a gift that I not only will treasure because of its intrinsic value," he said formally, "and because of the national figure portrayed on the dial, but because of the esteem with which I regard you and your family."

He replaced his gold watch, which Letty surmised had cost five time as much as her gift, with the mouse watch; then he turned to Robert Desmond. "Have you brought the necessary contracts for me?"

"Indeed," Robert replied and removed a sheaf of stapled papers from his briefcase.

"Thank you," Muhammad Abn said. "I shall be back in a moment." He took the papers into the bedroom and came out a moment later empty-handed, and Letty knew that the Saudi lawyers were scrutinizing the contracts.

"Come," Muhammad Abn said, "look at the view of my beloved Paris." He opened the door to the balcony, and they stood looking down over the Champs Elysées to the Etoile. "It saddens me that this will no longer be my playground," he said solemnly. "I will not be able to leave the Kingdom of Saudi Arabia as frequently as I have been accustomed to doing in the past. My father's reputation must be maintained, and in many ways he was a hard man." He sighed. "Shall we go inside?"

When they returned to the living room, the contracts were neatly stacked on the coffee table. Muhammad Abn leafed through them quickly, and then looked up quizzically. "I do not seem to find the space for my signature."

When Robert Desmond made a slight move, Muhammad Abn turned to Letty. "Perhaps, Madame . . . ?"

Tears stung the back of her eyes, and she thought, *I must not cry!* "Here," she said gently, realizing that he was showing her the greatest possible courtesy and the highest honor. "Please sign on the dotted line."

The Heron clapboard was festooned with pink, which was Letty's favorite color. Hattie had been preparing the dinner, it seemed, for three days, and Charlotte, who was staying the week in Angel, had baked beans and honeyed ham in one of her large ovens, and a turkey in the other, and Letty was upstairs in the master suite taking a nap. "You've got to be beautiful for your birthday," Charlotte had said, scooping out a handful of pink beauty mud, "and there is nothing so relaxing as a facial."

Luke Three had taken the bridal suite at the Stevens Hotel, and he lay in the king-sized bed alongside his new wife. "T'am," he said, taking her in his arms, "have I said that I love you in the last five minutes?"

She turned her almond eyes toward him. "No, but I want

you to be my husband again." She paused. "It is wonderful that Uncle has taught me how to speak English, so that I can say to you all those things that I wanted to say when we first met."

He nodded. "Yet somehow we didn't need to converse. I loved you from that first meeting."

"And me, you," she said simply, holding out her arms to him.

He felt her soft, smooth skin that was different from any other skin that he had ever touched, and he luxuriated in her presence. Then he very slowly and dexterously moved toward her until he felt her moist warmth. He kissed her again and again, knowing that their lovemaking would take a very long time, because she could not yet accommodate him fully.

She responded to his kisses—this "rubbing of the mouth," as she referred to it—and she allowed herself to float on waves of exquisite feeling. At last, and much too soon, Luke thought, although she had twice shuddered, he felt his essence pour into her, and she held him tightly. Afterward, they lay in each other's arms, and then he arose from her embrace. "We must bathe and get dressed," he said.

"Is it time for Grandmama's party?" she asked, and he kissed her one last time before he nodded.

Luke and Jeanette were dressing in the upstairs bedroom at the Heron clapboard. "Damn," he muttered. "Will you help me with this cummerbund?"

Jeanette laughed. "If you live to be a hundred, Luke Heron, you'll never be able to dress yourself formally. And just thank God that you're over those miserable shingles, and that doctor had the gall to suggest those welts were caused from nerves!" She snapped the gold clips together. "I might as well do your tie, also. And when I finish, will you zip up my dress?"

He laughed. "Yes, if you'll let me kiss the back of your neck."

"Oh, no you don't, Luke, we can't start anything right

now." She paused. "However, later, if you have the inclination . . ."

Patricia and Lars, who were dressing in the small bedroom next door and could not fail to hear the conversation, exchanged glances. "I could tell them a thing or two about stress," Lars whispered. "*Years* of it, in fact."

"Yes," she agreed. "Yet that was all over when you experienced your last trip, over a year and a half ago." She paused, lipstick in midair. "I hope that every person in America reads your book."

"I do too," he quipped. "We need the money!"

"That's not what I meant, and you know it! But if people know that the first bit of alien substance taken into the body changes the chemistry, you will have made your contribution. They must know the danger of experimentation."

"Yes," he said, and his eyes were very concerned. "And it's appropriate, too, that I finished the book here in Angel. You know something, Pat, I've felt Sam, Born-Before-Sunrise, around here all day. Have you felt his presence, too?"

She nodded and shivered. "Yes, but I didn't want to mention it because I felt you'd think I was imagining things."

"Imagination or not," Lars said quietly, "he's here."

Downstairs, in Muhammad Abn's suite, Clement and Sarah had finished dressing and were sitting quietly on the sofa. "I didn't really mind giving Luke Three and T'am the bridal suite at the Stevens," Clement remarked, "but this bed has got to be the hardest in the entire state of Oklahoma!"

"I agree, dear," she answered, running her hand over her electric-blue silk skirt, "but we'll go back to Kansas City tomorrow, to our newly decorated house, for one blessed week before we have to go to London, where Billy Nestor is conducting. I really don't want to go, but I suppose we must, since you're supposed to introduce him." She paused and looked at him with amusement. "I do hope you do a better job than last time."

"You mean at Hollywood Bowl?" He lighted a cigarette thoughtfully. "You know, Sarah, I've wiped that entire night out of my mind. Drunks do that, you know, a lot more frequently than they admit. But the best thing that ever happened to me was that fall backstage."

He held up his left arm. "If I hadn't fractured my elbow and Max hadn't put me in that funny farm, I'd still be making an ass of myself wherever I went." He took her hand. "Have I ever thanked you for sticking by me?"

"Only a thousand and one times, that's all."

"Then a thousand and two times won't hurt. By the way, for an old man who's just passed his change of life, and with the alcohol out of my system, have you noticed my performance has been improving?"

"It's true," she said with a straight face, "your singing is better than ever."

"I wasn't thinking of my voice." He laughed. "Jesus, Squaw, you can be dense sometimes."

"Yeah, Hotshot," she replied, "and doesn't it just get to you?"

Charlotte took the turkey out of the oven and called, "Jean, Jean, it's time to carve!"

He came in from the back porch. "Let's speak in English," he said slowly. "I want to talk a lot today and I must . . . practice."

"Put the slices in this pan, Jean; then while the turkey is in the warming oven we can go upstairs and change. Brigitte was down a moment ago, concerned about how she looks. I told her for a six-months-pregnant lady, she looked gorgeous." She paused. "It's too bad that you must go home next week."

He nodded. "But the journey is very long. She must be treated well in the last months. Also"—his eyes sparkled— "he must be born in France."

"But how do you know that it will be a boy?"

"Aunt Letty says that all the Heron firstborns are boys."

Charlotte gave him a long look. "Well, of course, if Letty made that statement, it must be true." She laughed.

"Why are you staring out of the window, Jean, instead of slicing the turkey?"

"I was thinking of *Maman*." His voice was distant. "She's here today in spirit. It was my last joy that she could come to America before that last great sickness."

Charlotte arranged the slices of breast meat carefully on the pan. "Did she know that she was . . . ill?"

He nodded. "But she did not know that I knew that the trouble with her legs was malignant."

Charlotte nodded. "Life is both funny and grotesque, Jean. It's really ever-changing. I'm just glad that I have your father."

"He's a good man," Jean agreed, "but I don't think his life has been very exciting—do you?"

Charlotte thought of Michel Bayard and Herr Doktor Professor Schneider, and the woman that she knew only as Mrs. Parsons, and she replied, "You're right, Jean, he is kind of a stick-in-the-mud and sort of plods along day-to-day. I suppose his life has been dull."

When the doorbell rang, Hattie was taking Sally Lunn rolls out of the oven. "Letty, would you get that, please?"

"Yes," she answered quietly. "You'd have me answering the door if the Lord himself was coming to call!" She looked out the window. "It's more flowers, Hattie, you'll have to go down in the storm cellar and hunt up another vase."

Letty opened the door and smiled at the young man. "Aren't you one of the Baker boys?"

He grinned. "Yes, ma'am."

"Well, tell your grandfather to come over for a piece of Angel cake after dinner, will you?"

"Yes, ma'am. By the way, the flowers are something special."

Letty glanced at the spray of pink orchids. "Well, who in the world would go to the expense of . . ." She opened the envelope and sighed gently. The card contained only four words:

Love,
Dwight and Mamie

Letty sat at the head of the table in the dining room of the Federal Restoration mansion, and looked down the long expanse of damask and spode and crystal and sterling at her family gathered together, and cleared her throat meaningfully.

Everyone stopped eating and looked at her expectantly. "I just want to say some things today that need to be said." She fingered the emerald necklace which Muhammad Abn had given her, which perfectly matched her green taffeta off-the-shoulder ballgown.

"First of all, thank you all for disrupting your lives and coming home. Secondly, I want to thank those of our circle who are here but can't be seen. Thank you, Fourteen and Jaundice, for lending me this big dining room, when mine was too small, and for furnishing the silver and everything.

"Sam, Born-Before-Sunrise, you're so real to me today that I can almost see your turban on the hatrack in the corner, and if I strain these old ears, I can hear Bella playing the piano and Torgo doing a run on the violin.

"Out of my own life, there are Luke and George and Bosley—and, I'm just vain enough to think that they may have gotten together somehow and just might be having a game of Faro with Poppa Dice. And there surely is a certain lady present—and she was a lady, no matter what people said—and I feel that Leona Barrett is looking on with approval."

She paused. "I know that the food is getting cold, but I've not finished yet." She picked up her glass of champagne. "Here's to all of you, whom I'll take in generations: Luke and Jeanette; Clement and Sarah; Mitchell and Charlotte; Patricia Anne and Lars; Jean and Brigitte; Luke Three and T'am, and Murdock, who is the latest, but not least, of the Heron and the Story clans." She paused. "Now we can eat."

"Not quite yet, Mama," Luke said, getting to his feet. He held up his glass. "Here's to you on your eighty-fourth birthday. God bless you."

As everyone stood up and raised glasses, Letty nodded. "Thank you, children," she said gruffly. "It's lovely having you here, but if you think I'm going to dissolve in a bucket of tears, you most certainly have another think coming."

She picked up her fork, eyes glistening, "And besides, you haven't seen the end of me yet. I expect all of you to disrupt your lives next year, when I'll be eighty-five, and the year after that, when I'll be eighty-six, and the year after that, and . . .

The Windhaven Saga
by Marie de Jourlet

☐ 42-006-4 **WINDHAVEN PLANTATION** $3.50
The epic novel of the Bouchard family, who dared to cross the boundaries of society and create a bold new heritage.

☐ 41-967-8 **STORM OVER WINDHAVEN** **$3.50**
Windhaven Plantation and the Bouchard dream are shaken to their very roots in this torrid story of men and women driven by ambition and damned by desire.

☐ 41-784-5 **LEGACY OF WINDHAVEN** $3.50
After the Civil War the Bouchards move west to Texas—a rugged, untamed land where they must battle Indians, bandits and cattle rustlers to insure the legacy of Windhaven.

☐ 41-858-2 **RETURN TO WINDHAVEN** $3.50
Amid the turbulent Reconstruction years, the determined Bouchards fight to hold on to Windhaven Range while struggling to regain an old but never forgotten plantation.

☐ 41-968-6 **WINDHAVEN'S PERIL** **$3.50**
Luke Bouchard and his family launch a new life at Windhaven Plantation—but the past returns to haunt them.

☐ 41-690-3 **TRIALS OF WINDHAVEN** $2.95
Luke and Laure Bouchard face their most bitter trial yet, as their joyful life at Windhaven Plantation is threatened by an unscrupulous carpetbagger.

☐ 40-723-8 **DEFENDERS OF WINDHAVEN** $2.75
Out of the ashes of the Civil War, the South rebuilds. Laure and Luke Bouchard continue to uphold Windhaven Plantation as Frank's niece and her husband forge a new frontier in Texas.

☐ 41-748-9 **WINDHAVEN'S CRISIS** $3.50
With the fires of civil war still smoldering, our nation prepares for its first Centennial—as the proud Bouchards struggle to preserve the legacy that is Windhaven.

☐ 41-110-3 **WINDHAVEN'S BOUNTY** $3.50
Left alone by a tragic twist of fate, Laure Bouchard opens a casino in New Orleans and struggles to defend the house of Windhaven against those who would bring it down.

☐ 41-111-1 **WINDHAVEN'S TRIUMPH** $3.50
As the proud South once again raises its head up high, the heirs of Windhaven must sow the seeds of a legacy that is both their birthright and their obsession.

☐ 41-112-X **WINDHAVEN'S FURY** $3.50
As a new age dawns in America, the Bouchards face new opportunities and dangers—and struggle to reconcile destiny with desire.